China Run

Also by Eric Clark

Nonfiction
DIPLOMAT

Fiction
BLACK GAMBIT
THE SLEEPER
SEND IN THE LIONS

China Run

by Eric Clark

Little, Brown and Company—Boston

FIRST AMERICAN EDITION

LIBRARY OF CONGRESS CATALOGING IN PUBLICATION DATA
Clark, Eric, 1937-
   China run.
   I. Title.
PR6053.L295C4 1985   823'.914   84-21794
ISBN 0-316-14491-6

BP

DESIGNED BY DEDE CUMMINGS

PRINTED IN THE UNITED STATES OF AMERICA

For Paul Chevalier

Acknowledgments

I would like to thank:
Miss D. Bayley, Institute of Civil Engineers, London; Professors J. W. Briscoe and W. W. Hay, both of the University of Illinois at Urbana-Champaign; Margaret Clark; Jonathan Clowes; Richard Cohen; Peter Deadman of the Clinic of Chinese Acupuncture, Brighton; Drs. Elisabeth and Iain Elliot; F; Herbert R. Hands of the American Society of Civil Engineers; Raymond Hawkey; Miss Rose Heatley; George Hughes; Peter Kelly, Editor of *Rail Enthusiast*; Martin Kerridge; Mrs. Joyce Pope of the Natural History Museum, London; W. H. (Bill) Turner; J. T. van Riemsdijk, Keeper of Mechanical and Civil Engineering, the Science Museum, London; Dr. Tony Whitehead; and all those people who cannot be named, not least those who helped me in China.

Early this century, when conquered China was no more than a semi-colony of the West, a group of resident Englishmen decided to import fox hunting for their amusement.

They gathered a pack of hounds, but the foxes had to be specially shipped from England.

The venture proved a dismal failure.

The reason, reported Emile Bard, writing in 1909, was a simple one:

"The animals could find no shelter in a strange country and were taken at once."

China Run

I

There were eighteen of us. Seventeen Chinese in their blue Mao suits and T-shirts and baggy trousers, faces as inscrutable as they are popularly supposed to be, and me. And, of course, the three steam locomotives, their smoke deflector plates like the huge ears of vast black monsters, looming above us in the arched hangarlike shed.

As steam and smoke began to distort their outlines, they took on the look of mammoth, prehistoric animals: majestic, full of a weird beauty with their round, black bodies, their shiny gold and red rod and wheel limbs. That, in a way, was what they were. Not long before I was born, a quarter of a million of them had roamed the world. Now there were perhaps 20,000 of them, half of them here in China, most of the others in India.

Two of the engines above me were silent, sleeping creatures, cooling after undergoing the series of tests a locomotive is submitted to before being sent into service. The third had just come on to steam. I closed my eyes and blotted out the other observers and the one-hundred-foot-long shed, and let my other senses delight in the moment. The subdued hiss of building steam, the comforting warmth radiating from the boiler and, most of all, the acrid, sulfurous smell that always triggered memories and emotions as vivid as that of any woman's perfume.

I opened my eyes again, but remained oblivious to where I was —

twenty miles from Inner Mongolia — and the world outside, the dirty, dusty industrial town of Tatung in China's northeastern Shanxi Province.

The locomotive on which my eyes were fixed was a QJ or March Forward Class. That might not have meant much to most people back in New York, but to me, a railroad man since I'd lost my heart to an old Consolidation at an Illinois grade crossing at the age of nine, it was a source of awe and excitement.

My Chinese hosts had ticked off facts and figures as we had toured the rest of the works, the forging shops, the pressing plant, the assembly sheds where overhead cranes made constant movement like giant arms. I had listened and remembered, because I was seeing something no one could ever see anywhere else in the world . . .

QJ, first produced in 1965, a modification of the HP or Hoping Peace . . . 127 tons in weight, ten driving wheels, each 1500 mm in diameter, 65,000 lbs of tractive effort at 85 percent boiler pressure . . .

A product of the last remaining steam locomotive factory in the world . . . What I was seeing was the birth of the last generation of a dying breed. In twenty years' time, perhaps, they would be gone. It wasn't even that they would die for all the right, unarguable, commercial reasons. We had started killing off the steam train back in the forties — not because it was obsolete but because our plants switched to guns and tanks, letting General Motors jump in and fill a gap that shouldn't have been there with diesels. Other countries had seen it as "progress," and rushed in to follow so they wouldn't be thought backward. Now the Arabs were helping deliver the final death blow — lending countries like India and South Africa cheap money to buy diesels that would burn their oil. Only China, it seemed, held out. And even here, manufacture of steam locomotives was down to one plant.

The locomotive being tested was in full life now. It had taken five hours to bring it to steam. In the fire box, coal would be glowing — orange, not yet white. Smoke was billowing from the chimney, most of it to be sucked into the huge, overhead duct; gusts of steam hissed from the cylinder drains near the front of the boiler, as though the locomotive was champing to use its enormous strength. First, though, it had to pass its tests. To this end, men were already checking the gauges wired to its body.

My guide, a round, smiling man, his skin shining in the heat, beckoned me to move closer, but I pretended not to understand, preferring to stay back, taking in the whole scene, for once an onlooker.

My eyes roamed over the other observers. Three, I thought, were women, but they were as shapeless as the men in their jackets and trousers. They wore no makeup. The impression was of a sexless, as well as a classless, society — but, in the few days I had been in China, I had already learned the classlessness was fake; maybe the other was too. All except the inspectors and two or three others were workers who had wandered into the shed simply to watch. They all talked animatedly but quietly in small groups. There was a lot of nodding, as though they were discussing technical matters, which they probably were. Men who work with trains love trains. That is a fact. It's not something I've found to be equally true with men who work with cars or airplanes or even boats, although some of them will.

One of the men caught my gaze and, by gesture, conveyed that the boiler was now being taken up beyond its normal, maximum, safe pressure. I nodded that I understood, not realizing that I had taken a step back instinctively until I saw his face start a smile. My instinct was due to the fact that if the boiler couldn't take the extra pressure, half the shed — and all of us — would vanish in the explosion. His composure came from knowing that the plant turned out one new locomotive nearly every day. The boiler would *not* explode; all the test would show was whether any parts needed tightening.

My guide came closer, forcing me to move nearer to the locomotive. He had met me at the station the previous night after the eight-hour journey from Peking, and had picked me up for the journey to the plant that morning. He reminded me of a Buddha; I felt that if you pushed him he would roll and bounce upright again like a child's toy.

"It is good, yes?" he asked.

"It is beautiful," I said.

5

He did not find the word strange. Although he was a professional guide and interpreter, I gathered he belonged to the plant and the town. He was a railroad man, like me. "Yes, beautiful," he repeated.

The outside gauges were all being disconnected now, and I felt myself being eased closer and closer. Beyond the locomotive, I could see men beginning to spray a coat of black paint onto one of the cooled engines.

"You want to go up?" He pointed to the cab.

Driving cabs of QJ trains are vast, the size of small bedrooms. At least eight men, including the driver and fireman, were already crowded into this one.

I made a token protest that I didn't want anyone to have to get down because of me — I'd already seen how space was cleared for foreigners in public places like restaurants and it embarrassed me. Nevertheless, I knew deep down nothing was going to stop me riding on that cab.

He went away, and I let my eyes continue roving. They stopped on a series of huge blackboards, covered, I had already been told, with performance figures. One, though, contained an oddly stylized chalk drawing of a middle-aged woman. It bore the look of having been there a long time; from the difference in the thickness of some of the lines, I judged it had been touched up on more than one occasion, to preserve it. I had been told what it portrayed: a woman, mother of one of the workers, who had fought against the Gang of Four. Her actual struggle had not been detailed, but I had been told early, so that its importance was clear. I had heard a lot about the Gang of Four already. It didn't seem to matter that the group, led by Mao's widow, Jiang Qing, had been in jail for over seven years. The evil of their presence, it seemed, remained hanging over China like a not-yet-exorcised demon.

My guide returned, and led me toward the locomotive. I could feel his sense of importance. A group parted, giving us more room than we needed to pass. They stared curiously, another experience I was beginning to accept as normal — all foreign barbarians were strange, a blond one over six feet tall only more so. These were working men, tough-skinned, but their lack of height made me feel both clumsy and vulnerable in a way I could not understand, and I realized I was stooping as men much taller than me often do at home.

We reached the foot of the engine's steps. My guide carried out a shouted conversation above the hiss of steam, and then stood back for me to climb up first. A space had been cleared for us near the driver. He was seated, his hand suspended near the controls that were all within easy reach. Cabs of Chinese locomotives are not only large; by the standards of the trains they pull, they are also luxurious.

My guide talked for a long time. The hypnotic singsong rhythm of his voice combined with the warmth and the feeling of being somewhere I belonged. Together they made my body remember it had not slept well for almost three days. The moment I had stepped off the plane in Peking the Chinese had begun rushing me around (everywhere, it seemed, except where I needed to be to do my job, but that was something I was prepared to forget for this moment).

The driver had skin crinkled like well-worn leather, and his hair was cropped so short that his scalp showed through. Every few moments, he would nod his head, turn to me in acknowledgment, and I knew my interpreter must be making the most of the little he knew of me — telling the driver probably that I was a famous engineer over here to help them build more railroads. Which was true in a way — although the actual job I was contracted to do was pretty tiny compared with the vastness of what had been done and what was still to be done.

There was a sudden silence, and I knew protocol demanded that I ask a question or two. I did, even though I already knew the answers. Although this was my first time in China, I had spent enough years in Africa and other countries in Asia to know the importance of formality.

Protocol satisfied, the driver turned his full attention to the controls. His hands were as leathered as his face, and the veins were gnarled like protruding lengths of string. But their touch as he wound the reverser into forward gear and began to move the throttle handle was as gentle as a lover's.

There was silence in the cab now; everyone was on edge to see how the engine behaved when it moved. One of the peculiarities of a steam locomotive — one of the things that makes it so special and so exciting — is that testing the parts gives no real indication of how well it will work as a whole. In that, it is like a living person — the parts all interact to produce something that is more than their mere total. It follows that it is also an individual.

Moving the throttle handle opened the valve to the cylinders; as the steam expanded, the pistons began moving, and almost imperceptibly at first the train began to ease forward along the rails that led the length of the shed to huge double doors.

The steam escaping from the open cyclinder drains billowed like huge exhausts of warm breath on either side of the locomotive. And as the engine breathed, it began to make loud sighing noises, whsssh, whsssh, whsssh . . .

We left the shed and went into brilliant sunshine. I shifted my gaze from the controls to the scene outside. Rails led off in every direction, but there were surprisingly few new trains waiting to be shipped into service; the need was so great, I knew, that many were moved the night they were finished, to go to work as far as two or even three thousand miles away. Around the yard stood three- and four-story buildings — workers' apartments because the locomotive plant was a town of its own within a larger town.

As we left the shed, hands waved from balconies and windows. Chinese trains have two whistles and two horns, all operated by foot pedals. Now, the driver sounded them all in a staccato song of triumph that echoed between the buildings.

The locomotive had built up some speed now, and the sound changed from the whsssh of moments before to an even more familiar chump, chump, chump . . . Almost immediately, though, the driver began to apply the brakes, sending a screeching sound back from the rails. The locomotive ground to a halt at the end of the test track. Without conversation, the driver put the engine into reverse, drove back to the entrance to the shed, halted, and repeated the sequence three more times.

Finally, the train at a standstill outside the shed, he removed his hands and turned to face his companions. His smile and the slow, deliberate nod of his head said it all: he was happy with the engine.

They all huddled back, smiling openly now, to let me leave the cab first. I swung down the steps, followed by the others. The sun was bright, but there was a chill in the air. Smoke and steam hung low like mist.

I realized that workers were clapping in unison. My guide, the driver, and others from the cab began to clap too, equally formally, not unlike Englishmen at a game of cricket. Self-consciously, I joined them, wanting to share in the collective emotion, despite its formality.

Still clapping, I stared up at the locomotive, sleek with moisture like an athlete who has warmed up. God help me, I was that child again, standing by the track on the branch line watching the Consolidation's rods going around as it eased away with its load of forty or more cattle cars. I felt my eyes fill with tears, something that nothing had made them do for a long, long time. It was a mixture of nostalgia, sadness, admiration, and the joy of sharing the moment with the men and women who had created such a wonder.

I was even prepared to start loving this whole vast nation, all 3,700,000 square miles of it, although all I had seen of it was an airport, parts of a city through windows, a hotel, countryside from a train, because it had made this morning possible.

Then fate, like a grown-up taking a bag of candy from a child, chose just that second to announce that the visit was over.

A newcomer whispered a message to my guide. He translated. I was expected back in Peking immediately. There was a train I could catch if I left. Now.

On the car ride from the plant to the railroad station I flopped back in my seat, looking, I realized later, like someone sulking. In reality, now that the excitement of the atmosphere of the locomotive plant had gone, I was just exhausted.

It was Wednesday. Eleven-fifty-seven A.M. Tatung time, which is the same as Peking time because even though the country covers more than three thousand miles there are no time zones. That meant, according to my watch, that it was just after ten the previous night in New York. I had left there five days before, via Los Angeles and Tokyo.

It had been less than a week since I had first heard about the vacant assignment in China. A fellow railroad engineer who had been going to undertake it had fallen ill. I'd jumped in — to everyone's surprise because it was a job for a less experienced man, which was another way of saying a lower-echelon, younger engineer. "It's like a neurosurgeon flying halfway around the world to do a tonsillectomy," one of my partners had said. He was exaggerating, of course, but he had a right to worry about how I spent my working time; he owned a share of me, so to speak. Still, he knew that Maddy and I had split up, even though, as we hadn't been married, he didn't take my pain seriously. So I had set off. And because I was on my broken-romance, jet-traveling, great-explorer kick, I had not bothered with a real overnight stop anywhere. I had arrived in Peking tired. The Chinese had then cooperated in my rage for activity by throwing me into an immediate set of excursions to tourist sights like the Great Wall and the Forbidden City. When I had objected, tiredly but politely, they had sped me off to Tatung with as little notice as they were now returning me. Perhaps now, at last, they would send me in the other direction, a thousand miles to the southeast, to the lower Yangtze Valley area, which was where the work had to be done.

The interpreter, who was in the front seat, turned and spoke, interrupting my thoughts, bringing me back to the present. Even though it was not raining, the car's wipers were on, clearing the light dust that seemed to cover everything. I had been told it was fine sand carried from the Mongolian desert. We drew into the center of the road to pass some mule-drawn carts. It was not a beautiful place. It looked like what it was, a poor and dusty industrial town. Its importance lay not in its looks but in the coal and soda deposits nearby. In turn those, and the fact that it was on China's northern border, made it a key railroad center. I was just glad I wasn't seeing it from the back of one of those mule carts in the winter.

"We are almost at the station. You have your case ready? We may have to hurry. We are a little late." He giggled, an obvious sign that he was nervous. He was probably worried about what to do with me if I did miss the train. Anywhere else he could have left me to catch the next one — moving me to a hotel to wait, if necessary. In China, you don't leave visiting foreigners alone, especially in a town like Tatung, which I suspected had to be high on the restricted list because of its strategic importance.

I caught his eye, and tried to reassure him. "We'll make it," I said. From his expression, it didn't seem to help much. We were in the land of the bureaucratic machine, I knew. Someone higher up had given orders that I should be shipped back to Peking. Down the line, the task had fallen on him. You didn't argue with the machine, you just did it. Unless, of course, you were at or near the top, but that was the way it was in a lot of countries.

I tried again. I patted my case. "I'm all ready to make a run the moment we stop." My hand left a mark on the case; some of the dust had settled on it, leaving a thin film. The dust outlined the squares where I'd once had some travel stickers. That was when I was young, before I knew such things were tacky. I could still remember removing them one night around two A.M. in a hotel room in the Philippines.

The car traveled the last mile or so with its horn blaring, forcing other road users to the shoulder. Most were bicycles, carts, or old trucks. One advantage of being in a country with no private cars is that provided you pull rank you don't have to worry about traffic jams. Though I hate such systems, I was glad about it now — I figured a thirty-second delay could have meant a front-seat cardiac.

My interpreter was out of the car the second we stopped. He was the first Chinese I had seen hurrying; I'd always thought it was not consistent with keeping face. I scurried behind him into the station. It was constructed solidly, Soviet style, like the hotel I'd stayed in overnight — both, I guessed, dated back to the early days after the Revolution when the Russians were friends and had sent in their hundreds of thousands of helpers and experts. Now, as far as I knew, the only good Russian was Stalin — not because he was dead (though that always helped in such relationships) but because after him the Soviet Union went revisionist and bourgeois.

There was a showing of tickets, an examination of my authorization to travel (in China, you don't move about anywhere when you want to), and then we were waved through. We took the steps to the overpass, with his feet moving three times to every step of mine. By the top, I was breathing through my mouth, and beginning to worry about him. On the straight, he managed to speak through the pants.

"We should be on time. Someone will be waiting to meet you when you arrive. I apologize that there is no one available to travel with you."

I found I was having to struggle to keep up. I'd been sitting around in New York for too long. My bag was heavy. As always on such a trip, it was packed to capacity. I tended to fill it with everything I might need if the visit was extended. Maddy had called it my home in a bag. She'd meant it viciously; what she was saying was that I was someone who wanted to live out of hotel rooms and a suitcase because I wouldn't grow up. I'd spent so much time hurtling from one country to another that I had ceased to have a real home. Even my speech had absorbed the words and rhythms of a dozen nations. "You don't even *sound* like an American," she'd screamed at me once. That was one of the times when she'd begun by talking about children.

We made the platform like two characters from an old movie, he going as fast as he could without actually running, I stumbling and grinning inanely at the staring crowds of people that we swept aside.

Later, my Chinese hosts were to tell me of a slogan, popular in the ten years of the Cultural Revolution, which had proclaimed, "Better a socialist train that is late than a capitalist train that is on time." This was obviously a capitalist train. It was already moving. The engine was well into the distance, beginning to build up speed. A long line of coaches was pulling out of the station behind it. We both stopped. My interpreter's face was full of frustration and concern.

Perhaps it was because I was still in my great-traveler mood, perhaps it was because he was a fellow train man. Perhaps it was like Maddy said, that I was just a thirty-three-year-old who wouldn't grow up. Whatever the reason, I began running, managed to get the door open on the final coach, and hurled myself inside.

When I pulled myself upright and got the door closed, I opened the window and looked back. My interpreter was in view still, but too far away for his face to be anything but a shape. I hoped it showed relief, or, at least, had managed to restore itself to inscrutability.

As he vanished from sight, I realized his hand had been making pointing, jabbing movements. It took several seconds for me to understand. He had been directing me to walk through the train.

Good cadre that he was, he did not want me to travel in the wrong class.

A walk through a Chinese train is an education, and one which I suspect is experienced by few foreigners.

The coach in which I found myself was occupied by several dozen peasants and three pigs. There were no seats. People stood or sat or crouched on the floor. In one corner, a noisy card game was under way. Several people were eating. There was an overpowering smell of pork fat and cabbage.

Although the car was crowded, men had pressed back to give me space. My bag was still on the floor where I had hurled it when I jumped. I retrieved it and, followed by curious eyes, I worked my way forward toward the rest of the train.

The car I left was, I found, the only one without seats. Those that followed on immediately were dirty and overcrowded, but had hard seats, six jammed into each pew. The corridors as well as overhead racks were crammed with sacks, bedrolls, and boxes. The deafening noise died as I passed through. Several people dropped their eyes, almost as though they did not want even that small contact with an unknown foreigner lest it compromise them in some undefined way.

Several coaches along, I was joined by a woman in off-white jacket and trousers which could or could not have been a uniform. She began remonstrating noisily the moment she saw me. I kept moving, hoping that she would tire but she remained at my heels. Despite the language barrier, there was no mistaking her meaning: I was in the wrong section of the train; I had no right to be here. Either they had chosen her because her features matched her job, or she had evolved to fit the work. Her squat, flat face had the markings of someone who had

had life bad, and was now getting her own back on whomever she could; it was a universal look, not necessarily Chinese — I'd seen it on prison officers, some army sergeants, not a few cops.

A coach further on, she achieved her desire. I found myself stepping straight in front of a PLA soldier, on guard, I supposed, because the train had come from the border with the Soviet Union. He was young, maybe no more than eighteen, and his green uniform was crumpled and the jacket was several sizes too large. But he had a machine gun slung at his shoulder and the moment he saw me it was obvious that my presence made him nervous. I stopped and waited while the woman talked with him. Then, at his gesture, I produced my papers. Either they meant little to him or I was something so out of his experience that he was taking no chances, because he signaled me to remain where I was, and the woman went forward, obviously to fetch more help.

He'd unslung the gun, which now dangled at his side. I didn't think he expected he'd have to use it, but his fear made me cautious. I kept my hands where he could see them and tried to keep my mouth in a fixed smile. His shoes made me want to tell him it was all going to be all right — they were canvas, well worn, with a gash on the toe of the left one.

The train swayed, sending me off balance for a moment, and when I righted myself I saw he had drawn back and raised the gun.

"Easy, easy," I said, beginning to sweat.

He launched into a stream of words, breaking his own tension, but leaving me no wiser and no more relaxed. With many languages, even if you don't recognize words, there is a tone that indicates some of the sense. With Chinese, nothing. The effect is a total inability in the hearer to understand, or even to guess at what is being said. It was something that chilled me now. Later, it was a fear I was to get to know well.

Because of the the boy's nervousness, I was glad when the squat-faced woman reappeared. She was accompanied by a man who wore a dark gray Mao suit and an air of weary authority. His face was disconcerting; the skin was smooth, the features boyish, but his hair had begun to recede and was flecked with white.

He spoke to me in what I recognized with surprise as Russian. I didn't know whether he'd understand me, but I felt that was something we had to get straight right away.

"I don't understand," I said. "I'm American."

He did.

"Show me your ticket and your papers," he said.

I handed them over with what I hoped seemed like resigned deference. With the pleasure of the locomotive plant wearing off, I was getting screwed up with China again. Still if I was going to throw tantrums, a train with a frightened boy soldier, an officious woman official, and an unknown cadre wasn't the place to start.

As he worked through the papers, slowly, carefully, I became concious of the blare of martial music that echoed through the speakers throughout the train. I'd encountered it on the way to Tatung. It was the Chinese equivalent of Muzak. The peasants had to listen to it. Foreigners and high officials who got to travel "soft" class, which is where I'd been heading, were able to switch it off.

"You are American? An engineer? You are here on holiday?" He spoke English with a faint American accent. I should have found it reassuring. I didn't.

"To work," I said. I tried to invoke some distant authority. "I was invited by your government. To study railroad construction." The moment I had spoken, I decided my language was not basic enough. I began to amend the sentence so that he would understand, but he waved his hand, arrogantly, dismissively. "I understand what you say," he said.

He handed back my papers.

"You are in the wrong section of the train." He spoke to the woman. I think he was telling her that she did right, because she retreated with what could have been a smile curling one corner of her lip. I got the impression that it would have turned into a full smile if the guard had shot me there and then.

I turned my attention back to the official, and began trying to explain why I had leaped aboard the train, but he was already turning to lead me away.

We left the crowded "hard" section of the train, and entered the second-class portion, that known as hard sleeper. It still wasn't lux-ury — three-tiered beds with thin mattresses — but it was obviously a big jump up. You could tell that from the occupants as we passed. They looked like supervisors or low-ranking party officials, men who worked with their heads and kept their hands soft.

My section of the train was beyond that. I wouldn't have reached it without an escort. There was another guard. It was also locked off. Impossible to know whether this was to protect the occupants from the lower-ranking cadres and peasants outside or whether it was to stop any foreigners inside from straying. Maybe a bit of both.

The guard unlocked the door, and we passed through. It was only a matter of feet, but it was like passing from the staff quarters to the guest bedrooms of a big hotel. The compartment into which I was led had lace curtains, white linen headrests, potted plants, and — mercifully — no music or barked announcements. On a table were flasks of hot water, mugs, and packets of green tea. There was a faint smell of cologne that could have come from some form of air-fresh-ening device, or from one of the three men who were already seated. They were all Chinese. The quality and cut of their jackets conveyed their ranking, but probably not as tellingly as the well-layered cheeks. Two were asleep; the other, a younger man, was studying papers from a leather case that lay open on his knees. He could have been a young executive taking the Shuttle.

My escort returned my papers at the door. "Your seat is here," he said.

I didn't say anything. I was staring down at his shoes. They were black leather, very new, very shiny. It was another look I was to get to know well.

"You must not wander the train again," he said. "It is not right." The word could have meant anything from "safe" to "legal."

"I'm just tired and hungry," I said. "All I want to do is rest and eat."

My seat was by the window. I flopped into it, exchanged a nod with the young executive-type who was now using a calculator, and poured water over some sprinkled tea. I placed the lid on the mug, and waited for the tea to drift to the bottom. The alternative, I'd found, was sucking water through narrowed lips to act as a filter.

I flipped open my bag — it was one of those cases that open at the middle, the kind the English call Gladstone bags — and took out Kissinger's *White House Years*. I'd only recently gotten around to it, and it was the China references that attracted me. I'd been doing a lot of background reading in the short time I'd had — that was my way about anywhere I had an assignment.

I opened the book, read a couple of paragraphs, decided again I liked the style if not the man, and set it aside. I didn't really want to read, but the open book was a good prop.

The train was straining now, beginning a haul up a long grade. The land was rocky, riddled by depressions, hard, exposed-looking. You didn't grow anything here; you tore it apart for what was underneath.

I risked the tea; it still wasn't ready, but I drank nevertheless. It made me realize I was hungry — I'd eaten early to be at the plant by seven-thirty. I considered going to look for something, but decided not to; inertia as much as anything.

Putting the book and mug aside, I reached into my bag and extracted a folder — the key notes on my assignment. I wasn't sure why I opened it — I knew most of it by heart, and if I was being summoned back to Peking for a meeting with the Railways Ministry it surely was not going to take place before the next morning. Maybe it was to show the young executive opposite that I was a worker of sorts too.

My eyes rushed over some basic factual notes: "Post Liberation 1949, 6,000 miles of railroad track, now 25,000, projected for year 2,000, 50,000 miles . . . Today manufactures nearly all its own rolling stock, track materials, and locomotives . . ." Actual figures followed. I'd penciled in the margin: "Only place left you can see a new steam loco running on a new stretch of track . . ."

A good place, in other words, to be a railroad engineer. In most of the world, there had been little real construction work since the beginning of the century. The name of the engineer's job was maintenance. Here, it was like being back in the old days of striking out across the continent to the West. The developed world was forsaking the train, had tied itself to the automobile. It had forgotten what the coming of the railroad had really meant — the complete revolution of people's lives as travel moved from the twelve miles an hour (maximum) of the horse to a new creature that could keep up fast and even speeds hour after hour. Here, it was still happening. Much of China was still moving from the bullock cart to the steam cart.

The door slid open, and a young girl with braids hanging from a white cap pointed at me, and said, "Eat. You come. Eat now."

I got up and followed her. I debated taking my case, but left it. One thing was certain — no one was going to steal it. Search it, maybe, but you expected that.

The official with black shoes met me at the door of the dining compartment. Like the coach I was in, it looked turn of the century. The dark, shiny woodwork reflected the glow of ornate brass lamps. There was an expanse of empty tables, and then, at the far end, about a dozen men, all drinking, laughing, and talking amid the debris of a meal. As I watched, one stood and drunkenly tossed a pack of cigarettes to a man across the aisle.

Only one other table was set, one to the immediate left of the door through which I had entered. The official gestured to it. The table covering, an oiled piece of cloth, didn't match the room's elegance. On it were a bowl and chopsticks, a glass, two bottles of beer that I already knew from my short experience would be warm, and three dishes of food.

I sat down, and began to fill my bowl. The official leaned over me. "You know them?" he asked. He could only mean the men at the end of the compartment.

I was genuinely surprised. "No. Why?"

He straightened himself with answering. "No reason," he said. He paused. "Enjoy your lunch," he added, and he was gone.

Three more dishes arrived as I ate, and I hurried. First, I was hungry. Second, rightly or wrongly, I sensed resentment from the other occupants of the dining car. They showed it in small but obvious ways — occasional nervous glances, voices that dropped in volume as they remembered that I might be able to hear them. At the distance, and with the background noise of the train, it would, in fact, have been difficult to pick out more than the odd, individual word even if they had shouted.

Even then, I would not have understood the language. It took me several minutes to work out that it was probably Russian. That made sense; the train had come from the Soviet border. The line west from Peking through Tatung was a secondary route to Moscow, though not highly favored or publicized now (for both the Russians and the Chinese, it took passengers too close to sensitive areas). I'd heard a lot of Russian spoken in the past — in Egypt after the Soviet experts had been told to leave the country. I'd been one of the American engineers who'd gone in to help pick up some pieces. I had had to learn the Cyrillic script to understand maps left behind, and the language's sound had become familiar from tapes that were forever being translated for me. The Russian I heard from the men in the dining car, though, was meaningless; only a few words conveyed anything.

Despite my haste to finish, they left before me. I had just started the soup, the last course in a Chinese meal. One halted the exodus near my table; he dropped his cigarette lighter and had to kneel in the swaying gap between the tables to find it. The others waited impatiently, silent, avoiding my look. The man looked sheepish when he finally found it. I watched him from the corner of my eye. He had the glazed expression of the very drunk. What drew me, though, was the difference between his features and his bearing. He was tall, bespectacled, pale, thin-faced, the epitome of a professor in some esoteric subject. His bearing, though, was stiff, upright, that of a soldier, even now when he was full of drink.

He caught my look, inclined his head, and in a minute they were all gone.

The Chinese official was by the door again when I left, but neither of us said anything.

The land outside was arid plain; in the compartment even the young executive figure was dozing. I read two more paragraphs of Kissinger, gave another quick flip through the folder, and joined him.

I woke a few minutes outside Peking, roused by music that someone had switched on inside the compartment. Two of my traveling companions had already left, the other was struggling into a topcoat.

I waited inside after we came to a halt, knowing that another guide would collect me. He did, but only after I pointedly had to ignore the gestures of two officials who wanted me to leave. He was small, wiry, and surly. I got the impression I'd kept him on duty late. I wanted to apologize; he'd probably started work around thirteen hours before; the chances were he had an hour's bike ride home after he'd gotten rid of me. But I found I had neither the words nor the chance, as he swept me through the vastness of the station.

It was after nine, an hour when many Chinese are going to bed. But the station was still packed: crowds sat on boxes, some playing cards, others eating. Groups stuggled on to escalators carrying sackfuls of belongings, throats were cleared at rows of spittoons, an official yelled orders through a loudspeaker.

Outside, it was almost dark. We came out into an enormous square. Buses were parked in rows at a large, open terminus. A solitary wall-poster to my right showed a woman in a pinafore lifting the lid of a pan and breathing in the scent of cooking with great relish. It wasn't J. Walter Thompson, but then it had little competition.

My guide led me to a waiting car, an old, dark-blue Fiat. There were curtains at the back, and a toy panda dangled in the front window. I got inside, clutching my case, and we drove off, the guide in the front. He'd said little, and I stopped struggling with my conscience and settled back in the well-worn seat.

The car drove north. There were few other vehicles, but a great noise of horns even through the closed windows.

We turned into Chang An Avenue — the Avenue of Perpetual Peace — the main east-west artery. There were more cars here, but they were lost in its vast width. On the far side of the road I saw the Peking Hotel, towering over its surroundings, and then the Tian an Men Gate where proclamations from the emperors were once lowered from a parapet to officials below. Mao had proclaimed the Republic from the same parapet. His picture was still there — one of the few still left around. The new pragmatic China hadn't actually declared him a nonperson, but it didn't want too many memories of him around either.

We made another turn from west to north, and twenty minutes later pulled off the road through guarded gates into the grounds of my hotel. It was neither as central nor as luxurious as the Peking, and the fact that I was there was probably a good indication that neither I nor my assignment was first-rate in Chinese eyes.

The hotel, nicely named the Friendship Hotel, was a small city really, placed in the northwestern suburbs, out beyond the zoo, on the way to the Emperor's Summer Palace. A series of buildings, gray brick with green tiled Chinese roofs, had been built campus style to house thousands of Russian technicians and experts in the early fifties. Now they held an overflow of businessmen and tourists, a resident population of "foreign experts," left-wingers with the China bug who helped with tasks like translating, and — it was said — the odd visiting politician or delegation that the Chinese wanted to keep out of sight.

I said a brief good night to the guide. For a long time after the car was out of sight, I stood on the wide sweep of steps to the hotel entrance, breathing in the evening air.

In front of me were the main gates, PLA guards checking all visitors. Chinese were not allowed inside unless they were expected. It was a bit reminiscent of the old pre-Revolution Shanghai Park with its sign "No dogs or Chinese." But this was to protect the Chinese themselves, from possible contagion. Whether they wanted it or not.

Finally I went inside. As I'd guessed, the dining room was closed. I bought a bar of chocolate and a bottle of Coke, and went up to my room. There was a note waiting, placed carefully on the old leather-topped desk, still complete with its inkwell and scratch pen.

I opened the envelope and walked across to the window to read it. It was a formal message advising me that I would be collected at eight-thirty the following morning for a meeting at the Ministry of Railways.

I tossed it onto the bed behind me. Perhaps it meant we were on our way. I realized I was too tired to care.

Reaching up, I began to close the heavy curtains. The street lamps outside illuminated the neat rows of plane trees that lined the street between the four-story buildings. A tour bus stopped beneath, and began disgorging its occupants. They had probably been to an opera or a duck restaurant.

Suddenly a new movement halted my hand. A short convoy of black Hong Qi cars, the limousines reserved for VIPs, passed below, and then stopped at a building beyond, across the street.

I stood in the darkened window a long time, watching the cars empty. Two men left one of the cars, then paused at the doorway to the building, sucking on cigarettes, as though reluctant to go inside.

Finally, in a rapid movement, I tugged the curtain shut. Kicking off my shoes, I found the Coke bottle, removed the cap, and drank deep.

Then, almost absentmindedly, I retrieved the letter, reread it, and placed it carefully on the desk.

I should have been pleased despite the tiredness; something was happening at last. But my mind was on the cavalcade of cars, and on the men who had stood outside, lit by the street lamp.

It was too far to see them clearly, but one of them had been unmistakable. A tall, scholarly-looking man. But standing stiff and upright like someone from the military.

The man on the train.

The shiver was only exhaustion, I told myself. But I dislike coincidences.

2

4 5

*T*he next two days passed in a series of meetings. Outside of the Ministry bureaucrats, I had anticipated some antagonism from any railroad professionals I met. I well knew that the job I was here to do was one that could have been done equally well by any competent Chinese railroad engineer. It called for me to look at the area between Nanking and Shanghai, see how traffic capacity might be improved, and give an opinion on various schemes for new feeder lines. But I was here precisely because I wasn't Chinese; my investigation would be the first, almost preliminary stage, of a report on which the Chinese could then raise funds if they wished from the World Bank. It was my professional impartiality that they were buying.

As it was, though, I met nothing but gentle cooperation. If no one actually rushed to volunteer the maps, papers, figures, and projections I needed to study before looking at the area, neither did anyone refuse to produce them once I asked.

I left the hotel soon after seven each morning — the Railways Ministry was a new, square concrete structure in the outer suburbs — and did not return until the evening. Although many of the officials with whom I met spoke English, I now had my own interpreter, a woman whose age I guessed as being somewhere between twenty-three and twenty-eight (exact ages, I'd found, were hard to gauge, whether with men or women). Her name was Chu Ming. In Chinese, the surname comes first. I called her, formally, "Miss Chu." Her attitude to me was, I think, best described as smilingly distant. Her presence, however, represented yet another improvement in cooperation. Soon, I hoped, I would get permission to travel the seven hundred miles to Nanking to begin work there. So far, all the Chinese were saying was "soon," which had all the come-on and lack of guarantees that I used to get from teenage dates.

On the third night I ate alone in the cavernous main dining room of the Friendship Hotel — Chu Ming had already pedaled off to wherever home was — and then went on working in my room. Even if I had not known the hotel's history, I would have guessed the rooms had been built for long-term residency. Mine had an outer hall that also served as a small sitting room or office. It was furnished with a large, old wooden desk and chair and a huge, overstuffed sofa. The walls were papered in a red and gold pattern which would have been blinding if it had not lost much of its color with age. The bedroom, beyond, had a large bed with a dark wooden headboard and springs that dipped like a hammock, a wardrobe, several chests of drawers, and an old-fashioned mahogany hat-and-coat stand. Beyond that there was a bathroom, with heavily stained white fixtures and water that trickled brown. The floors throughout were bare. It had the air of not having been touched since the Russians had left. I liked it.

I worked until well after eleven, long after I heard many of my neighbors go to bed (or, at least, heard the echoing sounds of plumbing that I imagined preceded the going to bed). Once, I heard a convoy of cars, and checked the window in case it was the Russians. But the cars passed. I had seen nothing of my Russian neighbors since that first night. Maybe they had moved on.

I fell asleep with my head still spinning with figures and with Chinese place names. Sometime after I descended into darkness there was a dream — a succession of huge, double doorways, each flanked with two dragons, not real dragons but the brightly colored pottery ones with open mouths that the Chinese use as trash cans. As each doorway opened, I found myself facing yet another closed one; a succession of doors, with no end in sight.

My body was wet with sweat when I awoke. The room was in almost total darkness; no sound penetrated from outside. There was no knowing whether I had been asleep for minutes or for hours.

The bedclothes were pushed back in a chaotic heap, as though I had been struggling with myself. I raised myself and leaned forward to straighten them.

Then I saw him.

At first, he was no more than a shape. But the instant I moved, he clicked on the table lamp near his hand. The light blinded me for a minute. When my vision cleared, I saw he was dressed formally in a suit but without a tie. That was less important than the fact that he held a gun in his left hand. It was small, the kind you imagine a woman carrying in her bag for protection, but his hand was slender, delicate, and in it the weapon did not look ridiculous.

I would have been more frightened if I had not recognized him. The man with the scholarly look and the military bearing. Curiosity damped down the fear.

"Please sit up slowly, and place your hands flat on your thighs. I promise you that unless you do something stupid, you will not be harmed."

His voice had a rough edge that, again, contrasted with his features; it was as though he had developed it that way as a deliberate antidote. He had a glass near his side. While I had slept, he had uncorked my bottle of Scotch and poured himself a healthy slug. As I watched, he reached out with his free hand, and drained the glass.

It was obvious that he was nervous; and that, suddenly, did scare me. I had grown up with enough weapons around to know that fear, booze, and bullets were not a good combination, especially when you are at the wrong end of the barrel.

"You were on the train," I said. "I remember you. I think you've got the wrong man." I was talking for the sake of talking. It was like being faced with a wild dog; you calm it first, then you worry about how to get away.

He reached out as though to pour more drink, but withdrew his hand at the last moment. "A good brand," he said, "good whiskey." Without changing his tone, he continued, "I had no choice. I saw you at your window the night we arrived. I know no one else. There is nowhere I could go."

"Why me?" I said. I had followed his orders. My back was beginning to ache, but I didn't think it was the moment to move.

"You're an American," he said.

It was a statement, not a question, but I nodded assent.

"I know," he said. "I heard Sokolov — he's one of our KGB companions — ask the conductor." He poured more whiskey, and in an unexpected gesture carried it over to me, placing it quickly beside the bed.

"You can get up," he said, "but please remember I will shoot you if I have to do so." He lifted the pistol. "And do not think I would be worried by the noise this would make. A gun like this is surprisingly quiet, and my experience is that people are unfailingly lacking in curiosity. The shot might wake your next-door neighbor, but I assure you that after lying awake for a few seconds he would sink back into grateful sleep again."

I believed him. I slid out of bed carefully, avoiding any sudden movements. Finding my robe on a chair, I covered my nakedness. Then I checked my watch — three A.M., later than I'd thought — and sipped the Scotch. It was neat, and it was early in the day to start drinking, but I wasn't complaining.

"Okay," I said finally. "Tell me what you want."

He had found another glass and poured it half full. He flopped in a chair, gun in one hand, glass in the other, and said, "I want a small favor from you, a very small favor."

He stopped talking, waiting for me to react, but I remained silent.

"You will be doing a great service for your country," he added finally.

"Suppose you just tell me," I said. I raised my eyes to a huge painting of a pagoda rising out of the mist; I'd found that hard drinkers hate to feel they're being stared at. Besides, appeals to my patriotism made me even more nervous.

"My name is Yakov," he said. "Boris Grigorevich Yakov. Colonel." The rasp was more pronounced than ever. "Your CIA know of me. They are planning to help me defect."

His eyes were searching for a reaction. I wasn't trying to hide one, but my face was set in numbed surprise.

"However," he went on, "I have a problem. I can wait no longer. Yesterday, my belongings were searched while I was away from the hotel — we are here on a delegation to discuss the border problem, only semiofficially, you understand. Last night, I overheard *things*." He accented the word. I didn't ask him to specify; he was already telling me much more than I wanted to hear. We had crossed a borderline where I ceased to be an innocent visitor; if he was telling me the truth — and I had no reason to doubt that he was — I was absorbing the kind of information that can get you pushed under cars or locked up in windowless rooms.

I couldn't leave; I couldn't jump him. I did the only thing I could do, took another gulp of my Scotch and let him continue.

"I believe they are getting ready to send me back to Moscow. They are only waiting for an aircraft. Perhaps I will be taken back unconscious, sedated. I have heard of such things."

My eyes moved to the door and the curtained windows.

"No one followed me," he said. "Do not worry — you are safe. There was one guard. I dealt with him. I think perhaps they will not find me gone until six or even later. They will not know where I am."

"They'll suspect you are still on the grounds," I said. The complex was miles from downtown Peking; in China in the small hours you don't just hail a cab or catch a bus.

"Perhaps," he said. "More likely they will think I had a rendezvous with someone who, by the time they realize I am gone, will have taken me far from here. Besides, even if they thought I might still be around, this is a vast place. Fifteen hundred rooms. I read it on a postcard."

"So what do you want me to do?" It was already obvious, but I needed him to spell it out.

It was as I had thought. He wanted to hide out overnight in my room. In the morning, when the room got its quick clean he would hide in the bathroom. I would be in there with him, pretending to bathe, so that the hotel staff would leave the room alone.

What he wanted me to do then was go to the U.S. Embassy, insist on speaking to a ranking official, and tell him what had happened. "If he's not CIA, he'll soon get them involved," Yakov concluded. "They will have me away from here fast, don't worry. It will all be over in a few hours."

I found his faith in U.S. intelligence and officialdom touching; I'd rubbed up against both a lot over the years in odd places. Like all overlarge pieces of machinery, they'd developed surplus bits that just gummed everything up. Still, it was no time to say that. And *if* I did go to the embassy, I had an interest in praying he was right.

"If I do what you ask, I'll be finished here in China." That was a secondary worry, but I was playing for time, thinking of alternatives. I couldn't see any except waiting until he let me outside and then yelling for the Chinese Public Security Department. That was unthinkable. I had no wish to hand him over to the Chinese. Nor, if I was mercenary, would it do me any good with them — they'd probably worry about my motives so much that they'd throw me out after questioning anyway. Besides, even though I didn't want to get dewy-eyed about it, if he was a defector with any real value, it was my duty to help.

I realized he was answering my objection, giving it more weight than it was worth. "Not necessarily," he said. "In fact, I would say not at all. There is nothing to connect the two of us. I imagine your intelligence people will be very discreet in removing me."

"What happens if they won't listen to me? If they say they haven't heard of you, think you're some sort of nut?"

His face went white, and I saw his hands tighten around the glass, empty again by now.

"They will," he whispered. "They will." But the thought obviously worried him. He leaned forward, his face suddenly conspiratorial.

"Tell them," he said, "that I have brought the VRR File."

"The VRR File," I repeated. It meant nothing, sounded innocuous except for the way he dropped his voice when he spoke the words.

"That's right," he said. "Tell them that."

He volunteered no more, and I did not press him. If I was going along with his wishes — and I saw no real alternative — I thought it best I knew as little more as possible. My problem, having decided to open the can, was how to keep the worms inside. The truth was I didn't want anything to louse up this trip. In engineering terms, it might be a bit of a joke assignment to my colleagues. But I needed it; I needed to be here, away from everything. Besides, seeing those trains at Tatung had triggered a lot of memories, made me anxious to get back to my roots.

We discussed a few practicalities in the next half hour. Like the time I should leave — nine o'clock, we decided, time for the floor waiters to finish with the room, not so early that my exit would look urgent. And how — by taxi, but not direct to the embassy in case the KGB men with the Russian delegation had some way of checking that. I would take the cab to the Peking Hotel, then walk. There was no problem about Chu Ming, my interpreter. My first genuine appointment was not until the afternoon; I had already told her I would be working in my room in the morning and would not need her.

The more Yakov drank, the more sober he seemed to get. The only effect I could notice was that his voice became more gentle, but that might have been because he saw that I was now coöperating. I had a soft spot for drunks. My father was one. Not a get-roaring-loaded, smash-up-everything drunk, but a quiet, rather sad one.

We settled down for the rest of the night soon afterward. It was after four. I risked a glance through the corner of the curtains at the building opposite before I went to bed, but the street was silent, peaceful.

Yakov made up a bed on the floor from cushions and spare linen from the top of the wardrobe. I fell asleep, wondering whether I shouldn't wait until he fell into drunken unconsciousness and then roll him outside, leaving him to gatecrash someone else.

I woke once, soon after it became light, and he was propped upright in his improvised bed, drink within reach, gun cradled against his chest like a lover.

When I awoke again, it was seven o'clock, and he was already cleaned up and fresh-looking, and two hours later I left on my way to the embassy.

The cab, which I obtained the regular way by going up to the hotel service desk and asking for one, dropped me at the Peking Hotel's west wing. I held out money, and the driver took the amount that he wanted and made me wait while he wrote me a flimsy receipt that I couldn't read.

A fellow visitor had told me at the bar one night that taxi drivers handed copies to Public Security at the end of every day. That way, they could keep tabs on your every step — for obvious reasons, not many foreigners tried to struggle with the public transport system. He might just have been right — he was an old China visitor — but I had put it down to the spy paranoia that seems to grip Westerners the moment they hit Communist countries. At this moment, though, I'd have believed it if someone had told me that the woman cleaning around the cars in the parking lot was an agent and her broom a disguised TV camera.

Because anything else would have seemed suspicious, I went inside and wandered through the series of tourist shops that stretched the length of the long lobby. I did one complete circuit, bought copies of *Newsweek* and the *China Daily*, the local English-language newspaper, and returned to the street.

I turned left into Chang An Avenue. I was no longer the only Westerner, as in Tatung, but among the hundreds of people who milled around I could pick out only a dozen or so of us. A crowd is supposed to be the best place to hide yourself, but not a Chinese crowd when you are an American. Because of that, even though I knew that outwardly nothing had changed, I felt vulnerable. How did I know the Chinese hadn't kept watch on the Soviet delegation, and had seen Yakov leave and enter my block? There were plenty of vantage points, and infrared glasses weren't high technology. Just as worrying, if Yakov had spotted me at the window and recognized me as the American from the train, wasn't it possible one of the other Russians had too? Maybe someone was following me right now.

I waited to cross at an intersection, and used the moment to turn around and look at the crowds who milled behind me. If I was being followed and if my shadow was Chinese, no way would I know. It wasn't true that all Chinese looked alike; it *was* true that it took your eye time to get adjusted — and there were so damn many of them.

My eyes flicked over the still-unfamiliar sights as I walked: the traffic cops in white jackets and white peaked caps conducting from wooden stands, their own bicycles parked at the side; the battered trucks and hundred of bikes, many laden with bundles, others pulling carts that you would have thought needed engine power.

Scores of tour buses passed, horns blaring as they worked through the bike-riders. I guessed they were on their way to the Friendship Store to stock up on souvenirs; I'd read that the Chinese cannot understand the Western preoccupation with shopping, but that if they were religious they would be offering up prayers for it.

I turned off before the Friendship Store. I hadn't been to the embassy yet, but I'd studied the map before setting out, and knew I had to make a left at the International Club. The area I entered had been specially built to bring most of the embassies together.

In its own way, it was like the jump from hard to soft sleeper on the train. There were no gates locking off the area from Chang An, but suddenly there were no Chinese in sight except the soldiers outside the buildings that could have been expensive suburban homes. They stood stiff under umbrellas supported in concrete blocks.

The trees were tidier, more ordered, here; I heard the sound of my own feet on the pavement and felt eyes following me. The day was beginning to heat up now, but was not warm enough to justify the sweat I felt on my hands. I shifted my case from right to left. It was my old faithful Gladstone bag, still overpacked with bits and pieces. I'd brought it because Yakov said it made it look as though I was keeping an appointment.

I missed the turn to the embassy, and didn't realize it until I saw a display case showing shots from American musicals on a side wall. I retraced my steps, found the main entrance. The Chinese guard paid no notice as I entered the short driveway; his job was to keep out the Chinese, not me.

The American flag flying over the compound gave me a feeling of reassurance. I chose the nearer of two modern buildings, and was met by a receptionist, a silver-haired man in a navy blazer who greeted me a shade less formally than a Rothschild's butler. I already had my passport in my free hand, and I held it out.

"My name is David Piper," I said. "I'm an American visiting Peking on business. I have some information of a highly sensitive nature that I would like to discuss with someone."

He took it in his stride, directed me to a small waiting area. A minute later, a second man arrived, took my passport from the receptionist, stared at me, and went away. I tried to lose myself in a copy of *Fortune* but it really stood no chance. I flipped the pile of other magazines, and got to thinking that the room would be a kind of paradise for the students who lobbied tourists to buy them imported U.S. magazines from the English-language bookshop. They couldn't buy themselves, because the shop would accept only foreign scrip, not real money.

I waited for nearly half an hour. Twice I wandered out but met blank stares. The waiting was increasing my nervousness, and it was making me more resentful that I'd gotten involved. Finally, a woman came for me, led me up one floor, along a corridor, and through an open door with no handle on the outside. The room I entered was bare of anything but a desk and two chairs.

A man in his mid-thirties, maybe two or three years older than me, sat waiting on one of them. He wore a white short-sleeved shirt and a tie with a club logo. My passport was in his hands, and he was flipping the pages like someone expecting to find a secret message.

He waited until the woman left. He spoke without raising his eyes, which did not make me warm to him. "What can I do for you, Mr. Piper? I understand you have some sort of problem."

There was a weary, emotionless quality in his voice that made it easy to guess what he thought: that I'd gotten into minor trouble like being caught dealing on the black market or trying to make a pass at a Chinese girl. He'd already decided I was some damned fool who hadn't remembered where the hell he was, and who now expected him to pick up the pieces.

His attitude made me go for shock value. "I'm at the Friendship Hotel," I said. "Top floor. Single room. Except that since around three this morning I've been sharing it with a man who says he's a Soviet army colonel with an arrangement with the CIA who are going to help him defect."

The pace accelerated after that. We changed rooms. A second, older man joined us. He had a hard, slim body, and tanned skin as though he used a gym and a sun lamp regularly. His mouth wore a greeter's smile that was not echoed by his eyes.

Mostly, he remained quiet as I repeated the story in detail. When he did speak, his voice was soft, the accent American but beyond that unplaceable; I guessed that he was a man who had reached a position where he got his way without shouting, and that the lack of accent meant that, like me, he'd lived in a lot of places. At the end, he asked me if Yakov had said anything else — given me a name "or anything." I started to reply, but he pushed across a pad, handed me a pencil. He wore a heavy signet ring.

I wrote down "VRR," feeling slightly silly. They both left the room, leaving me alone. I thought of all the spy movies I had ever seen, and imagined frantic code messages to and from Washington. Or perhaps they were simply debating how big a nut I was . . . Part of me was still refusing to believe what was happening.

The older man returned twenty minutes later. He had plastic cups of coffee for both of us. Since I'd last seen him, he had taken off the jacket of his tan suit as though he'd been involved in a flurry of activity. The pocket of his shirt was monogrammed with what looked like RA. He kicked the door shut, and sat on the edge of the desk. Before he spoke, I could tell he was going to be conspiratorial and reassuring, maybe with just a touch of patronizing thrown in.

"I guess it would make you happier if your uninvited guest moved on as quickly as possible. Yes?"

There didn't seem to be an answer to that. I sipped my coffee. It was fresh, black.

"Okay." The man looked at his watch theatrically. "It's quarter past eleven. I'd like you to go back to your hotel, stay in your room. That won't look strange?"

I explained that I didn't expect my interpreter until the afternoon, that I'd already told her I'd be working alone in the morning.

He continued. "Okay. You'll have to skip lunch. I want you to go back, tell the Russian what's happening, wait with him.

"At one-forty-five two men will arrive and take him to the elevator. Don't worry, there'll be no one else about. At the same time, a tour bus will unload its passengers at the side entrance, the one that leads directly to the main restaurant. You know it?"

I did.

"Fine. Yakov'll join them. He doesn't have to do anything, nor say anything. As soon as he's there, they'll all leave again. You don't have to know anything that happens after that. Just take my word, it'll all go smoothly. Tell the Russian that."

"And me?"

My voice was subdued. I was impressed by what had been arranged so quickly, despite an instinctive distrust of the man. The machinations also made the situation seem much more real.

"You go on as before. This is just an interlude, a couple of commercials in the middle of the late-night movie. Only difference is that it never happened. Okay?"

He handed back my passport, and escorted me out of the room and along the corridor where he handed me over to a secretary. His movements were spare but agile; I could imagine him doing his daily pushups and spooning wheat germ on to his breakfast yogurt. He shook hands formally with a dry, firm hand.

"You weren't in 'Nam?" he said.

"Too young," I replied.

For a moment he looked as though he felt I'd been born too late just to annoy him. But the smile on his mouth faltered for only a part of a second. Then, he retrieved himself immediately. "We appreciate this," he said. "We really do."

He called me back as I neared the elevator. "I doubt we'll meet again, Mr. Piper. But if you ever need me, call the main number, ask for Andrews. Okay?"

Downstairs, I retrieved my bag. I had left it under the eye of the receptionist. I noticed that the pile of magazines had been squared neatly. Perhaps he'd been checking that I wasn't making off with one. I thought it more likely that, to him, the magazines were for looking at as a display rather than for looking through. Momentarily, I'd destroyed his decor.

Outside, pausing on the step, blinking in the sunlight, I felt for a minute as though I had just been initiated into some secret society. It was almost a disappointment when the guard at the gate did not spare me even a glance.

At that time, it still seemed what Andrews had said it was — just some interlude, and a mildly amusing one at that.

All that ended at twenty-three minutes past twelve. I know the time exactly because I looked at my watch the moment before I opened my hotel door, just to check how long I had before Yakov was collected.

Until then, everything had been completely normal and without event. The walk back to the Peking, the approach to the service desk and request for a cab, the ride back . . .

Then I opened the door.

Yakov was gone. I forced myself to enter, closing the door behind me. I checked the bathroom, half-expecting to find a body. Nothing. Nothing, that is, except that everything had been ripped apart. The mattress was crisscrossed with knife slashes, the sink had been torn away from the wall, boards had been pulled up from the floor, paneling from around a radiator lay in strips.

I poured a drink, downed it neat, and wandered among my belongings. My camera had been opened and hurled aside; the film extended from it like entrails. A can of talcum had been split apart, and the powder emptied over the floor. Suits lay scattered, tailing their strips of lining.

I hesitated, unsure what to do. I decided I had no real alternative. I picked up the telephone, waited for a long time before the hotel operator answered, and then asked for the embassy.

Andrews was on the line, matter-of-fact, within seconds of the call's being answered. He obviously realized there must be an emergency.

"You forgot something, Mr. Piper? Something about the partner you mentioned?"

I took the cue. "That's right, Mr. Andrews. With everything else, it slipped my mind. I forgot to say it doesn't look as though he'll be coming over after all. In fact, I'd hoped to hear from him today, but I haven't."

"Look, Mr. Piper, I've got an appointment not too far from your hotel. Just about to leave, in fact. Why don't I drop by?"

I said that would be fine, and we hung up.

While I waited, I checked the corridor, and then peered carefully through the window. Neither provided any clue, nor any cause for worry. At the far end of the corridor, I could see one of the floor waiters sitting reading. Outside, there were half a dozen or so Chinese on bicycles going past. No parked cars, no one watching. Nothing.

I started to pour another drink, and thought better of it. I could need all my wits. No way could this room be put together again.

I carried my Gladstone bag in from the door, dumped it near the bed, and then made a slow tour through my belongings. A solitary page of printed paper lay on the floor. My eyes found others, and I realized that the searchers had dissected the book I was reading. I guessed that was one way of dealing with Henry Kissinger.

Andrews arrived within thirty minutes. He must have left immediately. He had the sense to tap on the door before entering; my nerves couldn't have taken the shock of the handle turning.

He walked around slowly, hands in pockets, pausing occasionally to poke something with his foot. He stopped at a smear of red on the wall near the bathroom. I'd already seen it, realized it was blood. It looked like someone had tried to steady himself against it with a blood-stained hand.

Andrews took toilet paper, wet it, removed the mark carefully, and then flushed away the paper.

He did not say anything, and I did not ask. It was becoming more obvious to me every second that I was in deeper than I had ever wanted.

He moved into the hallway, stopped at the desk, and looked down at some sheets of paper that had been rifled through but left. "These yours?" he asked, lifting the pile.

They were my notes on what I needed to do, in particular all the places I needed to visit, when I was finally allowed to leave for Nanking. I explained. He flipped the pages until he found the list of place names, began to read them aloud. His pronunciation was sure, impressive, like someone who had studied it hard and used it a lot. I was surprised. Over the years I'd bumped into a lot of diplomats; those that spoke a foreign language always seemed to be in a country that didn't use it.

He finished reading. "You going to all these places?" he asked.

"I was. Mostly, they're towns that might need new rail lines linking them to the main track. At least, that's what the figures suggest. It helps to look, ask a few questions on the spot, get some impressions."

"And it's been here all the time, lying on this table?"

"Yes, I guess so." I didn't conceal my puzzlement; I couldn't see why he was so interested. But he did not explain.

Andrews replaced the paper, walked through to the bed and stared down at the springs and stuffing that had burst through the mattress. "The Chinese are gonna love this," he said, partly to himself.

The smile had gone, and without it he aged. I guessed he was early fifties. I suspected he didn't like aging. His hair was carefully combed and sprayed, to make the best use of what was there.

He turned to face me full on. "You don't know what they were looking for? Yakov wasn't carrying anything, didn't show you anything?"

"Only a gun. Like I told you, he wore a suit. He could have had something in the pockets. I wouldn't know."

"And he said that he had *that* file?" He still couldn't bring himself to speak the letters aloud; or, perhaps, he'd forgotten them.

I nodded.

Andrews continued to stare, deep in thought. Then he said, "You've got to report this. No question."

He moved over to where a floorboard had been lifted, and ran his hand underneath. "Must have been loose," he murmured, "made them suspicious . . ."

He straightened and gave me his full attention again. "What we want to do," he said, "is make sure that you aren't bothered more than necessary. I'd suggest that you tell them a story that's basically true, but that leaves a few things out. What I'd say, Mr. Piper, is that you left your room this morning and that everything was normal — get it? No mention of a man calling on you for help. You set off for the embassy simply because you needed some advice. You told us you'd been waiting around for permission to get out of Peking — say you wanted embassy guidance on whether there was anything you could do to get things hurried up."

He paused long enough to make sure I was listening closely enough.

"You talked with a man called Donaldson — medium height, glasses, fair hair, slight limp. He's commercial. Okay? Then you came back, found this, didn't know what to do, called us. I was in Donaldson's room when the call came, on my way out. Offered to look in. All right so far?"

"I'm listening."

"I came, saw, said you must have been robbed by another foreigner — Chinese don't behave like this. I couldn't wait with you — my appointment. Suggested you call the desk, get them to bring the Public Security."

"They'll know I called the embassy, but what if they taped the call? I asked for you."

"I shouldn't worry about that, Mr. Piper. Just take my word that it's not their scene. The Soviets and a lot of others, yes. But it's not the Chinese style, and they haven't got the equipment. If you were a visiting nuclear physicist, well, just maybe they'd bug you. But unless they know something about you that I don't know, Mr. Piper, I'd guess they wouldn't waste any valuable equipment on you."

He was watching me carefully to see if I was satisfied. My face must have told him I didn't believe him.

"Shit," I said, kicking a low stool that lay on its side. It moved a few feet, but made no discernible difference to the look of the room.

He smile what I knew was meant to be reassurance. "Don't worry," he said. "Don't look upon this as trouble. Regard it as a unique experience. A dash of excitement in your life." At least we'd progressed from an interlude in the late-night movie.

The questioning, gentle but persistent, polite yet unyielding, went on until well into the evening, and was then resumed the following morning. It took place first in the hotel, then in a room in a police station nearby.

The room was bleak, with hard chairs and a large bare table. There were two windows, but high, out of reach, and the only view was peeling green paint and my two interrogators. One spoke in London English between sucking on discolored, protruding teeth; the other, who sat with eyes half-closed, interrupted occasionally in Chinese. He had a bad cold, and had to keep dabbing away mucus.

Throughout the questioning, I kept my answers simple and short, confining myself to what was asked, and no more. The same questions kept reappearing in slightly different form. I knew what they were waiting for was for me to contradict myself. Then they would try to open up a gap. Andrews had warned me. Even without that, I think I would have remembered. I had been questioned in South Africa once. They have had a lot of practice there.

Apart from the use of repetition and the persistence, there was no attempt to use pressure. When I wanted to go to the washroom, they led me there; if I said I wanted a drink, more tea was brought. From time to time, they would leave me alone, and then I would try to gauge whether they believed what I was telling them. Nothing they said or did gave me any indication.

On the morning of the second day, I asked to see someone from the embassy, not because it was something I really wanted, but because I suspected it was expected of an innocent man. My interrogators noted the request without comment, and having made the demand I did not press it.

Once, I found myself wondering what my interpreter, Chu Ming, thought of all this. Probably, she'd already been reassigned to someone else.

Finally, on the afternoon of the second day, I was led outside, helped into a curtained car and driven off. I thought at first we were returning to the hotel, but we continued downtown. I knew it was pointless to ask questions, and I contented myself with staring out, enjoying seeing ordinary people after a day and a half of confinement.

Winds had brought the first bad dust storms of the year, and people walked huddled, many with their faces covered with masks and scarves.

We stopped not far south of Tian an Men Square in what I recognized from my maps and reading as the old Legation Quarter. It was here that foreign diplomats and troops were concentrated until Liberation. The buildings — embassies, clubs, hospitals, barracks — had been built in a mixture of early twentieth-century European styles from the mock-baroque to the pseudo-Gothic. Much of the area had been demolished; other buildings were coming down, and a haze of rubble dust swirled in the air with the sand brought by the winds.

Though the foreigners and most of their buildings had gone, the area still had a cutoff feeling. The shady streets were almost empty of any Chinese.

The car drove through the guarded gateway of one European-style building that did remain. We passed the imposing columns, and got out at the rear of the building. Flanked by my two interrogators, I was led inside and handed over to waiting uniformed guards who took me up one floor in a service elevator.

The room which we finally entered was impressive in the way no other office I had seen so far had been. There was a desk, deep in papers, a conference table and chairs, and — at the other end of the room — a sofa and collection of small lacquered tables.

On a side table, coffee bubbled in a percolator. Nearby there was a board of carved jade set with red and black Chinese chess pieces. The walls were hung with examples of calligraphy. Even to my untutored eye, they were works of great art.

What impressed me was not the luxury — I guess you would have seen more in the office of any big international company vice president — but the individuality. I knew I was in a country where that was not an admired characteristic; to be an individual you had to be in a strong position or daring. I got the impression that the man behind the desk was both.

He stood as I entered. He was solidly built, a big man for a Chinese. His hair was short-cropped, a steel gray, the same color as his smartly cut Mao jacket. He wore gold-rimmed spectacles which he had pushed high on to his forehead as though he had taken a pause from reading. There was a mole on his right cheek; I knew the Chinese considered them lucky.

He saw my eyes take in the calligraphy. He walked across to one that held my look.

"You are drawn to this one?" The voice had a faint American accent. It could have come from first-generation Chinese Americans I'd met in the States.

I wasn't particularly, though I nodded assent to be polite.

"Interesting," he said. "It is one of my favorite works too. It is by Chang Yü-chao. He has very few followers because the brushwork is very difficult to achieve. Perhaps that is a characteristic we both admire."

He moved across the room and began pouring coffee, incongruously into small, delicate, porcelain tea cups.

"You like coffee, Mr. Piper? Sugar? I am afraid I have no cream."

He sensed my question, and he answered it without being asked. "I have been fortunate enough to enjoy an extended stay in your country. I found much that I liked." He held out my cup. "And this, to which I am addicted. Perhaps I am the first victim of a new opium invasion, Mr. Piper. Can you imagine a coffee war?"

He moved to the rear of his desk, and sat down heavily. "Of course not," he continued. "Our two countries are too good friends. That is why we are so determined to get to the bottom of your unfortunate experience. Someone must be punished. We must be sure it never happens again." He rasied his head, looked straight at me. "It is out of character, Mr. Piper," he said. "Perhaps you know that.

"I do not claim we are a country without crime. There are bad people everywhere. Nor do I deny that the belongings of foreigners contain many items that would be valuable here. But few foreign friends ever get robbed, even those who walk alone at night in the loneliest of places, let alone in what should be the special safety of a hotel . . ."

He paused, as though to let me contemplate why foreigners should be left alone by thieves. I imagined it was because if they were caught they were shot or locked away for twenty years.

He was smoking, a cigarette in a bamboo holder, and he removed the still glowing butt and replaced it immediately with a fresh one. His hands were smooth, the fingers long and thin, a contrast with the rest of his appearance. A musician's, I thought. Or a calligrapher's.

"Yet your room is entered, searched with a destructive thoroughness, and all at a time when the chances of the thieves being surprised are not inconsiderable. They must have thought the prize a valuable one, don't you think?"

I was concentrating on sipping the coffee and trying to look like an innocent victim of circumstances. I had not been told the man's name, nor where I was. It had to be Public Security; whoever the man was, he didn't spend the rest of his time chasing petty criminals. I was getting the big guys. I was becoming certain that the best I could hope for at the end of all this was to be thrown out of the country. Maybe they wouldn't even be that nice. I began to see the headlines — "American held by Chinese, State lodges protest."

I tried a resigned shrug. "I've told you all I know. I can't imagine what anyone was looking for. They must have made a mistake, gone to the wrong room, thought I was someone else."

I was not prepared for the photograph that he took from a drawer and thrust toward me. It looked like a much-enlarged passport or visa photograph. The face had a tight, intent expression. It was Yakov.

"This is the man who asked you to hold something for him." A statement, not a question.

"I've never seen him before."

It was obvious, even in my tired state, that my face must have betrayed my lie, and that my questioner, expressionless though he remained, must have seen it. I expected him to press home his advantage, but the man simply left the photograph where it lay, stood, and walked over to the windows.

My eyes followed him. I noticed for the first time that the windows were double-glazed with fine mesh between the layers. They weren't made like that to keep out cold or noise. Whoever the man was, he had need to protect himself.

My mind began to drift away into more worrying fantasies: what if the Chinese believed that I was actively involved; that somehow my presence in Peking had to do with the Russians? No doubt there was a report on file somewhere of my being on the same train with the mission from Tatung to Peking. I could protest, of course, that I had no control over my own travel movements, but nevertheless it was a strange coincidence . . .

The man was talking again. His back was still turned away from me, and I had to strain to make sure that I had not misheard the words.

". . . to your hotel. I hope the coffee does not keep you awake. You must be very tired."

And, as if at some unseen signal, the door opened and two men entered to lead me out and down into the silent compound and the waiting car.

It was twenty minutes to midnight when I arrived back at the hotel. The staff on duty stared at me with curiosity. They must have known about the raid on my room, wondered if and when I would return.

I had been transferred to another room. My belongings had been placed in stacks on the bed. Some were fit only for the trash barrel.

At the end of the corridor, a man with brilliantined hair and shiny black shoes was on duty. He had made a note in a pad as I arrived. It was not hard to guess what he was.

I was too tired to care much. I poured a drink, flopped into a chair, and woke with a heavy head about four. I stripped, got between the sheets, resolving to sleep until at least noon.

It was not to be. Before nine, I received a note by hand from the Ministry of Railways. Fifteen minutes later there was a telephone call from Andrews. Half an hour later a car was taking me to the embassy.

Andrews was waiting for me in the same blank room. "Won't they think this suspicious?" I asked.

"They would be more suspicious if we didn't want to know what you'd been through and what they've been asking you. We've been pressing for access to you for the last twenty-four hours."

He took up his old position on the edge of the desk.

"Tell me about it," he said.

I did, starting with the questions at the hotel, then the police post, and finally the European building.

"Describe the man," he said.

I did. He left the room, a secretary brought coffee, and he returned minutes later, photographs in his hand.

"Is that him?" He pointed with a silver Parker at a man on the edge of a group. They were stiff as though on a reviewing stand. It was winter and they all wore heavy topcoats and fur hats. Nevertheless, I had no doubts.

"That's him," I said.

He took back the picture, squared it neatly with the rest.

"You're honored," he said. "His name's Feng Shen. We think he's head of the First Bureau of the Department of Public Security. A big fish in a big outfit."

"*Think*?" I said.

"Nothing's certain here," he said. "You know anything about Public Security?"

I said I didn't. Part of me didn't want to know any more either, but curiosity made me keep quiet. Andrews was obviously in a mood for talking.

"Imagine all the police departments, the FBI, a chunk of the CIA and some of the prison service all brought together," he said. "They're

44

the eyes and ears of the State, and frequently the judges and the prison camps and the executioners as well. They run everything from traffic cops to making sure that whatever today's party line is no one bucks it. Nearest equivalent is the KGB, and I doubt they come quite up to it. You could say their job is to keep a billion people in line, but even that's not quite all of it."

He sipped his coffee, and I thought he'd finished, but he continued.

"What's special about Chinese Security is that it has always seen its job as knowing everything that's going on, the good as well as the bad. So it has a great machine involving all the people. Each street, for example, has its own committee, and it's someone's job to report on what everyone is doing or saying. You understand? It's something that's duplicated in every place, at every level — school, work, home.

"What's more, if people don't see and if they don't report, they can get to be considered guilty too. Great setup, huh? It's not just because they are Communists, though that helps. It dates back before then."

He stood and cracked his knuckles. "You know what parricide is?"

"Murdering your own parents," I said.

"Right," he said. "Let me tell you what the punishment was. The guy himself got cut to pieces. That was just for starters. Younger brothers were beheaded, local high officials were reduced in rank, neighbors living to the left and right had their ears cut off because they should have heard and reported, and those living in front had their eyes put out because they should have seen and prevented it." He cracked his knuckles again. "That's the tradition. Understand that I'm talking of a long time ago. But this is still a country where every man really is his brother's keeper — or God help him."

"And the man who questioned me. Feng Shen. Where does he stand in all this?"

"He worries about foreign spies," he said. "The First Division deals with counterespionage."

"He thinks I'm one?" I said.

"They think all foreigners are," he said. "But you — no more than most, I'd guess."

I remembered the note that had been delivered from the Ministry of Railways, found it, showed it to him.

It was confirmation that they wanted me to move on to Nanking to investigate on the spot; I was booked on a plane that afternoon. As far as they were concerned, it seemed that the Yakov affair might never have been.

"You want to go on with it?" Andrews asked.

I had been thinking about it since the note arrived. I didn't like being pulled in for questioning; cops and spooks give me goose bumps wherever they are, more so when you are seven thousand miles from home. At the same time, they hadn't pressured me, and they had let me go. Additionally, the embassy had known what was happening and had been keeping a watchful eye on me. It must be obvious to everyone that the Russians had followed Yakov and grabbed him. The Soviet delegation had to be the real target now, not me. Added to all that was the fact that I had no wish to return to New York, not yet.

Andrews was waiting for my answer.

"That's what I came here for," I said.

"They're not sure of you," he said, almost changing my mind. "They want to keep an eye on you. That's what all this is about. Keep your nose clean and they'll let you get on with the job you came to do. Do anything strange . . ." His voice died.

"Why should I do anything strange?" My voice rose in genuine anger. "Christ, I haven't done anything. I didn't want to get involved in this fucking thing."

He was a man used to emotional displays. He dealt with them by pretending they hadn't happened. He returned to the desk, leaned down over me. "You're sure, absolutely sure, that Yakov said nothing else, did nothing else. You've told me everything?"

"I've told you everything." I didn't have to fake the weariness in my voice.

"Okay. And I guess you're right to go on with it. It's what I'd do. I'd say it's all finished now."

He pulled over a pad and began to write.

"The area you'll be working is between Nanking and Shanghai?"

I said, "Yes."

He stopped writing, and slid the top sheet over to me. There were two addresses, one in Nanking and the other in Shanghai.

"You'll find that when you're there, Peking is a hell of a long way away," he said. "Memorize them. If you need help, go to one of them. Say my name. They can make contact with me."

I started to grin, began to say something joky, but he had turned away and was busying himself with a pocket diary.

"Got them?" he said finally.

"Guess so."

He retrieved the sheet and placed it in a plastic bin marked "Burn."

On the way out he decided to join in the joke. "Just in case," he said. "Nothing's gonna happen. You're going to wander around, do a job, go home, enliven a few cocktail parties with your experiences. Humor me, though — I get paid to play I Spy. Any problems, you make for one of the addresses."

He patted me on the shoulder as I left, and I decided I liked him less the more friendly he was. Something else troubled me and I didn't realize what it was until I was halfway through my packing. It was what he had said about security in China and how everyone watched everyone else. What bothered me was not the content. It was the way he had said it. Not just flat, professional; I would have expected that. But envious, almost.

Two and a half hours later I was airborne in an old British Trident, knees around my chin, and chain-sucking hard candies that the stewardess had handed around, a pack for each passenger. The biggest surprise had been that Chu Ming was waiting at the airport. She was across the aisle now, three rows ahead. She turned and smiled at me, signifying, I supposed, either that all was forgiven or that the Chinese were trying to lull me into a false sense of security.

It would have been more effective without the farewell scene at the airport. From the steps I had looked back, seen the black limousine parked nearby on the edge of the runway, a group of men beside it.

Most looked like bodyguards and hangers-on. One wore his jacket over his shoulders like a cape. The way the others stood a foot or two behind him stamped his authority.

Feng Shen.

If Public Security were trying to call attention to me — the only foreigner boarding the plane — they could not have done so more effectively.

3

Ꙭ ⱶⱵ

*T*he next day they gave me a train.

First, they made me work for it, exchanging formalities with railroad officials in immaculate blue uniforms, listening to seemingly endless speeches, poring over maps and more figures.

But then they gave me the train.

We left the Railways Ministry's regional headquarters building in midmorning, and I knew we were heading for the station, but I had no idea what to expect. We went in procession, a car in front, a car behind, and for the first time I felt like Somebody. Outside, it was hotter, brighter, fresher-looking than Peking, and there were wide boulevards shaded with huge cedar trees.

Nanking has a population about the same as metropolitan Boston, but is so spread out that parts feel rural. When we stopped and got out, I could see the Purple Mountains flanking the city to the east. Somewhere up there was the mausoleum of Dr. Sun Yat-sen, father of the Republic. To the west, I knew, was the Yangtze that had already flowed nearly four thousand miles from Tibet and was now within two hundred miles of the sea.

Surrounded by officials, I was led through a side entrance and over a footbridge to a siding. The moment we reached the train, the officials stood back beaming, and Chu Ming listened to one of them, and then said, "It is for you."

The engine was a diesel, and it had been polished until it looked like a museum exhibit. It was modern, Chinese-built, a class I recognized — a Dong Feng W 1800 hp. I seemed to remember it was a product not of Tatung, but of Talien, in Liaoning Province, one of the country's five locomotive plants.

The officials were staring at me with anticipation, and I sensed that Chu Ming was having to fight not to prompt me, a rude barbarian, to show my gratitude.

I didn't think words were necessary. My expression was plain. It is not unusual to have a train placed at one's disposal in developing countries — it is the most obvious way of providing an engineer with a method of travel and a base. Somehow, though, I had not expected it this time.

And if I had, I am not sure I would ever have anticipated anything as stunning as the single coach.

That was older than the engine — 1930s, perhaps even 1920s. It dated back to when foreigners controlled the railroads — they had first been built, after all, for the benefit of occupying nations, from Japan to France, Russia to Italy, who shared parts of the country ninety years ago.

This coach was German, and had been built as a director's salon — a hotel room on wheels for high-ranking dignitaries or officials. I climbed the steps, conscious of the looks. The inside was paneled in dark wood, and contained deep armchairs and lace-covered tables. Curtains screened two bunk beds, and behind a partition there was an ornate, white enamel hip bath. The windows were hung with curtains, and one wall was dominated by a large watercolor of a lake. White lilies in pots scented the air.

My hosts followed me into the coach. Tea was poured from flasks, and there was another formal speech. Chu Ming translated. Perhaps because of the setting, perhaps because of the relief after the previous days, I found myself staring at her. I knew I hardly needed to listen to the words — the occasional ones like "peace" and "friendship" and "great people" told me all I needed to know.

She was taller than many of the men around her, perhaps five feet six. Chinese women have much more delicate skin than women from the West — something technical involving the pores — but Chu Ming's face was browned, that look of someone who has worked outside in the wind and the sun. Her eyes had laughter lines, and her face was broad at the cheeks. As if in keeping with some new spirit, the sober blue clothes of Peking had been exchanged for a multicolored shirt. It hung loose, though, hiding any shape that it might have covered, just as the wide slacks betrayed no trace of legs underneath.

The speech ended, and I replied in the same safe platitudes — a short speech developed and refined in a dozen countries. Then I listened more carefully as it was explained that the engine and coach were for my exclusive use at all times. The driver would remain with the locomotive, sleeping in the special compartment behind the footplate.

Using the track between Nanking and Shanghai, I was assured, would present no problems. It was double track, as I knew — an up line and a down line. Also, the driver had a radio. He would report to signal control whenever I wanted to go anywhere. The unspoken message was that other trains would be held if necessary. It was the rail equivalent of the system used on the roads by official cars which shone lights and sounded horns signaling other vehicles to clear the way.

I got the feeling everyone genuinely wanted me to be happy. They would like me on their side. It wasn't just a question of the Chinese needing backing for a loan; it was the more prosaic and immediate case of local officials seeking support for works in their own area. The principle was the same as buying a man a good lunch or sending him a case of bourbon at Christmas. In this case, they knew I was a nut about trains, so they gave me this beautiful, working, grown-up toy.

The feeling of mobility, of freedom, after the events of the recent days was a heady one. Even before the last of the officials left, I knew what I wanted to do — sit back in the coach and simply travel.

I would order the driver to go to Shanghai and back, less than four hundred miles, a day's journey. It was a ride I could justify, to others, to myself. This would be my first, overall look — before getting down to examining parts of the track and the surrounding area in detail.

A problem arose immediately, but I was in no mood to let anything interfere with the day I had promised myself. Chu Ming, it emerged, had to attend a meeting. She had intended to do so in the early afternoon when I, like the Chinese, was expected to rest for an hour or two. I solved that by convincing her that once she told the driver what I wanted to do, I had no further need of an interpreter. At Shanghai, I did not even intend to leave the train.

I suspect she had been ordered to give me latitude — as Andrews had warned, they were still curious to see what I would do when left alone. In any event, she agreed reluctantly but quickly. She would arrange, she said, for food to be brought on board further along the line so that I could eat in my coach. Without actually saying it, she made it clear that I should be back by nightfall. I did not protest, and half an hour later we were on our way.

The train worked its way through the sidings until we reached the main track beyond the station. We waited a few minutes until a freight train passed, heading south like us, and then we were off. I had taken up a position on the observation platform at the rear of the coach. It was still only ten-thirty, but the day was already baking — the previous day it had topped ninety degrees — and I welcomed the breeze that movement brought.

We were in countryside almost immediately. Apart from the hills to my right, the land was flat, rich with wheat fields and rice paddies. Strange canvas grain tents flanked the track. Even in this rich, fertile area, plows I saw, were pulled by men or animals. The peasants wore straw coolie hats against the sun. There was the occasional, isolated factory with belching chimney. But mostly, you felt nothing had changed since Marco Polo had visited China seven hundred years before.

I stood outside for almost an hour, delighting in the harsh clarity of the colors, made more brilliant after the grayness of the cities with their absence of bright clothes, neon signs, or billboards. We slowed almost to a standstill to pass through a sleepy-looking station, and I smiled at the sight of a wasps' nest snug inside a public loudspeaker.

I went inside for a brief period, and played at work by staring at an unfolded railroad map. Though the track over which I was traveling constituted a mere one hundred and fiftieth of the country's rail lines, it was vitally important, running as it did through such a rich, comparatively highly populated area, never far from the vast Yangtze River, to China's largest and most important commercial city. According to my figures, a hundred and sixty trains a day used this track. The Chinese, trying to maximize use of what they'd already got, were determined it should be more.

From time to time, I stared out, made occasional notes, but more for the pretense; real work could wait until tomorrow. Then I could begin a preliminary assessment of the optimism or otherwise of Chinese plans. I already knew from my briefings in New York before setting out and from my background reading that engineering problems could vary widely in the area. Completing a supplementary line from Nanking to Shanghai a few years before had proved a slow, hard task — complex geological structures and quicksands had made bridge design and building difficult. On the other hand, a more recent, albeit much smaller, operation — a feeder line leaving the track at Fengyang — had been completed with no apparent problems at all.

After a while, I gave up even the pretense of work, and explored the coach. Cupboards promised much but yielded little, and that a curious, motley collection — a jar of candies, an old copy of the *Asian Wall Street Journal*, and a fan. There was also some beer. I removed the cap from one with the bottle opener on my Swiss army knife, a constant companion, drank deep, and scanned the front page of the *Journal*. I saw the Dow Jones was down three points, the construction industry was taking a new beating, and defense salesmen were flocking to Japan. I tossed it aside; with permission to travel I'd lost any nostalgia for the outside world.

There was a speaking tube that connected with the driver. I picked it up, tried a few basic sentences. Seconds later, a stream of Chinese emerged. I replied, *Xie xie*, thank you, and settled down with my beer.

We stopped soon afterward at a small station. A lone factory belched smoke on the hillside, and neat vegetable gardens extended almost to the track. I began to climb down only to be met by men carrying cardboard cartons of food on board. Almost immediately after they left, the train pulled away again. Inside the boxes were fruit, cold meats, boiled eggs, steamed buns.

As I started to unpack, the train began to slow once more. Finally, it stopped on an otherwise deserted spur. I climbed down and made my way along the track to the engine. The driver was sitting cross-legged at the foot of the steps, already eating. He smiled, pointed at me, and then at his bowl. The meaning was clear. Eat. Then, without pausing to see whether I understood, he pointed to the sky, then ran his palm across his brow. Next, he bent his head to one side and made a snoring sound. All of that was equally unmistakable — it was hot; after eating, we should rest.

I considered bringing my food outside, but the man had already transferred his attention back to his bowl. I returned to the coach, knowing that even here, miles from any observers, the division between us had to be taken seriously. The classlessness was theory, not fact. Chu Ming, for example, would never eat with me — she would sit in a separate room. Attempts to protest met the response that anyone working in China quickly comes to know: feigned incomprehension followed by a swift move to another subject.

As it was, I ate inside, finished quickly, and climbed back out onto the track. It was shortly after one. The driver was lying in the shade of the engine. He opened his eyes and lifted his head as I approached. I gestured that I was going to walk along the track. His face registered no response, but I knew he would not leave until I returned, no matter how long that was.

I began walking. The track ran straight — I remembered reading that that was a reason the Chinese had so hated railroads at first; according to superstition, anything straight was thought to be un-lucky. Nothing stirred in the flat fields on either side of me. In the distance, a solitary cloud hung lazily in the still air like a puff of smoke.

I stopped after about four hundred yards. The heat was beginning to hit me. I squatted to rest before starting back. The quiet was almost unnerving. It took a few moments to realize what was so strange. Then I did. No birds. Mao, I'd read, had had a thing about them — millions had been slaughtered by worshipful peasants. There was also the question of DDT. The Chinese used it like kids sprinkle sugar on their cornflakes. They'd probably killed off all the insects on which any bird could live.

There were rice paddies on one side. An hour earlier, an hour later, they would be busy with people. Now the peasants who worked them were somewhere else, resting like the driver. In the near distance, beyond them, there was the only sign of habitation — low, small buildings. They shimmered in the haze of heat.

I turned my eyes back toward the train, still reluctant to move. Suddenly, way beyond it, I made out signs of movement. A road ran parallel to the track for several miles. Along it, now, moved a pall of dust. It was the only sign of life in this place. As I watched, it became a vehicle — it was still too far to make out whether it was a car or, more likely, a truck.

Gradually, it became a car. It was the first I had seen since the train had set out from Nanking, and I kept my eyes on it. Cars are not common outside cities in China — it's said that the whole country contains only 500,000, fewer than U.S. automobile plants produce every single month, none of them privately owned.

As it neared the engine, the car began to slow, and then stopped. Men got out and I saw the driver move out of the shadow of the engine to talk to them. Their voices were low, a distant background murmur, and from here the group had an unreal quality. Because of that, it took me several seconds once it had happened to realize that the driver had been grabbed and thrown to the ground. By that time, he was already being hauled to his feet. One man had him from behind, and the other was hitting him across the face. The scream of pain cut through the distance between us.

I started to rise, and I saw a third man had joined the group and was pointing along the track in my direction. Instinctively, I dropped back into my crouched position. I didn't think anyone had seen me, although they must know roughly where I was by now. I slid onto my stomach, only my head raised. As if at a command, the three men returned to the car, and it shot off immediately — that meant there was a driver: at least four men. It stopped almost immediately, about a hundred and fifty yards away from me, at a point where the road began to curve away from the train.

The three men got out again. I could see their faces from here. The side of one man's face was misshapen. It looked as though he had suffered a terrible burn or some other accident. It added to the atmosphere of menace. I could hear the men's voices clearly raised. Side by side, they began to move purposefully in my direction.

The car, I realized, had gone. Moments later, I noticed where — craning my head, I saw it had stopped about two hundred yards beyond me, where the road neared the tracks again. A fourth man got out. He cradled something in his arms. Even at this distance, it was obvious it was a rifle.

I found myself reviewing possibilities in a curiously detached way. My escape along the track was blocked — not that there seemed anywhere to go in that direction. My return to the train was cut off. *If* I could hold them off, there had to be a train soon. But I couldn't — and even if one came into view this second, the moment I tried to stop it, I exposed myself to my pursuers. No, the only chance lay in the paddy fields and the cluster of seemingly empty buildings beyond. There might be someone there. It was the only hope.

Already I had wasted time. I had to move. I rolled sideways and down to the bottom of the slight embankment, hidden still by a patch of high ground. The rice paddies began about thirty yards away. Once I broke cover, I would be seen. I estimated I now had a lead of about a hundred and twenty yards. Would that be enough? I was in reasonable shape — although a spell in New York and office desks and business lunches had softened me, I had forced myself out into the park to jog every morning. What of my pursuers? Were they soft, city-dwellers? A lot depended, I realized, on whether they wanted to kill me or grab me. Even as I moved, I concluded it had to be the second, and that heartened me, though I purposely stopped short at thinking about what they'd do once they did have me captive. The only thing worse than being tortured must be being tortured to reveal something you don't even know. You can't even give up when you reach breaking point.

Every second waited was a wasted second. I eased myself to my knees, flexed my muscles as best I could to loosen them up. And I moved.

The shouts came immediately. There were no shots, though.

My feet hit the rice paddy. I miscalculated my entry, stumbled, and began to fall. Panicking, I staggered forward, struggling to right myself.

I managed to get upright, and then to develop a crude rhythm. The water was a little more than ankle-deep, and the mud sucked at my feet like weak magnets. I wasted more seconds stopping to rip off my shoes, but it helped and I quickly made up the time.

I risked a glance over my shoulder. My pursuers had gained a little ground when I stopped, but I was regaining it now. My height gave me some advantage. One stopped and leveled a pistol when he saw me turn, and shouted words I did not understand. They could only have been a call to stop. But I knew the man was bluffing. Even if they did want to kill me — which I doubted — the man's body would be racked with his exertion, his muscles would be trembling. At the distance involved, he would be lucky to hit an object the size of a train, let alone a man who was moving.

I fell twice. My limbs were heavy now. The pull of the mud grew stronger. The pace slackened but got more punishing. My body felt like a slowed-down sequence in a movie.

The shouts behind died away — my pursuers were having to put everything into keeping moving. My mind began to hammer. *No birds, no birds, no noise. It's a trap.*

Suddenly the buildings were much nearer. *A trap, a trap, keep back, they're driving you that way.* It was all planned, and I had fallen for it. But now there was nowhere else. I slipped, hit the muddy water hard, and gagged as I swallowed some. I staggered to my feet and moved again, arms flailing to give me momentum.

And then I realized the truth. The buildings were all deserted.

They were only walls. The roofs had gone. The windows were shuttered, the doors locked and padlocked — precautions that had long since ceased to be necessary.

There was no one. I was still on my own. I kept moving. They would give me some cover. And who knew what was on the other side? Maybe nothing; maybe just more open fields. But hope kept me moving.

There was a thudding in my head and a sound like waves in my ears. My chest was heaving in great sobs. All of me was now concentrated on keeping my body moving and I did not hear the helicopter until after its shadow had settled over me.

Then, for the first time, I heard firing. I saw that it was drifting in to land ahead of me. I tripped heavily again, and this time there seemed no point in getting up. I made only weak resistance when two sets of hands lifted me and hauled me into the helicopter, which soared off the moment I was on board.

The flight lasted perhaps an hour. The three uniformed PLA guards who kept me crouched in a corner looked so jittery that I did not even dare look down at my watch.

Once we landed, I was swept out immediately, head bowed under the still whirling blades. My eyes absorbed some low, green-painted wooden buildings, a concrete square, and a tower surmounted with communication aerials, before I was hurried inside. The room they took me to had a table, a camp bed, and the ubiquitous stuffed chair.

I decided we had to be on a small military base, and that this was a duty officer's room. I was left alone. Minutes later someone entered, handed me blankets, and made it obvious he wanted my clothes. They'd nearly dried in the heat. Without them, I felt more vulnerable, but also more human — the mud had stiffened into thick cakes. Soon afterward tea and a bottle of Japanese Suntory whiskey were delivered. The man who placed them on the desk returned again almost immediately to remove a map from the wall. To me, it looked like any routine map of the province, but who knows what is regarded as secret to a people convinced the rest of the world is populated by spies and barbarians?

I improvised the blanket into a togalike garment, alternated sips of tea and whiskey. There was no window. I searched the room but found nothing useful. I thought we'd flown north and were back somewhere in the Nanking vicinity, but that was little more than a guess. I tried the door. It opened. A guard poked a rifle toward my middle, and I closed it quickly.

I moved back not the room and stretched out in the chair. The fluorescent light overhead hissed, a fly buzzed angrily in a corner. Above the smell of whiskey, there was one of garlic: meals had been eaten in this room.

Questions surged through my mind. Were the men who had been chasing me the same people who held me now? Was this an elaborate way of making me vanish? But, if so, why? The answer was chillingly obvious — Feng Shen had never believed me. It would, however, have been difficult for him to hold me too long for interrogation; the embassy knew where I was, and Sino-American relations were important. But this way . . .

If they were the same men, though, why the shooting? Had there even been any gunfire? Could it all have been hallucination? And if they were not the same men, how could anyone have known that I needed rescuing?

Any moment, I expected the door to open and an officer to enter. Someone here must speak English; if not, it would not take long to ferry someone in.

When the door did open, three hours had passed — and it was only a man with my clothes. They had been cleaned, and were still hot from the pressing. I pointed to show that I had no shoes, and soon afterward I was given a pair of canvas sneakers. I imagined they were the largest available. I managed to get them on my feet with the laces removed.

They finally did come for me two hours later, two officers, both bespectacled, one around fifty, the other little more than half his age. The younger one spoke. "We would like you to come with us." He spoke hesitantly; the accent was bad, like one of those old Charlie Chan films; I guessed he'd been studying from tapes or records, without much chance to converse.

"I'm an American citizen, a guest of your government. Someone tried to kill me." It was an exaggeration; all they'd tried to do was catch me, with, I suspected, the idea of sticking lighted matches under my fingernails until I came up with the magic formula or whatever it was. But it seemed a time to keep it simple.

The voice was gentle, but firm. "Please come. Time to talk later. There is something we wish you to see."

We crossed into another building. The air was hot even though it was now evening. The room we entered contained only a wooden bench. The walls and the floor were bare concrete. Along one side there was an open drain like a urinal.

Three Chinese sat upon the bench, watched over by wary guards. I supposed they were the men who had pursued me. Two were bent forward as though winded, the other leaned back, using the wall for support. He had a narrow gash across his forehead, and blood had dried at his nostrils. There was no way of knowing whether he had bled during his capture or as a result of questioning since.

One of the guards yanked the two men bent forward, lifting their faces to my view. All three were young. One was trying to grow a mustache which looked not unlike one I'd had as an adolescent. None of their eyes met mine. I got the feeling they were like puppies who had already been beaten into submission.

"You know them?"

"No. Who are they? Are these the ones who chased me?"

It was my role to answer questions, not to ask them.

"Come." I was being moved on again, deeper into the building. We entered a corridor that had a more solid, more important feel. Lights were shaded, paint looked fresh, and there was a scent of polish from the wood-block floor.

We stopped at an unnumbered door. The younger officer knocked, waited and then entered. I was escorted inside behind him. The room was large and dominated by one enormous table, light dazzlingly reflected in its highly polished surface. Chairs around it were spaced and squared with precision. Only one was out of place, drawn back at an angle, and occupied by a big man. He had his jacket draped around his shoulders; his hand was raised to lift a cigarette holder to his lips.

"Tom Carr," said Feng Shen. "I think it is time you told me who he is."

Anger grew and seethed inside me. I wanted to burst with rage, scream at Feng, grasp a weapon — any weapon — and go berserk. My earlier suspicion that the Chinese had arranged the "attack" on me so that I could disappear seemed confirmed by Feng's presence. If we were near Nanking, Peking was about two hours' flying time away. Feng could have got here easily in the time available — but he would have had to be ready to set off. No doubt, by now, the engine driver had reported the kidnap to the local Security Bureau; equally certain, the Chinese authorities would soon be assuring the American embassy that everything possible was being done to find me.

And, of course, in the meantime, I was available for any questions that anyone cared to ask. By any method. I certainly wasn't against answering any questions about someone called Tom Carr. It was a name that meant nothing to me. Nothing at all. I suspected, though, that that would be no more than a starter.

I fought down the anger and a stab of fear; neither was going to help me. "Why are you going through with this charade?" I said. "I don't know anyone called Tom Carr, I never have, I bet I never will. What worries me is that someone tried to grab me or kill me. I don't know how the army and you got involved, but as you seem to have saved me, thanks. Now I'd like to get back to Nanking and my hotel. I take it we're not far away."

Feng disregarded everything except one word. "Charade?" He repeated it as though uncertain as to its meaning. "Ah, charade." He had placed it. "People play charades. Children at parties. A game."

He sucked deeply on his cigarette and gave a barely perceptible signal of command with his free hand.

Two guards grasped my wrists from behind, sweeping my arms high, giving me no time to struggle. My head was forced downward until it almost touched the floor. A third soldier stepped forward,

61

paused with feet in front of me, and even in my contorted position I caught the flash of an unsheathed bayonet. Pain shot through the whole of my body. My arms felt as though they must leave their sockets.

"There is a descriptive phrase for what is being done to you," said Feng, conversationally. "You would translate it 'the jet aircraft.' It is what you look like. It was very popular during the Cultural Revolution. Those who were being helped along at their struggle meetings were often made to stand like that, sometimes for hours. Afterwards, it is very hard to walk. I know from experience."

I understood what he was saying — that he'd been a Cultural Revolution victim — but there's an incontrovertible fact about pain: your own matters a damned lot more than anyone else's.

Feng moved, stood over me, and said, "Look at me."

His shoes were in my full vision. They were patent, had the shine of those of Spanish grandees who never got off their horses lest they'd pick up dust. Someone had spent a long time working on them.

What I did was childish, was a retreat from my decision to keep my anger screwed down tight. But there's a limit you reach. I cleared my throat, and spat, covering his toe caps with gobs of spittle.

His anger was immediate, and despite the pain that came it was welcome. I had set out to provoke and I had. It was my will that had triumphed over his, infantile though the game might be.

The price was high, though. At an unseen signal of command, my stretched arms were raised even higher, forcing me to choke on a scream.

"Look at me!"

I thought I could give him that. I swiveled my eyes upward. The figure above was a distorted blur through the pain and the sweat that ran from my forehead.

"I have no desire to cause you pain, but you must have respect. Do you understand? Respect."

There must have been another signal because, without warning, my wrists were freed, letting me fall clumsily to the floor. I lay for a while staring at the tip of the bayonet. I was starting to be less and less certain of everything; they didn't seem to be keeping to the rules I'd formulated for them.

"Please get up now."

No one helped me, and it took a long time. My limbs were slow in obeying commands. The three soldiers had moved back, but remained alert, watching me. Feng had returned to his chair and was lighting yet another cigarette.

Another unseen command, because one of the soldiers stepped forward and drew out a chair for me to sit down. I debated whether to stay on my feet to show that I was uncowed. I decided if I didn't sit, I'd probably fall. So I sat.

"Carr," repeated Feng gently. "Tom Carr. Who is he? Your contact? Your controller? A code name for someone? For you?"

"I told you, I've never heard it before. It's true."

Feng disregarded the answer. "Why are you here in China, Mr. Piper?" I began to reply, but Feng waved me into silence. "The Ministry of Railways approached a major company in New York, one with whom they had had dealings in the past. They expected them to send over one or more of their staff. Yet that company turns to a smaller firm, in which you are a partner, and it is you who is sent. Why is that, Mr. Piper? Did it provide good cover? Were your masters waiting for such an opportunity?"

"It's a small job," I said wearily. "Small, though important. I'm just here to make a preliminary assessment, prepare the way for a full-scale study later. That's when you'll get lots of engineers and economists running around all over the place. In the meantime, all it needs is one man who's done this kind of thing before. That's why I was asked."

I studied his face. He didn't seem impressed. "Anyway," I added, "how could anyone know there would be any approach from the Ministry of Railways?"

Feng lifted his head, and unhooded his eyes. He said nothing, but the answer was in his look. Oh, God, I thought, he believes that someone in the Ministry was got at, bribed, to concoct a nonnecessary job just to get me here.

Feng saw that I had understood. "Were you ever in England?" he asked. It was a country I didn't know; even though, way back, my father's family came from there, and my mother's from Wales, the whole continent of Europe was one that was alien to me. I seemed to have been everywhere else — Africa, Asia, Latin America, Australasia even. Still he didn't really want an answer, and I let him continue without interruption.

"England," repeated Feng. "I was there for a time. An interesting country. They have an intriguing phrase that their police issue to newspapers when someone is detained. 'A man,' they say, 'is assisting us with our inquiries.' "

Feng stood, turned his chair around, and mounted the seat like a horse. "You are assisting us with our inquiries, Mr. Piper." He went on, "Where were you recruited?"

"No one recruited me. I was never recruited."

"Was it at the university? You went to the University of Illinois at Urbana-Champaign, studied in the department of civil engineering." I didn't react to his knowledge; it was something the Railways Ministry could have checked easily with the basic reference books.

Feng continued. "What made you decide to become not just any sort of engineer, but the kind who travels around the world and visits many countries?" Feng lifted his cigarette. Ash had formed, a good half-inch long, and he considered it carefully before leaning forward and flicking it delicately into an ashtray.

"Excellent cover, would you not say, Mr. Piper?"

He would have been even more suspicious, I thought, if he'd known that at the time I was at the University of Illinois, virtually no one else wanted to go in for railroad engineering. The railroad industry as a whole was in decline; the course was barely attended. Unlike other students, though, who were concerned about careers, and money, and status, I was hooked on trains — and saw it as a way of escaping to out-of-the-way countries where railroads still had a present and a future. In a world with fewer and fewer trails to blaze, I wanted to find one.

Although I remained silent, Feng must have thought I was about to speak because he raised his hand, and said, "Respect, Mr. Piper. Remember, respect.

"And then," he continued, "you arrive here just in time for a man to vanish. By coincidence, of course, at the same time that thieves disturb your hotel room and no other."

He beckoned, and one of the soldiers picked up a folder and handed it to him. Feng spoke quickly in Chinese and the three soldiers left the room.

"Why did the Russian come to see you? Are you Tom Carr? What did he say to you? What did he give you?"

"I don't know anything about a Russian, and I have never heard of a Tom Carr."

Feng leaned across, opened the folder, extracted a sheet of paper, and slid it across the table.

It was a photograph, rows of squares, each containing fingerprints. Feng passed me the second sheet, more of the same.

"You must think us a very backward people, Mr. Piper. Strange, is it not, when it is normally we who think of you as the barbarians?"

He paused to allow me time to consider the significance of what I was seeing. He continued, "If you were back in New York, would not your first thought be that a man who has been in a room leaves his fingerprints? Those fingerprints, it will not surprise you, belong to Boris Yakov. Before you protest further, perhaps I should add they were everywhere in your room — even on your razor, which he must have used to shave."

"He must have waited until he saw me leave the hotel, and then used my room."

It sounded feeble even to me, but I knew that I would be crazy to concede a single point. I could, in theory, tell Feng the truth: explain how Yakov had come in the night, how I'd gone to the embassy, and how when I returned no one was there. That would have had the benefit of fact and simplicity. But I knew that if I confessed that, it would be only the start. Feng would be convinced there were other layers waiting to be peeled away one by one. And who could know when the last layer had been removed? Yes, best to admit nothing.

"Mr. Piper," said Feng evenly, "you are a liar. But you will find I am a patient man and that I have a great deal of time." He reached for his folder again, extracted another photograph, which he slid to me facedown.

"Now *when* did you first make contact with this man?"

I turned the picture over. It was Yakov. There was no mistaking the man. But it was not an enlarged portrait like the picture Feng had showed me in Peking.

This Yakov was lying on his back, eyes open but unseeing. Dead.

Feng left me alone with my thoughts after that. No doubt he expected me to brood, see the error of my noncooperation — and then spill all.

Not that there was much to spill. Again, there was a temptation to tell what I did know. After all, I was no more than an innocent bystander who'd got dragged in on the fringes. But I *knew* that once I told that to Feng, he'd never let up. He'd tell himself that if I was prepared to concede a story that fitted the facts he had, I must be doing so only to conceal another, more important, version.

Over an hour passed. I was brought tea and some small pastries. I even began to wonder whether Feng had left me alone for the night, and whether I should try to sleep.

I realized that what I did need to do was urinate. I opened the door, and made gestures to the guard. On a bad day, he could have misunderstood. He only nodded and led me along the corridor and beckoned to a door. It was a small, windowless closet, and I finished and returned outside.

At that precise moment, a crash and shouts echoed along the corridor. They obviously came from nearby. My guard looked about in puzzlement, uncertain what to do. He solved the problem by heading for the sound, but with me in front of him as his prisoner.

A door was open, and three men, two soldiers and a civilian, were already inside. My guard joined them, gesturing me to stay back. I obeyed him, but the scene through the doorway was clearly visible.

The civilian was one of the three Chinese I had been shown earlier.

He lay on his back, his legs drawn up against his abdomen as if in pain. His face was a dark purply red; one eye was closed, the other bulged open. What drew my eyes, though, was his right arm. It was twisted, contorted almost, the elbow in the air. The hand was invisible. It had been stuffed inside the man's mouth. The other hand, the left hand, was still locked onto the elbow in the air. It looked as though he had used it to supply pressure downward, jamming the other fist deep into the mouth and throat.

The guards knelt around him until Feng appeared, touching nothing. He saw me, barked angry orders, and I was led back to my room.

This time I did not try to sleep. I had little doubt that the man had committed suicide, even though the physiological mechanics were beyond me. I sat, hunched, the scene still sharp in my mind. I did not particularly mourn the man; he had meant me harm. But I dwelt on the manner of his death. I did not know then that it was an age-old Chinese method of suicide when there is no implement available.

I did know that it must have been a horrible kind of death to undertake. A man who went through that could have done so, surely, only if he had known he faced an even more terrible alternative.

When Feng finally returned it was as Mr. Nice Guy. I had fallen into a short sleep, and wakened sweating and shivering. I had seen death many times, and had been hurt and made mortal. But this one stripped me of resilience, threw me back on my isolation and my fear. Even in sleep, my mind had kept imagining the happening of such a death — the man's struggle to die pitted against the deep desire to live. To pull a trigger, slash with a razor, swallow a pill — they were one thing. To plunge a fist into your own stretched mouth, ramming back the tongue, disregarding the pain and choking, refusing to back away from death even though parts of you must be screaming to live . . .

Feng was in the room before I saw him. He nodded to a guard behind him, who put down a glass and left the room immediately.

"Drink," said Feng. "You will feel better."

It was sweet brandy, not unlike Spanish Fundador.

I drank it, and immediately regretted it. What I needed was not booze, but a pint of orange juice and a cold bath.

"The man was a fool," said Feng. "Suicide is for idiots and cowards. It is too big a price to pay to avoid answering a few questions."

His voice was dismissive; I sensed that it was the last time he intended to refer to the subject.

I started to speak, but thought better of it.

"I want you to look at some more photographs," he said.

He began placing them on the table. They weren't holiday snapshots. A lot of them showed Yakov, dead, laid out on a mortuary dissection table. There were others, of the back of a tall building, a courtyard and scores of parked bicycles in the foreground. I thought vaguely that I recognized it, and Feng confirmed my guess. The back of the Peking Hotel, the photographs taken from a narrow side street. A window and a spot on the ground were marked with crosses.

Feng leaned and pointed. "We think he fell or was pushed from there." He stabbed again. "His body was found at that point."

He paused, and I wondered whether I should repeat my protest that I knew nothing of Yakov. I decided to continue my silence. When Feng spoke again, I realized the pause had been for effect. "There were many marks on him. Not just the fall. Do you understand?"

His hands searched for a photograph of Yakov and placed it squarely in front of me. "You see the burns?" he said, his tone even. "Look" — his fingers moved near Yakov's throat — "there are a group there. Cigarette burns. Very bad. Very cruel." Another pause, and then he added, almost as an aside, "They broke his fingers too, one by one."

This time he wanted a reaction, and I gave him one, the safest: "*They?*"

"The Russians, Mr. Piper. It is obvious, is it not? Our late Yakov was fleeing from them. They caught him, and either killed him after torturing him or he died trying to escape." Again, he paused. "Why, I wonder, would they torture him, do you think? Had he taken something with him, something he no longer had when they found him? Perhaps they even thought he had given it to someone. Or told that someone where it could be found."

68

I wished I hadn't finished the brandy. Now I did need it.

He picked up a small tape recorder that I had not noticed before. He pressed a button, and I thought for a moment he wanted to tape-record an answer from me.

But instead noises emerged, strange attempts at what was vaguely the same sound, over and over again, like someone learning to speak.

With a shudder, I realized one attempt sounded like "Tom Carr" — the name Feng had kept repeating. Equally, though, it could have been Shumdar, or Some Car, or Omcar.

Feng clicked off the tape. "Yakov was not quite dead when he was found," he said. His tone was conspiratorial. "He murmured something."

"*That! That's* what he said!" I pointed at the recorder and began to laugh uncontrollably, the result of the tension and the disbelief. "That's why you asked me if I know a Tom Carr!" It was now obvious what the sounds on the tape were — whoever had found Yakov, probably a passerby, was trying to repeat into a microphone the garbled sound he might or might not have heard.

Feng was patient. He waited until my laughter died.

"It is good you are amused," he said at last. "Perhaps you are right. Perhaps it is nothing." Another of his pauses; I was learning that he was a master at them. Then the jab: "It is a pity that others are not so sure, nor are they so certain you know nothing."

I waited. At last we were getting to the heart of what he wanted to say.

"You haven't asked about the people who tried to seize you," he said. "At first we thought they were scum in the pay of the Russians. However, it seems we were wrong." A faint smile touched his lips. "Not all of those we brought here were as anxious to avoid answering questions as the man you saw." I picked up the brandy glass; although it was empty, it gave me something to do with my hands.

"It emerges," he continued, "that they were ultra Leftists, followers of the Gang of Four. Although such people are rooted out daily, like murderous weeds some continue to survive. Sadly, some still remain in high places — I speak to you with frankness. They dream their vain dreams of returning to power some day. They have their own spies, often among us." He nodded his head sadly as he spoke, as though soliciting my sympathy. "They must have received reports of what had happened — a member of a secret Russian delegation dies after talking to an American in his room." (He raised his hand to still my protest.) "Foreign intelligence men from your embassy take a not inconsiderable interest. Like me, they wonder what the Russian carried on his person or in his head. Like me, they suspect it must be valuable and much worth having. Like me, they wonder if you are the key . . ."

I set down the glass. My hand was steady. I noted it, and was foolishly proud of myself.

There had to be more, so I waited. "The fact is, Mr. Piper, that you are a marked man. Whether you know anything or whether you do not — and let us say that I give you the benefit of the doubt — there are people determined to talk to you. Not nice people. The Russians, of course. Now, the followers of the Gang of Four. If you had not been rescued in time, I do not think they would have been as gentle as I have been."

He stood, without warning, and opened the door. Two guards entered, and he spoke to them quickly.

He turned back to me. "They will return you safely to Nanking," he said. "As you surmised, it is not far away. You will wait there until I decide what is to be done with you. I will arrange for men to guard you."

And, for the second time, he turned me loose.

4

The hotel was just beginning to come to life when I returned. Dawn had broken on the way from the army base to Nanking. The car dropped me in the driveway and waited until I reached the main door. They didn't need to check that I went inside. A parked car was already stationed near the exit gate, a man with the inevitable shiny shoes was sitting in the foyer.

I disregarded him, went upstairs, and found my room. My suitcase and my bag lay on the floor, still unpacked — I'd only arrived in Nanking a little over thirty-six hours before, hard though that now was to believe. I had slept in the hotel only one night, and had removed from the case only those items I needed. Not that I was carrying much: I tried to travel light, and the slash-happy characters who had raided my room in Peking had reduced my number of wearable garments by half.

The room smelled stale, and I opened a window and breathed deeply. There was little noise from outside. High walls masked the sight, and the sound, of the wide road that passed the hotel. Clearer than the occasional car or truck was the croak of frogs from the garden below.

I kicked off the ridiculously small sneakers I had been given at the camp and stretched out on top of the bed covers. I had decided that I wasn't tired, and that I would lie and wrestle with my problem.

The next I knew it was nine o'clock. I staggered up. During the four hours that I had slept one of the floor waiters had placed two flasks of water in my room — one boiled but cold, the other hot.

I used the hot to mix instant coffee with powder from a jar in my bag — like Feng, I had my addiction. There were a few packets of sugar, something I rarely used. I decided now was the time I needed some instant energy, and added the contents of two.

Sipping the coffee, I resolved my problem with surprising speed and ease. There was only one thing to do, I decided: call Andrews. It was pointless trying to decide whether I wanted to stay in the country or not — anytime now Feng might decide that he wanted me out. Surely the fact that he had let me go so easily meant that he believed I knew nothing. If that was so, surely he would be happier with me back in the States — unless, of course, he was playing some devious game with the Russians and/or the Gang of Four supporters. What that all meant was that my own decision could wait, because it might never be needed.

I picked up the telephone beside the bed, waited until the hotel operator found someone who spoke good English, then asked for the embassy number. The voice took my instructions without interruption. "I will call you back," it said.

I started to ask whether there was a delay, but the line went dead.

I sat for a long time, then got the same person again. There were delays in calls to Peking, I was told; I would be called.

"How long?"

It was not known.

I said I might leave my room, but would remain in the hotel; would they page me? The voice repeated I would be called when the number was obtained, and again the line went dead.

I risked going down to the foyer. Chu Ming was sitting primly in a chair against a wall, upright, shoulder bag held on her lap. She looked like someone in a waiting room, ready to be called in for a job interview. I watched her for a while before she saw me. She had tied her hair in a bun, giving her the look of a stenographer in a thirties movie.

We met halfway across the lobby. If this had been the right movie I'd have reached out there and then, unpinned her hair, her eyes would have misted over, and I'd have scooped her up into my arms. Trouble was, this was all too real and besides, at the back of my mind there was a faint unease about the way she'd been detained in Nanking at a meeting the day I'd been given my train. I realized there was no way she could know what I'd do that afternoon, but perhaps the gang who had tried to grab me planned to hit me wherever I was. And maybe, just maybe, she knew, and had been ordered to keep out of the way.

"I am glad you are all right," she said.

"You know what happened?"

"I was told that some bad elements had tried to attack you, but that thanks to the intervention of the People's Army you are safe. I am glad. It would have been a shameful thing for our country if you had been harmed."

It came out like a taped weather report.

"You were told the details?"

I felt her stiffen. "It was not felt necessary for me to know more than the basic facts."

"What are your orders?" I asked.

"Orders?" She spoke the word as though it was one she'd never heard before.

"Instructions, then."

It was obvious she did not like the way the conversation was developing. Nevertheless, delinquent though I was, it was her job to humor me. "I was told that although the danger is now past, officials of the Public Security Department will accompany us discreetly for your protection. I was also told that it was felt best for the time being that you remain within Nanking. This is only until it is certain that all those who tried to harm you are detained."

I could almost hear the sigh of relief as she finished that she had got her lines right. "So what do we do?" I asked.

This time her reply was spontaneous and her surprise genuine. "There is no work that you can do here in Nanking? And there is

73

much sightseeing that you should undertake. This is an ancient city. Also you have not seen the Yangtze River Bridge. Everyone should visit that, especially you, an engineer."

She was right about a lot of things. The bridge was one. The Chinese had built it in the late sixties after foreign experts had said that it could not be constructed. It stretched for four miles across the river, providing a vital road and rail link with the rest of the country.

More important, she was also right about the work. In theory, I could do everything I needed to do without looking at a stretch of track, an acre of countryside, or a single plant. It could all be done on the maps and the figures. It wouldn't be as good, it wouldn't have any flair. But it could be done. And as it was only a preliminary report it would do. Still, I wasn't admitting that — not least to myself.

"I'll work around the hotel today," I said. "In my room."

"I will wait here," she said, waving at one of the chairs. "I have many papers that I should read. It will give me opportunity."

I did not argue. If she wanted to sit around it was nothing to me. I returned to my room, checked again about my telephone call. This time it was a different voice, younger; he'd find out. I held on until he returned; there were "indefinite delays" on all calls to Peking, he said, and hung up before I could say anything else.

I made more coffee and tried to force back a growing fear. Laying out papers on the bed, I played with work. After two hours, I called the operator again. This time there was not even any pretense at friendliness or helpfulness. "When it is possible to connect your call you will be told," the voice snapped.

Downstairs, I found Chu Ming in a corner of the lobby, working through her papers. She had a ballpoint pen in her right hand, and was using the point to trace down the columns so that she would not miss anything. Orders to the faithful, I thought: today's instant beliefs. But I only guessed; I could have been way out — for all I knew, the sheets contained the latest recipes.

Reluctantly, she set off to investigate the situation about calls to the capital. She returned after twenty minutes, just about the length of time that I guessed had been judged right. The information I had been given was "unfortunately correct." There were indeed "problems of a technical nature." Under questioning, it emerged that such problems might continue at least until tomorrow. I knew she was lying; she knew I knew. I turned away, shaking my head. It was my only protest. It wasn't her fault. She had a role to play, and she was doing it as well as she knew how. The man with the shiny shoes had a smirk on his face as I passed, and anger joined the frustration as I made it to the stairs.

Back in my room, I decided I couldn't hold back the obvious any longer. Although Feng had released me, he had cut me off from any help or contact just as effectively as if he had detained me.

Nanking was a city with, as far as I knew, no resident foreign community. There were no foreign consulates, companies, airline offices, banks, or newspaper representatives. Andrews and the embassy were seven hundred miles in one direction. The nearest other city with Americans was Shanghai, two hundred miles in the other. Neither were vast distances — if I was back in the States. Here, they were as awesome as they would have been in the days when man had to go everywhere on foot or horse.

In China, you can't just move about anywhere you like. Travel on trains means permission. You can't rent cars because there aren't any to rent — or even to buy if you had the money. Aircraft have the same problems as trains — only more so.

I'd realized all that, but I had forgotten that telephoning too is dependent on Chinese cooperation — or, in my case, permission. The only way you can make a telephone call legitimately as a foreigner is through the service desk of the hotel, or — if you can find one — at a post office.

The alternative for all practical purposes does not exist. There are no pay phones. Telephones are rare in private homes, restricted to those judged to need them. A shop might have one — but use would be dependent on the shopkeeper's speaking English and being prepared to help — a dubious proposition, because why should a foreigner be making a call under such circumstances unless he had something to hide?

And, even if one did cooperate, that would still leave the problem of the operator. Would he or she even connect a call from a foreigner without first making checks?

If that were not enough, in my case there was also the added problem of being accompanied by my own personal guards wherever I went. Whichever way I looked at it, it did not seem good.

It was, I realized, a situation that Andrews at least had anticipated. He had even said that if I had problems Peking would seem a hell of a long way away. He had given me an address here in Nanking, as well as another in Shanghai. That immediately raised one problem — try as I might, I could not remember it! The number, yes; the street, no.

I told myself it was a temporary blockage, that if I didn't sweat too hard it would come to me. Part of me feared, though, that I just hadn't memorized it properly — that, back in Peking, I hadn't tried hard enough to store it away because the possibility of needing it seemed so remote. Finally, it did come — but only after I traced my finger over a map, street name by street name. Once I saw the word, it all came flooding back.

That only left one problem: I had to get to it. That was not going to be easy — but it should not be impossible. I doubted whether I could do anything during daylight, but at night I should be able to leave the hotel for long enough to reach the address. Once there, I would leave a message for transmission to Andrews.

His help might not be needed — perhaps I was reading too much into the current situation. Perhaps it was exactly as it had been presented to me — in a day or two, once investigations were completed, I would be allowed to continue. Or, at worst, I would be shipped back home.

Each time I tried to believe that, though, I kept remembering the Gang of Four supporter with his fist jammed down his own throat, and I started thinking again how desperate and scared you would have to be to kill yourself that way.

I did not know what was at stake. I had no idea what Feng Shen would do next. I did know I'd be crazy to sit back and wait for whatever was coming to me.

I made Chu Ming happy that afternoon. I asked to go sightseeing. It was a bit like a Sicilian courtship — me, the girl, and two heavies. Still, it achieved its purpose. It gave me a chance to see the layout of Nanking and, most important, to locate the street I wanted and its distance from the hotel. Although I had already found it on the map, Chinese maps and street plans are often of limited use — for one thing, I'd found that several scales can be used on the same one: half an inch in one direction can be a mile, in another five.

On our return, Chu Ming asked whether there was anywhere I wanted to go during the evening — the menu included an acrobatic display, a Peking opera, and a basketball match. I declined, saying I would see her in the morning, ate and walked in the garden outside the hotel. It was a fine evening, hot but not blisteringly so like the day, but that was not my reason for wanting to be outside — I was plotting a path from my window, across to the wall and over into the street. Without appearing to take too close an interest in the walls of the hotel itself, I convinced myself it could be done — I was on the second floor, a narrow but maneuverable ledge ran the length of the hotel within reach; if I inched along about twelve feet I would reach the branches of a cypress tree.

I had reckoned without the determination of the Chinese to look after my welfare. When I returned to my room, a workman was just finishing covering the inside of my window with fine wire netting. A hotel official explained the reason: to protect me from mosquitoes. No use pointing out that I hadn't seen or heard one single mosquito; no use protesting no one else seemed to need the same protection.

Nor was it a surprise to find later that Comrade Shiny Shoes took up an overnight position in the corridor leading to my room. No chance at all of leaving by the door without being seen.

So I did the only thing I could do. I caught up on my sleep.

The following morning I rose at six-thirty, made myself coffee, and decided whatever happened I had to get to Andrews's address that day. Unless, of course, the telephone link with Peking was suddenly restored; but everything told me that just was not going to happen.

77

My best hope, I concluded, was to compile a day's itinerary of sightseeing — in the hope that, somewhere, I would be able to break free. Depending on just where in the city we were at the time, two or three hours should be long enough to reach the address and then return to the hotel. Once back, I would apologize for having drifted off alone; in a tone of righteous indignation I would complain I was tired of being accompanied everywhere. I hoped that it would be in the guards' interest to believe me. With any luck, they would not even have widened the search before I returned, although I realized I could not depend on that.

With the aid of a guidebook and a map, I drew up my list to put to Ming. Luckily Nanking was not short of sights — it had several times been the capital of the country. Chiang Kai-shek had been the last man to give it that status; my U.S. guidebook told me he had bequeathed it handsome buildings; my other book, published in Peking by China Tourism Press, said he had made it a "consumer city infested by KMT bureaucrat-compradors." I suspected they would have been interchangeable with Shiny Shoes (whom I'd twice checked was still on duty and awake): bureaucrats usually are.

That finished, I began to sort with painstaking care through my belongings, separating items that might be useful if suddenly the situation worsened and I was forced to make a run for it.

Where, and how I'd run was a different matter — not one I chose to think about. Another glance at the map only confirmed the near-impossibility of such a step. Peking was much too far. The nearest "safe" place, Hong Kong, was twice the distance to the south. There were ports along the Yangtze. Big ocean-going freighters could go as far up as Hankow, way beyond Nanking. I could try to get aboard one, but I assessed my chances as about the same as the Pentagon asking for a decrease in the defense budget. Between me and Shanghai was two hundred miles of rich agricultural land, dotted with lakes, crossed by canals. A mere seven hours by train — but even if I could board one I suspected the alert would be given long before I was halfway there. It would be ridiculously easy to pick me up.

I stifled such thoughts and concentrated on my sorting. Mainly, it was a distraction — a way of feeling that I was doing something. Never seriously did I think it would be needed. The most important items were maps — one of the city, another of the province. I left the others. First, they would have been too bulky, folded flat under my shirt, and second, I hoped that if someone did check my belongings the absence of only two would not be noticed. I wrapped them in polyethylene bags — I have always carried an assortment, having found them invaluable for a host of uses, from preserving soil samples to holding dirty laundry.

The others were obvious — a small tube of antiseptic cream, money, my Swiss army knife, matches, a small flashlight. Finally, although even then as part of the game it seemed crazily dramatic, I played at putting together a tiny survival kit — the kind the books had urged me to carry at all times when I had started backpacking as a boy.

I started by removing the inner workings from my pen. I then sorted and discarded items until I was finally satisfied. At the end I felt anything but James Bondish, but there was a slight feeling of reassurance, and that was all I could hope for. My improvised survival kit contained two aspirin tablets, some nylon line, two Band-Aids, four matches that I'd waterproofed with a candle left in my room, and a couple of needles from my sewing kit. When you travel a lot in isolated places, you carry most things that you might need. The needles, though, were a little special — before I packed them I magnetized them. I did this by extracting from the doorframe of the wardrobe one of the small magnets that held the door closed. I then stroked this along the needle several times, always in the same direction, from the point to the eye. I knew that if the needles were allowed to revolve freely the eye would always point north.

Having done all that, I felt a little childish. I'm not sure I would have continued if I hadn't wandered over to the window and if I hadn't peered out through the netting. Below, I could see one of my two guards conferring with two other men near a stationary black car.

My first thought was that they had come to get me. I returned to my small pile of odds and ends and, shakily, finished filling the pen barrel. The needles might seem like a joke, but without the ability to find north and south I was finished if I had to go on the run.

Quickly I packed everything into my clothes. The pen went into one of the breast pockets of a denim jacket — despite the heat, I would make sure I carried it everywhere I went. I made use of all my other pockets, without making it obvious — trousers, shirt. Most important of all, I spread about me the contents of a bottle of water purification tablets, all wrapped tightly in more plastic bags. In China water did not appear to be safe to drink anywhere, including big cities. Even the Chinese boiled it first.

I checked my watch. Almost time for breakfast. Taking my jacket and a guidebook, I left my room. I would stroll in the garden until it was time to eat. If they were going to pick me up, it might as well be outside my room.

Nothing happened. I walked twice around the drive, ate two boiled eggs — breakfast was always the one Westernized meal of the day — and drank two cups of coffee that tasted like the bitter essence of some Chinese weed. The dining room was cool, with an enormously high ceiling and revolving fans. The sense of space was accentuated by the fact that I was placed at a table surrounded by an island of empty tables.

In any event, there were few other diners, and I was the only Westerner. The others, judging from their clothes and the women's makeup, were overseas Chinese. Every few seconds someone would look at me as though I had dribbled egg down my chin, and as soon as I had finished I moved into the lobby to wait for whatever happened.

What happened was Ming. The smile was warming, even if she still worried me.

"You would like to go sightseeing?" she said.

"I would like to go sightseeing," I agreed.

She had her own list of "must" places that we should visit, but it was not very different from mine.

Late in the morning, rejoining our car outside the city museum, we walked near the group of overseas Chinese I had seen at breakfast. One of the women was about the same age as Ming, and I caught the look that passed between them.

The visitor — from Hong Kong, I thought —wore tight jeans and a sleeveless blouse which showed the line of what bust she had. Her hair was waved, and although her makeup was discreet by any standards but Chinese the lipstick made a gash of her mouth like that of a vampire in some Dracula film. She took the steps into the museum with delicate difficulty: the high heels made her move with the same care that her ancestors would have had to adopt with their bound feet. Her buttocks were out of a Levi's ad.

Ming's body, on the other hand, could have been a boy's under the loose-fitting clothes. Her shirt today was bright — yellow flowers on a white background. But there was no makeup, no trace of scent; her hair, jet black, was again tied in a practical bun. As I slid into the car I wondered what she thought of the other woman — contempt? envy? curiosity? I realized I did not know. Ming, like the country, was an enigma. Correction. More of an enigma. I had learned a little about China—even though it might be naive or turn out to be wrong. But about Ming I knew nothing.

I did know, and the thought came suddenly and apparently from nowhere, that of the two women she was the one who interested me. The shapeless clothes and the mystery of what they concealed — just the obvious sign of the greater mystery — excited me more than the blatancy of the other.

I slid into the back of the car. Ming, emphasizing the gulf between us, sat in the front beside the driver. She turned her head, and I caught it in profile. Put it down to tiredness, strain, the longing for some kind of contact, but I began to wonder what would happen if I touched her. Not now, but when we were alone. Not touch-touched, but just touched gently — fingertips on a hand, an arm, a shoulder.

The driver said something, collapsed in a fit of laughter, and spat noisily out of the window. He looked back, checked that our security companions were ready to follow, and pulled away.

It got rid of dangerous thoughts. I turned my mind back to real, immediate problems. So far there had been no chance at all to break free.

That remained the situation for the whole day.

I didn't even make an attempt. I was so closely watched that it would have been doomed to failure. Instead, I concentrated upon seeming cooperative, completely harmless, hoping to relax them so that something was in my favor once the time was ripe.

I was still relaxing them when we returned to the hotel. I felt obligated to insist she check on the progress of my call to Peking. Technical problems were still defeating the combined talents of the Chinese telecommunications service.

I had expected it, but I hoped my show of disappointment would soften her up for my next request.

I wanted to go to the Peking opera, I said.

She looked uncertain, was not sure there would be tickets at such short notice. Finally, she said she would check. She did — it took a long time; it must have needed a lot of clearance.

When she returned, she was smiling again. We must be ready to leave for the theater in thirty minutes.

5

The theater was a square white building surrounded by single-story shops. Now, at six-thirty-five, they were all closed. The building itself could have been anything from outside, except for one showcase containing stage photographs of men with long beards and women with elaborate headdresses. A sheet of paper, covered with ideographs, was pinned nearby; for all I knew it was a review from the local newspaper saying the show was a hit and not to miss it.

The streets leading to the theater were crowded with Chinese on foot. Most, it seemed, were heading for it. Once we got inside, I couldn't see how they would get seats — the interior was vast but in the gloom it appeared that almost every seat was already taken.

Ming led me to seats about a third of the way back from the stage, and sat beside me. I looked around: our two chaperones had taken up positions two rows behind. I doubted it was discretion; from there they could see everything I did.

The theater was crowded not only with people but with a noise that seemed to echo back from the walls and ceilings. It was as though I had stumbled into a reunion of people who had not seen each other for months. They were dressed as casually and drably as they were the rest of the day. It was oddly disconcerting, even though my guidebook had warned me about it, and even though I myself wore a sport shirt, my denim jacket, and jeans. It was hard to forget that

I belonged to a society that still regarded the theater as something for which you at least changed your shirt.

It was even more unnerving, then, when Ming leaned over to translate parts of the single-sheet program. Perfume. Just a hint, no more. But definitely perfume.

I began to wonder if I had got it all wrong. Perhaps the reason I had been turned loose, given this limited but pleasurable freedom, was so that Ming could encourage me to confide in her. Perhaps we had the Chinese equivalent of a Mata Hari situation — as a nation, I had no doubt they were skilled in it. Ming would be under orders to be pleasant, to encourage me to relax, to talk. After all, I had no one else to turn to. If it was true, it was interesting to wonder how far she would go. The Chinese were supposed to be puritanical. But then it would be for a cause. If I wished it, would sitting next to each other in the theater become lying together?

The curtains opened, exposing the musicians on the side of the stage. Like the audience, they were in their everyday clothes. They had no scores in front of them. My eyes scanned the unfamiliar instruments — a lute, two stringed fiddles, drums, bells, cymbals, a moon-shaped guitar . . .

The stage was almost bare, the way it was to remain. I leaned closer to Ming, more to check the perfume than anything else. "There's no scenery," I said.

"It is traditional," she said, no attempt at a whisper even though the orchestra was now playing. Here, I understood, if you wanted to talk, you talked. "But more and more theaters are adding scenery. They try to attract the young people."

I looked around. In the dimmed houselights, I saw what she meant. Most of the audience were middle-aged or old. It also gave me a chance to check my guards. One had sunk deep into his seat and looked as though his eyes might be closed. The other was reading his program notes.

That's the way, I whispered to myself. Get engrossed or be as bored as hell. Anything to keep your mind off me.

The first act lasted almost an hour. The whole of China is a culture

shock, but sitting through a Peking opera is like having all the strange-
ness distilled and poured over you.

It is singing, dancing, drama, acrobatics, pantomime, all combined.
Shrill instrumental sounds wrestle with the falsetto voices of female
impersonators. Aristocratic ladies in elegant costumes compete for
attention with court officials in robes with cascading sleeves, embroidered with dragon patterns. It is an assault on every sense.

Gradually a pattern of sorts emerged. The masks, I saw, all had
their meaning. The central character tonight, Judge Bao, had his face
painted in a mask of black and dark brown, with a white half-moon
on his forehead.

I attracted Ming's attention by touching her hand, which was resting on her lap. She reacted as though I had stubbed her with a lighted
cigarette. If she was under orders to be especially nice (and *that* was
only my theorizing), she was going to find it temperamentally difficult.

"The mask," I said. "What does it mean?"

I think she was relieved that my request was so routine. "The moon
means night. The judge is in communication with ghosts who come
at night."

At the end of the act we streamed into the lobby, an excited,
chattering horde. A few people drifted out into the street. It was still
daylight — not yet eight. For what I was about to do I would have
been much happier if it had been dark.

My head was still ringing with the strange music, my eyes still
filled with the garish colors of the masks and the costumes.

"How much longer does it last?"

She mistook the reason for my question. "We can leave now. It is
a special taste. As I told you, many young people in China prefer the
movies and dance dramas."

"No," I said, almost too quickly. "It's good. I like it." We had been
jostled into a corner. The lobby was no more than a large rectangle,
the street on one side, the entrance to the auditorium and various
doors on another. People were giving me a little more space because
I was a foreigner, but there was still little room to move. "It is strange,"
I added, "but interesting."

"There are two more hours, I think," she said.

"If I get bored, I will tell you."

That satisfied her. It also left me with a dilemma. There would probably be at least one more intermission. It would be darker then. Should I wait?

"You would like a drink?" There was a booth at the far end of the lobby. It was serving soft drinks.

"Please."

I did not offer to get them, first because of the language, and second because I wanted her out of the way.

Ming looked around and caught sight of one of the guards about ten yards away. The other was not in view.

"You will wait here," she said. It could have been a question or a command.

"I will go to the lavatory," I said, "and return here."

I began to move before she could say anything. I kept my eyes on her. I saw her speak to the guard. He nodded, and looked after me. I did not think anyone would be worried. The lavatory was through one of the doors the length of the lobby from the street. I suspected the guard's companion was in the street, watching the doors.

I was gambling that there would be some way out of the lavatory to the street. All I needed, I reckoned, was a few minutes' start. It would be easy to lose myself in the warren of narrow streets near the theater. I didn't think the guards would call in more help immediately — first, they would try to find me themselves, hoping they would not have to reveal they had lost sight of me.

As it happened, the lavatory offered no way out. It was almost as crowded as the lobby. People waited to enter cubicles without doors to use holes in the concrete. There were windows, but to reach one I would have to climb in full view of several scores of people. Foreigners are given a few allowances for eccentricity, but I thought that would exceed them by about a million percent.

I waited until a group left together. Making myself as small as I could without actually dropping to my knees, I moved behind them, using them as a shield. Once outside, I began to skirt the wall, using the crowd to hide me. I found another door, opened it, slid through, and entered a passageway. I passed a small office, a door opened. Someone called after me, but I pretended not to hear.

I turned into a second passageway, took some steps down and then more up, and finally came to a room with a window showing daylight. I had to move a packing crate to help me climb high enough, but the window opened easily and I hauled myself up, slid through, and dropped down into a narrow alley.

I figured out that one direction would lead to the front of the theater, the other to the rear. Even though it would mean a wider circuit to reach my destination, I decided the back was safest.

I retrieved my jacket, which I had tossed out of the window ahead of me, and began moving. I wore rubber-soled shoes, and they made no sound on the packed-earth surface.

I did not see the guard until I emerged from the passageway. He was the one who had been missing from the lobby. Mistakenly, I had thought he would be covering the front. He saw me a fraction of a second later.

Instinctively I drew back, and began to turn. He came after me, just as instinctively. Unbelievingly, I saw his hand was moving to slide under his jacket. It was an action I had seen dozens, perhaps hundred, of times — in the movies. But never with a Mao jacket before, even if it hung loose and had the top buttons undone. That slows things.

I was not capable of doing anything clever or elaborate. Maddy had taken twice-weekly karate lessons on the grounds that I left her alone so much (a hint that in my absence she had to spend twenty-four hours a day fighting off other men), but my own regular exercise had been limited to that daily jog and occasional tennis. Over the years, though, I had been forced into the odd fight, and knew the two things that counted were being fast and vicious. I launched a mule-kick at his kneecap while he was still fumbling, then went down on him with all my weight. I am not in the heavyweight league — a hundred and fifty-five pounds — but he was a good twenty-eight pounds less than that. Besides, he had already hit his head on the side of the alley on his way down, something I realized too late to stop my follow-through movement.

I hauled myself off him and got to my knees. He lay still, his arm still bent inside his jacket. His breath was so soft I couldn't hear it. I checked his pulse at his throat. It was there, but fast and very feeble.

I felt the sweat of fear bead my forehead. Christ, I thought, he may die.

I checked under his arm, trying to be gentle. If there had been nothing, I would have felt even worse than I did. But it was there — a pistol, an automatic, black, much-handled. Its butt was wrapped around with tape, its owner's customizing.

At least I had acted in self-defense; if I hadn't moved quickly he could have killed me. It could have been me lying there, my blood darkening the earth. That was some consolation for my conscience, but I doubted it would help if the Chinese grabbed me. The only question then, I suspected, would be whether I lasted as long as a trial.

I took the gun, sliding it into my waistband. I wasn't sure why — again it was instinctive. It was hidden by my jacket. I checked once more that my companion was still alive and then, irrationally, retraced my steps toward the front of the theater.

I was more cautious this time, peering carefully before emerging. All the implications of what had happened had not dawned on me yet, but I knew I had crossed a line.

There were lots of passersby. No guard. But there was Ming, looking frightened and lost all at once. My absence must have been noted. The other guard was probably searching the theater. The only plus from that was that the man I had injured would probably be discovered soon.

There was no indication that Ming was about to move back inside. It was foolhardy for me to wait any longer. There could be a scream, and a general alert, any second.

I removed my jacket again, using it this time to cover the pistol, which I withdrew from my waistband. The safety catch was on, and I left it that way. I didn't want to shoot anyone, least of all Ming. I did want to frighten her into doing what I ordered.

I stepped out into her full view. Worry turned to relief on her face, and as I neared it began to change to sternness — I was due for a reprimand.

I waited until I was close before exposing the pistol. "This may sound pretty heavy," I said, "but unless you walk slowly in front of me toward the car, I'm going to have to shoot you."

She hesitated, and I said melodramatically, "I've already hurt one man; I've got nothing to lose."

Chinese, particularly those brought up during the ten years of the Cultural Revolution, have been taught foreigners are capable of anything. She moved.

The car which had brought us to the theater was parked about a hundred yards away. It was empty — the driver had left it. The door was open, but there was no key in the ignition. Among my normally useless qualifications is the ability to start a car without a key. But here was no place to start lifting hoods and crossing wires.

Now, though, I needed a car. On foot, I had no chance of getting out of the neighborhood before the security man's body was discovered. I noticed the faint grin of triumph flicker across Ming's face. In the space of a few minutes it had changed expression so often as to be personal proof against inscrutability.

In desperation I scanned the street. Then I saw it: twenty yards further away was a second car, the security men's black Mercedes. The few passersby were giving it a wide berth. It too was empty. It might be just as useless, but I had to try. I gestured Ming toward it.

Curtains were drawn, screening the back windows. I tried the driver's door. It opened. The key was in the ignition. I imagined leaving it there was an offense against the Security Department rule book, but they must have learned over the years that no one steals a Public Security car.

I didn't have any choice.

"You drive," I said.

I made her walk around the car, get in the passenger side, and slide across, me behind her all the time.

Suddenly it came to me that in a country where cars were few, qualified drivers must be rare. I started to ask whether she could in fact drive, then stopped myself — I had no desire to feed her excuses. She turned the key, moved into gear, and eased off the parking brake. For all I knew, all guides had to take driving lessons.

The car jerked forward, almost stopped, then jerked again. I raised my free hand to steady myself against the windshield, and I realized that I was shouting that I would shoot her if she did anything stupid.

She continued driving, slowly, less jerkily. "I am not used to cars," she said. "It was a mistake." She sounded as scared as I felt.

We reached an intersection and stopped. The roads were busy with pedestrians and bicyclists, but there was little motor traffic.

"Turn left," I said. I hoped I sounded decisive, but I still didn't have my bearings. At least, there were no one-way streets, roadworks, or traffic jams.

I finally managed to synchronize the streets we passed with the map in my mind, and I gave more directions. For a while we joined a major boulevard and accelerated past a line of trucks. At a cross street, still manned by a traffic policeman, we were waved straight through. I wiped my forehead and wondered how much he had seen of the car's interior.

We entered quieter streets. The buildings all seemed to be workshops or light industrial plants. I checked a street name against my notes, a difficult process because they were in ideograph. We were within walking distance of the street I wanted. I did not dare go too near — the parked car would be too great a giveaway once it was found.

I ordered Ming to stop the car. Then I waited until I made sure no one was within sight, and we both got out.

I was afraid she would try to resist when I opened the trunk and ordered her inside. I felt bad about what I was doing, but I knew I would feel a lot worse if the security man's friends got their hands on me. I remembered a report in Western newspapers before I ever got to China about an attempted hijack, and how the passengers had swarmed over the men, beating and kicking two of them to death.

While threatening Ming, I tried to make my voice persuasive. "There's plenty of air," I said. "You'll be all right. They'll find you within half an hour or so."

"I can't bear being confined," she said, but she did as I ordered. I locked the trunk. On reflection, I pocketed the keys. The longer it took her rescuers to free her the longer it would take them to find how great a time start I had.

The address was no more than fifteen minutes away, but it was a long, jumpy walk. There was a patch of vacant land, with newly built square houses beyond, and I passed a group of kids playing table tennis on a table improvised from a concete block. They stared, and I smiled, but none of them rushed off to report that some foreigner was wandering about alone.

The encounter made me even more cautious. I paused before making a turn into the street that I wanted. It was just as well. Two men, both Chinese, were about thirty yards ahead of me. Their backs were to me, but I froze. They started to cross the street, and I caught the profile of one. I seemed to recognize him, a thought I dismissed immediately as a product of my nervousness.

They approached a long, low storehouse. One lifted his hand and knocked at a wood door set into the front of the building. He must have been holding something hard in his hand, a key or a coin perhaps, because the sound carried. The moment before the door opened and the two men entered, the other man turned and looked along the street. I pulled back quickly. I didn't feel he had seen me, but I got a clear view of him. The left side of his face was discolored and misshapen. And suddenly I knew where I had seen him before. Near a train. On a hot, lonely afternoon, when I had nearly died.

I could not tell from this distance whether the building he entered was the address Andrews had given me. The odds seemed to be that it was. Alternatively, it was an adjoining one from which he and his companions were keeping watch.

Why? The answer was obvious: they had expected me to run for cover ever since I had been returned to the hotel here in Nanking. But how did they know this address? I had not written it down, had told no one. There seemed only one answer: bad security in Andrews's office. I knew he'd take every precaution against that, but perhaps it was a question of the professional getting too careless, underestimating opponents he regarded as mere amateurs.

Even while I was thinking this I was on the move again. I headed back in the direction of the car. For the first few minutes my only thoughts were of getting out of the immediate neighborhood. Then I began to sweat over what I would do next.

My original aim in going to the address had been simply to get a message to Andrews — I wanted him to know where I was and that I needed aid. The confrontation with the security man had raised the stakes. Suddenly I had needed somewhere to hide until Andrews could get that help to me. But the way things had panned out now I was completely on my own. I'd failed to contact Andrews's man; help wasn't on the way; I had no hiding place. All I had was one security man — badly injured, maybe even dead.

I doubted that Security was gentle with people who did that. Furthermore, what I had done would only confirm suspicions that I did know something. Why else would I have broken away? They would be keener than ever to make me talk. Again I remembered the man who'd committed suicide with his fist thrust down his throat . . .

It was growing dark. I broke into a run. Christ! What was I going to do? I could hardly return to the hotel and give myself up apologetically. But what was the alternative?

I slowed as I reached the empty lot, but the boys had gone. Finally the car came into sight. It looked undisturbed. No one was in view. There was no noise from the trunk — if Ming had tried yelling or banging on the inside, she had stopped.

I was still operating instinctively, letting panic dictate my movements. I opened the car doors first, only then the trunk, suddenly apprehensive that I would find Ming gone, or suffocated.

She was still there, and safe, screwed up with her hands against her mouth like a small child seeking protection. She turned her head and looked up at the noise of the trunk being opened. Her eyes showed nothing, not even dismay that it was me and not a Chinese. I had to urge her several times, pulling on her arm, until she climbed out.

"I want you to drive again," I said. There was no need to feign gentleness. I felt bad about what I was doing.

"I can't," she stammered.

"Yes, you can. It's not far." I led her to the door, helped her inside, then got in beside her.

Despite her protestations, she switched on the engine as though sleepwalking, and pulled away gently and easily. I gave her directions. My voice sounded strange.

I'd decided that the first thing I had to do was get out of the city. Within it, there was nowhere I could hide. Once outside . . . But it was no good even thinking about that now.

The traffic was light and I made Ming drive fast, reasoning that speed would not seem unusual in what was so obviously an official car. One reason that I'd made her take the wheel was that I felt the car would excite less curiosity if it were driven by a Chinese — that was, of course, if there was not yet an alert out for it.

I kept thinking that if I was in any danger before, now I was struggling for my life.

The sky was dark now, and the lack of light helped and gave some comfort. The Chinese do not waste money or resources on street lighting; nor is there reflected glow from office blocks or illuminated roadside signs and posters. Cars, even in the open country, drive with only their parking lights on.

I began to search the glove compartment. There was an apple and a small flashlight, both of which I pocketed, a newspaper and cigarettes, which I left. There was also a large flask filled with a sweet liquid; it tasted like heavily diluted plum juice. I would keep that too.

We were on a long, straight road now, empty except for a truck or two. I saw that we were passing an institutional-type building, a school perhaps, set back behind a deep courtyard that was covered with parked bicycles.

"Stop!"

She turned her head, alarmed and puzzled. But she did as I ordered.

"Reverse. Back into that driveway, by the courtyard."

She fumbled, found the right gear, and did as I asked.

I took the key from the ignition so that she could not drive off, got out of the car, and quickly heaved two bicycles into the trunk.

I'd moved without conscious thought from the moment I'd seen the bikes. Later I realized that must have been the second my sub-conscious finally decided that if I was going to get out of this country I had to start doing things on my own.

I returned to the car, panting with effort.

"Let's go," I said, handing back the key. "Fast."

"They'll be missed," she said. "Reported stolen." She was beginning to compose herself. I would have to watch her more carefully.

"We'll be long gone. Just get going."

We continued to drive toward the hills. I watched until I saw the surrounding countryside change the way I knew it would — we had come this far sightseeing.

Ten minutes later I ordered Ming to turn off, onto narrow, winding country roads.

I saw the gap in the trees about half an hour later. We stopped and, with her beside me, I investigated on foot. Satisfied, I returned to the car. It was probably as good as I would find. Pines and heavy deciduous trees I did not know grew back from the narrow road as far as I could see. It should be possible to drive the car back thirty to forty yards.

Ming had begun to shiver with nervousness and exhaustion, and I drove this time, trying to get as deep into the wood as I could without leaving a trail of damage that would give it away. I drove slowly, letting the slope carry me when it would, not using any lights at all. Finally, I halted at the edge of a gully. I got out and checked. It was about eight feet wide and four feet deep.

I made Ming sit with her back against a tree where I could keep her in view. I lifted the bicycles from the trunk. They were black — the Chinese adopt the old Henry Ford approach, not difficult when you are producing to satisfy long waiting lists — with no gears. The wheels were padlocked so they would not revolve. There were tools in the car, and I snapped the locks. I pushed the pieces of chain into my pockets to dispose of later. Sooner or later someone would surely link the stolen bikes with me, but I saw no reason for helping them.

That done, I reached into the car and released the parking brake. I pushed until the car began to move. Then I leaped back, letting the Mercedes's weight do the rest. It hung for a moment, then collapsed into the dip. The noise seemed immense, and I regretted my action immediately. Surely someone would come to investigate — I had no way of knowing how far away were the nearest homes. The fear added urgency to the task of clearing the trail the car had left. I did the best I could in the darkness. Finally, I covered the parts of the car that remained visible with shrubs and weed painfully torn from the hard earth.

Then, sweating, coated with red mud, I collapsed on the ground.

Ming moved and I lifted myself quickly, and spoke, making my voice harsh. "Stay where you are. Don't move. Don't make me do anything."

She settled back, without speaking. Five minutes later, I tied my belt around her ankles. If she wanted to loosen it, she could, but it would take a vital few minutes.

"There's nowhere for you to run," she said. "You'll not get away. They'll find you." Her voice was flat, matter-of-fact, not bitter. It made it more, not less chilling.

I moved a few yards away and made myself moderately comfortable, seated against a chestnut tree. I did not reply. Maybe she was right.

Nevertheless, run was what I was going to do. My conviction had grown that there was no real option. As I saw it, the only alternative was handing myself over to a torture chamber, a prison camp, or a firing squad — maybe all three in that order.

It was a little after ten-thirty. A bat swooped between branches above. A small, dark shape scurried across the undergrowth a dozen yards away. A squirrel, I thought.

The day's heat was gone now, but even here under the trees it was not cold. The earth was dry — although it was supposed to be the beginning of the wet season the rains had not yet begun. On the run that might be a problem. I had spent enough time in the wild, right from backpacking as a kid, to know that drinking water is far and away the biggest priority. In an area with so much agriculture — which meant irrigation — that should not be insurmountable.

My mind began to review my resources. I had the clothes I wore, the items I had packed into my pockets that morning, and the minimum of food and water — a bar of chocolate, some hard candy, an apple, and a flask of some sweet drink. I also had two bicycles. Why had I taken two? The answer came immediately — even though I had thought nothing through, I had known I had to keep Ming with me.

My only chance, I reckoned, was to get to Shanghai. There, I had Andrews's second address. If that failed, there were Western offices and even consulates. How they would help, I did not know — I'd still be within China. But they provided some hope.

Besides, I had to get to Shanghai first. Two hundred miles. Pointless dwelling on the difficulties. They were obvious. I would just have to do what I could, moving by night, hiding by day. At least, by making a run, I had nothing to lose. But I did need every break I could give myself. That meant taking Ming. Without being able to read signs, translate conversations I might overhear, I was a deaf and blind man. Not that there was much alternative. If I relocked her in the trunk of the now hidden car, she might die before anyone found her. If I set her free, I would lose whatever small advantage I might have.

I checked my watch again. Not much more than four hours now until the first glimmers of light. We would rest half an hour, no more. Then move. I wanted to be as far away from the car as possible.

6

I used one of the magnetized needles to find southeast, the direction we now had to keep heading, suspending it from a piece of the nylon thread. It is possible to navigate using only the stars, and in the past I had done it. First, you look for the Big Dipper, then let your eyes follow the two stars at the end of the bowl. They are called the "pointers," and in a straight line from them is the North Star. Tonight, though, with cloud drifting overhead, it would have been easier in theory than in practice.

I relied on the needle often, lining it up with distant landmarks, then using them as markers. Ming, who was obeying my orders in an unemotional silence, rode a few feet ahead of me. It was nerve-racking because I had no way of knowing what lay past each bend, behind every clump of trees or bushes or beyond each dip. The map I carried was nowhere detailed enough for this kind of traveling; it showed only the major topographic details and main towns. We had to stop many times and proceed slowly on foot, sometimes making detours for houses that *might* be near. Once we alerted dogs; their howls pursued us as I urged Ming to pedal as fast as she could manage.

Soon I estimated that we were probably averaging not much more than about five to six miles an hour, perhaps double the pace an experienced walker would hope to keep up in hill country. To have traveled faster, though, represented too great a risk. Constantly, too, I had to be wary that Ming did not try to break away.

The roads we took were unpaved and pitted, but at least the hills were gentle. After the first hour, though, I felt the aches begin. I was using unaccustomed muscles. For Ming, as for many Chinese, bicycling was as normal a method of movement as walking. If she tried to break away, I had problems. I was bigger and stronger, but this was no time or place to get involved in a race. Any control I had over her came from threats and her fear. I knew it was mostly bluff on my part. Though I would grasp her, even strike her, if she was within reach, I would not use the gun. Not that it would be much use in any kind of pursuit in the darkness anyway. I had handled a pistol enough to know its limitations — and mine. Except as bluff, in fact, the gun was an embarrassment, surprisingly heavy and uncomfortable.

I insisted we take frequent short breaks: I had found from experience it was sensible. Halfway to dawn I gave us each some chocolate. Although we were both thirsty and sweating with the effort, I left the flask untouched. Vaguely I remembered that when liquid is scarce it is best not to drink for the first twenty-four hours, allowing the body to use up what it has instead of simply excreting an excess.

Well before the first signs of light I began to look for shelter, knowing that the day would be an even greater problem than the night. There were few features that would provide good cover. At last I decided upon a small copse. It was not ideal. If anyone was searching it was too obvious a place — it stood out from the surrounding landscape. However, it was the best available.

I hid the bikes as convincingly as I could, and then we burrowed into the undergrowth. Again, I tied her ankles. She did not resist.

"You're crazy," she said.

"Maybe," I said. What else could I reply except that she was right? At the same time I knew I was no more crazy than any animal which runs when it is being hunted.

She busied herself clearing ground for her back. "They'll be searching for us now," she said. "If they know you have that gun, they will shoot you first. You would be better giving yourself up."

"Try to sleep," I said. I brushed away some ants and changed position. Ming's tone reflected her exhaustion, but I knew I should tie her more securely. Nevertheless, I dismissed it: save it for the movies, I told myself. I was determined to sit, awake but resting, until she fell into a deep sleep. Then I would doze, no more, ready to move instantly at the slightest sound or movement.

That, at least, was the rudimentary plan. The first part went well. Ming fell asleep almost immediately, her jacket hugged around her like a shawl. Strands of her hair had broken free from the pins and they trailed across her cheek, giving her a waiflike look. I stared at her as the sun rose. There was a streak of red dust that reminded me of the Hong Kong Chinese woman's mouth. When Ming shifted in her sleep, I saw a button had been torn loose from her shirt.

The sight of the sun and the heat from the ground began to soothe my limbs with their warmth. The ache in my legs and across my back dwindled to a not unpleasant throb — the kind of feeling you get in a sauna after a good workout. Once or twice I closed my eyes, let myself drift, but I remained awake. After a while, I crawled to the edge of the copse to see whether I could see anything in daylight that would help me place my location. In the distance peasants were working in the fields. Already the land was beginning to shimmer with heat, reminding me of my thirst. I sucked at my mouth, trying without success to make saliva. We had lost a lot of water through sweating during the night. We would have to drink as much as we could find whenever we found it. But for the day we had only the one flask, and I kept to my resolve not to touch it. Ming, I realized, had not asked to drink from it once, even though she knew it was there, and even though she must also have been finding it hard at times to think of anything else. It confirmed my view that she was a strong woman.

Looking back into the copse from the edge, I could see nothing of the bikes, nor Ming. Satisfied, I returned and decided I could safely doze for half an hour. It is something that I have always found easy, an inherent facility refined by many years of use. All I have to do is give my mind a time, or tell it a set number of hours, and it wakes me.

That morning, flat on my back, head turned toward Ming, who was about five feet away, I told my mind "thirty minutes" and closed my eyes. Despite the hard ruts in the ground, waves of sleep pressed down on me immediately.

It was a dog's bark that woke me. I crash-surfaced through layers of sleep, groping for the pistol like some trigger-happy gunhand. The dog was outside the copse, but it was yelping as if it had found something. I decided that it had to be our scent, and I felt my stomach lurch and my palms begin to sweat.

Ming began to move, quietly, stealthily, but the slight sound made my head snap toward her. I saw she was carefully untying the belt. Ming obviously knew what I only suspected: in the Chinese countryside a dog certainly meant an owner nearby. She was getting ready to run, to scream.

I rolled over toward her, pushed her down with my weight. I pressed the pistol into her side, and cupped her mouth with the other hand.

"Don't say anything," I hissed.

Her body was quivering with sobs of what could have been either fear or frustration. She tried to bite my hand, but I dug the gun barrel harder into her ribs.

"Don't forget I'm a crazy man," I said. "I've got nothing to lose."

We lay, our faces down toward the earth. I could almost hear her trying to will the dog's owner: *Come nearer, come nearer, see us.*

The dog stopped barking, and the sound was replaced by a scuffling noise. Then there was a shout, a man's voice. It was some way away, but that was small comfort. For all I knew he was calling to his companions, "Come here, the dog's found something."

I had to move to get more weight onto Ming, afraid that she would manage to break free for a vital few seconds. My senses were all sharpened; I could smell the dried sweat on my own body, the warm earth, even the trace of the flowery smell of her scent. I peered into the undergrowth, vainly trying to make out what was happening. I began to wonder what I would do if we had been seen. Would I use the gun?

Even as I wondered, I knew that once even our rough whereabouts became known I was as good as caught. My hope at the moment was that Chinese Security would not be quite sure where I was — as they suspected me of being involved with American intelligence, they might well assume that I had contacts with whom I could have gone to ground. Equally, they might conjecture that I had an escape route leading in another direction, perhaps to one of the river ports. But once my presence was known, or suspected, in a given area, Security could swamp it with men. My freedom would be short.

Both of us were shivering now, despite the day's heat. Then, gradually, the noise both of the dog and of the man's voice receded. Ming tensed as though about to make a bid to break loose before it was too late, but I tightened my hold on her mouth and hissed a warning.

I waited until I was sure the man would be well away, then released her and edged away. I pointed the pistol like an angry finger. "Don't say a word, not a word."

Keeping my eyes on Ming, I stumbled, crouching, to the edge of the copse. The man was far away, the dog running ahead.

I returned, and Ming pulled herself upright. Her face was smeared with earth, and there were leaves in her hair, which now hung free of pins. She began to brush herself, removing debris.

We were both breathing hard, and staring frozen at each other. I saw her eyes properly for the first time: an amazing pale, sea color. I remembered her body under me, and a part of me stirred. It was the tension; it needed somewhere to go.

She dabbed at her cheek. It was bleeding a little. It had been scratched, perhaps by a twig or my nail. I found my handkerchief, folded it to a clean corner, and handed it to her. Then I poured her some of the sweet liquid from the flask, using the cover as a cup. "Drink," I said. "You'll feel better."

I could see that she did not want to take it, but her thirst was too strong to resist. She took the metal cover and tried to force herself to sip slowly.

"They'll get you next time," she said. "You know it's only time."

"Finish your drink," I said, "and then get some sleep."

But she did not, and neither did I. Hours later, after an eternity of facing each other in silence, darkness came, and I uncovered the bikes, took a bearing, and we moved off again.

We traveled farther that night, perhaps because I was more confident, or more afraid, or less cautious. I do not know. Perhaps it was also the realization that traveling would become harder the hungrier we became.

We finished all the sweet liquid, and shared the apple before we started. I rationed the chocolate, square by square, as an incentive on the hour, whenever we stopped for a short pause. We found some food — fruit, including newly ripened strawberries. Not enough to renew strength, but enough to satisfy hunger — shortage of water had dulled any real want of food.

Later that night, though, the rain came at last. It came with the suddenness and the force of a rent being torn in the sky. One moment we were riding in the warm, dry darkness, the next we were being pummeled by raindrops the size of grapes.

It was useless trying to continue. We struggled along on foot, pushing the bikes, until we found a yew hedge. We crowded against its sheltered side.

"Will it last long at this force?" I had to yell even though we were close together.

"I don't know." There was no anger in her reply or in what I could see in her expression. The awesomeness of the rain had made us companion-survivors even if not allies, albeit temporarily.

I got out two of the polyethylene bags I had brought along, and held them out, one at a time. They filled quickly. I added water purification tablets, left them for ten minutes, and then we both drank our fill. That done, I filled the flask and knotted the bags. With any luck they would not burst unless they were dropped.

If the rain continued, we would have no worries about drinking water. But it brought a new fear: if it went on with this ferocity even the slowest traveling would be difficult.

I sat, hunched, feeling the ground around me turn to mud, not fighting the first flickers of regret and depression that started to enter my thoughts. Then, as suddenly as it began, the rain began to ease. By any standards it was still heavy, but movement would no longer be like fighting through blankets of water.

To celebrate, I shared the last of the chocolate. I also made a silent promise that I would stifle any further feelings of depression. It didn't take much experience of the outdoors to know that without the will to survive I didn't stand much chance. I couldn't afford any self-pity.

Bicycling was more difficult than before the rain, with the water weighting our clothes, softening the ground, and making the going harder. At the same time it helped to hide us, and this urged me on to greater speeds and fewer bypasses. Before dawn the rain stopped, and our clothes dried on us as we rode. Movement was mechanical now; every effort had to be invested in the act of pedaling.

I ordered a halt soon after three. There was at least an hour of darkness remaining, but I doubted whether either of us could have kept going much longer. Besides — and this was the main reason — we had stumbled on an abandoned building. Only parts of the walls remained. There was a road nearby, narrow but paved. That forced me to hesitate briefly, but behind the building there was a gully through which we could retreat if necessary.

One corner of the ruin had escaped most of the rain. I used our jackets and two more of the bags to provide some insulation from the ground. It should not be too bad if we slept with our backs against the wall. I was so exhausted that I knew that sleep, even in such a position and despite the aches, would not be difficult.

Ming was reluctant to sit. It emerged that she was suddenly afraid of the presence of snakes or scorpions. I knew next to nothing of the wildlife of China, but I suspected both must live in the area — in the case of snakes, there were probably many varieties. Like most creatures, though, they prefer to keep away from man. Provided we didn't do stupid things like push our hands into gaps in rocks, I decided they were low on our list of worries. Nevertheless, I made a great show of kicking up the ground to show that our only companions were a few insects. Finally satisfied, she all but collapsed on the ground.

Both of us now desperately needed to sleep, but there were three things that had to be done. First, I made us both drink more water — I knew from past experience that it was all too easy to let water depletion bring on a state of lassitude before you knew what was happening. Second, despite Ming's fears about poisonous creatures, I insisted we remove our shoes and socks. Unlike the rest of our clothes, they were still damp. We could not risk any kind of foot infection.

The third made me hate myself. Because of our physical state, I doubted that Ming would try to escape. But after the incident of the man and the dog, I knew I had to be cautious. Somewhere Ming had found a ribbon to tie back her hair. I ordered her to remove it. Then I used it to bind her thumbs. She did not struggle.

I awoke soon after first light, and checked the knots. Her thumbs had begun to swell. Still half-asleep, I thought for a few seconds, then freed her. She parted her hands immediately, sighed, and turned into a new position. Her eyes opened briefly, but her breathing did not change. I waited awhile, then I slept again too.

When I awoke next, the sun was high. Ming was awake too, but she was not trying to go anywhere. There was no need. The shouts that we both could hear must have made it obvious to her that all she had to do was wait.

"You'd better not move," I said.

I lifted myself and looked over the wall. The open truck was parked back along the road, perhaps half a mile away. I counted nine men. They were heading out into the fields on either side of the road. There was no possible doubt about what they were doing.

Searching.

My mind spun. How could anyone know we were nearby? Or was it some awful coincidence — that they were not after me, but in pursuit of someone else who had committed a crime locally.

Ming moved, and I turned quickly, but she was only studying her thumbs and the pieces of ribbon that had bound them.

At first I misunderstood her expression, thought she was angry that I had cut the material. "It was too tight to untie," I said, "I had to use a knife." Then I realized that what her look really said was, why had I released her at all? That was not a question to answer now, even if I were sure; besides, I suspected any warmth or show of pity I displayed might be taken for weakness, encouraging her to resist.

My eyes and my thoughts returned to the truck and the men. One man seemed to be directing the others. Apart from him, they looked like peasants. The local militia? I began to calm down. Surely, if they *knew* I was in the area, there would be more trucks and more men. Whatever China is short of, it is not people. Therefore, I told myself, they were probably searching a wide area: this would be only one of many trucks and many parties strung out along the roads. Perhaps we had been spotted by someone: a man or woman, unable to sleep, gazing through a window in the darkness? Or perhaps the car had been found and its theft linked with the bicycles. Might it then be possible to work out how far we might have traveled, and to have arranged search parties at points on all the routes out of Nanking?

They were searching slowly; it looked as though they planned to make a day of it. Perhaps it was a pleasant respite from the daily chore. In time, the copse would draw them: of that there was no doubt. I peered around and checked the gully behind us. No problem there. We could leave unseen. The worry was what we did after that.

I caught Ming's eye and I thought she was going to mock me, but her voice was almost sympathetic. Perhaps it was because I had unbound her thumbs. "You have a better chance if you leave me," she said. "I promise not to shout until they find me."

I smiled but didn't answer. Even if she was telling the truth — and this was not a time to test it — I still needed her with me.

I had just decided that the only hope lay in leaving the bicycles and making a run across the fields when I saw the cloud of dust. The blazing sun had already dried the earth. It was way beyond the truck, perhaps two or more miles distant.

More trucks. It could not be anything else, I decided. It should have made me move immediately, but curiosity held me. Besides, I told myself, better to have some idea of what I was up against.

The cloud came nearer. I wished that I had glasses. Then I realized it could not be trucks. It was too slow-moving, and unless it was a vast convoy of vehicles it was too spread out.

Just what it was became clear a few seconds later. Bicyclists. Hundreds of them. But from where? Then the memory came flooding back. I remembered an article in the English-language *China Daily* I'd seen one evening in Peking. It was about the recent craze for mass bike rallies, taking city youths out into the countryside, closer to what the newspaper called "the real life." Cynically, I had wondered at the time whether it was not a craze inspired by the authorities to get some of the vast number of unemployed off the streets.

Whatever the reason, the fact was that hundreds of bikers were now heading in our direction, and were almost upon us. The men searching had seen them too and had stopped to watch. But I doubted they would try to stop them. Why should they? And, besides, if they did, the result would surely be chaos.

I saw they would pass by us within minutes.

It was my chance. Provided that I could frighten Ming into remaining cooperative.

"Come on," I said. "We're going to join them." I grasped her wrist and pulled her, producing the gun with the other hand. "I know what you're thinking," I said. "That here is your chance to cry for help. If you do, I'm doomed. I know that. But I promise you now — if you say one word, I'll start shooting. At the end of it there will be seven people dead. They're all kids. Think of that. Now move!"

I reached out as though to tug her again, but she was already moving. We manhandled our bicycles along the gully and toward the road. I kept her in front of me.

The first riders had reached us. "Just smile and wave," I ordered, as we scrambled down. "Remember, you start talking, I start shooting." The effort and my fear gave a breathless panic to my voice. I touched my cheek to brush away a fly, and felt the stubble. I must have looked rough too.

The bikers took up the whole width of the road, and they stretched back several hundred yards. They rode, bunched in small groups, talking and laughing. As riders saw us, they stared or waved. The bikes were like ours, ordinary town ones. The absence of gears must have made the kind of touring they were undertaking punishing, no matter how fit they were.

They hid us from anyone standing near the truck, and I began to yell "Hello" and wave my arms as we neared the road.

"Keep beside me," I yelled to Ming. Then we were moving with them, uncertainly at first as we tried to adjust to their pace.

They had cleared a gap for us to join them, and the boy in front of me turned, his face cracked with pleasure. "Foreign friend joins Chinese friends. Yes?"

I tried to forget that I'd told Ming I would shoot as many as I could with the seven rounds in the pistol. "Yes!" I shouted.

Despite the fear, there was a heart-pounding excitement about it — like being caught up in the crowd at the Big Game or joining in the applause at the end of a great concert. The kids around radiated youth and vitality and warmth. I felt oddly at ease. My legs ached, my eyes burned with lack of rest and the sun, my stomach ached from lack of food, and the pace we had to meet was greater than I would have chosen. But I found I delighted in keeping up with them, that I gloried in the sweat that sucked my shirt to my body, that I warmed in their wordless companionship.

I turned to Ming, my face beaming. My smile died, and the sweat on me became cold. She was talking to the boy beside her, quickly, softly; even without knowing the words, I knew she was talking in the way of someone who has little time to say what she has to communicate.

I didn't dare shout to threaten her. Who knew how many of the young Chinese around would understand my words? English was being widely taught to today's youth.

Instead, I yelled, "You're neglecting me." It made her turn her head toward me.

"I was only telling him that you were touring the country and that I am your guide," she said.

I moved my hand imperceptibly, a gesture she understood. Moments later, we dropped back.

"What did you tell him?" I whispered.

"Nothing."

Riders began to overtake us, forced either to do that or to slow down. For some minutes I tried to keep my eye on the boy with whom she had spoken. He turned once and our eyes met. He had a shock of dark, untamed hair, and I could imagine enjoying asking him questions about his life and answering his about living in the States. Now, though, I had to fear him. I half expected him to shout, to urge his companions to grasp me, but Ming must have warned him about the gun. What he would do, I thought, was sound the alarm at the next town we reached. Before then, I suspected, he would quietly brief his friends. There would be much status, I was sure, in capturing a foreign spy. It was the kind of thing they wrote stories about. I had seen them — cheap, little cartoon-strip picture books sold on street stalls. With difficulty, I had even bought one — the man had been reluctant to part with one to a foreigner. I couldn't understand the captions, of course, but words were hardly necessary. You could tell the baddie even if he wasn't the only non-Chinese: he wore a fedora and dark glasses and stole the plans. He came to a very bad end, of course, and the Chinese who apprehended him became heroes of the State.

The road curved, then began to climb, gently but enough to make me strain. I turned to look at Ming. She was concentrating on keeping moving. Like me, she was tired and weakened by hunger.

I had to stand up on the pedals for the last few yards of the hill. Bikers around were cheering me on, but I hardly heard them. I was still dwelling on what would happen.

At that moment the pressure relaxed, and I became conscious that the noise around me had changed. I lifted my head and saw that the road now stretched in a straight line downhill.

At the bottom of it was a ribbon of houses. A town.

7

As we coasted down the long hill, it became obvious that what lay ahead was really a sizable village. Beyond the ribbon of houses were small, industrial-type buildings, and then a square.

The bicyclists around us began yelling and pointing; arrivals were obviously high spots of the tour. One who had ridden up on my right removed his hands from the bars of his bicycle and began miming lifting food from a bowl into his mouth.

It was meant for my benefit. "Ah, food," I said loudly.

"Yes. Food." The word was taken up by those around like a chant.

Despite hunger, food was far from my mind. Uppermost was fear — about what would happen once we arrived. I imagined that the boy to whom Ming had spoken would seek help, quickly and quietly, while his companions kept watch. Almost as powerful as this concern, though, was a liking for the youths around me. In a very short time since my arrival in China I had moved from a curious neutrality about the country to a loathing for its system and the realities of life. Because of the needs of international diplomacy China might at present be the goodie as far as the United States and the rest of the West was concerned, and the Soviet Union the baddie. As places in which to live I doubted if there was much to choose between them. The American visitors that returned with misty eyes and glowing reports were, I now believed, just like the Westerners who toured Russia in the 1930s — seeing nothing of Stalin's purges or the injustice and inequality built into the system. That, however, did not stop me feeling good thoughts for the people — for the ordinary kids, not the politicians or the fat cats or the military men, all with their privileges and power.

I just hoped I didn't have to hurt any of them. Even more, though, I hoped none of them was going to hurt me.

I tried dropping back further into the pack, but it was difficult. Everyone was moving more slowly now, content just to make the occasional turn of the pedals to keep the pace steady.

Even if I had managed to drop to the back of the group, I am not sure what I would have achieved. Vaguely, I thought we might be able to drop out, leave the road, and gain at least some minutes before the biker whom Ming had alerted was able to tell his story.

It proved impossible. The nearer we got to the village the more the riders bunched. I found myself so close to Ming that I had to concentrate on not touching bicycles. I began talking to her in a loud whisper, hoping that the words would not be understood any further away.

"I know you've given me away," I said. "If there's shooting, lots of people will be hurt. Don't you understand that?"

A bike cut across me, and I had to swerve away. I jostled myself back into position. Ming's face was turned in my direction; at least she was listening.

"Just help me get through," I went on. "I'll turn you loose soon. If you're so sure I can't get away, it won't make any difference. It could save some of these people being killed." I drew slightly ahead of her, turning my head so that I could see her face. "If they do take me," I said, more loudly now because the noise around us had grown, "I will tell them that you helped me escape in the first place. I will tell them that only afterward did you change your mind." I thought I saw new fear reflected in her eyes, and I pressed on, hoping I had an additional weapon. "I'll tell them," I yelled, "that you made me promise that I would take you to America." A definite flicker this time. I twisted the knife. "And give you money once we got there."

I had to turn back to the road to avoid an accident. Anyway, I had now done all I could. We were still not at the village. I saw that at the approach, the road forked. The right fork, the major one, went through the village; the other ended up near some industrial buildings. A policeman on a raised dais was on duty at the fork, as though he had been expecting the cyclers (as perhaps he had). As the first riders reached him, he directed them toward the left. Even from this distance, it was clear why. The street was jammed. Now I could hear the music. We had chanced upon some sort of festival.

The activity below kept me safe for a few more minutes. I began to work my bike toward the right of the road, forcing others to give way to me.

"Do what I do!" I yelled to Ming.

I knew what I was going to do now, with or without her. From the corner of my eye I saw she was following my example. We were almost at the fork now, but on the right of the road as I wished.

I pulled upon my back brake, turned the handlebars, and launched myself into a skid, just as we used to do as kids when we raced around a dirt track. The bike hit Ming's, and we both screeched to a halt at the feet of a group of children. I pulled myself to my feet as quickly as I could, grasped Ming, who was on the ground, and hauled her upright.

"Move," I said. I was trying to smile for the benefit of the crowd.

She did not seem to be hurt, but I wanted her away before the shock wore off.

The stream of bikers was still being directed left; the boy to whom Ming had spoken would have been forced that way, was probably now dismounting, preparing to fetch help. Over the heads of the crowd I saw the policeman. He was staring toward us. His face betrayed his problem: he couldn't leave his post yet, but he wondered what was happening.

"Shout to him that everything is all right," I ordered Ming.

I grabbed the bicycles, pushed one toward Ming, and began wheeling the other. "Come on, hurry," I said, my voice hard. There was only one way to go without exciting more curiosity: on, further into the village.

At first, the crowd was thin enough for us to move. People fell back; eyes followed us every step, more curious here than in the cities. I suspected that for some of them I might be the first Westerner they had seen. Soon, though, there were too many people to allow passage for us and the bicycles. It became obvious that we would have to leave them. With them at our side it was becoming almost impossible to stir at all. What we had to do was get through the village and out at the other end. I was reluctant to abandon the bikes, because once we were free of the crowds, how would we travel without them? I knew, though, that I was being foolish — unless we moved fast there would be no more traveling. Finally, we left them, parked as best we could against a wall.

I held Ming's hand and dragged her with me. The press of the crowd hid the sight.

Even more so than before, my height now singled me out. I towered over the crowds that milled around us. It helped me keep moving, but I also knew that once pursuit began it made me an easy target.

We broke out into a clearing. Two figures on stilts, their heads encased in giant, laughing masks, towered above us.

Ming started back, and the crowd burst into laughter.

Holding tightly onto Ming, I skirted the edge of the clearing. "What is it?" I asked, bending down to her.

"I had forgotten," she said. "It is June the first — Children's Day. It is their own special day. In Peking, there are usually only parades. But here the village is making a festival. That is why there are so many people — they will have come from many *li* around."

We began to struggle through another crowd. Ming, thankfully, was offering only token resistance. Or, perhaps, more likely, she was now waiting for the right moment.

I kept looking back, but could see nothing except the crowds. In another clearing, we passed child acrobats, balancing on monocycles. Further on, oblivious to the noise, a small group of children, ribbons like butterflies on their carefully dressed hair, were listening to a story from an old man.

Suddenly, at the same time it seemed, we both became conscious of the smell of food. What looked like flat doughnuts were being dispensed from a booth. I found money and pressed it into Ming's hand. "Buy some — buy lots," I said.

I watched, and listened to the laughter of the crowd, impressed at the foreigner's appetite, as the food was layered on sheets of paper. Further on, despite the fear of pursuit, we quickly bought bottles of orange drink. I drained two almost without pause. The old woman behind the stall cackled with laughter.

I sensed it rather than saw it at first — a wave of movement behind us. Seconds later my fears were confirmed. Over the heads of the crowd, I could just make out people being forced aside to open a passageway in the distance.

There was no doubt. The biker Ming had alerted had talked to the police. Our pursuers were after us now.

I tugged at Ming's hand. "Let's hurry," I said. The food and drink was held against my body by my other arm.

"What is it?" she said.

"Nothing." No point in letting her know help was near.

I tugged again, and this time she moved with me.

The crowd became even more solid. We were hemmed in at the side by single-story houses, their doorways on the street. Many had alleys running between them, but I was reluctant to turn off. The road was the most direct way through the village.

It became clear, through, that at the ever-reduced speed at which we were now moving our pursuers would rapidly reach us. The best hope was to take one of the alleys, hoping to make a detour that would bring us out farther along the road nearer the exit to the village.

I'd stopped, and Ming was sensing my uncertainty. I could feel her fear running through me. Perversely, it strengthened me.

There were two alleys within easy reach. I had no way of knowing where either would lead, but it had to be one of them.

There were shouts from behind — words amplified by a loud-speaker. I saw Ming was straining to make out the words.

"This way," I said, pulling her with me. It might as well be the nearest alley.

There was an old man performing card tricks on an upturned box at the entrance to the alley. His audience had moved somewhere else. As we came within his sight, he waved a handful of cards, hoping he had found a new one. And not just any audience — a foreigner, a barbarian, whose presence would then attract others. Ming passed him without any trouble, but as I neared he stood to clutch at my sleeve. Trying to sidestep him, I knocked over the box. The cards that went flying looked ordinary enough, mass manufactured, well worn, but perhaps they were already carefully shuffled and arranged. He fell to his knees, picked up a few, and then, raising his head high, he began to wail like someone who has just heard he has lost his whole family.

I joined him on the ground and tried to help him retrieve the cards, reckoning that the loss of time was less important than the extra attention that was being called to us by his noise. But rather than pacifying him, my action drove him to new anger. He snatched a card from my hand as though I was stealing a trade secret or, more likely, laying a curse on his act. Then he began making imploring noises to the crowd nearby.

If Ming had acted then, I would have been finished. It only needed her to shout that I was a foreign spy or criminal and I think I would have been overpowered by a mass of people even before I could have tugged free the pistol. But though she did not step forward to help, neither did she get involved against me. Perhaps she was afraid that too many people would get hurt. Perhaps my threat that I would implicate her was having some effect. I knew that Chinese women who consorted with foreigners were treated badly. Sleeping with a Westerner was regarded as prostitution, and women were sent to camps or prisons.

I got to my feet, and pushed her ahead of me. "Keep moving. For God's sake, keep moving," I said.

When I looked back, the crowd was watching, but not following us. Another alley cut off to the left, parallel to the street, and we took that. We were among the houses: primitive, square shells, cooking stoves outside in small yards. Normally they would be occupied, people lazy or busy outside, but because of the festival they were deserted.

Suddenly we came out into a wide passage with a square of open ground on one side. It led only one way, to the left. That, if I had not completely lost my sense of direction, was back to the main street that we had left a few minutes before. To the right, the passage extended a few yards and then came to a halt against a high wall. It was pointless considering trying to climb that: the square was crowded with more people.

To be more precise, with people — and with one enormous dragon.

The dragon was obviously the high point of the festival. It was being prepared now, out of sight of the main crowds a few hundred yards away. It looked as though it was almost ready to begin its procession through the village.

The beast's giant papier-mâché head, jaws gaping, was already man-high in the air. Behind it trailed its body — silky material over a frame, multicolored, and covered with scales of gold and silver. Men were at various stages of working themselves into the framework. Those in position revealed only their legs and feet.

"Some size," I said. It was impossible as yet to gauge the dragon's length, but I guessed that when all the men were in place and the sections spread out it could be a hundred and fifty to two hundred feet, perhaps even more.

"I've never seen one before," said Ming. Briefly, she seemed to have dropped her open enmity. "I knew they had them in some of the villages — they removed them from their hiding places after the fall of the Gang of Four. You do not see them in the cities, though — the party is still not sure about them. Some say that even though the dragon is a symbol of China it is also a remnant of old superstitions and is a reminder of the emperors."

The Chinese who were preparing the dragon had seen us. They were staring at us with a curiosity that seemed friendly. One man began to beckon us nearer.

"Do as he wants," I said. "But don't say anything except what I tell you to say."

Ming did not move immediately. She was looking at me as though trying to make a decision. Finally, she spoke. "If I do as you wish, if I help you out of the village, you promise no one will be harmed?"

"I promise," I said.

"You also promise that I will go free, but if we are both caught you won't lie about me?"

It was hard to believe it was happening; it was like being asked to recite the Boy Scout oath in the middle of placing a bet with a numbers runner. Her face, though, was serious.

"Yes," I said. "I promise that too."

She began to move. "We should do as he wants," she said.

The moment we were near, the man who had beckoned launched into a monologue. He was small, round, with the kind of stomach you can rest your hands upon. Others around gazed at me, but remained quiet.

At the first pause in his speech, Ming translated briefly. Her sudden cooperation and the travelogue quality of the scene brought new feelings of disquiet. I wanted to get moving, but there was nowhere to go. "He says," Ming was continuing, "that his grandfather directed the making of this dragon. It is two hundred and fifty feet long, and it needs thirty men to operate it. He says it is ready to move now; he just awaits a signal that all is ready in the streets, and then you will see."

A thought began to grow. "Ask him where it will go," I said.

She was surprised; so was the man when she translated.

"Through the village," she said at last.

"No, I know that. What is its route from here?"

It was clear he regarded this as a strange question, but the man answered.

"From here, it goes to the main street. Then to the right and — "

I wasn't listening. "You're sure he said 'to the right' first?"

"Yes."

That meant the early part of the dragon's route would take it toward the other end of the village; near the edge it would reverse its direction and work back the way we had already come.

There was another burst of speech, but this time it called for a reply from Ming.

"What is it?" I asked nervously.

"He wonders whether you have a camera. He thought you would like to take a picture." The man was proud of the dragon and of the foreigner's interest.

"What did you tell him?"

"I said that you are an artist, that you remember the detail, and will paint it later from memory."

"You what?"

"There had to be a reason. A foreign visitor without a camera is like a cart without a wheel." Neither her voice nor her face betrayed any amusement.

The men around were beginning to fidget nervously, anxious to start. My nervousness had also grown, but for a different reason. The route the dragon was to go would take it away from our pursuers . . .

I had to act quickly, before the dragon set off.

"Ask him how it works," I said.

Ming looked bewildered. "You can see," she said. "Men stand inside, holding the — "

"Just ask him."

She did.

He obviously found the question as naive as Ming had, but he answered. I hardly bothered to listen to the translation. "Now ask him if it's difficult," I pressed on. "Can the men see where they are going, or do they follow the feet of those in front? Then ask him if they have rehearsed how to make it wriggle."

This time Ming did not hesitate: she had understood what I was trying to do — maneuver the man into letting me experience what it was like inside the dragon.

The interchange seemed to take an eternity. Any moment it could be too late. I interrupted the last reply. "Ask him if I could try it. Tell him anything that you think would help — that I'm a respected party member back home, a friend of the Chairman, anything, but try to get him to agree."

The man listened to Ming's request on my behalf, his head to one side, giving him a coy, babyish look. At the end he smiled, and spoke briefly. "What did he say?" I asked.

"He said you are too tall; you would find it uncomfortable."

"Is that all?"

But she was talking again. "You must be quick, he says. And only a little way. You must leave before you reach the main street. Do you understand?"

"And you?"

"You had best be quick. He could still change his mind. Here, where he says . . ."

"But you?"

"He would not allow a woman. It would be pointless asking. It would not be right." There was no resentment in her voice, no surprise. Just a finality.

I wondered if she would use the opportunity to disappear; she would find it easier to vanish into the crowd than me. There was now nothing I could do about that.

Two men were holding a section of the dragon high above their heads so that I could slide underneath. Inside, I placed my hands on the struts of the bamboo frame as directed, bending forward a long way so as not to loom too far above the men in front and behind.

It was like being inside some brilliant, multicolored tent. The light through the silk painted a pattern on the back of the man a few feet ahead of me. He turned his head and smiled, and I forced myself to respond, a nervous grin.

The order to move came moments later. The first I knew of it was a tugging movement along the frame. I tested my hands on the smooth surface and concentrated on the feet of the man ahead, determined to copy his steps like someone having his first dance lesson. Seconds later, we were off. It was harder than I had thought. There was a pattern — so many steps forward, then to one side, more forward, then to the other side, all to make the dragon writhe and twist as it moved.

We slowed and I almost went too far forward. Our feet began shuffling on the spot, like runners before a race. The man ahead turned again, and this time he spoke in Chinese. It was easy to guess that he was reminding me that this was the time for me to leave, but I grinned inanely and did nothing. I could see he did not know what to do.

Suddenly, from outside, music joined the babble of voices.

I felt the dragon begin to turn, saw the shift of movement through the silk.

It was turning left. Back the way we had already come. Toward our pursuers.

I wondered if I should slip out from under the silk skin now. But then, almost immediately, the dragon began to move in the opposite direction. The sudden switch almost made me stumble and fall. I heard the crowd's yelling rise to a new peak. The man ahead was doing some very complex foot actions now. I realized what was happening — the dragon was being made to twist and turn and coil on itself. When finally we straightened, the direction was clear — we were going right after all.

Through the silk I could see shapes and swirls of movement outside, but no more. I knew if anyone in the crowd dropped their eyes, they would see the lower half of my jeans and my Western shoes. More likely, though, I thought, their eyes would be occupied with all the activity above.

Several times as we coiled upon ourselves the crowd had to rush back screaming to give us room. The noise echoed inside, ominously frightening — it would sound like this if they rushed forward to grab me. Suddenly the crowds seemed to become even more tightly packed. The dragon slowed again, almost to a halt, and I guessed we had reached the end of the village and were about to make a full turn. I could feel the heat of the crowds now; their shadows darkened the inside of the skin; they were within a foot or so.

I moved. Dropping as low as I could, I rolled into the street. I had to scramble upright quickly to avoid being trampled, but people moved back to give me room. Faces I saw were filled with laughter; onlookers seemed to take my appearance as just another magical ingredient of the festival. I fought myself into and through the crowd, and finally I came out beyond them.

The scene was an almost identical copy of the other end of the village — a few straggly houses, then a dirt road through fields. Depressingly, the land was frighteningly flat and without cover for several miles until it reached a group of low hills. Once I began moving away from the village I could hardly fail to be conspicuous.

I stood, watching, wondering whether I had any other alternative. A figure appeared from beside one of the houses. Ming.

For a moment, my feelings soared at seeing her. Then the pleasure was replaced by fear. Something told me that the only reason she was waiting there was because she had already informed on me.

I began to turn, calculating my chances of fighting my way back through the crowds. Then I saw that she was beckoning. As far as I could tell, she was alone. Was she trying to get me to move near enough for police, hidden in the house, to jump me before I could draw the pistol?

She moved in my direction.

"Quickly, quickly," she said. "There is not much time."

I looked behind me. The crowd was taking no interest in us; they were preoccupied with the dragon dance.

Ming turned and hurried back the way she had just come. Reluctantly, I followed. She stopped beside a bicycle with a small wooden cart attached. In the cart were an old jacket and a pair of straw coolie hats. She put one on and handed me the other and the jacket.

The coat was loose even though it was short. I wrapped it around me, then put on the hat.

Ming was already in the trailer, seated, her legs curled underneath her.

I wheeled the bicycle a few yards along the road, and looked back. The crowd was moving away, following the dragon.

I got on the bicycle and began to pedal.

8

*It took a little over an hour to reach the hills, and the moment we did I collapsed full-length on the ground.

Ming stood watching me, from beside the cycle and cart. When she saw I was recovering, she produced a bottle of the sticky orange drink we had bought earlier and carried it over to me. I pulled myself upright and forced myself to drink slowly. Water, cold, fresh, sparkling water, would have been better, but the fact that there was anything at all to drink was a minor miracle.

"You managed to hold on to one," I said, forcing myself to stop. I handed the half-empty bottle to her to finish.

"Three," she said, producing the other two. "And these" — there were five, perhaps six of the doughnuts, squashed together in one mass now. All were contained in a canvas bag that I had not noticed before. She saw my look. "I stole it," she said. "With this." She pointed to her shirt, and for the first time I realized that the bright yellow-flowered blouse she'd worn since Nanking had been replaced by a more than discreet dark blue one.

She looked down, fiddled with a button, suddenly obviously embarrassed by what she had done. "I thought the other was too bright, made it too easy for people to see me. This was in a house, and I took it."

I began to laugh, but her face stopped me. "It was theft," she said.

To me, it was a crime hardly worth being added to the list, but I returned to the drink. My shirt was soaked with sweat. It would take more than a bottle of orange drink to replace what I had lost.

I looked up at the sky. It was absolutely clear. Not a sign of a cloud, and no wind to speak of. The rains of yesterday had obviously been a false start. It was five o'clock, but still uncomfortably hot.

Standing, I looked around. There was no shade immediately available. Nor was the cover good enough to hide us until dark. I returned to the bicycle, and reluctantly we started to move. The track grew steeper, but it began to look more promising and I pressed on.

We came to a small plateau on the side of the track. There were a few stones, an old ruin, little left now but the foundation. Beyond it there was a sudden drop where the hill fell away.

I walked over and looked down. There was an old path, now overgrown, snaking down the hillside, which was steep but not as sheer as I had first thought. About thirty yards below there was another large shelf of ground. On it, my eyes picked out shapes. Gradually it dawned upon me what I was seeing. It was an old graveyard. The ruin behind me had probably been a temple. Some of the graveyard was hidden by overhang. It was a perfect hiding place. It also had another advantage. I needed rest, and despite what Ming had done I still feared she might try to escape when I slept. I could not bring myself to tie her up again. The graveyard was so located, though, that she would find it hard to flee without alerting me.

I called Ming over. "Down there," I pointed.

"What about the bicycle?"

With effort, we might just be able to get it down the path; I doubted whether we would be able to haul it back. It would have to take its chances up here, buried in bushes.

I hid it as best I could, then we started down the path. It was harder than I'd thought. Several yards to the left of the path there was a ribbon of lighter color where it looked as if there had once been steps, now collapsed and overgrown.

We slid the last few yards, both of us breathing heavily. Now that we were on the ledge I could see that the disused path continued farther down the hillside, but it was even steeper than the one we had just taken. Nevertheless, if anyone investigated from above it gave us a back route for escape.

It was the immediate scene, however, that drew me now. There were about two dozen graves, most of them marked by exquisite small carved pagodas. I thought they were probably those of the monks who had been attached to the temple above. I knelt before one, elaborate with false doors and carved animals. I turned my head to speak to Ming, but she had moved well away, and was lying on the grass. I could sense that she was uneasy.

Walking over, I said, "You should try to sleep."

"I do not like it here," she said.

"We'll move as soon as it is dark," I said.

I sat beside her, and despite her unease I heard the sound of her breathing change, as she drifted into sleep.

I had wanted to ask her why she had not run, why she had returned to me. Perhaps I had caused more fear than I knew with my threat to say she had cooperated if we were caught. Perhaps — and this was a thought that had been growing ever since we had left the village — her orders from Feng Shen were to stay with me.

I knew I should sleep too, but the graves drew me. I walked back and stood among them. I felt a shiver, not from any chill in the day but from the presence of death. Even the bones of these men, hundreds of years old to judge from the graves, had crumbled beneath the earth. There were no moans, no shrieks — nothing but the soft, cheerful noise of cicadas. There was no smell, except the soft perfume of grasses. The men whose bodies had been carried down the hillside, buried here, had gone. The earth that covered them had hardened, been watered, and baked, had brought forth generations of plants and grasses, spanned wars and revolutions. Millions of people had been born and had died. The men were no more than markers. And yet the fact that they had existed and that this was their place lingered. A reminder that this was the way it all was: after all the action, all the ambition, all the doing, all the feeling, this was the ultimate, the only undeniable truth — grass and earth and bones of men with forgotten names.

Finally, I moved so that I was screened by the overhang. And, like Ming, I slept.

The scream could have been an animal in pain — high-pitched, long.

I was on my feet almost the second that the sound woke me. It was night, but there was a bright moon. I strained my ears for further noise, trying to place a direction. There was silence, and I turned to see what Ming was doing, but the ground where she had been lying was clear. She had gone.

The shouts began soon afterward. I could make out the voice, though not the words, although I already knew by then it must be Ming. The sound came from above. It was obvious what had happened. My earlier fear had been well founded. She *had* tried to escape. What I had not bargained for was that my sleep would be so deep that I would not hear her as she struggled to climb back up the hillside.

I had tied my jacket around my waist, to prevent stomach chills, and I undid it and pulled it on as I began to climb. I began grasping at the undergrowth, using it as leverage. I skinned my hands in my haste; a bush lashed my face, drawing blood from my forehead. Well before I reached the top of the slope, I was having to wipe sweat from my eyes so that I could see.

At the top there was stillness all around. I began to shout. At first there was nothing, and then there were more cries.

"Piper, Piper. I am hurt. Help me."

I placed the source in the darkness and began to move as quickly as I could, but with all my senses alert.

Nevertheless, I saw the split in the ground only at the last moment. I froze immediately. My heart was hammering. One more step and I would have followed Ming.

I moved my hand around until I found a tall bush that I could grip as much for balance as security. Only then did I dare to give my attention to the hole.

I couldn't see Ming, but I could hear the rasp of her breathing. Somehow she must have managed to halt her fall inside the shaft.

"Piper, are you there?" She spoke more quietly. She had heard my approach.

"I'm here. Take it easy. I'm coming to get you."

The problem was I didn't know how. The gash in the ground was about six feet wide and twice that long, narrowing at its ends. Because of the undergrowth it had been visible only at the last moment. I could see the marks in the soil where Ming's feet had skidded, the torn plants where her fingers had tried to grasp support in vain. Part of the edge had broken away, and earth was still trickling into the hole.

I tugged at the bush to test it and then, satisfied, I leaned forward. The gap was a funnel. Inside, it fell at an angle of about forty-five degrees. Only half of it was visible, and that barely. The only part of Ming I could see was her hands, her fingers (it seemed) dug deep into the earth about ten feet below.

I tried leaning a little further, but my movement disturbed the ground. Some stones joined the soil trickling into the shaft. I froze again. I heard them bounce on the side. I strained to hear them hit the bottom. But nothing. That probably meant it was deep. Just how deep was academic. If Ming couldn't hang on, she was as likely to be killed by a fall of fifty feet as she was by a drop of five hundred. Even if she wasn't, I would never get her out once she slipped.

The noise of the earth and stones frightened her.

"Piper, I cannot hold much longer. My fingers will not take the strain."

"You must hang on. You understand? You *must*."

My mind was considering possibilities as I talked. She was too far away for me to reach. I could make out no hand- or toeholds that would enable me to climb down — and trying to make ones would probably result in sending earth pouring down on her. I had nothing with which to improvise a line.

"I will try. But there is nowhere to rest my feet. It is too smooth."

"Try. Move your feet sideways. There may be something — a plant, a hole, anything. Just something to ease the strain. Try. But gently. *Gently*."

"I'm trying, Piper, I'm trying." Her voice was strained thin by the effort.

I leaned further forward, forcing the bush to take more of my weight. I tugged experimentally. The roots appeared to be deep.

A strangled cry, silence, and then the unmistakable sound of earth trickling.

"What is it? What happened?"

The sound of her voice was a relief, but not the words. "Piper, one hand is free. The earth came away as I moved. I fear I cannot hold much longer."

"Hold on, damn you! Hold, fucking well hold!"

The obscenities were screamed to relieve my own frustration, but even more in the hope of pumping fresh energy into Ming. She would know the words, resent them. Anger might bring a little extra strength.

There was no reply, but I could hear her gasps now, and I knew there was little time left. I again tested the plant that steadied me, then crouched as best I could and tested the earth near the hole with my fingers. It was hard, smooth. Unlikely, I thought, that it would crumble unless there was force such as the girl's fall had been.

I pulled myself upright again, and moved back to where I could stand with ease.

"Don't leave me. Don't leave me."

For the first time I realized she must be able to see me.

"I'm here. Keep holding. Whatever you do, keep holding. I'm coming to get you."

I stripped off my jacket, shirt, and jeans, tied a leg to a sleeve, then spun them to give strength. The resultant rope was still nowhere long enough to reach Ming, but I had known that.

Next, my fingers suddenly alien, I fumbled to tie one end around my ankles. I stuffed my shirt under it to act as a pad. I attached the other end to the bush, as near to its base as I could.

For a moment I stood absolutely still, glorying in the night, the moonlight, the breeze on my skin, the faint smell of mimosa . . .

Was I not just ensuring that the earth would claim two lives instead of one? And it was *her* fault if she was in danger. If she had not tried to escape while I slept . . . But it was not a thought that worried me.

Part of me even hoped that if I died and was found, by some miracle I would be buried in the old graveyard on the hillside. Not since I was a boy was there anywhere I had felt I belonged. I would not mind this place.

I dropped to my knees, squirmed forward, and began to half-crawl, half-slide into the opening, headfirst. I tried to progress at an angle, partly to reduce the steepness of my descent, partly to steer myself away from Ming.

I spread myself wide to maximize the friction, used my hands and toes like claws to scrape the surface of the hard earth. The "rope" was still slack behind me; Ming was below and to my right. I lifted my head, and then the slide began. It was as sudden and stomach-lurching as losing your feet on ice — total loss of all control and then, before I could do anything, it was over.

Only I was not lying on my back on the ground; I was hanging upside down, swinging in the blackness, the improvised rope and my ankles taking the full weight of my body. For a moment, I thought of the strain on the material, on the knots, on the bush, but I forced myself to dismiss such imaginings.

Then I wondered about Ming. I could not see her. Had my slide sent her plunging to her death?

"Are you all right? Are you all right?" It was her voice.

I reached out for the sides of the funnel, and turned myself carefully on the rope until I saw her shadowed figure.

"I'm all right," I said, although there was a pain across my stomach and I wondered whether I had broken or torn anything. "Are you still holding on?" A crazy question.

127

I began to work my way toward her, using the wall as a lever. Then I was by her, one arm around her waist, steadying her, providing her safety net.

Except there was no way of knowing whether the line would support two people.

"Keep your hold as long as you can," I ordered.

She squirmed and tried to dig both hands back into fingerholds. Her body was heaving, and at first I thought she was crying, and then I realized it was the strain.

The extra weight bore down, and I felt the pressure on my ankles through the pad.

The rope held. But for how long?

"We've got to climb out," I said.

She did not argue.

"Have you the strength?"

"I'll try," she whispered.

"When I tell you to begin, you must start using my body like a ladder. Pull on me. I will try to help. Use the sides as a lever for your feet. Do you understand?"

"I understand." The breath of her reply was warm on my face. Her body, part of its weight supported by the friction of the wall, felt like that of a child in my arms.

"All right — begin!"

She began to move. Her efforts sent the rope spinning, and I felt fresh strain. Fear gave me renewed strength. I reached between her legs, pushed upward on her buttocks. She was trying to pull herself up. Her hands and my body were wet with sweat.

"Move, damn you, move! For Christ's sake, pull. Don't stop. Pull, pull, pull! Keep going. Go, go, go!"

I could see nothing but a red haze. I began chanting aloud as much to hold on to my own consciousness as to encourage her.

She hauled herself higher and higher, and suddenly the weight of her shifted. She was using my feet as a step and I knew she must be nearing safety. My head was pounding no with an awful hammering I could not control.

Then there was no weight at all. The release of the pressure of her body sent my head spinning forward; my face crashed into the earth at the side before I could reach out to try to steady myself.

Then I was swinging in the blackness, a carcass on a butcher's meat hook. I wondered if I could jackknife my body, grasp the line above my feet, haul myself up. But I knew there was no longer any strength left in me.

Useless to fight now. My eyes were wet, not just sweat, but tears. Tears for myself and my life.

I closed them and saw the red earth and the graves and I felt the shadow grow, and then there was no more.

9

Ming was kneeling above me, wiping my face with a damp cloth, when I opened my eyes. I reached up and touched my face with my fingers. Sticky. Blood! I moved my hand into my vision, and then laughed. The stickiness was orange drink, all she had to wet the material.

"How did I get out?" I asked. My fingers were exploring my head and body, probing to see if anything was hurt. I remembered the pain across my stomach, but all I felt everywhere now was a numbness.

"I pulled you," she said. "You were very heavy." She giggled. "You are a big man."

An owl hooted in the near distance; it was the only sound except that of our voices.

My hands were still probing, and she saw and understood. "I don't think you are hurt anywhere," she said. "I looked." She giggled again, and I saw it was embarrassment. "You have some scratches on your face, but you do not seem to have struck your head. I think you fainted because you were upside down."

I pulled my wrist within my vision, and checked the time. Only forty minutes had passed since I first heard Ming's cries for help. I could not have been unconscious for more than a third of that time, probably less.

Remembering her cries made me think of our pursuers: would

anyone have been near enough to hear? If they had, I suspected they would have made their presence known by now.

She helped me lift myself into a seated position; her touch was both surprisingly strong and gentle. I felt a wave of nausea rise, but I held myself still and breathed in deeply and it went away. Common sense said that soon I — we? — had to move on. But not yet. I needed rest.

"What about you?" I asked.

"I am all right. Like you, some scratches, but nothing bad. I was lucky."

"We must clean them," I said. "We can't afford to have infections. I have some antiseptic cream." I reached down, and realized for the first time that I was nude except for underpants.

Ming had untied my ankles. I unraveled my clothes and dressed. The gun was still there — Ming had not touched it. I pushed it into my waistband. Then I used the cream on her face and hands, and stood before her, bent, while she did the same with me. There was enough only for a smear; I hoped it would be sufficient.

We both sat down, and she separated two of the doughnuts from the sticky pile.

"Could you eat?" she said.

I took one, and bit. The sweet, syrupy taste was what I needed. I drank a little juice and swished the mixture around my mouth.

"It's good," I said, in the tone that Michelin inspectors probably reserve for three-star restaurants.

She laughed. The moon was still full, and I could see the laughter lines around her eyes widen. I was very glad she was not dead.

"Why didn't you run away?" I asked.

"I tried. You had said I could go if I helped you get out of the village." She did not add that she had doubted I would keep my word, but it was implicit.

"Not then. When I was unconscious."

"Why did you save me? You could have killed yourself."

Thunder broke. It was some way away. When I looked up, the sky above was beginning to fill with clouds.

"There'll be a storm," I said, sidestepping the question in what I recognized was a very Chinese way. Any answer could only have been maudlin. It was like the old query about why people climb mountains. I had saved her because she was someone in danger. That was it. Period. Or was it? Didn't the frenzy I had felt, the risks I had been prepared to take have something to do with *who* needed help? God help me, she stirred feelings in me. Some of them were ones of guilt, at what I was making her do, at the risks I was making her take. But not all of them.

I bit into more of the doughnut, and chewed. My mouth was so dry it was hard to swallow. I moistened my lips with more of the liquid. Ming was doing the same. We were like animals enjoying a kill. The thought did not disturb me. To survive we had to be like animals. Keeping alive was what mattered, nothing else. There was more thunder. I hoped the rain would come soon.

"Why are they chasing you?" she asked at last. She was gazing down at the earth. I got the impression it was a question she had asked herself a lot while I lay unconscious.

"You don't know?"

"I know what I was told."

"Which was?"

She hesitated before replying. "I was told that although you are an American you were in league with a Russian visiting this country who gave you some information before he died. I was to watch you, encourage your confidence, help you if you asked. There was a name particularly I was to listen out for."

"Tom Carr?"

"That's it. Or something like it. Who is it? What is it?"

"I don't know." I saw her disbelief. "I honestly don't know."

The thought struck me that she was still obeying her instructions; even now, she was trying to find the answer to the question for her masters. Even as it began to develop, though, I dismissed it; this, I believed, was no more than true curiosity — she wanted to know what kind of man she was with.

I stood and tried a few steps. I thought I was fit to set off again. But just a few more minutes, I told myself. I sank back to the ground.

Neither of us spoke for a long time, and then I said, "You might as well know the truth. It cannot cause anyone any harm. If only your security men had believed me . . ." And I told her the story, condensed, but with all the salient facts. How Yakov had come to my room and I had gone to the embassy and when I had returned he was missing. How Feng Shen had questioned me, and how Yakov was supposed to have spoken a dying word.

I also told her of how, in Nanking, I had meant only to get a message to Andrews by visiting an address, not to go on the run like this. "I did not mean to hurt the man," I said, "but afterward there was no turning back."

Cloud had covered the moon, and I could no longer see her face, but at the end of my monologue, she said, "And that's all?"

"That," I said, "so help me God, is all."

There was another long silence in which I finished the doughnut and the drink.

"You have had much luck so far," she said. "You will need a lot more if you are to escape."

"Ah," I said, "that famous revisionist luck."

"You Americans are funny people," she said. "You joke at moments of such seriousness."

"You giggle when I ask you a question that embarrasses you or angers you."

"You mean you joke to hide your fear?"

"I joke to hide my fear."

She began dusting her clothes with her hands, although she must already have removed all the earth possible.

"I cannot imagine you ever being afraid," she said, and she giggled again, and began to busy herself immediately. I recognized her remark for what it was: a very personal statement.

I fetched the bicycle and cart and started to check it over. She would have to come with me, I told myself; I needed her as much as ever, and I still could not afford for her to be found. Now, I thought, she owed me.

"Where would you have gone?"

Her reply had an intensity she had not used before. "Not to inform on you. I have an uncle — my father's cousin, really. I think his village is not that far, perhaps eighty or ninety miles from here. I thought that traveling alone I might reach him. A Chinese woman by herself could get a lift. I know he would help me."

Suddenly, I had many questions. "You know where we are?"

She looked surprised that I should ask. She obviously had great faith in my needle-and-thread navigation. "I recognized the name of the village that we were in," she said. I opened the map, and she located it for me. We had traveled farther than I thought, but Shanghai was still about a hundred and thirty to a hundred and forty miles away.

"And your uncle?"

His village was not marked, but she pointed to the approximate spot. The nearest town I recognized was Soochow. If we managed to get there, Shanghai was only sixty or so miles farther on. Help in covering that final lap — and in getting into the city — might tilt the balance in my favor.

"Surely one of the first places that Security will have checked is the homes of all your relatives and friends," I said. "They couldn't know that you haven't helped me of your own accord. I'd doubt they are short of manpower to investigate everything. And with a village roughly in the direction they must now know we are traveling . . ."

I finished checking the bicycle, and Ming got to her feet. She obviously took it for granted that she was coming with me. Good.

"I thought of that," she said. "I know that as soon as we vanished they would consult my files, and what you say is true. They will have questioned not only relatives and friends but also acquaintances, people with whom I have worked, persons whom I hardly know. But I do not think they would find my uncle's name. You see, on their files he has been dead many years."

I waited for her to explain.

At last, she said, "When the Russians were here, when they came to help us, there were many, many of them. You knew that?"

I did. I had seen their work everywhere I had gone.

"When the split came between our two countries, those who had worked alongside the Russians became suspect. My uncle was one. He was sent to the country to rehabilitate himself. You know the meaning of that?"

I nodded to show that I did.

"When what you call the Cultural Revolution began, my father saw that my uncle was in danger again. He had settled well in the village, had been accepted, had done many good things. The danger, though, was from the center, from Peking. My father was a man of some power. He arranged that my uncle's security files were altered — to show that he had died. In effect, that closed the files. My father had to tell me so that I would never try to make contact."

I noted the past tense in speaking about her father, and the word "power." There was a lot that I wanted to ask, and she had opened the gate for me. But for now I confined myself to the main point. "You have seen nothing of him since? That was, what, fifteen, sixteen years ago? He may really be dead for all you know."

"No. We have corresponded. There are ways. I made contact when my father died. I have even been to the village once. I made an excuse, pretended I was someone else. He had been in an accident. I had to see him."

"And what help did you expect if you reached him?"

"I don't know. Transport, I suppose. He would have access. And he has friends, some important. I know that."

The big question. "If he could help, do you think he would help me too?"

The first spots of rain fell. I began stretching open the plastic bags to collect as much as we could.

"We would have to ask him," she said.

It was as easy as that.

The next hours were more nerve-racking even than the days before. Not that anything untoward happened. We forged on in the rain that fell increasingly heavily, seeing and hearing no one. The reason was that suddenly again I had been given hope. Its existence brought fear.

If you believe that you have little or no chance, all you can do is keep going, depending on some kind of miracle to preserve you. But now there was the new fear that someone would take away the chance that I had suddenly and unexpectedly been given.

My legs were almost too weary to keep the bicycle going, and after the first hour when we broke for a rest Ming tried to insist that we should exchange places. I refused, but at the next stop I saw the sense of it. I traveled in the cart, huddled up and soaking wet.

Well before dawn, which came late that day, we found a gully on the edge of an old, unworked quarry. If we had had any kind of covering I would have insisted we stripped and tried to dry ourselves. But there was nothing, and we were too exhausted. We fell asleep, several feet apart. I woke once, and she had moved close to me, and we were holding each other for warmth. The next time I awoke, she had moved away again, and the sun was high and I was dry.

Later we talked a little. As we finished the doughnuts, eking out each and every bite, trying to disregard the hunger pains in our stomachs, we agreed that when darkness came again we would try to steal food. We would also attempt to find a telephone.

We found one about an hour after dark. The overhead telephone lines led to a small, isolated plant, deserted now. Breaking into it called for care rather than skill. The small group of concrete buildings were surrounded by a wall topped with no more than a token amount of barbed wire.

Nevertheless, climbing over it took me a long time: all my limbs ached and the weakness brought by effort and scant food meant that even simple tasks now taxed me. Once over, I crouched for several minutes, motionless in the shadow of the wall, watching for any sign of movement or occupation, but also recovering myself.

Finally, satisfied that I was alone within the walls, I found a side entrance, secured only by a bolt, and let in Ming. She smiled as I opened the door and whispered that all was quiet; yet again, I found myself impressed by her buoyancy and her strength.

Together we paced the outside of the main building. I checked for signs of an alarm, although I believed the chance of finding one must be small.

At the back of the building there was a window open about an inch. Behind the glass was a layer of wire mesh, but it was only tacked to the frame. I got the window open wide and ripped away one side of the netting. The gap was still too small for me, but by silent gesture Ming persuaded me she could enter. Minutes later, she let me inside.

The building was little more than one large open space. In the center were rows of grinding and polishing machines. Containers were full of what looked to me like chunks of semi- or even nonprecious stone. Partially completed statuettes were spaced around on work benches.

Three cubicles down one side of the floor acted as offices. There was only one telephone, and that was inside the only cubicle that had a door. It was black and heavy, like something around the time of World War II. Next to it, arranged carefully on the cheap, modern desk top, was a tin ashtray. On the wall there were two portraits of the Chairman — whoever ran this plant was obviously not taking chances on his loyalty being questioned.

We paused nervously before the telephone for several minutes, before finding places to sit out the night. For Ming, we pushed together two chairs to improvise a bed of sorts. I found some sacking which would do as well.

I had a sudden impulse to ask Ming to pick up the telephone and ask the operator for the village's number. But at this time, almost eleven o'clock at night, all good peasants were long in bed. We had racked our minds for some excuse that would enable us to call late at night, convincing whoever answered the village's communal telephone that it was necessary to fetch the uncle. But we could think of nothing short of an excuse of such import that news of the call would spread throughout the surrounding area.

Dawn, however, was a different matter. Ming was to pretend that she was the neighbor of a niece with the news of the birth of a boy baby. Despite all attempts at sexual equality, I'd already learned it was boys that you shouted about — even the Chinese admitted that some girl babies were still smothered at birth.

Ming thought that would work. There could be no way of knowing what time this plant would open, but certainly we should have at least an hour to get away. The biggest risk was that we would then be traveling in the light. We had decided that, depending on what Ming's uncle said, we would return to the quarry before setting off again that night. It was easily the best hiding place we had yet found.

Ming searched the building in the hope of finding food. There was nothing, not even tea dust. There was water, and a kettle for heating, and we risked a small fire and drank boiled water.

"Peasant's tea," said Ming, and she laughed again.

There was a great deal I wanted to ask her, but after we cleared away and disguised all traces of our water boiling, we dozed separately, each with our own thoughts. I dwelled briefly on life back in New York, wondered not very deeply about what Maddy might be doing, and thought about my mother and Dick, my younger brother — he'd had to take on the farm equipment business in Ashfield, Illinois, after my father first became ill. He had only recently forgiven me — he had thought it was my duty. I had written before I left for China. It struck me that they would not be worrying about me; often months passed without a letter from me when I was abroad, and then there was usually a stock opening about the pressures of work . . . As far as they — and others — were concerned I was just away, doing what I liked doing most.

I woke Ming shortly after four. There was a temptation to tell her to try phoning not her uncle but Andrews instead. Except that would mean putting in a call to the embassy in Peking (for Nanking and Shanghai, Andrews had given me only addresses, not names, so trying to telephone there was pointless). Even if there wasn't a special alert, I suspected any Chinese operator asked to connect a call with the U.S. embassy at this time in the morning would be suspicious. At the very least he would listen to the conversation and report it. Always supposing, of course, that there was even a duty officer at the embassy to answer the call. And if there was, what could I say without completely betraying our whereabouts to whoever was listening? . . . No, that idea was hopeless. So I said nothing, just watched as Ming lifted the telephone receiver and called the operator. She had no number; only the name of the commune. We waited twenty anxious minutes until the call was connected.

Ming launched into her long explanation of why she was calling, who she wanted. I watched her face, trying to gauge the reaction she was getting.

Presently she covered the mouthpiece. "I insisted I must break the news myself. They are fetching him."

She noticed that I was looking at my watch nervously. "I won't be long," she said, but her eyes turned toward the doorway too. Once the call was finished it would take us several minutes to leave if we were to hide the traces of our break-in.

I heard the voice come on at the other end of the line, saw the relief come into her face. She began to speak. Then I heard the click, loud and harsh, and then the dial tone.

"The line has been broken," she said.

She was still holding the receiver, her face pale, her hand tight with tension, when another voice boomed out of the earpiece. Even at a distance I recognized it as someone new.

"He is asking who is on the line," she whispered to me.

"Hang up," I said.

We left as quickly as we could while resealing the entrance window behind us. We stole three sacks. I huddled under them in the cart while Ming pedaled.

We arrived back in less than the hour I had calculated. We both collapsed and said nothing. Ming's smile had gone; for the first time she looked completely drained of all strength.

We had taken a big risk. And what had we achieved? Nothing.

10

We spent the day trying to rest, considering what we might do next, and worrying together and separately whether the voice that had broken into the telephone call had any significance.

As the day passed and nothing happened, I began to lean more and more to the view that it was meaningless — that the break in the line had been no more than China's lousy telephone system, and that the voice was coincidental, maybe just someone trying to reach another number.

I even began to regret that we had run so quickly without trying to reconnect the call. Apart from anything else, if the break had no significance, not persevering could only have aroused suspicion at the far end. However, even in my frustration I realized that to have stayed longer, to have gambled on not being disturbed by someone arriving at the plant, could have been suicidal.

Ming slept much of the time. Her face had lost most of its vitality; the skin had paled. Once I touched her forehead. It was damp, but she seemed not to have a temperature.

I settled back, facing her, seated with my arms around my knees, watching her in her sleep, and feeling guilt that I had got her into this. Guilt and a lot of tenderness. I felt another stomach cramp and began to shiver despite the heat, and I knew that if we were to keep going we must have food. I remembered as a youth having the old "3-3-3 lesson" drummed into me when I started to go wilderness camping — three minutes without breathing, three days without water, thirty days without food. Survival times. After thirty days without food, I wondered, what hell of a shape would you be in?

In the early dusk we discussed it, and reluctantly I agreed that Ming should forage for food. That meant, in practice, fruit. It was too dangerous to attempt to raid a home; we might be able to steal vegetables from a peasant's patch, but that presented another problem — human excrement was the fertilizer that would have been used. Unless we could cook the vegetable we stole, we ran a very real chance of being immediately laid low with gut trouble. That was a risk we couldn't take. A fire, it was easy to decide, was completely out of the question.

An hour later Ming returned and slid down beside me.

"Was it all right?" The hour had seemed a long one.

"No one saw me. I got this." She held out her hands. In them was a large melon. Her face was creased in that smile that I was growing increasingly dependent on having around. She looked better. The rest, and no doubt the excitement of the search, had done her good.

She threw the melon at me and I caught it laughing, for a brief while two playful children. I reached in my pocket for my knife, and the pistol fell from my waistband and bounced off a rock. Ming jumped back, her face no longer smiling.

She said nothing, but it was easy to read her thoughts: through my stupidity the gun could have gone off, perhaps injuring one of us, but certainly attracting attention.

I picked it up and swung it so that she could see clearly. "It's not loaded," I said. "No magazine."

"When did you do that?" she asked.

"A long time ago," I said. I began to laugh. "You don't think I would have carried a loaded gun, do you? I might have shot someone by mistake. I carried the gun to frighten you into obeying me, not to hurt you."

She dropped her eyes demurely, coquettishly. "You are a strange man, David Piper" — except that the "David" came out "Davide" and long, as though someone French was trying to pronounce it.

"Now that you know, there's not much point in carrying it," I said.

I scraped some earth away with a piece of rock and buried it. Then I picked up the melon and began cutting.

I know that it cannot have added much to our bodies nutritionally but the flesh was soothing, refreshing, comforting, even filling, all in one. We ate two pieces each, slowly, without talking, just catching each other's eye from time to time.

If we were to get any farther that night, the time was nearing. Neither of us made any movement, nor did we say anything. Ming may have been waiting for me to take an initiative. Perhaps she thought my silence meant I was planning the next move.

I was certainly thinking, but not about setting off. It came to me that to continue as we were doing was crazy. We had had a great deal of luck — we could not expect it to continue. Besides, the Public Security Department now knew roughly where to start looking for us — from the moment we had joined the bicyclists we had left a series of clues that should not be hard to follow. Secondly, and perhaps even more important, we were growing steadily weaker. The loose waist of my once-tight jeans was a constant reminder of the difference between our intake of food and the energy we were using. In practical terms, the distances we covered were going to get progressively shorter, and with the exhaustion we would become increasingly careless. Soon hunger and tiredness would start playing hell with my judgment — if it had not done so already.

The truth was that I just didn't see us making it. The girl alone, perhaps, but both of us . . . I told myself I was not being defeatist, simply realistic.

I broke the silence. "I won't stop you if you want to go on alone," I said. "You would stand a thousand times better chance. I'd understand. It's pointless for us both to get caught."

"You have no chance without me," she said. "With me . . ." She shrugged. "But without . . ." Her voice dropped.

I unfolded the map and stared at it, as though seeking inspiration. My mind started to flirt with giving up. I fought it, but it was hard. A voice kept whispering that I couldn't be any worse off — that, sooner or later, I'd be freed and allowed to go home. It also kept saying that it would be the best thing for Ming. I *knew* neither was true — the chances were that I'd just vanish; as for Ming, I guessed that the mere suspicion of her complicity would mean prison camp or banishment to some forsaken spot in the far north.

I came up with a solution of sorts. It did not involve giving up; in practice, it might mean an end to the running by ensuring we were caught; but that was different.

"I don't think we should move on tonight," I said. "This is a good hiding place if they were suspicious about the call and manage to trace it. Besides, I think you were right in one vital thing — we do need help. We're not going to get far without it."

Then, such as it was, I outlined my idea: that the following morning Ming should travel into the nearest town, visit the post office, see if it was possible to get through a call to Andrews — I didn't think we dare attempt a second call to her uncle. There was some risk in trying to make such a call, but nothing like the ones involved if we'd tried from the plant at four A.M. She could also investigate whether there was transport we could use: a siding where we might hide aboard a freight train, a parking place where trucks were left overnight . . .

She listened, and agreed by not protesting. I fell asleep feeling that she had read everything that had passed through my mind.

She left before dawn, reckoning that she would be less conspicuous entering the town with others traveling in from the surrounding countryside to sell their wares.

We unbolted the cart from the bicycle. She filled one of the sacks we had taken from the plant with twigs and leaves and tied it to the handlebars. It looked as though she carried produce for sale.

With her clothes battered from sleeping rough and from the rains and with her hair again tied back in a demure bun, Ming looked the part. She was safe as long as no one had her picture and there was no check on papers. We thought it unlikely she would be picked out as a stranger: according to the map, the town was a sizable one.

As she prepared to move off I fought an impulse to hold her. Instead

I contented myself with an almost brotherly squeeze on her shoulder. "Take care," I said.

She didn't reply, but seconds after setting off she turned and raised her hand. Soon she was lost to view.

Briefly, the dark voices of a few hours before returned — once in the town, she would make straight for the local Public Security office. Or she would be recognized and held the moment she arrived. Whichever, I would not see her again. The first I would know of what had happened was the arrival of a squad of the People's Liberation Army or the militia.

I went back to my now familiar nest in the quarry, allowed myself a slice of melon, and settled down to watch the dawn break, and to wait for the soldiers to come and collect me.

She returned early in the afternoon. Her face was beaming, and before I could say anything she had taken the sack off the handlebars and opened it on the ground.

There were fruit, cold meats, pastries, and bottles of mineral water. There was also a block of soap, a piece of cloth, and — most unexpected of all — a straight razor.

I reached out for it. It was not new, but the blade was as sharp as if it had been. "People always sell things they no longer need," explained Ming. "It was on a tray with other things. No one would be suspicious that I bought it."

She had anticipated my question. I spread my arms. "But all this," I said.

"I was a wife at the free market to sell and also to buy. What else would I do?"

Still holding the razor, I lifted my other hand, and felt the stubble. I had not seen my face for days. I knew Chinese men needed to shave only rarely. To Ming I must look bad, almost like some animal.

"Looking at me has been giving you nightmares," I said. "That's why you bought it."

She took my gentle mocking very seriously as though afraid I had genuinely misunderstood her motives. "I thought that you should shave in case we have to go among people," she said. "If you look presentable, you might get away with it. But with that beard . . ."

I could hardly cease staring at the food. But I knew it was time for my Lawrence of Arabia act — that part in the movie when he deliberately goes without water just to show he can do it.

My action was less dramatic, but it took me about as much willpower. I picked up the soap and the piece of cloth and walked away until I reached a shaded, deep puddle still not evaporated by the sun.

I remained within Ming's sight, and I heard her begin to speak in protest, but I pretended not to hear. Nothing was going to ruin my gesture.

Shaving with an open razor, without a mirror and without hot water, is not easy. To say that is to use understatement on a par with describing Libya's Gaddafi as a man who isn't fond of Jews or Jimmy Connors as someone who knows how to play tennis.

When I had finished, I felt over my skin carefully, mainly to check whether parts of me were still attached, and whether there was much blood. Some, I expected. Damage seemed to be confined to two nicks. I finished the antiseptic on them. Then, with the cloth draped around my shoulders, I wandered back to Ming.

"What do you think?" I said, turning my head so that she could see both profiles.

She dropped her eyes. "There was no need," she said. "I did not mean to offend you."

I wanted to reach out, assure her that the last thing she had done was to do that, but she was already spreading a sack as a cloth and producing food.

"It was me I was offending," I said. But either she did not hear or she did not understand.

We both began to eat, slowly, chewing carefully, knowing that our stomachs were not strong. After several minutes I paused and said, "Okay, what's the bad news?" There had to be some, otherwise she would have told me about the telephone call the moment she returned.

"I went into the post office," she said. "I waited until there were many people. But I saw men checking the faces of callers against some sheets of paper. I did not dare risk it. Was I right?"

She knew she was, but I reassured her.

"You said not to attempt to call from a hotel, so I looked around and bought food at the market. Then I returned."

She briefed me on the vehicle traffic and on what she had been able to see of the railroad station. Neither sounded very promising.

I thought she had finished, but she added more, almost as an afterthought. "There are some tourists," she said.

"You saw them?"

"I saw a tour bus outside a hotel."

"This isn't a tourist area, is it?"

"There is always shortage of accommodation. Perhaps they house people here on the way to Nanking, or to Wuhsi, or Soochow. The hotels there may be full." I understood: I had heard complaints in Peking of people having to stay thirty and more miles outside the city. The Chinese, wanting foreign currency, were anxious not to turn visitors away. The hotel shortage was just part of a larger paradox with which they were having to live. Foreigners were also a virus — their very presence, with their clothes and expensive cameras and seemingly unlimited money, set a bad example. At the same time, however, the Chinese needed them. The State was solving the problem in a neat way — housing visitors away from the beaten track and the ordinary people.

"Tourists," I said aloud. That probably meant Americans or Europeans or Japanese. If I could get a message to one, he should have no problem telephoning Andrews. But what could I tell him? What help could I expect from him? I would have to trust that he had developed some sort of network: wasn't that part of his job?

Ming focused on my expression, mistaking it for resignation.

"Are you thinking there is nothing more we can do?" she asked.

I noted, and liked, the use of the word "we." I reached for a pastry and bit into it with definite abandon.

"Thanks to you, we're back in business," I said, and I explained.

I felt good the next morning. I risked a few more flicks of the razor over my face. And I ate. That was real luxury.

It took longer than I had anticipated to reattach the cart to the back of the bicycle: the problem lay in tightening the bolts enough for them not to work loose on the way. In the end I had to use a couple of stones, one like a chisel, the other as a hammer.

Nevertheless we were on our way soon after sunrise, again planning to join the equivalent of the morning commuter rush. I sat in the back while she pedaled. I made myself as small as possible, my knees under my chin, and my head drooped forward. A sack, and the coolie hat, left only my eyes uncovered.

In my pocket I had a folded note already written. It contained the words "Andrews" and "U.S. Embassy," together with the brief message, "Friendship Store, Wuhsi, three days, 6 P.M.," and the embassy phone number.

The hope was that the tourist would pass the message and that Andrews would have time to arrange for someone to be there. We had chosen Wuhsi because it was a big town, used to seeing streams of foreigners, and because Ming knew of somewhere there where she was sure we could hide out in safety.

Near Wuhsi is Lake Tai, one of the five largest lakes in China. Because of its beauty and because it has a reputation for healthy air, many high officials have resort houses on its shores. Ming knew of one such house on one of the lake's one hundred or so islands. She had accompanied a visiting Yugoslavian party leader on his visit there. She was convinced it would be unoccupied now. Although, after the outbursts of rain, the day was now hot and clear, Ming said the weather was not typical. June, on and around the lake, marked the start of a gray, depressing rainy season. The first rain was called the "Plum Rain."

The journey took around an hour, and as we neared the town I heard blasts of martial music being played over outside speakers —

daily reveille for all stay-in-beds. It was hard to imagine anyone needed it. As we passed the first houses the road was bustling with other bicycles, ancient open trucks, and manpowered carts of all descriptions. Shouts mingled with horns and hooters, bells with shrieks and laughter. Although I knew hardly any of me was visible, I huddled down even further.

Ming turned off the road, along a narrow dirt track, and out onto another road. At last we reached the hotel that she had seen the previous day. She parked in the shade of a plane tree across the street from the entrance drive. Leaving me balanced in the cart, Ming squatted on the pavement and began to eat a piece of fruit.

The hotel was new: concrete, a lot of stainless steel, and glass. It looked as if it had been built on a tight budget. If I had to classify it architecturally, I'd say Airport Hotel 1960.

The idea, simple enough if all went well, was that I should try to lobby one of the tourists as they left the building. Just how and at what point would depend on circumstances. Ideally, what I wanted was for one of them to venture outside before breakfast. Then I'd throw off the sack and the hat, hurry across the street, speak briefly, and pass the note.

We had decided that it was something that had to be done by me, not by Ming. Shaved, hair washed, clothes brushed, I looked reasonably human. The important point, though, was that I was an American. That, we thought, might make the tourist I approached take it seriously. Ming, on the other hand, would be automatically suspect: a note passed by her would quickly hit the nearest trash barrel. The visitor would conclude, not unnaturally, that he or she was being drawn into some horrible danger or being compromised by the Chinese.

The trouble was that no one left the hotel, and at ten past seven I was beginning to feel the onset of panic. Ming appeared relaxed, crouched in the street; I couldn't help worrying whether we were conspicuous.

I was wondering whether we should ride around the streets and return later when my tourist appeared. Or, more precisely, a lot of them appeared. About twenty, in a snake, like kids being led out of school. They were accompanied by two Chinese guides, one at the front, the other bringing up the rear. They disregarded the tour bus, took a sharp right in the street, then another, and began to vanish from my view.

Ming began pushing the bike the moment they went out of sight. We traveled for several minutes. I could not see where we were going. I heard a sharp blast from a whistle, and we stopped. I realized we had reached a crossing controlled by a policeman. There were more blasts, and then the sound of voices raised in argument. An ancient truck stopped behind me. Without looking, I knew the driver was staring down at me, and I huddled inside myself. Finally we started off again. As we passed the policemen I saw he was directing a man pushing a cart not to move from behind some imaginary line. The man was obviously being delayed for some infringement. I sent him my silent thanks for occupying the policeman.

There was no way of communicating with Ming. Nor could I know what had happened to the tourists; I could only hope that she still had them within her view. Suddenly we stopped, and Ming pushed the bike and cart into a space between many other similar vehicles.

She parked and leaned over me. "When I say 'Now,' take off your hat and get up quickly," she said. "We are at one of the markets. I came here yesterday. The tourists have been brought here. I can see them now."

There was silence, and I knew she was waiting for a moment when no one was looking in our direction.

"Now!"

I had rehearsed the movement in my mind. One hand pushed aside the sack, the other removed the hat, and almost simultaneously I rolled myself off the cart and up into a standing position.

In practice, I ruined it a little by getting a cramp in my left leg and doubling up after a couple of paces. No one seemed to notice, and a few seconds later I was mingling with the crowd.

Free markets are part of the post-Mao, pragmatic China which decided people work better if you hold out a carrot now and then for them to nibble. They exist so that people can sell goods on their own behalf — usually produce or animals in excess of what is due to the State. Not only do they exist, but they are a part of China the authorities like to display to foreigners. One of the old China hands I'd met in Peking had told me they were not quite as new a phenomenon as the Chinese liked to pretend — before, though, they'd operated underground, "and they called it the black market."

In this one there was no attempt to merge with the crowd for me. I was an attraction every step that I took. Heads craned upward to look at me; a group followed just to see what I would do; I stopped once to get my bearings and found that I was ushered to the head of a line for shirts.

It was easy, though, to keep my eye on the tourists. Like me, they towered over the Chinese shoppers. They had split into smaller groups. I picked out a couple who were pausing every few feet to take more pictures. They were in the late fifties or early sixties, both small and square-built, not unlike many of the farmers and their wives with whom I'd grown up. When I reached them, the man was photographing the woman against a background of brightly colored songbirds. The birds — the Chinese catch them and keep them as pets — were confined in small cages, laid out for display on a trestle table.

I waited until he had finished taking the picture. My immediate plan was to step forward and to offer to photograph them both together, but he moved away, leaving her alone. A scrawny chicken, in a wire-netting box, had drawn his attention; maybe he was a farmer.

Moving beside him, I began talking immediately. It would have been nice to strike up a casual conversation, win his confidence, gauge his possible reaction to my request. But I didn't know how long we had. Seconds, maybe.

"Please don't look startled or do anything strange," I said, making my voice as Midwestern as I could. Over the years I have lost my original accent; with moving around so much I've developed a new one, an amalgam of many influences. As Maddy had said, sometimes it didn't even sound like that of a native American anymore. Something told me, though, that a good Midwestern voice would give him some confidence in me.

"This isn't a joke," I went on. "I'm an American, a visitor like you. Except I'm in trouble." He didn't say anything, but I felt him stiffen. "I don't want you to get involved," I rushed on, "but I have to get a message to the American embassy. The phone number and the name of a man is written on a piece of paper I've got here in my hand. I want to pass it to you. Will you call them? Not from here, but when you get to your next hotel later today. Just read them the brief message that's on the paper. That's all. There is no risk, I promise you."

From the corner of my eye I could see other tourists heading in our direction with one of the guides.

"Will you do it?" I asked urgently.

He didn't speak, but he moved his hand next to my side. I slipped him the note, and he pocketed it.

"Thanks," I said. It seemed inadequate, and an anticlimax, but I couldn't think of anything else short of a full speech.

Still he said nothing. He had decided that taking the note was enough without actually talking to me.

I backed away, saw Ming, and began to follow her.

As soon as no one was watching I would resume my position on the cart.

What happened after that was dependent on what opportunities arose. I felt full of optimism. It did not fade even briefly when I failed in my attempt to buy a bottle of Coca-Cola moments later. There was a table with cans of Coke like islands in a huge bowl of ice and water. It was confirmation that, whatever I had thought, the town definitely was on the tourist map. Ordinary Chinese don't buy Coca-Cola — I'd forgotten the actual figures, but I knew a can cost something like a half-day's pay. Still here I was, obviously a tourist, thirsty, feeling like celebrating, and with money I otherwise had no way of spending.

I held out a note. The man pushed it back, wouldn't take it; no change, I guessed. The sight of the Coke was making my mouth water, but I couldn't afford a scene. I smiled, shrugged, and moved on. I couldn't know at the time that the reason he would not accept my note was that it was real money. Foreigners visiting China can use their dollars, pounds, francs, or yen to buy foreign currency certificates or scrip from banks or other exchange outlets. Only these notes can then be used to buy some imported items like Scotch, British and American cigarettes, periodicals. It was this special currency that the man wanted. Nor could I know that, because of my action, I was leaving behind yet another sign of my move toward the south.

I I

We continued to travel southeast, following the railroad as best we could. It was somehow ironic that this was the track I should have been riding in my director's viewing car, cosseted as a guest of the State.

I wanted us to get to Wuhsi as fast as we possibly could. In a straight line it was about sixty miles away. The best possibility, I had decided, lay in trying to hitch a ride on a freight train. We would have to gamble on being able to leave it before we entered the town.

I remembered some major work taking place on an embankment not too far to the south of where we were now, and this might be the place to try to join a train. Provided, of course, that we would also be able to find somewhere nearby to hide ourselves and the bicycle and cart. To say we were depending on a little luck would have been like saying Atlantic City needed the odd gambler. But I was experiencing that special anything-is-possible kind of optimism.

The sun was hot and on the back of the cart I itched and sweated under the sacking. I did not dare remove it, though. Although the road was not busy there was enough traffic for me not to take risks. The land was changing the farther south we moved. The red, dry earth of Nanking had gradually become darker and richer-looking. The leaves here were greener and lusher. Wheat fields alternated with rice paddies.

We were never far from the track, and I saw three trains pass, one diesel and two with belching chimneys. That day at Tatung seemed a long, long way away.

Through the gap between the sack and my hat brim I watched the peasants at work in the field. There was a lot of laughter and horseplay; it all seemed very safe and innocent.

Every so often a cart with ungreased wheels would pass us, and until I became accustomed to the noise the screech startled me.

At midday the fields emptied as people went home or found shelter for the universal afternoon rest. Ming stopped in a spot which provided both shade and cover — to continue would have been suspicious — and we ate.

We remained silent, almost as though we were complete strangers who had chanced upon each other. We were cocooned inside our own thoughts. I stood up, disturbing her mood. "I have to go into the bushes," I said. The euphemism sounded strange after what we had shared, but our relationship, still delicate, still uncertain, depended on such formalities.

We had stopped near a pocket of land that had not been cultivated. Grasses and weeds ran unchecked. It looked as though it was waiting for someone to develop it. Back home I would have guessed it was owned by some speculator holding on until someone wanted to widen the highway or build a drive-in. The railroad passed about twenty yards away. Beside the track, just within our view, were three old cars that looked as though at one time they might have been used for housing.

I walked toward them. The undergrowth was so high I had to make detours to reach them. As I got nearer I saw that the windows had gone and that most of the woodwork had been stripped — taken, no doubt, for firewood or as building material. I urinated — the point of my walk — and then looked inside one. Most of the floor had collapsed, and weeds grew through the gaps. There was a dusty, mousy smell. Something scurried in the corner, but too fast for me to see.

It was a perfect spot to hide the bicycle and cart. With a little luck, they might lie hidden for days. Did we dare to leave them, though, and travel on foot from here? Perhaps we should also stay until darkness, then follow the track, seeking the works that I remembered.

I turned, startled, at a sound. It was Ming. There was concern on her face. She must have worried that I was away so long.

"What are you doing?" she said.

I did not reply immediately because I had caught sight of something I had not seen before — a truck, among the undergrowth, some thirty or forty yards ahead. It must have been there when we arrived, but not visible from the road. There was no way from here of knowing whether there was anyone with it. If there was, we were lucky we had made so little noise.

Ming saw it too. I drew her into the cover of the wagons.

"We could hide the bike here and steal that truck," I said.

"They'd find it and know where we had gone," said Ming. Her comment surprised me; I had thought her first protest would be about the driver of the truck.

"They're fools if they don't already know which way we are heading," I said. But I knew she was right. You cannot hide a large truck the way you can a bike and cart, and once it was found Security would have a precise area in which to search.

"I'm going to take a look anyway," I said, and before she could protest I began working my way in the direction of the truck, dropping low like John Wayne crawling toward the Apache camp.

The driver was there, but almost impossible to see until I was only a few yards away. He had placed a blanket on the ground and was stretched out on it. He represented two firsts for me: I'd never heard a Chinese snoring before, nor had I seen one drunk. The second surprised me more than the first. The Chinese, like Jews, are people who rarely drink to excess, and are contemptuous of those who do. This Chinese still had the bottle in his hand. He'd had the priorities of the drunk well in mind, having recorked it before he'd passed out. While he was asleep the sun had moved around, and his head was no longer in the shade. He was going to feel pretty bad.

The truck was East German and looked about twenty-five years old. The back, covered with a canvas hood, was piled high with cabbages behind the tailgate. The smell in the heat was almost overpowering. Which concerned me less at that moment than the way the truck was pointing. Southward. The way we wanted to go.

I hurried back to Ming and explained the situation.

"Burrow down in the cabbages?" she repeated, her face wrinkling with distaste. "We'd suffocate."

"We'd choke a bit and smell awful at the end," I said. "But not suffocate. And it is going the right way."

"But we don't know where."

"Its destination has to be a good few miles away," I said. "Otherwise he wouldn't have stopped here — he'd have kept going." I was not as confident as I sounded. He might just have wanted to get his drinking in first. He could be heading for a place two miles distant. But I was willing to risk that.

"Besides," I added, "he has to be making for a big town — there aren't any for quite a distance." Without rechecking the map I wasn't sure that was true. But it seemed to tip the scales.

"We'd best hurry then," she said.

It took both of us to manhandle the bike and cart. It proved impossible to uncouple them again: I had hammered the nuts home too tightly. We broke away more rotting floor inside one of the carriages and heaved the vehicle into the space. Then we covered it with all the rubble we could find. From the doorway it was only a shadowy shape in the gloom.

Finally satisfied, we made our way toward the truck. I went first to check. The driver had stopped snoring but had not moved. I waved to Ming to join me.

The ripe smell of cabbages almost drove her back, but I was already clearing a space into which she could climb. I followed her, and we wormed our way into the pile until only our heads and arms remained free. The cabbages felt slippery and alien against my body, almost like creatures. We built a barricade of cabbages between our heads and the tailgate to hide us from view.

It was thirty-five minutes before we heard him move. I knew because I kept checking my watch. The smell had become slightly less nauseating with familiarity, but not much. Both of us needed activity to distract our minds. I heard the man drag himself to his feet and curse. Then there was the sound of his swallowing from the bottle, followed by a bout of spitting and long urinating at the side of the truck.

He came around to the back to make a cursory check on his load. A few cabbages had rolled near the space above the tailgate. He tossed them deeper into the truck, one by one. They landed near our heads, and it was a struggle not to move. I heard him spit again, and moments later the truck rocked as he climbed inside and started the engine.

Because of the wall of cabbages, which I did not wish to disturb in case the driver checked again, we could not see out of the truck. It was a strange feeling. I could only guess at the speed we were traveling from the sound of the engine and the feedback from the unpaved road. I put it at no more than thirty miles an hour. I figured we should wait for ninety minutes, which with luck would have carried us forty to fifty miles, and then look for an opportunity to leave the truck. There were lots of possible problems, of course, not the least what we would do if the driver stopped to unload before then. That, though, was negative thinking.

There was one false alarm when he did stop, but it was only so that he could urinate again. Half an hour later, we worked our bodies loose and crawled to the tailgate. The road behind us stretched in a straight line for several miles. Just then we slowed, made a turn, and began to climb a gentle hill. The vehicle was moving more slowly now, but I held back, waiting for better cover on the sides of the road.

The driver shifted gears as we continued to climb. The roadside was perfect now, and we were moving at no more than gentle jogging speed. On both sides of us were tiers of tea trees. Most important, beyond them on our right I could see the glimmer of water in the distance. It stretched so far that I thought it had to be the lake. Because of the heat haze it was impossible to gauge its distance with any real accuracy. Certainly many miles. Perhaps ten.

The engine began to gasp as we slowed even more to take a curve, and I whispered to Ming, "Are you ready? Shall I go first?"

"Yes. I'll follow."

I struggled for some leverage and started to raise one leg over the tailgate.

Then, with a shudder, the truck stopped.

It was only when the engine was off that I realized how it had masked every other noise.

The sounds that reached us now were chilling, strange but at the same time universal in the message of pain and suffering they conveyed.

There was the steady boom of a gong, a softer thud of drums, the clash of cymbals, and rising above it all the wailing sounds of human voices.

"A funeral," murmured Ming, unnecessarily. We had both frozen.

"What a time to choose," I whispered back. Like her, I was speaking for its own sake. The nearness of death, even when it is that of a stranger, makes you want to protect your exposed places with trivia.

Death, though, seemed somehow incongruous from the back of a truck of strong-smelling cabbages — it was as if we were actors who had stumbled into the wrong play.

Ming took me literally. "The time will have been chosen because it is the most auspicious hour and date." She saw my look and rushed on in the same whisper, "There are still people who believe such things. Old people. Sometimes it is kind to humor them."

I was only half-listening. I was amending my own words. As far as we were concerned it *was* a good time to choose. It was an excellent place to leave the truck.

"Let's go," I said.

"Now?"

"Yes, now."

I clambered over the tailgate and dropped to the ground. She followed, and I reached out to take her weight. The flesh of her thigh gave under my hand, and I felt another shiver that had nothing to do with the funeral. She felt it. "What is it?"

"Nothing. Let's hurry."

We slid into the trees before looking back. The driver had left his cab — strange how we had not felt the movement — and was standing facing the funeral procession. That was still twenty-five yards away. He had removed his cap, and his head was bowed. I guessed that about now he would be feeling the need for another drink. It was a heady time for anyone to contemplate death.

I thought that the procession might pass us — there was room alongside the truck — but it began to turn. We watched, lying on our bellies, lost in the moment despite our own problems. The ritual of death has always fascinated me — perhaps it is the dark side of my Welsh ancestry: my mother's great-grandfather had fled Wales, not for economic reasons like his neighbors but because he liked the sound of America. What intrigues me is how universal needs are satisfied in often very nationalistic ways. I had once sat eating delicacies with hundreds of others around funeral pyres at an Indonesian mass cremation, and on another occasion I had talked and drunk myself into oblivion at an Irish wake. Different means; same end.

At this moment there was nowhere we could go. But even if there were I would have wanted to remain.

The procession was headed by boys carrying banners, each of them covered with Chinese characters.

"What do they say?" I whispered even though there was little likelihood of anyone's hearing anything above the noise of the band and the mourners. A solitary horn had now joined the sounds.

"They all say things in praise of the dead man." I was about to ask how she knew it was a man, but she continued with the same tone of apology I heard before: "These are all old customs."

I wondered if she really felt as censorious as she sounded, or whether she was reciting the party line, parrot-fashion. But I said nothing; it was no time to start an ideological debate.

After the boys came the band, followed in turn by children carrying round paper wreaths and a huge white paper horse. I did not have to ask about them — they had to represent the objects that the corpse would need in the next life.

Next came the coffin itself, placed upon a cart. A man walked beside it, beating two pieces of wood in time with the steps of the bearers. Finally, there were the mourners. All were dressed in white, the Chinese color for grief. At the point at which the procession turned off the road, the women among the mourners dropped out and began to retrace their steps.

"The women do not got to the grave," said Ming. "They return home to wait." I had already guessed that, but I was amused that despite Ming's deprecation of the ritual she knew what was happening.

The procession moved from our sight, and a few minutes later the truck drew away and continued its journey.

With it gone, I could just glimpse the procession again, working its way down the hillside. It stopped among a cluster of conical grave mounds. The music stopped, and the silence was painful.

I saw a glint of light followed by a sudden spiral of smoke, and I knew they were burning the paper wreaths and the horse. Beyond that I could make out nothing, but I imagined the coffin being placed into a waiting grave. There were words, too low I think to have understood even if I had spoken Chinese; then more silence, and the unmistakable sound of earth falling on to wood. The noise came in short bursts as though soil was being thrown, handful by handful.

Minutes later they returned to the road; many of them were already removing their white robes. We watched until the road and the land were deserted, as though the funeral had never been. From this distance even the grave mounds could have been something else. At least his family had somewhere to mourn him. In the city I knew that cremation was compulsory.

"We should go," said Ming. I studied her face. The funeral and its ancient ritual had embarrassed her. She wore the expression I would have had if I'd been showing her around Washington, D.C., and we'd happened upon an old lady being mugged.

"Will anyone return to the graveyard?" I said.

She did not like the question, misunderstood the point of it, thought I was still being curious for curiosity's sake. Nevertheless she answered. "Not today. Usually it is not until the third day."

I was not sure she was right about the third day; maybe that was the way it was at some funeral she had attended once or heard about. But, within the greater ritual, there are always variations of practice — not just from area to area but sometimes even from one hamlet to another. However, I thought she was probably correct about the grave being left for at least twenty-four hours.

"Good," I said at last. "Then that's where we'll hide until it's dark."

It was an uneasy few hours, concealed within the graveyard, shielded from sight by one of the many clumps of yew bushes. We talked very little, and although I was not tired I pretended to sleep so that we would not have to converse.

The new grave mound was like a scar on the hillside, and it kept drawing my eyes and my thoughts. What kind of man? Was he old, young? A man with a wife? Children? Did he die suddenly, unexpectedly? Or was it at the end of a lingering illness?

It struck me that images of death had twice punctuated my flight. First, there was the monks' graveyard, much older than this place. Now this. Was it some horrible portent, like the dead man's hand in poker?

I shuddered, then cursed myself for such thoughts. But I was glad when darkness came and we were able to move.

There was no need to use the needle. I had noted the direction of the water, picked out landmarks which we could follow. The countryside was ideal for providing cover, but the wealth of trees and plants made traveling slow.

It was three in the morning before we reached a hilltop that looked directly down on the water. There was no doubt it was Lake Tai. It was a clear night, and I could pick out the shoreline, and the shadows of some of the many islands.

We spent the next hour finding a place where we could hide for another day; it was obvious there was no chance at all of finding Ming's island that night. We made a shelter of sorts among tall pines, and burrowed into it.

In the confined space the smell of cabbage rose from our clothes.

I wrinkled my nose and turned toward Ming, but she was already asleep. I lay awake for a long time and finally, just before dawn, I risked leaving her alone and reclimbed the hill. From the top I looked down on the lake and took bearings, using the map and points that Ming had described. The two main ones — a group of islands called Three Hills and a small peninsula named Turtle Head Islet — were easy to find. The islet had a small lighthouse at the point where the turtle's head would have been.

It was a breathtaking dawn. The rising sun turned scudding low clouds into balls of fire. The grayness of the hillsides became shades of green, dotted madly with the orange and red of fruit on the trees. Pavilions and towers rose out of the lake.

I left it reluctantly and returned to Ming. I was glad I had noted my path well; she was completely hidden until I was only feet away.

Rain came again late that morning. It woke us both.

"I think it is the Plum Rain," said Ming. "I told you about it."

It fell steadily all day. The spot in which we lay was protected. We had the plastic bags and the sacks for our beds. There was food and a little drink left. It was strangely cosy. Just one thing disturbed me, and it was late in the day when I realized exactly what it was: the relative paucity of wildlife. We saw a little — some squirrels, frogs, a small deer that was gone so quickly that it was barely a flash of movement, swarms of tiny white moths. And there were a few birds — I recognized a variety of titmouse as well as pigeons.

But I am sure that in any equally wild place in most other countries I would have seen more. I had read of China's sledgehammer attack on agricultural and disease-carrying pests. I was deeply grateful on one level — we had, so far, not been bothered by mosquitoes. But what we were experiencing here in the forest was one of the results.

We left our hiding place early that evening, masked by the grayness and by the drizzle that obscured the land like mist.

At the lakeside, we disregarded the first boats that we found. It was obvious that they belonged to fishermen. Such men, I reasoned, would be certain they left their boats well secured, and would be most suspicious if they found one gone.

The second group we stumbled upon looked more like pleasure craft. They were moored not far from a collection of newly built buildings — one of the many clinics that had developed around the lakeside, Ming said.

The boats were flat-bottomed and made, strange as it seemed, from concrete. Ming assured me it was common locally. I untied two, and found them light and easy to handle. Poles had been left in the boat. We climbed in one and took the other in tow. I reasoned that taking two might make the owners believe they had drifted loose — after all, who would steal *two* boats?

Despite my careful bearings and Ming's description, it took most of the night to find the island. Patches of mist kept swallowing us, hiding everything from view. My efforts kept me warm, but in the damp I could see that Ming was shivering.

From the water, there was no sign of a house on the island. But Ming said she was certain — and there was no mistaking the work that had taken place to clear a landing space.

I maneuvered the last few hundred yards as carefully as I could to make no sound. We didn't speak, not even in a whisper.

Ming stayed with the boat while I explored. The whole island was little bigger than the gardens of a country estate. The house became visible within minutes of setting off. I approached carefully. There were wooden shutters inside, drawn over all the windows. Ming was right.

All the doors were locked. It would have been easy to force one, but messy, and I did not want to leave obvious signs of our presence. I found a window with some play in the frame and managed to slip the catch with the blade of my knife. It opened outward. That left the shutters, but here I did not mind some force — once they were pushed together again there would be no sign of entry from outside. I pushed and strained until they began to gape, then got a branch through the gap. It was easy then to reach through until I found the catches with my hand.

Inside, I searched the rooms slowly in my best burglar style. But, quite apart from the closed shutters, it had been obvious the house was empty from the moment I entered. It had that feel and smell: starved for sun and air.

I got Ming and then, even though I was tired, I searched *outside* until I confirmed what I had suspected must be so — that the island had its own boat.

I stripped off my clothes then, reentered the concrete boat, and poled it out into the lake, its companion still in tow. A southwesterly wind was building. It would help carry the boats away from the island.

It was also swirling the mist, making it hard to keep the island in view. I waited until I could see it clearly, then slid into the water and began swimming. I had to stop several times to tread water while I got my bearings before I reached land again. Once there, I picked up my clothes and entered the house.

Ming had not dared use any light, but dawn was coloring the rooms. She was in an American-style kitchen, heating water on a butane gas burner.

I strode on past to find a bathroom. It had an air of coming back to breakfast after a morning swim on a holiday for two.

I just hoped no one else would decide it was a good time for a real holiday. Like the house's owner.

12

We decided that we would sleep the day in relays so that one of us was always on watch in case anyone came. I found it impossible to believe that the house was left completely unattended, although all the signs pointed that way. Ming, on the other hand, found my disbelief equally hard to understand — no one would enter and rob such a house unless he was completely crazy. He was certain to be tracked down. And then . . . She made her fingers into a gun, and uttered a shooting sound. Perhaps she was exaggerating, but she had made her point.

Ming insisted that she should take the first watch on the grounds that the swim had taken what little strength I had left. I agreed on the promise that she would wake me in two hours' time. As with many of our plans, the theory and the actuality proved to be far apart.

It was nearly thirteen hours later when I woke, and Ming was asleep, curled kittenishly in the overstuffed chair that we'd moved near the window so she could keep watch on the landing strip. There was a half-full cup balanced precariously on one arm, a sure sign that she had hardly moved in her sleep. I removed it carefully and, equally gently, brushed away wisps of hair from her eyes. She stirred, but did not awake, and I left her. Both of us needed rest, drink, and nutritious food, in that order.

Outside, the mist had lifted and the late afternoon sunlight carved a thin gash through a light drizzle. I could pick out a junk and a large barge in the distance, but there were no small craft. Either it was not the time, or the weather, or both.

Despite the rain, I walked down to the shore, then navigated the island as best I could. I confirmed it was small, more of an outcrop. It had been left wild with bayberry trees. They hung heavy with their matte, gray-green fruit. I plucked one and crushed the berry, and its heavy scent filled the air. The color reminded me of something, and then I realized. Ming's eyes. I had seen no other Chinese eyes like them.

The boathouse, which I had already investigated briefly when we arrived, was carefully landscaped into the wild scene, so that it was only visible from one direction. The boat had a small outboard. The walls were hung with fishing gear.

I started back to the house. It was one story, little more than a square with a bulge at one corner where it had been extended. I followed it around. At the back, which faced east, there was a veranda hung with vines which overlooked a rock garden. Beyond that there was a pond surrounded by drooping willows. I walked to the edge of the water; fish — carp, I thought — moved lazily among the waterlilies.

The carp gave me an idea, but I left it for now. I wanted to explore the inside before the light faded. The main room was L-shaped. At one end was the chair where Ming still slept, at the other was the American-style kitchen, complete with refrigerator and stove. Both were fueled by portable gas containers. There were three other rooms: the main one was a bedroom designed and equipped like a deluxe hotel. It had white and gold built-in furniture and a portable television mounted on a unit facing the bed. It led into an equally luxurious, albeit impersonal bathroom. The third room occupied the extension. It was a cramped box room with a pull-down wall bed and a washbasin. I guessed it would hold some servant or bodyguard.

Except for the overstuffed chairs and the Chinese paintings of rivers, mountains, and animals, the house could have come straight from the pages of any U.S. real estate brochure. The floors throughout were tiled; a rug lay carelessly by the bed like some expensive trophy. When I thought of the way people were living only a few miles away, I realized the man who owned this had to have real pull. Maybe Ming pretending to shoot anyone who dared despoil such a place wasn't exaggerating; maybe you only got the bullet in the head when the authorities had finished being really nasty to you.

Even with two of the blinds open wide it was getting hard to see. I quickly checked the drawers and cupboards. The wardrobe was empty but for one robe: white cotton, embossed, in English, with the name of the Hotel Okura, Tokyo. I recognized the name: one of the best hotels in the city. The kitchen was well equipped with cans, most of them with labels I couldn't make out. They included orange juice — a mad luxury in a part of the country where fruit grew everywhere. I opened one and drank deeply.

Later I would check the effectiveness of the blinds. For now, I inspected the lamps. I dropped one, and it clattered on the hard tile floor. Ming moved with a start and I hurried over to reassure her. Her eyes were wide open, but she was still asleep, like someone in a trance. I took one of her hands and smoothed it. She closed her eyes and began breathing more easily.

The room was dark now, and I needed light. Not knowing how much longer Ming would sleep, I closed the two blinds I had opened, lit one lamp, and turned it low. Then I walked around the outside of the house to check. I could see nothing. I returned inside, increased the light, then checked again. I decided it was safe.

I was still nervous, though. Despite Ming's certainty that the house would be unguarded, I thought it likely that at the least the local Public Security Bureau would keep an eye on it. That might mean no more than daily, even weekly, observation from a boat on the lake. Nevertheless, in the daytime particularly, we would have to be cautious.

We had the great advantage that the house had been designed to give privacy. This was most marked at the rear. The view of the lake from the veranda would have been spectacular — if the owner had not decided to retain the trees to hide the house from sight.

The house made me realize how filthy I was. I looked down at my hands: the ingrained dirt etched patterns like a network of veins. My body was heavy with the odor of dried sweat. My clothes, wet through so many times, were stiff and stained.

I returned to the bathroom and figured out how to get hot water. It would have been pleasant to soak myself, but I was still too nervous to relax that much. There is a special fear at the thought of being caught naked. After I washed my body, I slipped on the robe and rinsed my clothes. It was hard to say which produced the most mud — me or them. I took my clothes outside and laid them on a flat rock. The warm air all around would dry them within the hour.

I went back and shaved. It would be good to say I felt like a new man; all I felt like was the old one but a little cleaner. Looking in the mirror, I decided I didn't look too bad — for a man who had been on the run for over a week. My skin, like Ming's, had lost much of its color. Black rings under my eyes reminded me of what served as wild nights when I was in my early twenties. Then I had thought they looked interesting. Now I saw they just made me look like a man in need of a week in a rest home. My facial features are pronounced — I've got a hawkish nose, too long a chin. Both had attracted scratches, which reminded me briefly and perversely of Maddy.

So that I wouldn't begin wallowing in my condition, I started to clean up the bath. I heard a noise and turned to see Ming backing away from the doorway, obviously embarrassed at having been seen watching me doing such an intimate or unmanly thing.

I pushed past her, leaving her alone, and a minute later I heard more water running. I returned to the kitchen and began gathering up odds and ends — an old-fashioned can opener, a broom handle, some cord from a drawer. That done, I put them together to form a rudimentary spear. I was after fish. The can opener, I reckoned, would be more effective than a knife, acting like a hook once it was inside the fish.

My first attempts were useless: the fish in the pond moved too fast. I returned and collected the flashlight I had seen earlier in a cupboard. I tied a piece of gauze over the lens to cut the beam and propped it up so it shone into the water.

It worked. The spear entered the first fish in the middle of its body and I yanked it out fast and clubbed it with a stone I had waiting. Kneeling in the early dark, the dead fish before me, the crude spear by my side, I felt a rush of blood heat and an exhilaration from having hunted and killed after being passive and pursued. I realized that I was gulping in air, the result of emotion, not effort. I carried my booty into the house, dried myself with the towel I had earlier discarded by the door, then returned to my fish with an expectant air.

As I had anticipated, it was a carp. His teeth were set in what really did resemble an evil smile. I slit his belly and gutted him quickly. If I had been behaving sensibly, I would have cut it into steaks, and fried them. But I was feeling more than a little high, and I cleaned him and then rubbed him inside and out with salt. I found oil and a pan, and started cooking the fish.

There was no shortage of equipment, nor of canned and bottled spices and sauces. I sorted out the ingredients I needed by sight, sometimes checking by tasting on the end of a finger. From them I made up a sweet and sour sauce of a kind in a small pan. By then it was time to flip over the fish and begin heating the oven.

It might have seemed absurd trying to cook Chinese food here for Ming — like walking into the George Cinq and asking the chef if I could put together a steak *au poivre* for him. Given the ingredients — and I am adept at improvising because my kind of cooking doesn't use measures or recipe books — I could have served up the carp in half a dozen different ways from memory. There's a Jewish way I like where you bake it with onion, garlic, tomato, parsley, powdered saffron, and pine nuts, adding a little wine near the end. Or a Hungarian way with potatoes, onion, sweet pepper, tomato, and some sour cream mixed with flour. Or I could have fried steaks of it in egg, flour, and breadcrumbs. But the ingredients available dictated what I should do.

I basted the fish, checked the oven temperature, gave it a couple more minutes, and then transferred the dish. I figured about fifteen minutes now. I put on water for noodles that I'd found and got the unopened bottle of brandy I'd seen earlier on my tour. I poured a finger, adding lots of water, knowing that my stomach might resent what was going to happen. It seemed a pity, though, not to live up to the Playboy in the Kitchen scene. I was sipping the mixture cautiously, noting in a detached way how the alcohol was hitting my central nervous system instantaneously, when Ming stepped out of the bathroom.

She was pink with the heat, and her hair was still damp. What was ludicrous, though — and a tribute to Chinese modesty — was that she had redressed in the grubby shirt and stained trousers. The drink and the temporary release from tension made me begin laughing like a kid whose neighbor has just farted in church.

Her eyes widened in genuine puzzlement.

"What is the matter? What have I done?"

"Oh Christ," I said, downing the brandy and water and pouring another one. "It's us. At the last count we were being pursued by your Security apparatus, the friends of the Gang of Four, and the Russians. Yet here I am sipping brandy and cooking like we've got the neighbors coming over for dinner. And as for you, you put your old, dirty clothes back on rather than walk around in towels, risking me seeing a flash of Chinese skin."

"There are not enough towels," she said defensively. She used the same tone she had used before all this started to recount production figures or detail the number of people who owned bicycles. "Besides," she continued, "it would not be right." Almost in the same voice, she added, "I would like a drink, too."

I reached for a glass, poured, added water, and handed it to her.

She sipped and began to gag. I moved to pat her back, but her prim-young-lady attitude held me back. She stopped coughing. "I am not used to drinking," she said.

I took the glass and added more water. "Nobody should really be drinking anyway at a time like this," I said. "It's only the asbestos-lined guts of old reprobates like me that can hold it after what our stomachs have been through."

I checked the fish as we talked. Another five minutes. The sauce was simmering nicely. Pity there were not a few strips of pepper that I could add.

"Are you really that, a reprobate?" she said. "That is someone who is a scoundrel — yes?"

I turned to see if her expression matched the suddenly mocking tone of her voice, but she had averted her face and was getting down bowls and chopsticks.

I didn't answer until I had strained the noodles and put them in a bowl and laid out the fish and covered it with sauce.

"No, not a scoundrel," I said, taking her question very seriously because suddenly it seemed important that she should not misunderstand. "More someone who has been around perhaps a bit too much and done a few things I don't like to think about late at night."

I set the fish in front of her. *"Voilà,"* I said.

She was trying a fresh sip of the drink now that I had added more water.

"Don't you think I'm a genius?" I continued.

She set down her glass, not saying anything.

"Here," I said, taking spare chopsticks and breaking away a piece of fish and placing it into her bowl. "Eat. Enjoy." Even to me my voice sounded strained.

She made the bathroom in about ten seconds flat, and I tried to disregard the retching sound and the fish eyes that seemed to have fixed themselves on me.

She returned, shivering moisture beading her forehead.

"I'm sorry," she said. "I think it was just seeing food. That and the drink."

I hoped she was right — illness wasn't something we could handle. I sat her down, gave her mineral water, and my two aspirin that had remained untouched in the pen survival kit. I moved the fish out of sight and filled a small bowl with plain noodles.

"Eat a few if you can," I said.

She toyed with a couple, then let me lead her into the bedroom. The bed was covered with quilts of satin brocade. She had started to shiver again.

"I'm sorry," I said. "It was crazy of me."

It was the kind of thing that Maddy had used to taunt me about —
the impetuousness that didn't consider the effect on others.

Her smile almost had me forgiving myself. "It's not you," she
said. "It was a nice thing to do. I am sorry I have disappointed
you."

I moved as though to help her into bed, but she waved me away.
"I'm all right," she said. "Please leave me. I know I will be better
soon."

On the way out I closed the door firmly. The fish was already
congealing under the sauce. I ate some slowly, chewing every mouth-
ful several times even though the flesh was like jelly. I knew I needed
the strength. Fish was good protein. It would have been just as good,
of course, if I had cooked the fish less elaborately. But the reason I
had done what I had done was the same as the one that had made
me start cooking in the first place. Railroad engineering much of the
time is a hard, dirty job carried out in tough, lousy places. I had long
ago decided that, like the Victorian explorer dressing for dinner, you
needed to cling to some civilized touches. Wherever you worked there
was always something that needed to be cooked — even if it was only
a hunk of frozen beef. So cooking is what I did.

I put the rest of the fish away in the refrigerator to eat later. I
washed everything and put it back where I had found it, and then I
wandered around removing other obvious traces of our presence and
my slightly damp clothes from the rock. I found a spot and buried
the fish guts. If anyone came I wanted us to be able to move quickly.
I made a bed in a corner, out of sight but within easy reach of the
main door, and I tested the brandy again, neat this time.

It took a long time, but finally I slept the sleep that comes only to
the pure in heart or the loaded with booze.

I woke several times in the night, and on each occasion forced myself
to make a series of checks. First, I peered through the shutters to see
whether anything was in sight — although why I thought my wake-
fulness should coincide with anyone's activities I do not know. Then
I looked at Ming.

She had sunk into a deep, dead sleep, hardly moving at all — the kind where an observer has to stand silent, ears straining, to catch any sign of breathing at all.

The last occasion on which I checked was soon after five, and light. This time she had moved. Since my last visit she had got out of bed, stripped and washed her clothes. They lay draped around the bedroom. There was no immediate sign of underwear, and then I realized that, still coy, she had hung it under her shirt on the back of a chair.

I stood looking down at her for several minutes. The covers were pulled high, and only the top half of her face was visible. Strange to think that underneath the quilts she was naked. Even now I had no idea of what her body looked like — her loose clothes had hidden every line.

I didn't dwell on the thought, though. Reprobate I might or might not be, but on the run at five in the morning with a mouth tasting of stale booze has roughly the same effect cold baths are said to have on boys at English public schools.

There was no excuse, though, for what I did before leaving. Oddly, to have been seen doing it would have embarrassed me more than was right. I belong to a society and a time that finds something peculiar in softness. I leaned forward, moved a hair from her forehead, and kissed her very gently.

The feeling lingered as I settled back into my corner chair and drifted back into sleep.

It was still there when the men came to check the house.

The rattle on the door handle wakened me. Even before I was fully conscious I had rolled off the chairs and into a kneeling position on the floor.

There was a second rattle, then the sound of voices. The sudden realization that they were not trying to whisper brought relief. Whoever was outside did not really expect to find anyone in the house. It was a routine check.

At that moment the bedroom door opened and Ming emerged. She was dressed, almost groomed-looking. I waved madly at her. She understood and hurried silently toward me, and we stood immobile together. I knew that unless they came inside there was no way they could see us. I could not stop worrying, though, that I had left something outside that would betray us — something small like a coin that had rolled out of my jeans as they dried on the rock.

I heard the men set off and then their voices along the side of the house. There were at least two of them.

"Who is it?" whispered Ming. "Have they found us?"

"I think it's just routine," I murmured. "They're checking the outside. If we're quiet they'll probably go." Inwardly I was not so confident. What if there was suspicion about the missing boats and they were planning to search more carefully?

There was silence, and then I heard the voices return. One of the men shouted and there was an answering cry from a distance. I wanted to look, but did not dare. Finally, there was silence again.

I waited for a long time before risking peering through a blind. I could see a launch retreating into the distance; I hoped it was theirs. I moved outside, wishing for the first time that I had kept the gun. We had got so far now that I thought I would probably have used it if I had to. There was no one. I returned.

"They've gone," I said.

Nevertheless, we kept out of sight the whole day in case they returned. Ming was better; she had been right — it was just exhaustion and tension and what we had been through. We ate the rest of the fish, and I cooked more noodles, and we drank a lot of tea.

There were still many things I wanted to ask Ming; some things I would not have minded telling her. But she kept a polite silence that was hard to break, and by the time I screwed up enough courage to try it was time to move.

13

We left in the middle of the afternoon. There was rain and sun, but I couldn't see a rainbow. I hoped that wasn't significant.

Ming had found capes and under these, with a fishing rod in full view, it might just have looked as though we belonged legitimately on the lake.

We sat out on the water for a while, getting our bearings, waiting for the right time to strike for shore. In the grayness of the day island peaks hung faint in the distance like mirages. As drizzle again turned to mist the water and the sky seemed to become one.

The lake — Ming had told me its name meant "Big Lake" and that it was originally part of a shallow sea — was busy. Barges, sailing vessels, small boats like ours, and junks crisscrossed continually, all of them seemingly suspended in space. A large cruise-barge, carrying Chinese at leisure, passed by. Its lights were blazing, illuminating windowpanes decorated with patterns of plants in translucent silver.

The passengers were probably day-trippers from Shanghai, said Ming — a reminder of how near, yet how far we were from the city. The noise of their chatter and laughter carried out to us, and remained long after the vessel had been swallowed by mist.

"This is the way I always imagined China before I came here," I whispered, waving my hand to embrace the tranquil, mysterious waters. In a parting in the mist a pagoda floated·in the distance.

"I wonder if I will find America as I expect it," said Ming.

It was the first time she had made any reference to the future. Her optimism pleased and surprised me.

"Do you know much about the States?" I asked.

She hesitated before replying, and I expected that she would say that she had received special briefings as a guide or had had access to U.S. magazines. Instead, she said: "My father told me much. He lived in America until he returned to help China. He had been in the United States since he was a boy."

There was a pause, and I was still absorbing what she had said, when she added: "My mother was American, but I do not remember if she told me anything. I was young when she died."

I kept quiet. It was a time for listening. Her mother's nationality explained why my threat to say she had cooperated had had an impact earlier — given an American background, the authorities would be much more likely to believe it. It also explained the strange, beautiful sea color of Ming's eyes — a color that seemed alien among otherwise Chinese features.

Ming began speaking so quietly it was almost as though she wanted no one to hear. "I suspect America will be like this lake today," she said. "The country my father told me about will exist but it may take me a long time to find it."

Then, with minimum pause, and the slightest rise in her voice, she added in the disquieting way she had, "What is the time? It is time for us to go? Yes?"

It was.

I drew in the line and began rowing toward the north bank, using the outline of Hui Shan Hill to its west as my marker.

We paused when the shore finally came into view, checking whether it was safe to land. Ming had warned me that this shore was busy, and that quickly became obvious.

Causeways divided lotus and water-chestnut beds; acres were dense with mulberry trees for the silkworms; and at one stage there was the discordant noise of a geese and duck farm.

We beached the boat on lush grassland near a peach orchard. I dragged it high on to the shore and left it there, the rod clearly visible as though its owner was nearby and on the point of return. Then, still wrapped in our capes, we walked until we found the road. We passed many of the convalescent homes and clinics for which the lakeside is also renowned and finally reached the hotel that Ming told me marked the nearest point of the lake before Wuhsi.

According to the map we still had a fair distance to go; about four miles. We passed peasants working in the orchards and the fields, and they stared. I tried to keep remembering Ming's reassurance that many foreigners would be attending clinics in this area — and for one to be out walking would not be unusual.

Much of the time I thought about what Ming had told me of her father and mother; I tried to prompt her to tell me more but she pretended to misunderstand my questions. Then she withdrew into herself. Without meaning to, I found myself staring at her.

Finally, she caught my look. "Is there something wrong?"

"No," I replied honestly. "Nothing's wrong."

The look of puzzlement remained.

"It just makes me feel good to look at you," I ventured.

She made no reply, acting as though she had not heard me. But moments later she began to sing, quietly to herself, a lilting, dancing song in Chinese.

As well as being a resort, Wuhsi is a large industrial city. We followed the main road right into the center, along wide, busy, tree-lined streets, and we reached the Friendship Store with over a half hour to spare. Cabs and buses for the tourists were drawn up nearby; a few cars, of privileged Chinese who could afford to shop in such a place, were parked separately.

We paused at the foot of the entrance steps.

"I will wait outside," said Ming.

"But they will think you are my interpreter," I protested.

"Tourists shopping the Friendship Stores do not need an interpreter," she said firmly. "Everyone will speak English." She smiled. "Just look acquisitive." She pointed to a row of minibuses. "I will be

177

near those," she said. "I will look like any other guide waiting for her party to return."

The store was on two floors, divided like an old-fashioned department store. There was everything from pads of writing paper at a few cents to antique jade at a price that would keep all the assistants in rice for a few hundred years. I wandered and bought a few small items — a fan, a book of poems, some bars of chocolate. The Chinese are wonderful at hand-wrapping everything as though it is a gift. After half an hour I looked as though I had bought presents for everyone back home.

I was still early. Nothing had happened so far. The waiting was hard because there was no way of knowing whether the message had got to Andrews, and if it had whether he had been able to act upon it. It was like waiting for the result of the big race when you've gambled your savings and the rest of your life's earnings on it.

I returned to the first floor. At the edge of the food section there was a short stretch of counter devoted to serving drinks. I bought a mineral water, and found a corner where I could watch Chinese cadres sorting through bottles and jars of exotic delicacies like crystallized fruit. Your view of equality, I had discovered long ago, depends upon just where you stand on the ladder of privilege.

A group of Japanese passed; they snaked in a line as though bound together by an invisible rope. They stopped and bought bottles of fizzy orange. I stepped back and positioned myself nicely beside the Westerner who had entered the section in their wake. He was short and almost as broad as he was tall, a pastiche of a tourist, in crumpled sky-blue trousers and a short-sleeved shirt. Sunglasses protruded from his breast pocket, and a Pentax and accessories swung around his neck like ritual jewelry.

"Mr. Piper," he said.

I soared with relief and excitement. I wanted to hug his fat body and tell him how great it was to see him. Instead, I said, "Don't tell me — you're from Rent A Spy."

"Swell," he said, "I come all this way, and I get a cheap comedian."

The Japanese tourists had us hemmed into a corner. "Did you arrange this?" I said.

He grinned, showing a lot of fillings. They worried me without my knowing why; perhaps I was getting sensitive. "No need," he said. "They're everywhere, like lice. You just wait around and they come crawling out."

I was glad I hadn't hugged him. Still, I didn't have to like him, just be glad he was here.

The Japanese had finished their drinks and were exchanging the empty bottles for small change that had been taken as deposits. They began to move off.

"Let's go," said my new companion. "As we near the doorway I'll leave you. You head for the exit. Someone else will take over outside."

We walked slowly in the wake of the Japanese, two Americans swapping impressions after bumping into each other a few thousand miles from home. He hadn't said anything about Ming, and I realized he probably did not know about her. I had said nothing in the note. If Andrews knew I'd taken her on the run with me, he probably thought I'd gotten rid of her. I shivered at what he might have imagined.

I felt conspicuous not talking and tried to make conversation. "Where are you from?" I asked.

He looked surprised. "The States."

The answer puzzled me. "Sure," I said, "I know that. Where in the States?"

Light dawned. "Oh yeah, where. Way back, Boston, but I've traveled a lot."

"Nice city," I said.

He gave me one of his best grins, and I caught the fillings again. I don't think I have ever seen so many in one mouth.

"Yeah, I like it."

The Japanese had stopped to examine some bottles of Chinese liqueurs.

"I used to have a friend there," I said lightly. "Used to visit him from time to time. His wife used to cook that great local pudding.

What's its name? Indian pudding, that's it. Real sweet stuff, but what a taste. Made with lots of honey, isn't it?"

We were on the move again. "Yeah, honey," he said, "that's it. As you say, great taste."

We entered the main hallway and he left me, saying loudly, "Great meeting you. Hope you enjoy the rest of your trip."

I made for the exit, starting to sweat a little. From the corner of my eye, I saw another Westerner start to follow me. He was taller but still well built and, except that he had no camera, almost identically dressed.

Outside, instead of waiting at the foot of the steps I turned right and kept moving toward the line of tour buses. I could see Ming in the near distance.

After the first bus I took a sharp turn, taking me between two vehicles. Then I turned and waited for the man following me. His face was angry and so was his voice. "You were supposed to walk out and stop the hell there," he said. "What do you think this is, some kind of game?"

"No," I said, "I guess I know it's serious." I dropped my parcels and his eyes followed them involuntarily. I had taken my army knife into my hand as I came down the steps. It remained closed. I didn't want or need the blade. I lunged with it protruding from my clenched fist. I connected with much of my weight. I felt it drive high into the space between his rib cage. Without a jacket, there was nothing to lessen the force for him. He made a cough like someone gently clearing his throat, then doubled over like a jackknife closing on a spring. I grasped the side of his head and crashed it forward on the side of the bus. My own head was pounding so much inside that I didn't know whether there had been much noise or not.

He lay still, and was silent. His passport was stuffed in his back pants pocket. I couldn't read it but I recognized the Cyrillic alphabet. I replaced it but took his money — we might need it. I rolled him under the bus, straightened and brushed myself down, and then retrieved my parcels.

Ming remained where I had last seen her. I made a detour to avoid the Japanese who were climbing on to their bus; a Chinese guide, with a clipboard, was on the step checking them aboard.

"What's the matter?" asked Ming.

"I'll tell you later," I said. I turned my eyes to the Japanese tour bus. "Find out where that's going," I said. "It must be one of the hotels. Say I missed my bus. You stayed behind to find me. Get them to give us a lift. We have to get away from here."

She did not argue or stop to ask questions. She made straight for the bus.

"They're going back to the lake," she said when she returned. "The Taihu Hotel."

"Tell them that's fine."

"I did," she said. "I said that you are staying at a clinic nearby."

"What's wrong with me?" I asked.

Despite the circumstances her mouth split in a wide grin. "Perhaps you have a persecution complex and think that people are after you," she said.

"Don't look now," I said, "but a figment of my persecuted imagination is just looking toward this bus and wondering what the hell is going on."

We had been spotted. By the man with the mouth full of fillings — fillings that reminded me of dental work I had seen in the mouth of an East European engineer I'd worked with years back.

He made a few tentative steps in our direction. We climbed aboard the bus and it began to move immediately. I looked back and saw that he was running toward a car, his camera bouncing in rhythm with his belly.

The guide came down the bus to talk to Ming, smiled a lot, and went away satisfied.

"They'll drop us at the clinic," Ming said.

I must have looked worried. "It'll be all right," she added. "We just stand waving until they drive off, and . . ." Her eyes became serious. "And what?" she continued. "Where do we go? What went wrong?"

"Go?" I said. "I don't know. The boat should still be there. Back to the island, I suppose."

I didn't know what we would do then. I had expected this to be the end. Although I had not let my thoughts linger on it, I'd anticipated that Andrews would have us met and whisked away; from that moment there would be nothing for us to do but follow orders. Now we were back on our own.

"Was it Feng Shen's men?" Ming asked. One of the Japanese turned around and I thought he had overheard us, but he simply wanted to smile. I smiled back.

"No. Unless he's employed by the Russians," I said.

"But how did you know?"

"Indian pudding," I said. I didn't try to explain, although it was very simple. Anyone who comes from Boston knows Indian pudding; although it looks weird a lot of people in New England are passionate about it. Even those who aren't know that it is not made with honey. Cornmeal, spices, and molasses, yes. But not honey.

The journey that had taken us an hour and a quarter on foot now lasted a fifth of that time. The driver was an expert at a standard tour-bus driving technique: you place your finger on the horn and keep moving.

As we neared the lake Ming moved up front to stand near the regular guide. She was planning to point out one of the clinics we had passed earlier.

She saw it, the bus stopped, and we both got off. There was a lot of head-bowing and smiling and waving. We started up the drive, planning to retrace our steps once the bus was out of sight. Then we would make for where we had left the boat; today I was hoping that the Chinese really did prove as law-abiding as all the fellow travelers said they were.

I had not anticipated one problem. The car that the phony American had made for had followed us. If I had not been so filled with my own cleverness at escaping, I would have noticed it earlier. As it was, I didn't see it until we were halfway down the drive and about to turn back. It stopped on the road and two men got out, neither of them the man I had talked with earlier. One thing was certain: they were no more tourists than he had been.

We stopped. "Who are they?" said Ming.

"The people who were waiting at the Friendship Store," I said.

"Russians?"

"I guess so." Though how they knew we would be there and how they had been able to move about China I did not know: I'd understood that since the Sino-Soviet split Russians were strictly confined to Peking.

There were more immediate things to worry about, though. Like, what did we do? The drive led straight from the road to the entrance to the clinic. There were trees on the left, and we could turn into them. But there was no way of knowing for how long they would give us cover, nor where we would have to emerge. The men from the car might be able to cut us off — with the man who had said he came from Boston there were at least three of them, perhaps four with a driver. Even more important, we were being watched by a small group of people outside the clinic. There had to be a risk that if we behaved strangely someone would call the local Public Security Bureau.

So we couldn't dive into the trees. We certainly could not turn back. We had to go on.

"What do we do?" asked Ming.

I looked over both our clothes. We looked pretty reputable, I figured; not the fugitives we so obviously were a couple of days before.

"Do they treat foreigners at this clinic?" I asked, starting to move again. The men by the car had made no attempt to follow us.

"I suppose so," she said, "Many people come here — foreign as well as Chinese, I think. All these clinics specialize in traditional as well as modern medicine."

"So tell them I need treatment," I said.

Her step faltered. "You would need an appointment," she said.

I stopped and exploded before I realized it. Afterward I rationalized it as a release of tension: for all I knew I'd just killed my second man.

183

In the thirty-three years up to coming to China the most I'd done was bloody a couple of noses. I didn't like being on the run; I didn't like what I was having to do to keep free.

"For Christ's sake," I hissed, "you're a smart lady, a key person in this setup. You've been chosen to accompany some important people; Feng Shen himself set you loose to spy on me. You *know* how to use the system, how to exert authority, scare people a bit. So scare them here. Tell them I'm someone important, that I have to be on my way to some crucial talks with people who matter. But say that I've got something wrong — say I've got this lousy pain in my gut and they've got to do something about it."

"They will want to know where we are staying, how we got here, where our car is parked."

My anger did not have to be feigned. "Say I'm staying at a government guest house or, better still, that we're passing through and we've sent the car away to return in three hours . . ." My voice trailed away. "Oh, God," I said, "you can tell them something, surely."

She smiled. "You swear a lot, David Piper," she said. "It is not polite in front of a woman. But yes, I will think of something. I will make them jump a little."

We entered the building. I wondered what the Russians would do. They might follow us, but I doubted that. They would know that we were not going anywhere except out the way we had come. In their place I would stake out the front and back, then wait.

The building was startlingly bare inside, with concrete floors and paint that was beginning to peel. A short, stocky woman in a white coat was just beginning to mount the stairs ahead of us: to my unpracticed eye she could have been either a doctor or a nurse. She paused at our entrance, answered a question from Ming with a terse statement and a pointed finger. Halfway up the stairs she spat noisily into one of the spittoons without breaking her step.

We took the corridor she had indicated. It ran in a straight line toward the rear of the building. Halfway along we found a waiting room, crowded despite the hour. Or perhaps evening was treatment time. All the patients were Chinese. Some looked as though they had been waiting a long time.

Ming spoke at length to a nurse. She went away but returned quickly. We were immediately ushered out into a passage and through a series of small rooms into a larger one. Heavy curtains served as doors. A desk stood against one wall. Prominent on it was a white acupuncture doll on a wood base. An unlit stove took up the center of the room. Two examination couches stood on either side of it. One was already occupied, but even before we sat a man was being helped down from it and out of the room. Two needles protruded from the back of his neck. I hoped no one would forget him.

A doctor joined us. He was late middle-aged, had unruly layers of thick graying hair, and inquisitive brown eyes behind half-rimmed glasses. His face had a frozen look as though he couldn't decide whether to be aggressive with us or servile. He and Ming talked for a long time while I stared at a huge diagram of an ear.

There was a pause, then Ming said to me, "I explained that you awoke this morning with a pain in your abdomen and it has got worse during the day. Doctor Lin says he is afraid from what I told him that it may be appendicitis. However, he says to tell you that in China, unlike in your country, an operation is not the first treatment. Here it is the practice to use acupuncture first. He will do this because of the urgency of your business, but he insists that you seek further help as soon as you reach your destination."

I nodded and replied through Ming just as formally — it was best to be cautious: there was a chance the man might know some English or that someone was listening outside.

I finished speaking and remembering the role I was playing I put my hand on my abdomen and grimaced. I was thinking that I was lucky about the nonoperation policy — I hadn't properly considered repercussions when I'd invented my symptoms.

On instructions relayed through Ming I exhibited my tongue, then positioned my right wrist on a small red and white cushion that the doctor placed near the edge of the desk. He touched the pulse side of my wrist with three fingers, and I felt him press lightly and then deeply with each of them in turn. That done, he repeated the process with my other wrist.

Next he led me to one of the couches. I began to strip, a Pavlovian reaction, but he signaled me to leave my clothes on and lie down. He probed around with his fingers and I gave a few grunts. Even though his expression did not change, I got a feeling he was puzzled. I wished I knew how someone with genuine appendicitis would behave.

His hands moved from my stomach and down toward my ankles without warning. He pulled up a trouser leg and pressed hard on my right shin. It seemed a fair guess that he was not probing that spot for nothing, so I let out a long shriek. That seemed to make him happier. He began talking to Ming again, smiling down at me a lot. He finished, and left the room abruptly.

"What's happening?" I said, starting to lift myself.

Ming stopped me, a hand on my shoulder. "He'll be back any moment," she said. "I think it's all right. He was suspicious when he first examined you, I think." She began to giggle. "I think your tongue was not horrid enough: you are too fit. But the fact that your shin was tender has confirmed his early diagnosis."

The doctor returned, washed his hands, and extracted four needles from a glass container. I craned my neck to look. They were each about one and a half inches long.

He spoke and Ming again translated. "He says he will insert these needles and leave them in place for half an hour," she said. "They should reduce the pain considerably."

He bent over the couch and undid the bottom buttons of my shirt. Looking up at him I realized that size too was comparative. The way he looked to me now was how I must have appeared to most Chinese.

I could smell garlic on his breath. I hadn't detected it earlier. Maybe his brief trip outside had been to chew a clove to ward off whatever evils foreign devils carried. I wasn't sure I was joking. He was nervous. I wondered whether he'd alerted anyone or made any telephone calls. I tried to remember everything I had read about acupuncture — could he paralyze me by inserting needles at key points? Such are the fantasies that you get when you are lying in a Chinese clinic pretending to be someone else so that you can escape Russians waiting outside! It didn't help that my total knowledge of acupuncture came from one barely remembered article in the *Reader's Digest*.

I did seem to recall that it was supposed to be painless. I hoped so. Everyone I guess has a special fear. With some it's rats or spiders, or having a tooth drilled, or standing on a high roof. None of those bothers me. Mine is needles. I've even been known to waive local anesthetic to avoid the hypodermic and damn the pain later.

The doctor inserted the first two needles, one each side of my navel. They barely penetrated the skin, and I felt myself relax. If this was all it was, fine. Then he pushed. First one, then the other. Fast, watching my face all the time. I suspect the first expression he saw appear was incredulity. The needles went in a good one and a quarter inches. The second would have been pain. That, like size, is comparative — and subjective. It wasn't great, body-arching agony. But it hurt, and not the way I would ever have expected. It was the sick, sudden pain that you get when you are struck hard on a muscle.

He didn't wait. He hoisted my pants legs, dabbed with the iodine pencil, and placed two more needles into the muscle halfway down my calves. The technique was the same — first the positioning into the skin, then the thrust.

At least my expression seemed to sweep away any remaining doubts. I thought I even saw sympathy. He fetched a damp cloth and wiped my forehead, talking as he did.

Ming translated. "He says he knows the pain in your stomach is great, but it should begin to ease quite soon. You must lie still and try to relax."

He left me alone, and Ming went with him. I didn't like the thought of the four needles inside me. I tried to peer around the room to distract myself. I was able to lift my head but no more. A nurse entered carrying what looked and smelled like a huge block of marijuana. For a giddy moment I thought that was what it was and it was for me. But she passed through another blue curtain and disappeared.

The doctor and Ming returned on what proved to be the first of regular couchside visits. He withdrew the needles in turn, pushing them home again almost immediately. Then he asked, "How is the pain now?"

After the second visit, I realized the right answer was "A little better" or "Much better" each time he asked. That presumably was how a real patient with a real appendicitis would have reacted. With luck it would also ensure that the needles came out in the shortest possible time.

On his sixth visit I answered, "The pain has almost gone." The sweat that still beaded my forehead might have seemed a contradiction, but he withdrew the needles — fast and with a little flourish like a magician whipping a handkerchief out of an empty hat.

I got to my feet just as the nurse returned. She still held the smoldering block. This time she was blowing on it.

Ming saw my puzzled expression. She knew what it was. "It's an herb: moxa," she explained. "Sometimes it is used for warming acupuncture points."

The doctor was talking again; he was also opening a small phial which he had taken from a drawer.

The needles he extracted this time were tiny. He gestured that I should sit and then, using tweezers, he inserted four of them into my left ear. He paused briefly to admire his work, then covered it with adhesive tape.

He talked as he worked, and Ming was having to work hard not to let amusement into her voice. "Doctor Lin says that normally he would want to see you again in the morning. As you must travel tonight, the needles he has placed in your ear will help until you are able to see another doctor. He says you should not get the ear wet. And also that you should try not to exert yourself."

He opened the curtain and called. The nurse returned, without her moxa this time. "He says that if we follow her she will show us somewhere to wait until the car returns."

I thanked him as much as I could. The nurse led us back into the hallway and toward the staircase. Before she could object I darted past a small group of parked wheelchairs and looked out of the front door. The car had gone from the end of the drive, but that meant little. We had been inside the clinic for about an hour. Most likely they had parked farther along the road and returned on foot.

The nurse was calling to me, and I hurried back. She led us to a room at the back of the building on the second floor. It was at the end of a long corridor and to get there we had to squeeze past a large bin of used laundry which looked as though it had been abandoned until morning.

There was tea waiting in the room and the nurse poured. She seemed reluctant to go. I picked up the cup and drank, filtering the leaves with my lips. I walked to the window and looked out. The room overlooked gardens and, then, the lake. It was galling to think that we were only half an hour from where we had left the boat.

The garden was full of huge shadows. There were many places one of our pursuers could have concealed himself. There was also a lot of open ground between the house and the lakeside if we tried to leave that way. The situation was not promising.

Finally the nurse left. I moved back from the window. If there was anyone watching the building, I had confirmed we were inside. But then they knew that.

I began to run through ideas of how we might get out of the clinic. I toyed with dressing up as a doctor — there were probably coats in the laundry bin we had passed. My height was against that. And anyone moving outside at this time would be immediately suspect. Particularly if he was heading toward the lakeside.

I poured more tea, hoping that it would give me some kind of inspiration. Then I realized I had already hit upon the key. Anyone or anything moving outside would be suspect! I had to capitalize on that fact.

"Wait," I said to Ming, making for the door. The look of puzzled concern was still on her face when I returned two minutes later.

I dropped the bundle in front of her — used clothing and bed linen I'd taken from the basket. I sorted through and found a coat and white hat which looked half clean.

"Put them on," I said.

Ming recoiled, but I thrust them toward her, and finally she took them and began to do as I ordered.

I tied the rest of the clothes into two bundles, one long and thin, the other smaller and rounder. Ming was dressed in the coat and hat now; one was too small, the other too long, but that would not matter — the Chinese aren't snappy dressers, and this wasn't the Mayo Clinic. Clutching my bundles, I ushered her outside, down the stairs, and into the corridor that faced the main door. We paused to confirm it was clear and then I hurried over to the wheelchairs.

Even with my jacket draped around the bottom of the two bundles they did not look much like a person sitting in a wheelchair. But that was close to and in reasonable light. Outside, from a distance, I hoped it would be very different. Anyway, I told myself, I had something extra going for the deception — people generally see what they expect to see. Whoever was watching the back of the clinic knew there were two people, a Chinese woman and me. When he saw a woman dressed as a nurse pushing a wheelchair with a slumped figure in it toward the lakeside, I gambled he would have no doubt that's what he saw.

We took the corridor that ran through to the rear of the clinic. We passed the turn-off to the waiting room; it was empty now. The design of the building was basic. The passage led to a door that opened directly onto the garden.

The sky was darkening quickly now. Nevertheless I would have liked to have waited longer. That, though, was too dangerous — there was no knowing how long it would be before someone visited the room we had left.

"Walk straight toward the lake," I said. "Then turn right and keep going."

"You're staying here?" Her voice was worried.

"I'll be close behind you," I said. "I'm betting that anyone who is there will think that it's me in the wheelchair. He won't do anything until you are out of sight of the clinic. They want us alive, so you'll be safe. By then I'll be near."

I was taking a lot of gambles, most of them with her life, but if I stopped to consider that too carefully we would both be doomed.

"I'm afraid," she said softly, and not for the first time I wanted to hold her.

"Me too," I said. Then I realized that the truth was probably poor

190

encouragement so I put on my best tough-guy act and added, "And that's good — it'll make me move faster."

By the time she was halfway to the lakeside I had plotted my route. I hoped any eyes would be concentrated on her. I ran quickly, first skirting the building and then making a dash for my first cover, some cassia shrubs.

I paused until Ming and the wheelchair were moving parallel to the lake. The obvious hiding place for anyone watching Ming was the lakeside itself where the grass was high. I thought I saw movement there, and decided I had to start my dash for the trees. Once there I kept moving, fast enough, I hoped, to get close to Ming before she moved out of sight of the clinic and thus entered the danger zone; slowly enough to keep down the noise.

I reached the edge of the trees and dropped into a crouching position. Ming's back was about twenty yards ahead of me; she was having to struggle to keep the wheelchair moving because the lakeside path was rutted.

Although I had anticipated it and had, in fact, planned for it, I could hardly believe the presence of the man who darted into view between me and Ming. His back was toward me.

"Stop! I have a gun." The words were in English. He did believe I was in the chair.

The light had almost gone now and the man's back was silhouetted against distant mountains. I was about to rush him when I saw that although he had his back to me he really did have a gun. I reached down around my feet. The best of the nearby broken branches wasn't much, but it was tougher than my flesh. I weighed it in my hand and then charged.

He began to move, alerted by the yell I uttered. Maddy used to make similar sounds when she practiced her karate — she said it paralyzed attackers. I thought I might as well try it; I knew I couldn't disguise the sound of my approach on the uneven ground. At the same time I began to swing the branch like a club. It caught him across the face. We collided and he fell back, trying to get his arms around me. He hit the ground with me on top of him. I recognized him as he went down: the man I had already knocked unconscious outside the Friendship Store. The sight of me, the memory of what had happened, drove him to a frenzy, giving him extra strength. We began to roll. He kept trying to smash his forehead into my face, but I kept my head close against him so that he had no momentum.

Still rolling, we reached the high grass. I caught a flash of water and thought, incongruously, that whatever happened I mustn't get my ear wet. His strength was telling. He managed to get on top; one of his hands was ripping at my hair, the other was clamped over my mouth and nose, trying to choke off air. I managed to break free just long enough to yell to Ming, "Get his gun!" and then I was struggling to avoid suffocation again.

Long, long ago, getting drunk with a madman of an Irish construction boss in the Philippines, I received a distillation of his lifetime's barroom fighting experience.

"No matter how tough they are," he had said, "you can always break their little finger. Bend it properly, and it just goes snap."

What he had not mentioned was the difficulty of keeping hold of slippery skin. But once you managed that, he was right. I both felt and heard the crack. It was followed by a piercing scream of pain. I swung myself above him, reversing our positions. Ming was hovering over us, holding the gun, and I took it from her and used it like a club until he was still.

Afterward I lay sobbing into the damp grass. When I looked up, Ming was motionless. With the white of her face and the robe she could have been a statue.

"We've got to get away from here," I said, dragging myself to my knees.

"Is he dead?"

I felt for his pulse, but couldn't find it. That was not conclusive; my hands were shaking and all of me felt heavy and numbed.

Still, I lied; I thought it would make Ming feel better. "He's all right," I said. Even to me it sounded like someone in a bad Western.

I staggered upright and tried to drag him to the trees, but he was too heavy. I rolled him deeper into the grass. It could only be a short time before someone started looking for us anyway. The clinic would be suspicious that our car had not returned — even if they had not yet found us missing from the room in which we had been told to wait.

I looked back in the direction of the clinic. There was no sight or sound of unusual activity — as yet.

I risked a few more seconds to extract the now battered map from inside my shirt. I crouched over it, Ming beside me, shielding the light from my flashlight with my body.

Jabbing with my finger at a spot on the far side of the lake, I said, "If I get us there, could you find your uncle's village?"

She searched until she found a town she recognized. "If we reached there," she said, "yes, I could find it."

"And his house?"

No hesitation. "Of course."

We found the boat twenty minutes later. The pole and the fishing rod were as we had left them.

This time I used the motor. Speed, not stealth, was our greatest hope now.

14

I t took most of the night to cross the lake. The sky was clear and there was no mist. It made navigation easy, but it also meant that we were clearly visible. Each time we neared an island, I worked out how we could use it for cover if need be. But the whole crossing was uneventful. We zoomed on like some noisy insect, and during the whole journey saw only three boats, all large working vessels, well to our south.

We talked little on the crossing. Ming was certain that the village was no more than four or five miles from the lake. Before that, though, we had to find the town that would give her her bearings.

Our first task on reaching the far shore was to sink the boat. I managed to hammer a small hole, using the short blade on my knife and a rock. Then I enlarged it, using the wood-saw blade. It is only inches long, but incredibly effective. Finally we piled the boat high with stones and pushed it out from the store. It filled and vanished from view.

The second was to find somewhere to spend the day. Our luck held. We found a hut that once must have been used by fishermen. Even now, half collapsed, it provided us with the cover we needed. We ate the chocolate I had bought at the store; there was water from the lake. Neither of us slept much, though, and never at the same time.

Throughout the day one question kept nagging at me: how the Russians had known of my whereabouts. The answer, when it came, was devastatingly obvious. I checked with Ming my understanding that Russians were confined to Peking. "It was true," she said. "They are still isolated from the people, but this last year they have been allowed to travel. Mostly of course it is officials who are located at the embassy and their families. There are a great number of them still, I think at least five hundred. But there have also been some from outside."

We fell silent, and I considered the irony. A few hundred Russians, only a percentage of them traveling outside Peking at any time, and I had chanced upon them when I had passed my message for transmission to Andrews.

I had handed the note to a Russian! I remembered how I had thought the group looked like Polish Americans. A chance in how many million? And I'd drawn it!

We left as soon as it was dark. The railroad going east from Wuhu ran near the shore, and we used this to navigate. We finally found the village only an hour before dawn. Ming left me crouched against the walls of an outside latrine on the edge of fields while she disappeared for what seemed a terrifying long time.

When she returned there was a man with her. He led the way to the cluster of houses. He moved quickly and did not talk. His feet were bare.

We passed a standpipe. I quickly took in a dirt road and a straggle of brick houses, and then we were being ushered inside one, and the door locked behind us.

The house had two floors. I glanced at the stone staircase as we entered and Ming understood my look. "Don't worry," she said. "He lives alone."

For one man, it was a lot of space by Chinese standards. In a town, a house this size could easily be shared by a number of families. Perhaps it reflected his standing in the village.

The main room was crammed with objects. There were three stuffed easy chairs, five upright chairs, a table, a bulky chest of drawers, a large, old-fashioned radio, a number of storage boxes stacked on top of each other, and mounds of books and old newspapers piled high on the floor. Photographs of the Chairman and Stalin were on the wall. One corner of the table was set neatly with writing materials. Her uncle saw that I was staring at them and he spoke quickly. Ming translated: "He says he is engaged in writing a history of the commune. He adds that it is a lengthy task because every time there is a change in the political climate in Peking the history changes again."

I noted his smile and returned it. "Tell him he has a job for a lifetime then."

Ming translated and his smile broadened. "Ten lifetimes," he replied.

I knew from Ming that her uncle — Wen Chang-tu — was in his late sixties. I would have found it impossible to guess. There was an agelessness about him. His head was completely bald and crossed with a darkened scar. His body was so thin that it would have looked wasted but for knots of muscle. Ming had told me that he was a building administrator before being sent to the country for reeducation. It was hard to believe that now. Here was a man who had evolved to survive his surroundings.

He continued talking, but it was obvious that it was small talk or family chat and Ming did not translate. Without stopping, he rummaged in a cupboard and produced a bottle of vodka and some tiny, ornate glasses. The foil around the bottle cap had rusted. Wen exaggerated his movements as he began to open it; he was making it clear that this was a moment of special importance. He drew the cork, sniffed the liquid, and poured two glasses. He began to put down the bottle, paused, then poured a third glass.

He handed them around, then held his glass outstretched in a silent toast before tossing back the drink. I did the same, remaining equally silent. He poured me a second measure, and he and Ming left the room. They returned minutes later with tea and small dishes of cold food.

That, and the vodka, made me want to sleep. Ming and her uncle continued their conversation; their voices became a blur, a metronome of sound. It was an effort not to close my eyes.

At last they must have gotten to practical things because Ming brought me into the conversation and began to translate.

"I have told him that you are being pursued and must get out of the country. I have asked him if he can help. He says that he will, but soon we must sleep. He says that we are safe here. No one comes, not even to clean; he does that. If there are visitors there will be warning, and anyone who comes will only enter this room. Soon he will take us upstairs. We are to stay there. Tomorrow, he says, our problem can be considered. He asks if that is acceptable."

It was.

Then I rememberd the telephone call we had tried to make; I asked Ming to find out what had happened.

She had already asked. "He says not to worry. He went to the telephone but when he finally arrived the line was dead. He told everyone that it was a lousy service, and that he guessed his niece would write. He does not think anyone was suspicious. Besides, he says, this is a tight community, only a few dozen people. People have no wish to involve themselves with what happens outside. They have learned from experience that it can be dangerous."

Wen led us upstairs soon afterward. The narrow staircase opened directly into a single room. There was one small window, heavily curtained. Light came from a single bare bulb. Again there were books piled on the floor. The most amazing object, though, was the bed — a four-poster, black-lacquered, draped in heavy embroidered silk. Wen must have sensed my surprise, but he said nothing.

Instead he pressed the bottle of vodka into my hand; I had not even noticed he was carrying it. Ming translated. "He says you may have problems sleeping after such a journey. He has always found a drink or two helps."

I took it and struggled to put together a simple sentence in Chinese with some of the few words I had picked up.

"*Duo xie Tong Zhi Wen,*" I said. Many thanks, Comrade Wen.

He inclined his head, and retreated down the stairs almost immediately, leaving us alone.

I looked around, and said, "We both sleep here?"

"He apologized for that," said Ming. "He said it would not be the first time that revolutionary comrades had been forced to share a sleeping place together."

Still clothed except for her shoes, Ming climbed into the bed.

"You can place a pillow in the center of the bed or sleep on the floor if you are afraid for my honor," she said.

While I was still absorbing the shock of hearing her speak in such a way, she lifted her head, reached out, and took the vodka from me. She drank from the bottle and returned it.

"If I need protection tonight, then surely you Americans are men among men." The smile remained on her face, and a minute later I realized she was already asleep.

The sounds of the village coming alive kept me awake for a long time despite my tiredness. I found the softness of the bed difficult to adjust to after sleeping on hard ground.

Then I did sleep and when I awoke it was shortly after eleven o'clock. Outside I could hear strident music from a radio.

I padded toward the window, taking care not to wake Ming, and cautiously peered from behind the curtain. The standpipe was to the extreme of my vision in one direction; two women were kneeling by it, scrubbing clothes on the ground. Ahead and to my right I could see three houses, all of the same fired-brick and thatched-roof construction. The street was unpaved and had narrow, open drains. There was straw strewn about — for the animals, I guessed, although I had heard none. A woman, bent with years, padded into view, and I retreated in case she lifted her eyes.

Wen must have been into the room while we slept because there was a bowl of cold water, soap, and a towel. There was also what looked like porridge, some cold steamed rolls, a flask of boiled water, tea, and cups. I went to the top of the stairs and listened. There was no sound. Wen had to be out.

Like Ming, I had slept fully clothed. I now removed my shirt and washed. I examined the points on my stomach and legs where the acupuncture needles had penetrated. There were small bruises and the fading yellow of iodine. I felt my ear. The tape was still in place. I decided to leave the needles for now — they were sterile and could do no harm.

Still clad only in my jeans, I began to eat slowly and steadily, starting with the porridge, which was bitter and watery but filling.

Ming started to stir, and I poured hot water over tea in the second of the cups and carried it over to her.

Her eyes were open. "Good morning," I said.

She pulled herself up, took the cup, but averted her eyes.

"What's the matter?" I asked puzzled.

"There is nothing the matter." But she turned her head away.

"I can see there is. Please tell me." I felt gauche, adolescent. I had done something wrong, but because of my naiveté I did not know what.

"Seriously, there is nothing."

But then I understood. "Christ," I said. "We're sleeping in the same room, in the same bed."

Nevertheless, I got my shirt and pulled it on. "Is that better?"

But I knew that was what it was. It had not been proper for me to walk around in front of her naked, even from the waist upward.

Suddenly she smiled and got out of bed. I turned my back on her while she washed, then sat facing her as she ate.

As soon as she had finished she pointed to our clothes. "We cannot wear these." She stood and fussed over the bed, which had been soiled by our trousers. The headlong rush since we had left the lake had left them stained with mud. They were no worse than they had been in the early days after we had left Nanking, but now that we were in her uncle's house . . .

"I guess we'll have to live with them for a while," I said.

"Rubbish! We can't stay in these. We'll . . . we'll . . . smell!"

I burst out laughing. We were on the run for our lives and she worried about our clothes.

199

She ignored me. "Besides, it is unhealthy. All I have to do is go downstairs where there is a barrel of water. I will take no time. I cannot be seen from the street." Obvioiusly delighted with her decision, she added, "Take off your clothes. You can wear a sheet."

"You don't think that's as bad as a naked chest?"

Her expression became serious. "That is different." She did not explain, but I thought I understood: not wearing a shirt had meant I did not think her feelings were worth considering; it had been an insult.

"Okay." I began to strip. "You'd better turn around."

She gathered the clothes, leaving me alone.

I used her absence to wash the rest of me. Finished, I wrapped the sheet tightly around me and settled down to drink more tea. I was suddenly anxious for Ming's return. I wanted to talk.

All the sounds seemed to come at once. The girl's light step on the stairs; the door below opening and closing with a bang; the gasp.

I was on the stairs beside Ming before I even realized I was moving.

Wen was inside the front doorway. He was not alone.

15

There was no time for anyone to scream. Afterward I was astonished and horrified by my speed and my violence.

I forced Ming out of the way, leaped the final few steps, and let the momentum carry me into the man at full force. My shoulder sent him hurtling back into the closed door.

In almost the same movement, I spun him around and got my forearm in a lock across his windpipe. I would have killed him without a doubt had not Wen and then Ming dragged at me and kept shouting.

Ming's voice finally penetrated. "My uncle says he's all right, a friend. Let him go!"

Finally I relaxed my grasp and staggered back. The man I had attacked was leaning against the wall, trying to suck down air. His throat was deep red.

"Put cold water on it," I gasped. "Do it before it swells."

Wen helped him toward the water barrel. I realized I was naked and picked up the sheet. Ming was staring into nowhere with glazed eyes. There was blood at the corner of her mouth.

"What is it?" I asked. "What happened to you?" I stepped forward, but she retreated so as to avoid me.

"It's nothing," she said. "I fell. I struck my mouth."

Wen returned, checked through the window that no one outside had been alerted by the noise, and then gestured for me to follow him upstairs.

He disregarded my presence until Ming and the man joined us a few minutes later. Both took up positions well away from me.

"I do not know how to say it," I began at last. "Could you explain that I thought it was someone I had to fear? I acted without thinking, afraid that if I did not he would cry out for help."

Ming did not translate. Instead, she said, "You thought my uncle would betray us?" Her tone was angry.

"No, no." I rubbed my forehead. "I thought it was someone your uncle had to bring home, someone he would have kept downstairs, someone who would have been none the wiser about us if we had stayed in this room as he ordered. Instead, there you were in full view . . ."

This time she translated and at great length. I hoped she was embellishing my explanation, working at it, being my advocate. If these people turned against me, I was finished.

Gradually I saw the men relax. Wen's companion began to nod, then he said something and the others laughed.

"What did he say?"

"He said that he understands, but he is not sure his wife will if his throat swells. Although she may welcome the fact that he cannot interrupt her . . ."

Like the others, I grasped the chance to relieve the tension, and I laughed for a long time. Then I waited, silent, embarrassed again, while Wen left to fetch tea and Ming and the man conversed formally together.

The man was young, perhaps in his late twenties, no taller than Wen, but where there was muscle on the older man, here there was fat. Not the fat of a large frame, but the soft, easy fat of indulgence. His glasses, which I was relieved to see were unbroken, had gold rims and tinted glass. His jacket was well cut, and he wore an expensive-looking wristwatch. It was not hard to place him as someone who worked at a desk or with his mind, doing not too badly, perhaps earning money on the side from favors dispensed. I remembered a line from my briefing in New York, "In China you work, or you work for the party." This man worked for the party.

My immediate instincts were not to trust him; but I did not see Wen as a fool, nor really as someone out to betray me (something he could easily have done by now had he wished, without this charade).

Wen returned, and we drank tea and made small talk. The man's name, it emerged, was Ho Teng-po. At the proper time the tone of the conversation changed.

Ming translated with a more formal note in her voice.

"Mr. Ho is a good friend whom my uncle has known since he was little more than a boy.

"Fortuitously he had to visit the village today over an interpretation of the party's plans; he also visited my uncle's home to look at the latest progress on his history of the commune. It is fortuitous because my uncle had meant to approach him over your problem."

There was a long pause and I sensed I was expected to speak. I said, "And he can help?" It was too abrupt; impolite. But Wen answered. Ming translated:

"My uncle says Mr. Ho has friends who bring in goods — things that are in short supply but for which there is a large demand. My uncle says that if it were not for the way our leaders now run affairs it would not be necessary. People would have what they want here." She paused as though considering whether she needed to translate the rest. Finally she added, "He says that such imports are not necessary in the Soviet Union where there are not such shortages." I stared at Wen but saw nothing in his face but sincerity. The man lived in a dream world. The Russians with whom he had worked in the 1950s had fed him propaganda and over the years since it had grown and grown, sustaining him in his loneliness.

Ming began speaking again, and the words jerked me back to the present. "My uncle says that just as Mr. Ho's friends bring things in they could take things out."

Ho must have gauged the point the translation had reached because he interjected, laughing, and Ming again translated, "He says he is not sure they have ever wanted to take anything out before."

"Ask him why." I caught her eye. "I know it's a crude question, but wrap it up as politely as you can. Ask him why they would do it."

The conversation with Ho continued for a long time before she translated his answer. "He says they would do it as a favor to him. And he would do it as a favor for his friend, my uncle."

"What else?"

"This is not the time."

"Please. I know that I am being rude. You can explain it is my barbarian way, but I want to know it all."

It was obvious that neither of the men liked what they sensed was happening. Wen busied himself pouring more hot water in the tea, Ho set his mouth in a fixed smile and giggled when he finally talked.

"Well?" I prompted.

"Mr. Ho says that his friends' friends may welcome some contribution to their costs, but that is something you could discuss with them direct. He for his part would be no more than a go-between. You must understand that he must convince them you are to be trusted. They put a lot at risk."

This time I was even more blunt, and I had to insist forcibly before my question was put.

"I have little money. How would I pay them?"

The embarrassment was open now. I wondered how many bad points I was accumulating.

The answer was less than specific, but enough to satisfy me.

"He says he does not know such things. He can only imagine they can be arranged. Perhaps, for example — and he is only guessing — you could write a letter for your bankers which they could present on arrival. He imagines your destination would be Hong Kong."

While Ming and I are still in their hands, I thought. A kind of self-imposed kidnap situation. Nevertheless, the practicality of such a scheme satisfied me.

There were many more questions I would have liked to have asked, but I knew I had gone as far as was possible. I forced myself to join in the small talk, smiled and nodded a lot and thanked Ho effusively when he left.

Moments later I heard the front door open and close again on Wen and Ho.

I turned toward Ming to speak, but she had her back to me. I was aware of her rebuff and suddenly felt very alone.

That night I made a bed on the floor. Ming did not protest; the chill that hung between us had not lifted. Wen had returned only briefly — there was an evening meeting he had to attend. Now, at eleven, I heard him downstairs, but I lacked the courage to join him and he did not come up.

Ming was asleep. I was not only awake but bursting with impatience to get moving again. The fact that something might be under way should have helped. Instead it was having the opposite effect, making me resent the lack of activity. The claustrophobia of the room, accentuated by Ming's hostility, made it worse.

I slid out of my improvised bed and switched on the light. Its beam was so weak I doubted it would disturb Ming. In my desperation for distraction I began to search through the nearest pile of books, vainly hoping there might be something I could understand. Not all the books, I found, were Chinese. Many were in Russian. Wen must have managed to hold on to them for over twenty years; I suspected that at times during that period he would have had to use a better hiding place than this.

One thick volume was obviously a Russian-Chinese dictionary. For lack of other stimulus, I started looking up Russian words I recalled from my time in Egypt after the Soviets left.

I soon tired of the pointlessness of it. Ming began to move restlessly and then to talk softly to herself. As I watched she twisted violently and would have fallen off the bed if I had not stepped forward and restrained her with one hand. She relaxed again, and I began to retreat, afraid now that I would waken her. It was too late.

"What is the matter?" she asked.

I continued to move back lest she should think I threatened her. "You had a nightmare. I thought you would fall out of bed."

"I woke you?" She pulled herself into a sitting position. Her hair, free of its bun, ran wild over her face, but she made no attempt to brush it back.

"I was awake. I couldn't sleep." I pointed vaguely toward the floor. "I was looking through the books. Hoping there was something I could read." Her eyes drew me; they were huge with wakening.

"They're all in Chinese."

"A lot are in Russian." I laughed softly. "But I can't read that either."

She looked surprised through her sleepiness. "I would have thought he would have destroyed them."

"He probably feels that keeping them up here is enough."

She lifted her hand to touch the corner of her mouth. The tip of her finger came away red. The cut on her lip was bleeding again. It was a small gash but in an awkward place, and talking had reopened it.

I found my hankerchief, but it was too grimy. I wet the corner of one of the towels and handed it to her.

"I'm sorry," I said. "I didn't mean to hurt you." I stepped toward her. "Here, let me do it."

Her head moved back instinctively.

"It's all right." I smiled. "I have my shirt on."

She smiled too, so I sat on the edge of the bed and carefully dabbed at the cut until I was satisfied that the bleeding had stopped. I started to rise and noticed her eyes again. All the laughter had gone. They were deep, serious, questioning.

I remained still, frozen. The silence grew increasingly heavy. Then, slowly so as not to frighten her but also to give her time to end the spell if she wished, I leaned forward and kissed the edge of her mouth.

"My father used to kiss away my hurt like that when I was little," she said, not moving.

I leaned forward again and brushed my lips on her full mouth. She did not respond but nor did she draw away. We stared at each other transfixed; her eyes were wider than ever, like a startled animal.

206

"I am afraid we are going to die," she said finally.

"All the more reason for this, then," I said, and moved my mouth on hers again. This time she lifted her arms, and when we had kissed she drew my head to her shoulder.

We were cautious with each other the following day as though the previous night had not happened. Not that much had taken place. I had lain with my head cradled on her shoulder as we drifted in and out of sleep. That was all. But we both knew it was a big step and that we could never go back.

It was not something we were admitting, though. Even when I found a mirror and began extracting the needles from my ear with tweezers from my knife, she kept her distance, although her help would have made the task much easier.

Oddly, this artificial gulf made it possible for me to ask some of the questions I had wanted to ask for a long time.

Her father, it developed under questioning, had been taken to the United States as a boy, had gone to a university, and had married there. When Ming was three, her mother had died; a year later her father returned to China. He had been welcomed and given a prestigious job.

As though he resented all the years he had spent in America and wished to atone for his betrayal, her father had raised Ming to hate the United States and its materialism. Perversely, though, he had taught her English.

During the Cultural Revolution, when many academics and intellectuals had been hounded, humbled, beaten, he had survived virtually untouched — his speciality was seismology and it was one of the few disciplines allowed to continue because of its possible practical value in predicting earthquakes.

Those years had affected him, though — more through what he had seen happen to colleagues than what happened to him. She was still small then, but remembered his telling her one story — he had spoken it almost to himself in a tone that mixed disbelief and a guilt that he was untouched but had not helped. A colleague at another institute, downgraded from heading a department to having to carry out the most menial manual work, had suddenly and unexpectedly been reinstated. His "rehabilitation" had coincided with the visit of a very important foreigner. Ming's father, who had been present, had celebrated quietly with his old friend. The following day — within hours of the foreigner's departure — the man was back cleaning corridors. It had all been a carefully orchestrated charade for the benefit of the visitor — it was important that he should carry home the message that all was normal at the institute despite reports leaking abroad. Two days later the man hanged himself. For the last two years of his life Ming's father had continued outwardly as though nothing had changed. To Ming, however, he began speaking of America in a different way, recalling the good, not just the bad. His talk verged often on the treasonable. For her it was exciting — and bewildering and frightening because she had been taught by her teachers and the whole propaganda apparatus of the State that if necessary you reported your parents' shortcomings as readily as anyone else's.

"He said things like the individual being important. To you that may seem nothing. But from childhood we are taught that it is working as a team that matters. All the prizes at school are for being a good member of a group. We used to recite a poem aloud. I still know every word."

She began to recite it, her head lowered as though shy.

> *I would like to be a tiny screw*
> *So that they can put me where they want and screw*
> *   me in tightly*
> *Whether on the arm of a powerful crane*
> *Or in the simplest wheel.*
>
> *Although I cannot be a machine all alone*
> *Although I can do nothing alone*
> *I can serve my country and the people even so.*
> *I know that if I stay in the background I shall soon*
> *Be nothing but a piece of rusty metal.*

"There is more," she said. "My father tried to teach me to laugh at such sentiments, but I am not sure he believed what he said completely. Nor that he had something to put in its place." She paused. "I think he converted from one faith to another and found no real truth in either."

As Ming spoke I sensed one reason for her mood this morning was that I aroused in her some of the contradictory feelings that her father had bequeathed to her.

She questioned me too, but much more indirectly.

"We read that in America people often marry and divorce casually."

I laughed, trying to lighten the atmosphere. "You mean have I married and divorced casually a lot of times?"

Her embarrassment was genuine. Not, I think, because I was wrong, but because I had been bad-mannered enough to tell her I knew what she was asking.

She protested, but I answered nevertheless. "Never married, never divorced," I said. "There are people like that in America." I paused. "My parents had been married thirty-six years when my father died."

She was looking away and I pressed on. I felt a need to tell her the rest of it. If I didn't I had a feeling it would never be said. "I did live with a girl," I said. "I guess that's pretty well the same as being married. It ended a little while back."

I thought she was going to remain silent, but she said, "Is that common in America, for two people to live together without marrying?"

"A lot of people do," I said. Then afraid that she would get the impression that America was all big city mores, I added, "But not all of them. Most people still marry."

"I think that is right," she said.

There was silence then, one that weighed more heavily as the day progressed. It did not break until the evening when Wen returned and called for Ming. Minutes later she reentered the upstairs room, and I could tell she had good news.

"My uncle says they will take us, not tomorrow, but the day after. That is not long."

An hour later we were allowed downstairs. We had been forced to wait until a neighbor delivered food for Wen. It was already on the table — one large bowl of rice, another like thick stew.

There was enough for all of us; I suspected it was meant to last Wen more than one day, but I ate. It looked unappetizing but tasted good. The main ingredients seemed to be cabbage and eggplant and small pieces of fat pork.

We finished quickly, Wen poured drinks from an unlabeled bottle of white spirit, and then he detailed the escape plan. Wen's knowledge did not extend far. The following night we would be moved to an outbuilding, and collected from there at dawn. From then on everything would be taken care of. As Ho had thought, our final destination was Hong Kong.

Ming returned to the room before me, leaving me to look through books of photographs that Wen had produced. I followed her fifteen minutes later, part of me anticipating that she had gone upstairs first to prepare herself . . .

The moment I entered the room I realized that my thoughts were fantasy. The light was still on, but Ming was in bed, face turned into the mattress, either asleep or feigning sleep.

I kicked off my shoes and retrieved the vodka bottle Wen had given me the previous night. I sat on the bed and drank deep. I needed sleep — there would be little the following night — but I was restless. Partly it was Ming's presence. God! How could she sleep so well?

I forced my mind away from her and upon Wen and the plans for our escape. But that was no help — there were too many unknown questions and they triggered off a score of fears. Even if I could trust Wen, how did I know I could trust the others. Ming too was worried. *"I am afraid we are going to die."*

Deciding that I must sleep, I corked the bottle, eased myself off the bed and tiptoed across to the light switch. I tripped over a book, bit back a curse, and waited to make sure I had not wakened Ming.

It was the Russian-Chinese dictionary. I picked it up and then, the light momentarily forgotten, I slumped on the nearest stool and flipped the pages, admiring the shapes of the Cyrillic script and the ideographs beside them.

My eyes blurred and my head began to reel with the vodka and with tiredness. A phrase began to sing in my head; it started as a whisper and grew louder.

Tom Carr. Tom Carr. Tom Carr.

Those words that the Russian Yakov was supposed to have said as he lay dying. So long ago it could have been another age.

As a distraction I looked up *Tomka*.

Nothing. I began to play with variations of the word.

Momka. Romka. Domka.

Then, changing the vowel, *Mumka, Rumka* . . .

I stopped at *Sumka*.

There it was, with ideograph.

I felt I had to wake Ming, discover whether I had found anything. Afterward I told myself it was only an excuse. Still, afraid of her reaction, I had to pretend it was all very serious.

Through half-open eyes she stared at the book, and then she translated in a voice husky with sleep.

"Case," she said. "It means a case. It says more. It is a special sort of case, one that opens in the middle."

She saw my face.

"What is it?" she asked.

I said nothing. But I remembered.

"What is it?" she repeated. She was wide awake. Minutes had passed in silence. I had moved away from the bed again and was seated on a stool, the book on my lap but my eyes not seeing anything in the room.

I was recalling the hotel room in Peking the night that Yakov had arrived. The picture in my mind changed — it was the same room but the way it was on my return from the embassy. Yakov had gone. The room was in chaos. I saw myself standing inside the doorway, frozen at the sight in front of me.

I kept the same picture in my mind, but changed the focus. As though using a magnifying glass, I studied the image of myself. My face was a mixture of shock, anger, and disbelief; my body was taut with surprise and fear; one hand had begun to rise, instinctively protective . . .

But the other hand. What was that doing? I zoned in even closer. The arm was extended straight down beside me. Unlike the other, it had not moved. It had its own job to do. Instinct had come into play here too. I could see the knuckles tightened, sense the tenseness in the muscles of the forearm . . .

My hand was protecting the case in my left hand.

The case became the object of all my attention. Black, an ordinary enough color. Heavy, because it was filled with all my papers and books. A hand case that went everywhere with me — but a slightly special-looking one: soft sides and hinged so as to open flat into two equal compartments. The English had a name for it: Gladstone bag after the nineteenth-century statesman. So had the Russians. They just called it *Sumka*.

Suddenly it was evident why I had become the focus of everyone's attention.

Sumka. So obvious they had all overlooked it. The one item that had been in the room overnight with Yakov, but not there when his pursuers had found him the following morning. Because it had been with me.

Sumka. Sometime during the night while I was sleeping fitfully Yakov had reached out for the case and secreted on it or in it a message or document of some sort.

But was that possible? Until I had fled in Nanking I had continued using it. I had seen nothing. But I realized immediately that meant little — provided that the items were small enough there were hiding places that I would never have chanced upon. The bag was old. How many times had I lost a pen through a slit in the lining, only to stumble upon it much later? The bottom of the bag, too, afforded a possible hiding place — it was double-layered for strength with, I imagined, space between the layers for something flat.

I lifted my head and looked at Ming. Her face was puzzled but she kept silent. I moved and sat on the bed and began to laugh.

"I think I know where it is," I said.

"Where what is?"

My laughter became more hysterical. Then I stopped. "I don't know what," I said. "Only where." And I explained.

At the end, she said, "But you don't know. It's only a guess."

"No," I said firmly. "I *know*. It's the only thing that makes any sense. He had to have something with him. No one has found it. They think he handed it to me, or told me where it could be found. That's why all this thing started. Where else could he have put it?"

My eyes remained on her, and then I realized that her look was not one of disbelief but of not wanting to believe. She wanted nothing to disturb plans that had now been made.

Her words confirmed that I was right. "It's interesting," she said. "But too late now. Your case is with your other belongings which you left in Nanking."

She got out of bed and poured more hot water on the leaves in her cup. I could see she was flustered. "They may all be back in Peking now. They may even be back in the United States. If they have said that you are dead, which I think they may have done, your belongings will have been returned. To the next of kin. Is that the phrase? Isn't that what they do?"

I found the near-empty vodka bottle, poured the remainder into my cup, and sipped, disregarding her look of disapproval. Until that moment I had not thought what I would do about my discovery; realization had been an end in its own right. Ming's words made me think about the present whereabouts of the case. The more I did, the more convinced I became that it would still be in Nanking, where I had left it.

I told Ming so, and I explained the reason for my certainty. "They won't report me dead or even missing until they have to — until I actually am dead," I said. "In the meantime they'll keep up the pretense that I'm away looking at railroad tracks. That's why they'll leave my things just as they are. Later they can fly someone in from the embassy to collect them. It'll look convincing."

She was silent, but I could tell that she thought I would return to Nanking. I hadn't decided that; perhaps she thought it because that would have been the Chinese thing to do. It was my duty as a member of the group. Whatever was concealed had to be important — after all, it was Yakov's ticket to the West and there was no indication that he didn't know its value. Thus it was important I secured it for my own country. End of thesis.

The trouble was I didn't think that way. I did things *I* wanted to do. I always had. I'd opted for freedom. Sometimes I got accused of enjoying it at someone else's expense — before we'd made up, that had been my brother's line. But mostly I knew it was jealousy: people finding excuses for their captivity because they hadn't got the guts to break out.

This time there was no doubt about what I wanted. No doubt at all. To get the hell out of this country. To be with Ming. To stay with Ming.

And yet . . . something nagged at the back of my mind. Duty? Conscience? A feeling I had obligations, debts that I should pay? A flickering thought that if I didn't go back I would never forget what I had done, would never forgive myself?

Balls! I fought it back.

Ming was still silent.

"Look," I said, "we need sleep. Nothing has happened, nothing has changed. All I have done, I think, is to work out where something is hidden. Now let's sleep on it."

I reached out, and began patting her hand as though I was comforting a small child. She drew back. She, at least, knew what I would do.

"I am not a baby," she whispered through clenched teeth. "You are a madman like all Americans. In the morning you will say that you must return to Nanking, and you will ask my uncle how it can be arranged." She began to sob.

I should have denied it, but I wasn't certain enough of anything to do that. I reached forward and held her forearms. "It'll be all right," I said. "Really it will."

She exploded. Her fingers gripped deep into my shoulders and she began to shake me. "You fool!" she screamed. "You fool!"

The fury of her attack drove me back. Then, as suddenly as it had begun, she stopped.

"I'm sorry," I said. "I'm a bloody idiot. Do you have a way of saying that in Chinese?"

Her face was still, her eyes drained of all anger.

"Come on," I said. "Go back to bed."

She did not move.

There was a fresh spot of blood at the corner of her mouth. "You've made it bleed again," I said.

Her hand moved to dab it, but I stopped her. "No," I said, and I bent and brushed the blood away with my lips.

I drew back and looked at her, but neither her face nor her eyes changed. The words when she did speak were soft.

"If you are going to be a fool," she said, "we may not have much time."

My face must have showed that I still did not understand.

"Do I need to explain?" she continued. "Please do not force me to be more brazen than I am being. Please let us go to bed."

Her breasts were even smaller than I had imagined, enlarged under her clothes by a stiff, pointed bra. They were hard, like perfectly round apples, and the nipples stiffened under my fingers.

I moved my face down and rubbed it in the warmth of her belly before venturing further. Her hips and thighs were broad. Between them she was childlike in her smoothness, and when I touched her with my tongue she made as though to stop me, fingers in my hair, and then relaxed.

When finally I entered her, she was tight but not a virgin. Making love, she was like two people. Her body moved and strained to give and take pleasure, yet her hands pulled the quilt high so that we should be hidden in our nakedness.

Afterward she was very still, and I gently wiped a tear from her eye.

We lay soaked in warmth and a present in which nothing else

mattered. I thought she had fallen asleep, but then she said softly and incongruously, "When were you born?"

"Born?"

"Yes, the date."

I told her: July 29, 1950.

There was a long silence, and then she said, "Tiger. You were born in the year of the Tiger. I am June 1958, the year of the Dog. It is good. Tiger and Dog, they go well together."

I waited but there was no more, and she slept.

She woke me during the night, her hands making soft patterns on my chest.

"I thought you were a puritanical nation," I said.

She knew the word. "Modest," she said. "Not puritanical. Communism has done that."

Her hand curled around me, felt that I was aroused. The darkness in the room was total, and I felt her slide on to me, begin moving.

It seemed a tactless thing to say, but I said it. "Do you take something?" I knew that in a nation where birth control was all but compulsory the pill had to be widely available. I did not know, though, how accessible it was to unmarried women.

She paused; her body lifted on me.

"If we live," she said softly, "I would like to have your baby."

The crossroad at which Maddy and I had parted. Yet I smiled.

"I would like that too," I said.

Then she lowered herself with agonizing slowness, and I arched to meet her.

16

My body wanted to sleep until it was sated; my subconscious dragged it awake as dawn was breaking.

I could smell the rich warmth of sex and sweat, feel the heat of Ming's thighs against mine. The four-poster was a nest. All of it told me to go on as planned.

Nevertheless, I lay and watched the room lighten, and I thought. Some of the thoughts were of age-old and often mocked virtues like duty and patriotism; others were very personal like being true to oneself; yet more were of the most fundamental things of all — staying alive and dying. Many concerned Ming. I could not have shared them with anyone else. It was not just that I would have been embarrassed to lay them outside of me — which I would. It was both more complex and yet more simple than that. At the end of it all it added up to a question: how would I feel about myself in years to come if I didn't go back? I laughed at the cult of the masses, rejoiced in my own individuality — but didn't I owe a price for it? Freedom didn't just happen. Wasn't this the time I had to pay? No one else could.

Ming turned in her sleep, and I wrapped my arms around her and dozed for a while, letting myself luxuriate in our togetherness.

The sound of Wen moving about below disturbed my pleasure; I raised myself and gently kissed Ming's eyes until she awoke.

We enjoyed the touch of each other's smile for a long time. We said nothing, and I traced kisses on her face with my fingertip.

Then, at last, she moved. She too could hear her uncle and knew why I had wakened so early. She made it easy. "We should go now if you wish to talk to him before he leaves."

I began to protest that I had not decided anything. But even as I started to speak I knew that I had. Then I tried to explain. But I stopped after a few words. There was nothing I could say.

We washed and dressed quickly, Ming first while I kept my face averted. Downstairs Wen hid his surprise at our early visit. He was finishing the remains of last night's meal.

I must have rehearsed in my subconscious what I planned to say because the words came easily. As far as I was able to judge Ming translated them impassively, not arguing my case or letting her own feelings intrude on them. Speaking carefully, I laid stress on the fact that I wanted to return to collect a document that a *Russian* colonel had given me. I did not, of course, add that he was trying to defect at the time or that his own countrymen had killed him. I lied by omission, and I felt a twinge of guilt — both because I liked and owed the man and because I was making Ming my accessory. But my unease was small: against what had happened and what was still at stake it seemed a small untruth, and one that would certainly not add to his danger.

Wen listened and said little in return. At the end he was noncommittal. Perhaps he just did not know. Left alone, we returned to the bedroom. We did not make love. We talked a lot, of small and inconsequential things. Like names. David, I told her, was the patron saint of Wales, land of my mother's anecestors. Ming liked that — to the Chinese, she explained, the family is really everything; the dead, traditionally, are as important and ever-present as the living. It dawned upon me that I had been wrong earlier: what I was doing in my decision to return to Nanking was far from being Chinese. A Chinese would have done it for more immediate, prosaic, individual, or family motives. But not, like me, for such vague concepts as conscience or State, despite what the party might wish.

Did Western first names have meanings? she asked. I said they did, but often people did not know them. I knew mine; my mother had told me. It meant "beloved," I said without any embarrassment. She liked that.

Her name, Ming, was composed of two ideograms that signify "sun" and "moon." Its meaning, she said, was "shining light." And I liked that.

The day passed comfortably, gently, both of us sensitive to the other's feelings, both mindful without voicing it that this could be a day by which we would have to remember each other.

We both hoped, I think, that Wen would return saying that what I wished was impossible; he had tried, but no one would help me. Then I would have done all that I could, and my conscience would have been appeased. There could certainly be no question of my trying to return without transport — Nanking might only be a hundred and forty or so miles away, but the journey had taken us ten hard days.

Wen returned in the late afternoon. First, he wanted to speak to Ming alone. They were a long time, more than half an hour. I still do not know what they said.

Then they came to the bedroom together.

Wen's face and Ming's voice were as impassive as they had both been that morning.

It had been arranged. Ho would take me. I must get ready to leave immediately.

As it happened it was the middle of the evening before Ho arrived, and another two hours before we left.

Ho explained that he would hide me at his house overnight. Just before first light the following day I would be collected and driven to Nanking. The journey would take the whole day; the driver had many calls to make at towns on the way.

In Nanking I would be dropped at or near the hotel soon after it was dark. Then I would have just one hour. Afterward I would be taken directly to Shanghai to join up again with Ming, who would have been moved in the meanwhile. For me it would mean one, perhaps more, change of vehicle — but that did not have to concern me.

At the end, Ho paused. His expression was blank, but I was not deceived. He expected praise. I gave it; he deserved it. I was impressed.

Before we set off I tried several times to arrange moments alone with Ming. We did not manage it until shortly before I left. Then we had only seconds, time in which to do nothing but cling to each other, wordless.

My transport to Ho's house was in an old motorcycle sidecar, beautifully preserved and elaborately decorated, attached to a bicycle with a small engine. The sidecar had a tarpaulin cover, under which I hid myself. There was no seat inside, and I stretched out on the floor, my head supported by a bundle of newspapers. The top speed we reached was not great, but the springs were rudimentary and the roads rough, and by the time we stopped I was in agony with cramps and with the jolting from the road.

Ho pushed the bicycle and sidecar into the courtyard of his house before pulling back the tarpaulin and hurrying me inside. There was no sign of his wife or of any children; perhaps he had none.

I barely had time to register concrete walls before I was ushered into a deep cupboard under the stairs. The door was closed, but Ho returned minutes later with a candle and matches, cold rice and apples. There was also a bottle — Wen's homemade crude liquor. I was still smiling at the sight when I heard the rasp of metal against metal — I was being padlocked in.

It was a bad night. The cupboard was clean; there was no trace of rodents; there were layers of blankets for my bed. But my sleep was disturbed by nightmares and each time I awoke I imagined fresh dangers and horrors until I brought my mind under control.

It added to my fear that it was nearly eleven hours — long after the first light — when the door was finally reopened. Ho explained nothing, but a covered truck was waiting outside, its tail within a dozen paces of the door. I waited until Ho checked, then ran across the open ground, my eyes screwed against the sudden light.

Ho did not get into the truck with me. "The driver speaks little English," he said. "But he knows what to do."

"You're not coming?"

"I have things to arrange here."

He slapped the back of the truck hard, and the driver switched on the engine.

Ho reached up and I thought at first that he wanted to shake hands. Instead, he pushed an envelope at me.

Before I could say anything, he struck the truck again, and it jerked forward.

We turned, and he disappeared from sight. I settled myself on the floor, in a corner. There was a hatch into the driving cab, but a curtain was drawn across it.

I peered down at the envelope for several minutes before opening it. It was pale yellow with tiny flowers in the top left-hand corner, the kind I had seen on sale in the Friendship Store. It was sealed — Chinese envelopes have no adhesive of their own, and I could see where the gum had run. Inside was a one-page note on the same decorated paper.

"David, my dear one," it began. The writing was large and carefully formed; the pain of committing deep emotion to paper was obvious in every stroke. For the message that followed the words were curiously formal, like a Victorian love letter, but — perhaps for this reason — incredibly moving.

I am taking the risk of insisting this is delivered to you, because who can know if we will see each other again. I think you know, but it is important to me to say I love you. I do not think I could have said the words aloud even if we had had time. I am told that the man who takes you to Nanking has orders to wait for you, even if you should be longer than the hour Mr. Ho insisted upon. But if you should become separated for any reason, there is a house in Shanghai. I do not know how you would get there, but I think if anyone could it is you. It was difficult getting this address and I have promised you will memorize it and destroy this paper. I will try to wait there until you arrive.

There were two more lines. They made me want to return, but I knew there was no turning back now. They said, "We are to leave soon, earlier than planned because security cadres have been making enquiries about the telephone call. I do not think there is danger, but it is better to be cautious."

There was no signature. The address was separate — a hand-drawn map on a scrap of paper with the address written in pinyin and in ideograph. I could not believe it would ever be necessary. This journey, to Nanking and then to Shanghai, would go smoothly. At the slightest sign of a problem I would back away. Still, I concentrated hard until I was as certain as I could be that I knew both the diagram and the address by heart — I hadn't forgotten the panic in Nanking when I thought I'd forgotten forever the address Andrews had given me.

The letter I folded and placed inside my shirt. The map I tore into the tiniest pieces I could, and one by one I floated them out of the back of the truck until they disappeared from sight.

We stopped three times on the way — twice to load cartons (one batch clearly marked with the name of a Japanese television manufacturer), once in a closed yard when the driver indicated he would be away an hour.

In his absence I risked leaving the truck, but only to stay crouched beside it. Using my grimy handkerchief as a blotter, I drew gasoline from the tank until I had filled an empty mineral bottle from the vehicle two-thirds full.

I worried about the smell of gasoline in the air when the driver returned, but he seemed not to notice it. He had food and drink. We ate separately, he in his cab, I in the back. He obviously wanted to know as little about me as possible.

An hour later, soon after ten P.M., we reached the outskirts of Nanking. There was a strange feeling about being back. I tried to console myself with the thought that it was the last place anyone would be looking for me.

We stopped, and unable to see where we were I thought we had arrived. The driver drew back his curtain. "Ten minutes," he said. "We arrive. Then one hour, I return. Understand?"

I did. In his basic, staccato English he managed to explain that he planned to stop at the hotel gates and distract the guard's attention. I should then be able to slip through into the garden.

In fact, when the time came, he drew to a halt just beyond the gates. I peered through the curtain as he climbed out, and saw him spread a map on the hood. Seconds later the guard joined him. Quickly I made my way to the back of the truck, dropped into the road, and darted through the gate.

I remembered it all well: the pathway flanked with lawns and trees, the circular driveway, illuminated by ornate lamps, and beyond them the square-built hotel, its name in red characters stretching the whole width of the main building.

I skirted the wall quickly, cut across the grass, and joined the drive. Once there I forced myself to walk slowly, a guest returning after a late evening stroll. The gasoline-filled bottle I held close to my side. A group of people came out of the main door; I heard them before I saw them and their laughter startled me. They stood outside taking the air before going to bed. Their voices, American, tempted me, drew me, made me long to run to them. But I knew there was no freedom that way.

Five minutes had passed. I reached the side of the building and followed it around until I found a window that appeared to lead into a storeroom. Then I moved back into the bushes to wait. The Americans returned into the hotel; their noise died as the doors closed behind them. I crouched motionless for twenty minutes. The rest of the hotel appeared to be asleep.

Time.

I stood up, pulled off my jacket and shirt, and wrapped the shirt around my right fist like a glove. At the window, I checked to be sure no one was in sight, then drew back my fist. The secret, I knew, was nerve and speed. I punched the window hard and straight. A neat hole appeared. Even in the stillness of the night there was little sound — no more than a few tinkles as fragments of glass fell to the floor. I reached in, unlocked the catch, climbed through, and put my clothes back on.

The storeroom led into the kitchen, which was better than I had hoped. I checked that the exit into the corridor was not locked before quickly piling up all the inflammable material I could find. There was a huge container of oil, and I used it liberally — I wanted smoke and smell.

Then, using my handkerchief and one of the matches from my survival pen, I turned the bottle into a Molotov cocktail. I lit the handkerchief taper and tossed the bottle into the oil-soaked pile.

It exploded into flame immediately. The speed transfixed me: I had to force myself to move. I left open the door into the corridor so that the smoke would carry, paused for a few moments to let it gather strength, then rushed into the main lobby, hand in front of my face, screaming, "Fire, Fire! There's a fire!"

At this time I had expected only one or two dozy Chinese staff on duty. The presence of the noisy Americans, still grouped together and reluctant to part company, was a bonus. They took up the "Fire" chant and rushed to investigate.

I ran over to the ancient fire alarm boxes and, hoping they worked, smashed one open and pulled the lever. An ear-splitting clanging began to echo through the hotel, mingling now with the sound of people shouting. I stood pressed against a wall as doors started to open and people began descending the stairs. Then I fought past to the second floor. The waiter's cubbyhole was empty, as I thought it would be by now. I scanned the hooks, removed the key I wanted, and began running in the direction of my old room.

A door opened and an elderly man looked out.

"Cosa c'è?" he asked in Italian — What is the matter?

I paused, struggled for the word, remembered, *"Fuoco."*

"Ah." The man turned and shouted the word back into his room.

I left him, checking the time as I moved. Fifteen minutes to the hour. Perfect.

I reached the door of my old room, inserted the key, and tried to turn it. It stuck. In my rush, had I taken the wrong one? Or had the room been sealed? I took it out, then reinserted it. This time it gave.

The sight inside made my mouth spread into a huge grin. The room was exactly as I had left it. There was an air of normality as though I had only slipped out for a stroll. An open book was beside the bed, a note-pad stood on the ornate writing table, a stack of laundered shirts waited to be put into the drawer.

And, on the carpet by the bed, was the Gladstone bag.

I opened it, ran my fingers along the lining, lifted the inner layer of the double bottom: nothing. But it was a cursory look. I checked the time again. Ten minutes. I had to move now. Best to take the bag with me. With luck no one would notice it was gone, nor connect me with the fire.

I reentered the corridor, locking the door behind me. The Italian and his wife were standing outside their room, cases around their feet. As I ran past they began struggling toward the stairs.

The smoke became thicker as I descended. Despite the confusion I skirted the inside of the hotel to avoid the lobby, found a side door, and unbolted it. Crowds were grouped in front of the hotel and a fire engine swept into the drive as I watched.

I had expected the gates to be unmanned, the guard drawn toward the building by the fire. Instead he was standing there in full view, waiting imperiously for any other traffic after waving through the fire engine.

No matter. I found a shadowed section of the wall. Thick creeper covered it and it was an easy climb to the top. As I lowered myself down the other side, in shadow and unseen, I saw the truck traveling toward me. Realizing no one could see me where I stood, I began to move forward to get into the driver's vision. The sound of revving car engines forced me to a halt. Two cars I had not noticed before roared into life. They shot across the width of the road, skidding to a halt in front of and behind the truck. Men leaped out as the cars stopped.

My escape route had been cut.

17

There was no alternative. I walked. Keeping in the shadows, I hurried away from the cars and the hotel. After a few minutes, when I was convinced I was far enough away, I hurriedly crossed to the far side of the broad avenue.

There was little traffic and no lights. I wondered how long it would be before the security men began searching the streets. From the way they had ambushed the truck they must have expected to find me inside. The driver might not talk straight away, and even if he did their first search would be of the hotel and the grounds.

The truth was that there was no way of knowing how long I had. My two priorities were, first, to get out of the immediate vicinity; then, to escape from the city itself. At least I knew the layout of the city from my previous study of maps and from the window of the sightseeing car.

The railroad station tempted me — but I knew that was no good. It was the first place where they would increase security, if they had not done so already. I debated trying to flag down a truck and hijacking it, but decided that was too chancy — road blocks were a real possibility, but of greater immediate fear was that the driver would not stop but would report me.

I saw only one chance. The river.

I took a side street off the avenue, zigzagging until I thought I was running parallel to it. Finally I reached the banks.

Ahead of me the water stretched out in the darkness more like a sea than a river. I could barely make out the far side. Downstream in the distance I could see the lights of the famous bridge. I walked along the banks until I found some cover, then squatted and settled down.

Gradually my eyes became more acclimatized to the inky blackness, although the river remained a frighteningly impenetrable expanse. I knew the currents were strong — I remembered the engineering problems of building the bridge.

I couldn't swim its width. Or, in fact, very far in it: that I knew. What I could do, I hoped, was swim out far enough to clamber aboard one of the chains of barges that plied the river day and night.

With nothing to do but wait I turned my attention to the bag. Using my flashlight, I emptied it carefully. The riverside was far from the ideal place but I needed to know whether I was right — or whether I had returned in vain. Moreover, I told myself, it would be too risky to try to swim out into the Yangtze with the bag. Even closed, it would rapidly fill with water and drag me down.

My first search revealed nothing. I worked on the lining with my knife. Again nothing. I fought back the growing feeling of anger and failure.

The handles! They were made of leather over a cylindrical shape of metal. Perhaps they were hollow.

I hacked with my knife until they came away from the case. They *were* hollow. I scooped inside with my little finger, double-checked with the flashlight, and finally with the thin knifeblade in case whatever it was had got stuck.

Nothing.

I switched off the light but kept on staring at the now dismembered bag, trying to place myself in Yakov's position.

What he had on him had to be small to be hidden in the first place (I still had to tell myself it *was* hidden). But how little? If it was only an instruction as to where the real material could be found, then very small — no more than the tiniest scrap of paper with a few words on it. That meant I would need to rip the bag apart completely — taking care, too, to check whether he had written anything directly on to the case's interior. And if it was the document itself? That too need take minimal space — I'd already decided it would have to be on microfilm. I knew something about such things — I had experience with their use for storing vast amounts of diagrammatical information. Somewhere I had learned that a square of 16mm film, no bigger than a thumbnail, could hold up to 20,000 words.

The light of a vessel came into view, but I disregarded it. Whatever happened I had to find what I sought first — or satisfy myself it was not there.

I risked another flash of my light, shielding it with my jacket. The reinforced edges were the next possibility . . . I placed the knifepoint on the stitches, and then paused.

The lock.

The metal casing around it was about three inches by two inches across. No more than a square inch or so of that was occupied by the lock itself. Taking great care, I began to prise it away from the leather.

The pieces began to flutter out. I grabbed the ones that had reached the ground, then proceeded even more casually, although I was certain I had them all.

I did not stop to count them, but I guessed there were about a hundred. The squares were smaller than 16mm — I thought Minox sub-miniature. The whole, compressed and squared, was no bigger than a sugar cube. On my — admittedly very rough — calculation it could contain anything up to 100,000 words — the contents of a very substantial book.

I thought very briefly on what it might contain. Details of military deployments? Weapons stocks and capabilities? Contingency plans? Names of agents? Useless even trying to guess. All I knew was that Yakov had thought it his trump card, and a lot of people were after it.

The Gladstone bag had contained some small soil sample boxes and I divided the film between two of them — I'm not sure why: perhaps

I thought it would spread the risk of losing it. Both were meant to be waterproof, but I further sealed them inside small plastic bags, which I knotted. Then I rammed the two small parcels into the deep, tight side pockets of my jeans.

I searched a little more in case I had missed anything. Then I placed the contents back in the bag and added stones. I tossed it out as far as I could. I lost sight of it before I heard it hit the water.

The night was hot but when I touched the river it was cold — snows in the north were probably melting by now, surging down toward the sea. I sat cross-legged, and remembered that in his old age Mao had swum here to prove his youthfulness: no one outside a chosen few knew just how long he had remained in the water. The claim, I remembered, was that he had swum a great distance. I even remembered, from a news magazine, a few lines of the poem he had written to commemorate his feat:

> *I have just drunk the water of the Changsha*
> *And come to eat the fish of Wuchang*
> *Now I am swimming across the great Yangtze.*

A strange poem to remember, but somehow it had stuck in my mind purely because it was so alien.

A steamer neared, its light defining its shape. I was surprised — I had thought only craft with a small draft would risk the river at night: again from my knowledge of the problems involved in building the bridge I knew the river was notorious for sudden changes in its soft floor and shifts in the channels that vessels had to take.

A steamer was not what I wanted anyway. I had to wait almost an hour for that — a tug pulling its string of barges. I judged as they approached they were about forty yards offshore.

The end of the waiting was a relief even though it also brought fresh fears. I honestly did not know whether I could succeed in what I was about to attempt. If I failed, I hoped I could regain the shore. If not . . .

I moved, knowing there was no alternative, and conscious action would still the fears. My shoes were already off and tied to my belt. I slid quickly into the water, gasping at the cold, and began swimming immediately, enough to add some warmth, not enough to drain myself too quickly. I tried to keep my mouth clear of the water: God knew what the Chinese pumped into the river.

Finally, knowing there was no more time and that I had done the best I could, I settled low in the water, silent and still in case anyone on board the tug was peering in my direction. The vessel passed about fifteen yards away and the wash caught me, spun me, filling my nose with water. I gasped, frightened for a second that it was over, and then, spurred by the black shapes sliding by, I began to swim toward them.

There were five barges, one behind the other, linked like a chain. I deliberated for too long before trying to grasp the stern of the fourth one, and I bounced back. Half-stunned, I struggled, seized hold of the last barge and hung there suspended, legs trailing in the water.

I realized that unless I called upon all my reserves of strength and acted now it would be too late. "Help me, help me," I mouthed, hoping someone was listening. The first heave left my heart pounding, my muscles burning, but it raised me a vital few inches. The second took my stomach onto the edge of the barge so that I was jackknifed over it. There was a cover stretched right to the edge. I contorted myself and then I was underneath, lying squeezed in a gap between bulging sacks.

Gradually my heart quieted. The cold had killed all feeling. I curled into a ball, trying to give myself warmth. I wanted to sleep; my body craved escape. My brain began to tell me that I *must* sleep, that it was essential and that afterward I would feel better. But I knew it was lying. I forced myself to keep repeating aloud that I must keep awake. I recited poems, worked through multiplication tables, listed Presidents . . .

Precisely two hours after climbing into the barge — an arbitrary time, but I knew I had to set one — I lifted the cover, confirmed dawn was still some way off, and slid back into the water.

I could make out the shape of the shore, and I swam mechanically. A wind blowing inshore helped me, and I hit the bank without realizing I was even near. I collapsed for a few minutes, then pulled myself upright and began walking.

The hiding place I found was little more than a deep depression in the earth, but it had to do. I dropped there, woke once as though in a nightmare, stripped off my clothing, which had begun to steam, and slept again.

As I drifted in and out of sleep my head kept echoing with the sound of trains. Once I thought I even heard a real whistle; I knew the track south could not be far away.

Trains were my one thought now; hitching a ride on one the only hope I had left.

I lay hidden all day and the first part of the night, reaching the track soon after three-thirty A.M. It was a bright night. I passed through a deserted station. An outside tap was a temptation, but I knew it was dangerous to drink. I used it to wash the smell of the river off my clothes — I did not bother to remove them; they would dry on me.

Beyond the station I found a hiding place in the grass and settled down to wait. Once day broke some of the trains would slow or even stop at the station. By the time they reached me they would be moving slowly enough for me to jump on board — provided that I was fast and agile enough. Desperation should make me both.

I heard a train in the distance. It passed through the station, whistles blowing, but without slowing — but then, at this time, I expected that. I followed its approach with my head raised in the grass. It was a freight train: I could see the glow of the fire and the silhouettes of the driver and the fireman.

I also saw something I had not expected to see. A third man on the footplate. I could make out no more than his presence. The fourth man at the rear of the rain was equally no more than a shape. But it was a shape that included a peaked cap and a rifle or machine weapon of sorts.

I forced myself not to panic. The fact that there were guards on this train need not be significant. It could be a specially valuable or dangerous consignment.

Nevertheless I waited with nervous impatience for the next. It passed a bare twenty minutes later. I could see no one other than the driver and fireman in the cab this time, but there was no mistaking the man in the doorway of the final wagon. He lit a cigarette as the train passed, and the match illuminated the green of his uniform.

My immediate plan had been destroyed. I had meant quite simply to ride a train to the outskirts of Shanghai, then leave it as I had joined it, and risk making the few final miles on foot.

But now?

Perhaps the guards would prove only a temporary measure; perhaps if I could hide out for even one day . . . Certainly, I knew there was no point — no hope — in trying to make the distance on foot again.

That meant a better hiding place than this, but near the track so that I could keep watch. I began walking. Daylight was not far away; I did not have much time.

Suddenly I saw a spur of track leading away from the main line, and I followed it. At the end of the loop there were various shapes: a collection of sheds, some open freight cars, an uncoupled steam locomotive. A road retreated into the distance. It was obviously a regular loading point for produce or materials brought in from the surrounding area.

As I watched, the rising sun began to tip the edges of the buildings. I looked quickly at the locomotive: it had the look of having been positioned here the previous evening for early morning loading.

If that was so its driver and fireman must appear soon, and begin to build steam. The fire had to be lit several hours before the engine was ready to move.

An idea was forming, but first I needed somewhere to conceal me for those few hours. The land around was flat: no hiding place there. That left the buildings. On examination the first three proved useless. One was an open-fronted bay, another a hut used as an office, and the third a store which, I saw through the window, was completely empty.

On a slope beyond and above the three was a fourth building. It was square, made from concrete and only three-quarters completed. It looked as though the builders had decided to leave it as it was. Material and equipment to finish the job still lay around, but they had the air of having been there a long time.

The wooden hut provided my only real find — a heavy kettle, half-full of water. I took a chance it had been boiled and drank deep from the spout. It was light now, and it had become obvious that there was only one possible hiding place, and that the best of bad choices — the flat roof of the unfinished concrete block. Nothing overlooked it, and it had a low parapet that would hide me from the ground. The trouble was I would roast there. But I had no choice.

I climbed painfully, dragging behind me a sack that had held concrete — it would provide some protection for my head and neck against the direct sun.

I stretched out on my belly and looked down on the locomotive. I took in every detail of it — let my eyes dwell with pleasure on the shine of its rods, the gleam of its brasswork, the fresh red of its wheels.

In a few hours, if all went well, it would be mine.

I planned to steal it.

The driver and a fireman arrived together, on bicycles, less than half an hour after I had settled myself. The fireman set straight to work firing the boiler. The driver squatted near the wheels and began eating food that he had brought with him in a metal container. I watched oblivious to hunger but when I saw him drink from a bottle suddenly desperate again for water.

I watched the two men carefully. The driver was middle-aged and did not look strong. The fireman was slight, but had to be in good condition because of the job he did. Their physical state was vital to me because if I was to steal the train I had to overpower them, and I could have felt a hell of a lot better than I did this morning.

I wanted to take the locomotive, not hijack its crew. It would be hard if not impossible to persuade any driver to produce the kind of ride I intended to make.

Gaining control, I decided, should not be hard — given my size and desperation. To ensure I had to use only the minimum force I would make the best use I could of surprise.

A truck arrived after about an hour, transferred its containers, and left. The railroad men still made no attempt to couple the cars; either they were waiting for more goods or — just as likely — they had a whole day to complete this one task. In a country where people far outnumbered jobs, it was obviously foolish to rush any work.

A maverick cloud covered the sun, and I welcomed the relief. I figured I still had something like two hours before the locomotive was ready to roll.

It kept drawing my eyes to it. A steam engine is a huge, awesome piece of machinery. The one below would weigh about a hundred and ten tons, fifty more with its tender added. It was of a common type known as the JF class — a workhorse commonly used on local lines or to serve a commune or a factory. It was the kind of locomotive for which I have a very special sort of affection — my love for trains is directed at *working* engines.

I like locomotives that do work better than any other form of transport could do it under the circumstances: the 2-10-2s that fight the winding mountainous route through the Andes in Argentina to the Chilean border; the great transcontinentals of Australia; the nineteenth-century German locomotives that still haul wood in Indonesia instead of standing on display in science and engineering museums . . .

There are railway fanatics, millions of them probably, who delight in special railway museums and preserved tourist lines. I have nothing against the pleasure people derive from them, but such engines are of no more interest to me than pet poodles would be to a naturalist specializing in lions in their natural habitat.

What really mattered now, though, about the workhorse below me was that I could drive it. It carried a driver and a fireman, but that was not strictly essential. Because the Chinese are a small people, their engineers have designed cabs in such a way that all controls are easy to operate. Furthermore — and most important — this train had a fully mechanical stoker: no need for a fireman to keep shoveling coal. Once the fire was under way all that anyone had to do was monitor the controls. It did not have to be fed manually at all.

So I could take it, and I could drive it. Provided that the tender was full of water and there were no cars attached, it had an operational limit of perhaps two hundred miles — more than far enough. I would not attempt to take it right to Shanghai — that would be too risky. But I should be able to get near, within say twenty or twenty-five miles, even closer perhaps, before deserting the train. Surely that would give me some real chance.

Only desperation could father such a scheme, but I kept telling myself it was not as totally wild as it might at first seem. There was double track all the way to Shanghai so I did not risk meeting another train head-on. I might meet a locomotive traveling in the same direction, but I could drive on sight and on my brakes.

My unauthorized presence on the line would be noted quickly and reported down the track, of course. But what would the railroad authorities do? A driver of a train cannot go left or right or choose the path he will take at a junction; such things are determined by the men who switch the points from outside. He is confined to stopping and starting and regulating his speed. They could, of course, decide to switch me off the main track and onto a siding. Alternatively, they could block the line.

I was reasonably certain, however, they would do neither of these things — particularly if I drove the engine full-out, which would probably mean seventy miles an hour. *If* they tried to switch me or block my path at that speed there would certainly be a spectacular crash. I would gamble — had to gamble — that officials on duty would quickly realize that there was nowhere I could go; that I would run out of track or steam within only a few hours. They could pick me up then.

That, at least, was what I would do in their place. I tried to disregard the fact that one man in a position of control with a different attitude could end my run quickly and dramatically. Not to say fatally.

There were added signs of activity below. The driver was walking around with an oil can. There was an exhortation attached to the front of the engine — a common practice. I could not understand it, but hoped it would be something appropriate for what I was about to try.

The number on the side of the engine was 702. That I knew had to make it pretty old. Numbers of JFs as far as I could remember went up to 2500. I doubted whether any numbered 500 or lower still existed. This one — 702 — had probably pulled its first carriages more than fifty years before on the South Manchurian railways.

I thought of the history it had lived through — in its time China had been occupied by the Japanese, had experienced Mao's Long March, seen the Revolution and the retreat of the Nationalists, survived the Cultural Revolution at a cost of millions more killed and disabled . . . I thought of the terrain through which this train would have battled, the goods it would have hauled, the men who would have driven it. Like all engines, it began to come alive.

The 702. It sounded right. The 702 to freedom.

The sound of a horn made me turn my head and I saw the dust of a truck in the near distance. It must be the rest of the day's load.

Watching the unloading and loading, I was nervous that the truck driver and his mate would stay until the locomotive pulled away. But after a communal smoke they left, shouting and waving as their vehicle retreated into the distance.

I watched it vanish from sight and knew that I could wait no longer. I slid on my belly to the rear of the roof, eased myself over the edge of the parapet, hung precariously by my fingertips for a few seconds, and then dropped.

I lay sprawled for a short time before making my way stumbling around the building. I waited until neither man was looking my direction, then began to slither down the slope.

I was still about twenty yards from the engine when the fireman turned and saw me.

18

⚜

I ran the last few yards like a sprinter unleashed from the starting blocks.

The fireman, who was about ten yards away from the engine, stood transfixed, shock etched deep into his face. Then he yelled. Ahead and above me, the driver appeared at the side of his cab to see what was happening. He turned immediately, and grabbed a metal bar. I leaped, my feet connecting with the third of the four steps, my hands grasping the rails. I propelled myself forward into the cab, my head a battering ram into the driver's legs.

My weight sent the man hurtling backward onto the floor. I heard the crack as his head hit metal, and I hauled myself to my knees, desperate in the hope that he was not badly hurt. Despite my frenzy to survive I had no wish to harm this stranger.

The sound of the fireman's feet on the metal steps made me turn just in time. My movement made the hammer miss my head, but it caught my arm a glancing blow that temporarily paralyzed it. Through screwed-up eyes I saw the hammer being raised for a second blow, and leaning back to give myself maximum room for momentum I drew in my right leg and lashed out. My foot caught the man high on the hip, swiveling him around, sending the hammer crashing into the side of the cab.

Rolling to my back, I drew in both legs together, paused to check my aim, then launched my feet into the fireman's stomach. The force sent the man hurtling backward, out of the cab, down onto the ground.

I lay for what could have been a few seconds or many minutes, breath rasping, trying to draw enough strength to stand. Finally I struggled to my knees and crawled to the edge of the cab. The fireman was lying below, holding his hands over his stomach, moaning gently, making no attempt to rise. I turned and gave my attention to the driver. He was breathing evenly and his color did not look strange — both good signs, I hoped. I lifted his head and found the gash; it was still bleeding but only slightly.

I half-climbed, half-slid from the cab to the ground, found the men's packs, extracted a bottle of water, and drank deep until I gagged. I tried my arm; it ached, but movement had returned. I wanted to rest but I knew that if I did I would find it hard to rise again. Digging deeper and deeper into my reserves I dragged the fireman to the small wooden hut, then returned for the driver, carrying him as gently as I could over my shoulder. I left them one of the water bottles, locked the door, and tossed away the key. Once the fireman recovered and decided to get out it would take him only minutes — the window was small but large enough for an exit. Alternatively, the door was not strong; but I knew fear would halt the man for a little while. And once the train was on its way I wanted him to escape and seek help. It could hardly add to my own danger, and it gave me some small consolation that I would not be delaying their getting medical attention.

My clothes were soaked in sweat now, and like a drunk I staggered the distance to the hand-operated points, set them for the main track, and returned to the engine.

Inside, I allowed myself a few brief moments of inactivity, seated in the driver's chair. I closed my eyes and breathed in the heady, familiar mixture of oil and smoke. I reached out and ran my hands lovingly over the main controls, shiny with the touch of dozens of railroad men before me.

The steam engine without doubt is one of the greatest of all of man's inventions. Of all his mechanical creations it is at the same time his most romantic and his most awe-inspiring. The power I now had in my hands was comparable with that of a waterfall or a volcano. Yet not only did I control it but it would respond to my lightest touch. According to my will and my skill it would ease quietly forward or roar through the country like a stampeding beast.

The familiar, nostalgic pleasure of the cab calmed me, and I set about my routine methodically. The first priority was to check the fire. I pressed the pedal and the fire door opened with a hiss, displaying a flickering bed of coal. All well there. Next I checked the steam pressure and the water level in the boiler — crucial, because if the level fell too low it would explode.

Satisfied, I made myself comfortable in my seat, reached forward and wound the reverser into forward gear. I removed the brake and opened the throttle. I was still nervous; I opened it too far, too quickly, making the wheels spin on the spot with a hurt, ear-splitting sound. I pulled back, wiped my brow, and tried again — this time with greater care. The engine began to ease forward. I kept the speed right down as we neared the main line, saw there was nothing in sight, and opened the throttle.

The 702 built up speed quickly. This was a track I knew almost by heart from studying maps and plans. The first station I would pass was about five miles ahead. Fighting the instinct to begin braking, I began working my feet on the pedals that operated the two horns and the two whistles — setting up a mad cacophony of sound.

The locomotive swept through the station at just over fifty miles an hour, but even at that speed I could see the amazement registered on the faces of the staff. Soon now the warning of a runaway train would be flashed ahead.

The exhilaration overcame all my exhaustion, made me forget any fears or doubts. Heroes who charged enemy guns must feel something like this. It was a glorious high.

I had the throttle wide open. Below me the rods were darting backward and forward, driving the wheels at almost maximum speed. I leaned out of the cab window, eyes narrowed, peering into the distance as far as I could. Smoke shrouded the fields we passed. My nostrils were again full of that special acrid, sulfurous scent.

My one hand was on the throttle; the other remained within easy reach of the brake lever. If I saw another engine ahead at this speed it would take a long time to stop. We flashed through another station. A man was screaming and waving a flag. I found I was shouting and laughing out loud.

The 702 was taking on a personality of its own now, singing, muttering to itself. A dozen voices merged into one distinct voice — the grumbling of the mechanical stoker, the chatter of the exhaust from the chimney, the pounding of the great wheels on the rails, the rattle of the footplate beneath my feet. A steam engine's noises are all its own — old-timers swear you can tell individual locomotives simply by the sound they make, and I know it to be true.

I looked at my watch and found to my astonishment that I had been traveling for over an hour — I was a good half way to my destination. I had the map which I had carried carefully since first leaving Nanking. On it I had picked out what I thought was the perfect place to leave the locomotive in order to make a getaway.

The first attempt at stopping me came twenty minutes later, and it was over before I realized fully what had happened. A detonator on the track provided what was meant to be the warning to stop. Almost immediately I saw that points had been set to send me off the main track into a loop.

At this speed there was nothing I could have done even if I had wished to do so. And the speed and the momentum of the locomotive was so great that the points had no effect. The engine continued forward, leaping the narrow gap, leaving a snake of broken rail behind.

Cold sweat broke on my face. The gamble had almost failed. They had tried to stop me. I told myself that the attempt had been made by one panicking individual. It would not happen again.

The exhilaration returned, greater than ever. If I was going to die I could think of no better way, no better place. I began to sing, my voice raised over all the noises of the 702.

> *Now listen to the rumble, now listen to the roar*
> *As she echoes down the valley and tears along the*
> *shore.*

Now hear the engine's whistling and her mighty
  hoboes call
As we ride the rods and break-beams on the Wabash
  Cannonball.

Now here's to Long Slim Perkins, may his name
  forever stand;
He'll be honored and revered by the 'boes
  throughout the land;
And when his days are over and the curtains round him fall
We'll ship him off to heaven on the Wabash
  Cannonball!

I finished and launched into another song, equally rollicking, and then my voice died away.

I was wrong: they were going to try again.

This time there was more warning — time enough to brake to a halt had I wished. The track stretched in a straight line as far ahead as I could see — and the barrier that had been built across the rails was visible for miles.

Impossible, of course, to know what they had used. What I did know was that a hundred and sixty or seventy tons of engine and tender traveling at seventy miles an hour would take a lot of stopping. I doubted that the barrier had that much strength. And me? I could hardly be better protected. I had all the size and strength of the boiler ahead of me to absorb the impact.

The decision was made within seconds. Horns and whistles shrieking, the locomotive smashed through the barrier, hardly slowing with the impact. Pieces of debris soared through the air and looking back I saw people still throwing themselves away from the track. My voice rose crazily, "We did it, we did it, 702!"

Yet I knew my time was limited now. I checked the map and my watch. We passed through one more station; fear flooded through me until I was satisfied there was no further ambush.

I knew we were nearly there now. Nevertheless it was a relief when at last I saw the river for which I had been waiting. Even from a distance there was no mistaking it.

I had already begun to ease back our speed. Now I reached for the brake.

Minutes later the locomotive finally slid to a halt halfway across the bridge that spanned the river. The scene was travel-poster idyllic. Below was the water, a stream of junks in the distance. On the far side, the country was heavily wooded, perfect for hiding until dark when I would begin the final miles of my journey. If I handled this right no one would be looking for me. Would Ming still be in Shanghai waiting? The thought came, only to be pushed quickly away.

I leaned from the cab, absorbed the view, and then turned my attention to the gauges. The water level, as I had planned, had now reached a level veering on the dangerously low.

With a quick movement I opened the blower to goad the fire, took a final look around the cab, climbed down, and began to hurry for the far side of the bridge.

Almost there, I heard an airplane. The fact that it might be looking for the train made me increase my speed. In a few minutes, when the pressure in the locomotive's boiler became too great, it would explode, bursting apart. Nothing could survive such an explosion — including, I hoped my pursuers would conclude, its lunatic driver.

With luck I would get away.

Suddenly I stopped and turned back to face the train. I could still hear the plane but not see it. The engine stood lonely and majestic in the center of the bridge.

I thought of its uniqueness, of all it had seen over the years, of the men who had handled it. Of how it had brought me this far, leaping rails, crashing aside obstacles with easy contempt.

In a flash of terrible certainty I knew I could not destroy it. It was my ultimate madness. I had almost killed several men, had gambled my own life. Yet I could not destroy this piece of machinery.

Resignedly, yet without regret and without fear, I began to retrace my steps, slowly this time. My eyes suddenly caught the flash of the airplane and I dropped instinctively to the tracks.

The move spared my life but ended that of the 702. As I lay facedown waiting for the airplane to vanish from view the explosion came, the waves of force crashing over me, setting the tracks shaking and humming with a weird funereal sound. I raised my eyes in horror, watched the engine split apart, make a jumping movement, then slowly begin to tilt as the bridge buckled beneath it.

Finally, gathering speed, the locomotive plunged downward and hit the water with a giant hiss that became a cry like that of a dying animal.

Still unable to believe what was happening, I dragged myself to the edge and looked down. The surface of the water was hidden by steam and as it cleared there were waves and then bubbles and finally just a widening slick of oil.

I peered until there was nothing to see but oil and then, conscious that I was crying great tears in silence, I stood and ran for the trees.

19

I remained within the cover of the trees for as long as I could, worrying less about the direction I was taking than the need to get as far away from the bridge as possible.

At the end of the woodland there was a wide stream. I tested its depth with a long branch. Then, satisfied, I slid chest-deep into the water and began to follow it. Its banks were wild with grass and flowers; I would be invisible to anyone in the surrounding fields. If anyone came close, or if there was a boat, I would submerge myself among the water weeds.

The bed of the stream was uneven, and the going slow. The water reflected the sun back into my face, and I kept dowsing my head to avoid heatstroke. After a while it was impossible to know what was sweat and what was water.

I came to a bridge that crossed the stream; it was narrow, the width of one vehicle, but I lingered in its shade, tempted to pause here but knowing that it was as yet too early to rest. I hoped they would think that I was dead, that I had dissolved into a thousand pieces with the engine. But it was basic caution to get out of the immediate area. Once I did that Shanghai was far from being an impossible distance away — only twenty or so miles. After what I had been through, I told myself, that was nothing!

The bridge had been recently built, the brickwork still its original color, the mortar unstained. On an impulse I left its shade, pulled myself onto the bank, and cautiously looked around. There were peasants working in the distance; a water buffalo plodded on the horizon. But it was more the landscape, the unchangeable face of this land, that concerned me. Finally satisfied, I slid back into the water and returned to the shade of the bridge.

I paused there for several minutes enjoying the cool before setting off again.

Half an hour later the stream turned back on itself, and I left it. After that I used what cover I could until I grew convinced that to blunder on further in daylight was foolhardy. I had traveled at least two miles from the bridge.

I found a clump of sycamore and burrowed myself into the ground near the base of an especially large one. My clothes dried on me and my head began to throb as though a large hole in my forehead was opening and closing. I wished I had brought water; I still had a few purification tablets.

Although I had not planned it, I drifted into an uneasy sleep. It was still light when I awoke. My head was pounding, my throat was swollen with thirst, my eyes blurred. How I felt, though, was the least of my worries.

I was surrounded by people.

They loomed over me, black shapes against the setting sun, heads bent like spectators at a traffic accident.

I scrabbled at the earth, panicky for a lever to pull myself erect. On the ground I felt especially vulnerable; any moment I expected a foot to crash into my face.

At last I managed to get to my feet. I screamed with rage inside; I had got this far only to be caught like some injured animal.

No one had moved or spoken and I took a lurching step forward, expecting them to fall upon me. But those in my direct path stepped aside, and for the first time I realized there was something odd about their faces.

It was the expressions. They were all the same. Detached interest.

Not triumph, nor elation, at catching me; not anger at who and what I was; not even pity for me. Just detached interest.

These were the faces of people who had chanced upon an unexpected piece of drama. It enlivened their daily routine; they were curious. But as for the rest I could have been an image on a television screen.

I took a second step, stumbled and fell, and hands grabbed me. I began to struggle, then I realized that the hands were holding me upright, not trying to detain me.

They released me almost immediately, and I noticed something else about the faces. All were young. The oldest — there were only about a dozen of them — was barely out of his teens. These were not peasants. They wore jeans and a variety of shirts — Western checks, sweatshirts with slogans, T-shirts with stenciled faces.

One stepped forward. He had "FAME" blazoned across his chest. He also wore the air of a leader. He was tall and rangy and was trying to grow a mustache. His hair was long enough to proclaim both defiance and the fact that he came from a family with enough rank to let him get away with it.

"Hey," he drawled in an accent that if I'd closed my eyes I would have imagined came from a Texan, "take it easy, man. No one's gonna hurt you."

Everyone remained silent, waiting for my first words. It registered that all of them were tall for Chinese. It came from being well fed since birth. I'd seen a few youngsters like this before, in Peking, hanging around the hotel, not caring much about the normal rules because mostly they could disregard them. These were the offspring of high-ranking cadres or army officers: the privileged, the kind who got the easy jobs and to whose antics the rest of the populace turned a blind eye.

What they were doing here, on the edge of a field twenty-odd miles out of Shanghai on a late afternoon, was something I would have to wait to find out. In the meantime my instinct told me the sensible reaction was to keep the atmosphere as light as my questioner's tone.

I looked about and shook my head in stage bewilderment. "I don't believe it," I said. "I slept a hundred years and I've waked up in Hollywood and they're making a movie about life on a Chinese commune. You're actors, yes — American actors, straight from Chinatown."

My questioner turned to the group and translated quickly. They all began laughing as though I was Richard Pryor halfway through his act. The trouble was that laughter is one thing; getting them to laugh with me, not at me, was something separate. I did not know which it was to be yet. There is a Jewish saying, "First the laughter, then the liquor, then the pogrom." I didn't know about the drink, but part of me was scared that they'd leap straight from the first to beating the hell out of me. Maybe I'd seen too many New York kids in gangs.

The boy gave me his full attention again and the laughter died.

"I'm Zhou," he said. "Like in Zhou Enlai. You heard of him? Great man. You call me Joe, yeah?"

I pointed to my chest like Robinson Crusoe meeting Friday. "David," I said. It seemed pointless lying about my name; there couldn't have been too many Americans camping out in the Chinese countryside.

As though no one else had heard, Joe turned and called my name aloud. They took it up, producing almost as many pronunciations as there were individuals.

I expected more questions, but Joe turned and began to walk away. "Lesgo, huh," he said over his shoulder. "Just stick with us." He paused for a second. "You can walk?"

"Yes," I said, "I can walk." I started after him, with the others bringing up the line behind.

A flicker of hope began to join the hammering in my head, but I forced it back, assuming it was too early yet to stop being scared. Joe led us about sixty yards and there, startlingly, was a road hidden from where I had lain by a natural incline. Even more surprisingly, parked there were two cars, both black with fins like 1950s Cadillacs. I must have shied back at the sight because there was more laughter from behind and a new voice, again in English though less confidently, said, "It's okay. We borrowed them."

We squeezed into the cars, me in the back of the lead one, a youth on each side of me. Joe was in front beside the driver. We swept past a group of peasants standing around a bullock cart, horn blaring and wheels spinning dirt. One of the boys beside me screamed back in derision.

Joe turned to face me, his mouth split in a grin. He flipped a cigarette from a pack of Winstons with practiced ease. I refused and he tossed it into his mouth and lit it with a small gold lighter, almost as one movement.

"Cool," I said. "Real cool."

That broke them up again, and they were still laughing when the cars stopped.

We had halted inside a small dell, screened at one end by a row of poplar trees and around the other sides by thick, closely grouped bushes. There were at least a dozen other cars, all with the same official look. There were also two open trucks, and perhaps a hundred kids in total. At the far end of the dell, in front of the trees, a portable stage was being erected.

Joe and his group led me toward it, spaced around me like bodyguards. We passed two barbecue fires, a musician unpacking a guitar, and a couple sharing a smoldering stick that looked and smelled in the still air suspiciously like the moxa I'd encountered in the clinic. This time it pretty obviously wasn't an herb used in acupuncture.

Two men and a girl met us halfway across the dell. The girl had heels about four inches high and a lot of makeup, reminding me of women I'd seen around bars in Hong Kong. She eyed me with the same neutral curiosity, while the rest talked, then I was led away and settled in a space in front of the stage.

Others came to stare, occasionally to ask a question of Joe, who remained, proprietorially, beside me. I had decided to speak only when spoken to, so most of the time I remained silent. Besides, I had to be dreaming. This could not be true. A girl brought me a bottle of beer and a hunk of charred chicken which I bit into immediately. It dawned on me I was an honored guest. Joe had turned up with the ultimate status symbol. A real live American bum in his battered Levi's!

Joe asked questions. Others strained to listen. He did not bother to translate my replies, leaving that task to others in the crowd who knew English. The questions were disconcerting in their irrelevance to where and who I was.

"You like the look? We look good, yes? Real American look?"

"Which part of the States you come from?"

"You think this real crazy, yeah?"

Only once was there a reference to what I might be doing here, and that came after the sound of a bursting bottle visibly startled me. "You on the run from somewhere? Yeah? Don't worry. No one's gonna get you here. I've posted lookouts. Not that anyone'll come." A voice interjected, "Not if they know what's good for them," and there was a lot of laughter.

The stage was completed, the wiring connected to a portable generator. The sky darkened and the music began — electric guitars, keyboard, drums, saxophone, and an old Rolling Stones number that touched a lot of chords. Eyes studied me, nervous for my reaction.

I waited until the last notes of "Street Fighting Man" died away, and then I erupted with enthusiasm. It was the kind of performance that would have won me an Oscar without need for a vote. I felt the relief spread. I might by any objective assessment have been no more than a barbarian on the run; to these youths I was the one true link with the inspiration for their amateur Woodstock, the only person who *knew* whether it was 100 percent.

I drank more beer and ate more chicken, and shared some of the moxa that wasn't moxa, but with care. I hadn't forgotten about the pogrom. The dell grew alive with light — from bonfires and headlights. Music boomed on without pause. There was a little dancing, but mostly people just listened. For what had to be an antisocial — probably illegal — event, it was oddly decorous. There were very few girls, maybe eight or nine. The closest I saw to loose behavior was couples holding hands and swaying in time to the music.

I drifted into sleep around two A.M. and woke to see the fires being

killed and the stage dismantled. Joe was still near me, but more subdued when he spoke. "We're returning to Shanghai," he said. The
accent was not so pronounced now that we were without an audience.
"We'll be there soon after dawn. You want to come?"

I gestured toward the other youths left around the field; some were
already piling into cars. "What about them?" I asked.

"They won't say anything. Not outside themselves. Or at least not
for a few days. It's too good a secret to let out." He began to laugh,
curiously shrill, and I realized it was probably the pot. "Hey man,
anyway, what are you? An imperialist spy? Where'd you come from?
Dropped by parachute?"

I began to say something, but he stopped me. I knew he didn't
want an answer; he didn't want to hear anything that might stop it
all from being a huge joke.

"Come on," he said. "Lesgo. We'll drop you somewhere central.
There's so many tourists about these days no one'll spare you a glance."
He led the way back to the car, stopped in the lights and called over
some friends. There was a hurried discussion and then one, the biggest, pulled off his sweatshirt. It was large and had hung loose on
him. It was also restrained — dark blue with a Levi's emblem.

"Take it and give him yours," said Joe.

I hesitated, then did as he said. My own shirt was stained and
streaked with dirt and some chemical color from the river. Wearing
it, I'd be suspect in any crowd.

Handing it over, I started an apology, but stopped. It was obvious
none was needed. The burly youth slipped it on with an air of triumph.
Perhaps it would become a special object for veneration — the actual
shirt worn by the genuine American who had stamped his seal of
approval on a pseudo-Stones concert.

The sweatshirt fit me well. "Good," said Joe. He fumbled in the
car, withdrew a flask of water and a cloth. I used them to sponge my
trousers and then to wipe off my face and hands.

We got in the car, Joe again in the front. The youths on either side
of me fell asleep minutes after we started off.

The sky grew lighter as the open fields gave way to factories and then urban sprawl. There was silence from the front. The only indication that Joe remained awake was the flare from his lighter each time he lit a fresh cigarette.

I could make out the city stretching endlessly before us now. Joe gave what sounded like an order and we stopped a few minutes later. The driver got out and returned with hot, fat, sugared pancakes. I bit into one, relishing the heat and the smell and the sweetness.

"Good, yeah?"

"Very good."

Joe checked his watch. I had already glanced at mine a minute before. I knew it was a few minutes to six.

"Lots of people will be moving in half an hour," he said.

"You too?" I said.

He saw the joke. "Bedtime for us," he said. "But other people."

There were already bikers and a few pedestrians.

Joe passed me another pancake. "We'll sit here for a few more minutes," he said. "Then we'll drop you at Zhongshan Road." He saw it meant nothing to me. "It used to be the Bund," he said, "before the name was changed." That did mean something: the Bund was the boulevard that ran by the edge of the Yellow River. Along it were the buildings that had once housed the big European companies in pre-Revolution days. I nodded to show I understood.

"There's lots of hotels, shops, busy streets around," he said. "And many Western visitors. I don't know where you are going, but you're on your own then. You understand?"

"I understand."

He stared at me for a long time, but I said nothing else. I could, I suppose, have asked him why he was helping me. His father had to be part of the System and it must be obvious that it was the System that was after me. Maybe that was why. What the hell! He was a teenager and rebelling. Protecting me must have been a pretty good way to do it.

Suddenly he gave a crooked grin. I got a strange feeling that he was trying to copy an expression he had seen in a gangster movie. "Lesgo," he said, and turned back to face the road.

Twenty minutes later they dropped me on the Bund. I got out, relieved to see there were already a number of people about, including some tourists staring down on the boats below.

Joe fumbled under the dash again and produced a pair of dark glasses and a baseball cap. He held them out through the window.

"Disguise," he said, pressing them into my hand. He clearly relished his role as conspirator: I did not snub him by refusing. I knew I'd have to discard them — I couldn't risk looking like a refugee from *Peanuts*.

The car took off before I could answer. It made a U-turn, its brakes screeching. I stepped back, leaned against the river wall, took a deep breath of sea air, and watched the car vanish. No one turned to wave.

20

I walked along the Bund slowly for a long time. Although I saw no other Westerners, there were few stares. Apart from being China's biggest city Shanghai is also its most cosmopolitan. The street itself — once the Wall Street of China — with its grand European-style buildings was reminder of that. Nor did my aimlessness seem out of place. Although the day's bustle was beginning scores still strolled or gazed down on the river. Others practiced their *Tai ji quan*, the beautiful, slow-swinging, rhythmically stretching Chinese exercises.

Tired and battered though I was, Shanghai gave me a lift. It *felt* closer to New York than anywhere else I had been since leaving home. People's expressions were keener; the noise of cars and bicycle bells and ships' horns had a purposeful quality. I thought under better circumstances I could be happy here.

After an hour I retraced my steps, turned into what was obviously a main shopping street and found a department store. I bought half a dozen items in different parts of the store, rather as I had shopped back in Wuhsi. The only characteristic the items had in common was that they were bulky. I figured that they added to my cover; who, I reasoned, would expect a man on the run to be walking around with a bag full of presents and mementos? I also bought a razor and some soap.

Next, back in the street, I found a bookshop and added an English-language guide and a map to my purchases. Finally I chose a hotel from the guide, and headed in its direction.

The first sight of the hotel, the waterfront Shanghai Mansions, confirmed that I'd made a good choice. It was large — probably twenty or more stories — and Westerners were already spilling out for their tour buses.

I squeezed past them as I entered the hotel. It was a temptation to grab one and blurt out my plight but I knew none of them could help me. As I'd expected, I found a European-style washroom on the ground floor. I soaked a handkerchief I'd bought and entered one of the cubicles. It had a solid, old-fashioned bowl and an elaborate tank mounted high on the wall. That occupied me for a short time. Then I shaved blind.

Only when I was back in the street did I let myself think about the address Ming had given me. My first instinct on being dropped from the car had been to go straight there. The survivor in me had told me that by now the pipeline might be closed. First, I was late. Second, although I had tried not to think of it, the security men who had turned up in Nanking must have learned from someone that I was going there. There were only two possible explanations for that — either someone in the escape plan had betrayed me or Security had tracked down Ming's uncle and made him talk. And that probably meant they had Ming too. I *had* to know. My plan was to walk to the address, looking as touristy and innocuous as possible. Hence all the preparation. If there was then any suspicion I would retreat — to the safe house Andrews had told me about so long ago.

I had found the address on the map. It meant following the river again before turning off into the old Chinese city. I stepped straight into the Shanghai that I had seen in old movies and read about a hundred times. Narrow streets carved a way through packed rows of tiny shops, cramped houses, and crowded restaurants. The noise of human voices was almost deafening; there were people everywhere. A man fought past, holding two scrawny dead chickens high above his head. In front of me an ancient lady hobbled forward, too slow for the crowd behind her — I looked down and saw tiny, bound feet, legacy of a time when small was beautiful. She had been one of the luckier ones — I'd read that when the Communists took power they had unbound thousands upon thousands of bound feet, not knowing or caring that it was too late, causing agonizing pain and crippling the women forever.

I found the house I wanted. It was a few yards inside a narrow alley. I let the crowd carry me past to give me a chance to look and to think. My glance did not help. The shutters were closed; the house could have been deserted. Or occupied. Without trying the door, there was no way of knowing.

Decision time, I told myself. There is a moment when there is nothing left but action. I turned and made my way back.

Two men grabbed me as I neared the door. They came from either side, grasping me by the elbows and carrying me forward. The crowd hid what was happening.

I started to twist away, but something poked me in the side. A gun. It had to be a gun. It froze my actions for a few seconds, but I had to attempt a break — even if I got shot. I couldn't let them just take me. Not now. Not after what I'd been through.

I poised myself to make my move. The man on the left must have sensed it because he muttered, "Please, please, keep moving. You must not stop." Something in the voice — the pleading, the desperation — made me accede.

I let myself be led away. We crossed a street, cut through a restaurant and out through a rear door into another alley.

Only one of the two men accompanied me out of the restaurant. He was about twenty-five, and his face had the same desperate expression I'd heard in his voice.

"What is it?" I said. I realized that through it all I had held onto my parcels.

He began to push me. "Go, go. You must go."

I stood my ground. "What is it?"

The door behind him opened, and the man's companion hissed something.

He turned back to me. "You must move, fast. It is no good. It is over. They raided the house. We have been waiting in case you came, keeping watch from nearby. Now go. Please go. We will try to lead them away."

I heard a shout and then the noise of a scuffle from inside and I began to run, leaving the bag behind; now it was nothing more than a signpost for anyone pursuing me.

Once out of the alley I forced myself to slow down. I came out into a wider street, stepped into the road, and was nearly hit by a bicyclist — a woman riding with one hand on the handlebars, the other nonchalantly holding an unwrapped piece of meat. I saw a gateway into what looked like a park and I followed an elderly man pushing a bamboo pram. He was singing softly.

It *was* a park, full of the kind of people doing the kind of things they do in parks everywhere. Children played, old men were reading newspapers, students were studying their books.

I paused in the shadow of a grostesque ginkgo tree; its trunk was so vast several people would have had to join hands to form a ring around it. I stayed long enough to satisfy myself no one had followed me and to try to check my position on the map. I thought if I continued through the park I would come out on or in Nanking Road, the street where I had already shopped. It ran from the waterfront, dividing the city in two.

I was wrong about my bearings, but I finally did find Nanking Road. Here, among the shops, restaurants, and cinemas, I felt more protected. I bought some ice cream and a fizzy orange drink. The crowds around me were so thick now that there was no way I would have known if anyone was following me.

Without thinking, I realized I was heading for the second address — the one I had memorized so dutifully before all this began though certain I would never need it.

It was north of Nanking Road, in a narrow street of old apartment houses, balconies alive with fluttering washing. As before, I walked the length of the street, this time trying to disregard the stares of small children and at least one adult in a window above.

The address itself was one of three small shops, no more than a window filled with traditional herb medicines, a doorway, and a single room. I tried the door, half-expecting it to be locked. It opened, yielding the heavy scent of herbs.

Still in the doorway, I listened, heard only silence, and self-consciously called out one of the few Chinese phrases I knew.

"*Ni hao*" — Hello.

A curtain opened at the rear of the darkened room and an old man emerged. He came forward without speaking.

"Do you speak English?" I said.

He bowed his head. "A little."

"My name is Piper," I said. "I was given this address."

He looked as though he did not understand.

"This address. I was given it. A man called Andrews."

Light dawned. "Ah, Mr. Andrews. He gave address."

"Yes." We were both grinning.

He half-turned and waved me toward the curtains. "Please, you will come this way."

I followed him, expecting that I would be ordered to wait while he made a telephone call or sent a message or even went out himself.

It was much less complicated than that. The curtain revealed a small room. The shopkeeper led the way through and opened a door at the far end. He stood back to let me enter first. The room was thick with smoke and heavy with the scent of bourbon whiskey. It was a room in which someone had been waiting a long time.

The door closed behind me, leaving me alone with the man who had been doing the waiting. He was smiling, but his eyes were as devoid of emotion as they had been the last time I had seen him.

"You're a resourceful man, Mr. Piper," said Andrews.

I was grinning inanely, hardly able to believe that I had made it when he stepped forward and hit me. The first blow landed in the pit of my stomach and I was still trying to protest that he had got the wrong person when the second crashed into the side of my head. He kicked me then and I blacked out; wondering why no one seemed to like me much anymore.

By the time I came to, Andrews was leaning against the far wall, a gun in one hand and a whiskey glass in the other.

It all seemed vaguely familiar, and then I remembered what it reminded me of: Peking, the Friendship Hotel, the night that Yakov called and started all this.

I pulled myself upright and started to say something tough to show him what a hard man he was dealing with. The only sound that came out was a sort of choking noise.

When I finally could talk all I said was, "What the hell, what did I do?" The only thing I could think of was that he suspected I had sold out to someone, maybe the Russians. But if he believed that I don't know how he squared it with my presence.

He didn't bother to answer, nor to indulge in small talk at all.

"The film," was all he said. "Where is it?"

"I haven't got it," I said.

"Shit." He said the word without emotion. He put down the glass and picked up an object from the table beside him. A silencer. He screwed it on to the pistol.

There was a flicker of something in his eyes, and it was not humor. "You went back to Nanking when you were well away," he said. "Made your way into your old hotel. Took a bag. You didn't do that because you needed a change of socks. Someone had told you where it was, and you went back and got it. As to it being film, I'm guessing — but I'm right, aren't I?"

I decided to try to keep the talk going as long as I could; maybe he'd regain his sanity.

"How did you know?" I said.

It hardly deflected him. "We have friends throughout the Security apparatus," he said. "They kept me posted." He lifted the gun and pointed it theatrically at the general region of my legs. "Now," he said, "hand over the film or tell me where it is, or I blow off your kneecaps. For starters."

His tone had not changed at all. I knew, beyond any doubt, that he wasn't bluffing.

258

I had caught an interesting inflection, though, on one of the words he had uttered. I pressed on. I had nothing to lose. I was telling the truth. I didn't have the film. *"We,"* I said, trying not to let fear creep into my voice. "Who's we?"

It worked. I guess everyone has a moment when he needs to confess, to share the big secret. Sensible drunks do it with bartenders they will never see again. He was sure I wouldn't be around long to tell anyone else, so he let me feed him my bait.

He laughed again, this time a real belly laugh, and allowed himself the luxury of another pull from the drink he lifted from the table.

"As I said before, quite a resourceful man," he said, nodding his head in mock congratulation. "Already you've figured that I've got two masters." His face clouded, and a thought struck him. "Your contact didn't say they suspected me? You guessed!"

I didn't know what he meant; I wasn't even sure what I'd guessed. But I wanted him happy. I nodded that he was right.

"You're from a farming community way back," he said. "I know that — had you checked out when all this started. Me, all I saw until I was thirteen was the inside of a tenement and some shit-poor streets.

"My old man went the political way. He was always with people who were going to change it all. Me, I went the other way. Got out, learned to swim in the right sea."

There were no windows in the room and the heat and the smoke started to hit me. I began to sway and he kicked me over a chair, one of the few items of furniture.

"Sit," he said, "but make just one move I don't like and I'll blow your balls off."

He resumed the monologue as soon as I sat down. "I saw early on that China was going to be important, that we couldn't pretend it didn't exist forever. I took classes, studied the country, learned the language. When the time came I was ready. Nothing political, you understand. Not like my old man. Just good career planning."

"So you came here?" I prompted him.

He put down his glass and lit a fresh cigarette. "I know what you're doing," he said. "Guess I'd try the same in your place. When you're gonna get bits shot off you even a few minutes' grace is worth having. Still, you've touched my weak spot.

"So, yes, I came over here. That was way back, before this crowd of old second-raters was running the country. Mao was alive. And you know what? I guess I really did start to believe. Not all that crap that pinko movie stars and fag novelists think they've witnessed, like people all being equal and nobody starving. No, I mean real gut stuff like a whole people who've been kicked around grabbing their own destiny by the balls.

"You know something? I started to weep inside after Mao died and I saw things going soft. Not soft nice-nice, but soft swimming with the tide, taking the easy way, encouraging people to be cynical and materialistic. You know what Mao wrote to his wife Jiang Qing just before he died?"

I shook my head, but he was already continuing. His voice took on the tone of someone reading the gospel in church. "He wrote, 'Man's life is limited, but the revolution knows no bounds. In the struggle of the past ten years, I tried to teach the Chinese people revolution, but I failed.' "

I still didn't understand; not least, I still had no idea who "we" were.

"He died believing that," he went on, and the emotion was thick in his voice. "He was wrong, though." His voice rose and I got a taste of the conviction and the passion buried somewhere in there. "Since they squashed the Cultural Revolution they've had purges, sackings, corruption trials . . . They've replaced thousands on thousands of officials, attempted to turn the army upside down. They tried Jiang Qing and the rest of what they call the Gang of Four. But they haven't dared execute her. And throughout the country there are still millions who believe as she did, forced to lie low . . ."

"The Gang of Four," I said, and I began to laugh uncontrollably. So they were his masters. Somewhere along the line he'd established links, probably at first as part of his CIA role to monitor all the factions. Then, privy to secrets from all sides, he had begun to help. Given even the little he'd told me about his background and his father,

I didn't find it hard to understand how he'd got more and more deeply involved.

My reaction ended whatever time I had bought. His face clouded with rage. The drunk, sober, was regretting his indiscretions.

"Shut your fucking mouth," he screamed.

I stopped laughing then. His face became twisted with the effort of bringing his anger under some sort of control. He was going to shoot me; that was obvious. But he was going to do it slowly, deliberately. He had an image of himself as a stylish operator, and he wasn't going to let it vanish.

With concealed effort he raised his gun arm slowly, almost lazily, like someone lining up on a can on a wall. Then to complete the effect he squeezed his mouth into a smile.

"For the hell of it," he said, "I'm going to blow one of your fucking kneecaps off first and *then* ask you about the film, just one more time."

I knew I was finished. There was no way I could distract him. Even if there had been, he was much too far away for me to try anything.

He turned his head slightly and bellowed an order in the direction of the door. I realized he was summoning the man who had brought me inside.

It wasn't much of a chance, but I tensed myself to be ready to move the moment the door opened. I told myself he might be off his guard for a crucial fraction of a second. But that wasn't the reason. It was as basic as breathing — you don't let someone try to kill you without doing something. Even if it's something useless.

The door began to give and I moved fast, flinging myself forward in Andrews's direction, my arms outspread. I screamed as I moved, hoping the sound might throw him for another vital moment.

The first shot echoed through the room when I was only halfway toward him. I didn't feel anything and my momentum kept me moving. I thought I must crash full into him, but Andrews was no longer there, and I hit the floor hard.

There was still firing and in what I thought must be my final seconds on earth it dawned on me it couldn't be Andrews — his gun was fitted with a silencer.

Then, suddenly, it was terrifyingly quiet. I was lying facedown and couldn't see a thing. Hands pulled me upright. I stood in the center of the room, swaying, wondering why I couldn't feel any pain. I looked down at my body and couldn't understand why there was no blood.

Gradually I took in the scene. A smell of gunpowder had replaced the scent of tobacco smoke. The room was full of small men in dark gray suits. They all had shiny black shoes.

I turned my head and saw Andrews. He was the smallest figure of all: just a crumpled, bleeding figure on the floor. His head was raised toward the door and his eyes were wide open. For the first time since I had met him they looked alive. That was the final irony; because he was as dead as his hero, Mao.

21

The car was a Mercedes. I was again wedged in the back between two men, but this time my hands were cuffed.

No one said anything, which was just as well because I was in no state for talking. I still hurt where Andrews had hit me, and a lump about the size and consistency of a small cannonball seemed to have formed in my stomach and was trying to force its way upward.

I was still reeling with the treachery of Andrews, and with his slaying. Replaying his death in my mind there was no warning, no chance for him to surrender. Just the door bursting open, men hurling me to one side, and then the shots, at least a dozen.

I tried to work out the direction we were taking, but the curtains at the windows were tightly drawn. The car roared through the streets, horn blaring. That, at least, told me one thing. My captors were Chinese Security. Not Chinese working for the Russians, nor Gang of Four sympathizers (who, no doubt, could have turned on Andrews), for either of these would have been more stealthy. That provided a grain of comfort — I would find out what had happened to Ming. I might even be allowed to see her.

Finally the car slowed and through the front window I caught a glimpse of a double gate and a high wall. We stopped and I was led out, my hands secured in front of me. I expected to find myself in some kind of prison or security complex, but the car was drawn up in a driveway at the side of a white-painted, European-style three-story house.

A side door was already open and I entered, one guard ahead of me, two behind. I was in the corner of a marble-floored hallway from which rose a sweeping staircase with rich red carpet. The house was obviously a holdover from pre-Revolutionary days, perhaps the home of a rich foreign merchant. As it was, it could have been in Paris or London or Vienna.

One man stood at the foot of the stairs and without speaking he directed us upward. I was led to a huge, circular room on the second floor. I stared around bemused, hardly able to credit the Louis XV furniture, the rich drapes, the heavy oil paintings.

I heard a cough that I could not place. Then one of my guards pushed me forward and out onto a wide balcony that overlooked a garden with lawns, trees, even a small lake. There was no sound of the street nearby.

There was a second cough and I turned my head. At the far end of the balcony was a man. His back was turned, there was a wreath of smoke around him, and his jacket was over his shoulders like a cloak. He turned slowly, but I already knew who it was, who it had to be.

"I can hardly tell you how pleased I am to see you," said Feng.

The room to which we moved was a dining salon, elaborately furnished. A long mahogany table was already laid with dishes of food.

At an order from Feng a guard removed my handcuffs. I rubbed my wrists to restore the circulation.

"Look," said Feng, waving expansively. "Bread. It is a long time since you last saw that. Specially baked for our foreign friends, obtained for you from the kitchens of the Peace Hotel. You see how much I honor your achievement in getting this far."

I wanted to ask about Ming, but I still harbored a hope that even if she had been picked up Feng believed I had forced her cooperation. Instead I asked, "Why did you kill Andrews?"

The sight of food was making me feel like vomiting.

"I understand he was just about to start shooting you into many pieces," said Feng, pouring from a brandy bottle and placing the drink within my reach. "I see from your face that he had already expressed his displeasure with you. I think you should be grateful to us. My men heard it all from outside. They had the room taped. Another minute and it would have been you looking like a leaking pan."

I stared at the drink, longing to lift it, but I left it alone. "But why kill him?" I persisted. "You could have arrested him."

Once I had said it, it sounded feeble.

"And what?" said Feng. "Locked him away somewhere to cost the State food money? Shot him later? Asked for him to be sent home? That would have been messy. We could have sent him back to Peking, kept him in place, tried to use him. But I fear that if we had done that we could never have trusted him. Besides, if the slightest thing went wrong my head would have fallen. The Gang of Four, you see, are monsters above monsters. That is something any of us forget at our peril." He waved at my glass. "Do drink. You see I tell you the truth."

I compromised and drank only half the glass. The brandy hit me immediately, acting like a touch from an electric prod.

"Good," he said, and smoothly continued his monologue. "Besides, I had convinced myself he had nothing to tell us. He thought that he spied on us. In reality, I have known of his activities for a very long time. It was inevitable this would happen some day. We Chinese have many old sayings, Mr. Piper. There is one that is very appropriate here. 'Predestined enemies will always meet in a narrow alleyway.' "

He gestured to a guard to refill my glass before he continued.

"When I heard of the train explosion I confess I did not know whether you were alive or dead. I still did not until you went to the house in the old quarter this morning. However, I ensured that Mr. Andrews received information that we believed you had survived. Already I was convinced that we had learned everything we could from him by subtle methods, but it seemed an excellent last chance to stir him into some frantic action and see what happened. I was not surprised when he tried to obtain a ticket on the first plane from

Peking to Shanghai — the journey takes less than two hours. Of course, I saw that there was a vacant seat."

I noted the words "last chance"; it sounded as though Feng had already decided to get rid of him before today. My main thoughts, though, were about how Feng had known of my return to Nanking and the house in the old quarter.

I feared I already knew the answer.

There was only one way of finding out. I asked him.

"Nanking," he repeated. "I knew from the start that you were heading toward Shanghai, of course. For all your resourcefulness you left signs. I also knew that Mr. Andrews had given you addresses in Nanking and Shanghai. I know you did not go to the first — my men had it under surveillance.

"Perhaps I should also tell you that I did all I could to minimize the search for you. I rather liked the idea of your being free — I wanted to see what would happen, what you might do, who might try to find you, what waves you would create. That's an American expression, isn't it, Mr. Piper? A very good one, I think.

"Besides, I had decided — prematurely, it was to emerge — that you knew nothing. You see, I had even deciphered Colonel Yakov's dying message. I had decided the word was *Fomka*. It is a nickname, meaning 'Little Thomas' in your language, and it so happened that there was a man of just such a name in the Soviet delegation. I thought our dead Russian comrade had been trying to tell someone that it was this man who had killed him.

"I could not prevent the hunt completely, of course. Too many people were involved. And there was a security cadre who nearly died. There were some sightings of you that were known to others beside myself — that time you joined the bicycle ride: I liked that one particularly. But there were some known just to me, and I kept it that way, Mr. Piper."

I drank more brandy and mulled over two facts: that the guard I'd injured escaping in Nanking outside the opera had not died, and that one reason why I hadn't been caught while on the run was that Feng had maneuvered it that way.

I gave him my attention again. I wanted to know the rest.

"The note that you slipped to a tourist for transmission to Mr. Andrews was something I kept to myself," he said. He saw from my expression I did not understand. "Ah," he said, "you thought perhaps someone had called Mr. Andrews as you requested? I'm afraid that what really happened was one of the guides saw what had happened and persuaded the tourist that he was the subject of a joke in poor taste."

He saw that I still looked confused. "I am sorry, Mr. Piper," he said, "your head must be hurting after all that has happened. But you wanted to know. Let it suffice that news of the note and its contents came to me. It seemed an ideal opportunity to leak it to the Russians — they too have their spies among us — pretending at the same time it had reached no one in authority in my department. All I had to do then was facilitate their request to visit Wuhsi, which followed shortly, as I knew it would. I wanted to see what would happen. My full intention was to pick you up immediately afterward. Unfortunately — or perhaps fortunately, as it emerged — you proved a veritable magician at vanishing."

He waved at the table. "Please, please, do eat.

"We really did lose sight of you then. Later, after a delay caused by incompetence that has now been dealt with, we finally heard of your attempt to telephone Comrade Chu's uncle. My men arrived at the village a little too late. You had already gone. We soon found out about you and your plans." Again he read my face. "Do not worry yourself. The man Ho talked quickly enough. No harm has come to the uncle — he is an old man. I think we will simply see he is moved to a new village, perhaps somewhere north." I felt again the flood of remorse and guilt that had been recurring since Nanking; I had needed the uncle's cooperation in order to survive, but now I was responsible for his fate.

He continued, "We were again too late to seize you at the hotel in Nanking on your return and by now I confess I did want to seize you, very much. Too many people were saying that you had been loose for far too long and were a danger."

I couldn't hold back any longer.

"The girl," I said. "Chu Ming. What happened to her?"

He didn't answer at first, and I rushed on, "She didn't want to come with me. I forced her, and her uncle. I had a gun . . . "

"Ah, Comrade Chu," he said finally. He lit the cigarette he had placed in his holder.

I thought he was about to answer, but when he spoke again all he said was, "Perhaps we will talk about her later. But first let me take up the conversation you were having with Mr. Andrews before we interrupted you. Before I ask you any questions, shall we search your clothes? You will remove them, please."

I stripped. One guard looked through them, checking seams, feeling linings, turning out pockets. Another searched my body.

They found little: one single, tiny frame of film, concealed in the waistband of my jeans.

Feng held it carefully and gestured for me to dress. Then he held the film up to the light. I knew it wouldn't reveal anything that way but I kept quiet.

"Where's the rest?" he asked.

"I think you should have that frame examined before we talk any more," I said, my throat dry.

He stepped forward and I braced myself, thinking he was going to hit me. But he stopped, turned, and left the room.

I poured myself a large drink of the sweet brandy and set out to wait.

Feng returned two hours later, his hands empty but for another cigarette. I had been dozing, my head on the table, but I raised myself when I heard the door open. I was just in time to prevent a guard from yanking me upright by my hair.

"Where is the rest?" Feng asked as though he had never been away.

"There are lots more," I said, striving to keep my voice calm. "All the same size. Only you know how much information each one contains or how much it covers. Was my sample of as much consequence as you thought it might be?" I didn't have to ask that; I could tell it was from the way he looked.

"Where are they?"

I refused to budge from my prepared stance. I had nothing to lose; that was my strength. "Lots more," I repeated. "Somewhere between here and Nanking. Hidden in hundreds of square miles of country. Safe, so they won't rot, I promise you that. But somewhere no one will ever find them."

"You'll tell us in time," said Feng, equally evenly. "Everyone does. I say that not to frighten you, but as a fact."

"Perhaps, " I said. "Perhaps you're right. Once you would have been, but now I don't think so. I think maybe you'll kill me first."

"What do you want?" he said.

"Freedom. And the girl."

"The girl could be tortured too. You have thought of that?"

I shrugged, forcing myself to seem more sanguine than I felt. "If you've got her, and I guess you have, I know she's doomed anyway. What you do will hurt me but I don't think it will change me."

Feng's anger was so sudden, so unexpected that I had no time to lift my arm protectively or to move my head. The blow from the back of his hand caught me across the face, knocking me from the chair with its force.

The guards moved to block me as I began to rise. But Feng had already gone, the door slamming noisily behind him.

They moved me to another building, a sack over my head, and when they removed it I was in a room without furniture, window, or light. They had taken my watch. At first I tried to keep track of time by counting until it dawned that it was a foolish enterprise, and I settled on the floor and tried to sleep.

I attempted to place myself in Feng's position, imagining the arguments that would be going through the security man's mind. What Feng now had to do was weigh the certainty of retrieving the film if he turned me loose against the possibility of doing so (no more, no matter what he had said) if I held out and had to be tortured for the information.

I thought that in Feng's place I would opt for certainty. What, after all, was my life or death to him?

I also thought that if I were Feng I would be happy to have someone able to tell the authorities back home about Andrews's death. Proof of his treachery might be a useful thing. After all, I couldn't see the U.S. government just sitting quietly back and forgetting the death or disappearance of a CIA man in China unless it looked as though his end had been in everyone's interest. My story would convince them it had been.

All these thoughts comforted me for a while until I realized I had forgotten one thing.

The only lesson I should have learned in China was that I had no idea of how the Chinese really thought at all.

22

*struggled when they came for me, but there were too many
of them, and they handcuffed my arms in front of me again and pulled
a hood over my head.

I felt the heat hit us as we got outside, and that probably meant it
was day; but the hood blotted out both sight and sound.

My head was still covered when the car jerked to a halt about an
hour later and I was hauled roughly outside. Unseen hands bared my
head, and once my eyes focused I saw I was standing in the shadow
of a Boeing 707, the markings of the Chinese airline CAAC on its
side.

"It will take you to Tokyo," a voice said. "Before disembarking
you will not forget to dictate a message for me . . ." I looked down
and saw Feng's face framed in the rear window of a second car.

"What about Ming?" Despair made me choke. I didn't want to win
this way.

Feng waved a hand through the window, and I felt my arms grasped
to force me toward the waiting airplane steps.

Feng's voice followed me. "I'd remember a very meaningful phrase
from your country, Mr. Piper. Don't push your luck."

He barked an order and the car screamed away. Like my young
friends on the Bund he did not even look back.

I paused at the top of the stairs, and turned; the car was already on the edge of the airfield. Apart from this one plane the runways were deserted.

A nudge from one of my guards sent me stumbling out of the daylight into the gloom of the plane. I almost fell. I placed my hand on a seat for support, and as my eyes became accustomed to the shade I saw that the plane was completely empty except for me and the guards. I was the only passenger.

"You sit. There." A gun poked me viciously in the side. "There. There."

I collapsed into a seat. It hardly mattered. There was no elation that Feng was letting me free. Just pain. I had lost the one thing that had kept me going through it all, the only person I'd ever met that I cared about more than myself.

I heard the door close behind me, glanced, and saw the guards had gone.

I started to get to my feet, but the plane began to taxi immediately. There was no waste of time, no waiting for clearance. The aircraft gathered speed, rose quickly, sending me crashing back into my seat. Then, in a cloudless sky, it banked over the sprawl of the city.

There was nothing I could do now. I gazed down, not really seeing, my mind filled with memories. Images unfolded in front of me — Yakov's body in the photograph, the shadow of the helicopter as I struggled through the paddy fields, Wen's hand trembling with excitement as he unwrapped the vodka, the cloud of steam rising from the river, Feng with his eyes blazing and his hand raised after the blow, the only time I had seen him display anger ..

And Ming.

I looked down at myself, ran my hand over my face. My clothes were dirty; I'd lost some weight; my cheek was still bruised. But I guessed that with a shower and a shave and a change I wouldn't look too different from the man who'd arrived in Peking, who'd stood and watched steam trains being made all that time ago. Yet I knew I was changed, forever.

A faint noise made me move my head and focus on the aisle. At the far end the door from the flight deck had opened and a figure stood silhouetted there.

My eyes were misted and all I could make out was that it was a woman. Tension made me want to giggle at the incongruity of it all. A stewardess to serve the flight's one and only passenger!

She came nearer but the sunlight and my tears made her no more than a shape.

Then a voice — a voice that I recognized — said, "I have come to take you home."

23

⊁ ⊀

We waited at Tokyo's International Airport, Ming still in the airplane, me high above in a private lounge set aside for Chinese use in the terminal's north wing.

I had three guards — although they must have known that if I was going to attempt a break I would have done so as I was led past hordes of arriving and departing passengers.

Two of Feng's men had been on the flight deck; more had been waiting when we touched down. I had dictated the message for Feng, but only after being allowed to move from the plane to the tarmac. On orders, the other guards had stood well back; I reckoned that the number of witnesses who had the plane in full view would deter them from trying to pull me back on board.

Besides, they retained their real hold over me. They still had Ming.

The hours passed. I was brought sandwiches I did not eat, drinks I sipped and pushed aside. It grew dark, but through the plate-glass window I could still see the Boeing below. For normal security reasons it was parked well away from other planes and illuminated by arc lights.

A telephone rang for the first time and a guard answered, but it seemed to be nothing.

Then it rang again and this time the man gestured me toward the window.

I looked out and saw the airplane steps being pushed back into place. I knew from that and from the sudden relaxation in the room that it was all over.

I did not wait to watch the Boeing's door open. Guards followed but did not try to stop me as I rushed out, took the emergency stairs down three floors, crashed through an exit and out into the night air. Two Japanese security men bounded after me, but my Chinese guards began screaming at them and waving ID cards.

Maybe I should have been scared, but what was happening behind hardly registered on me. All I saw was Ming being led across by the man to whom I had given the message.

We neared and stopped.

The man spoke mechanically. "Head of Bureau Feng thanks you for the parcel. You may both go."

He said nothing else, and I stepped forward and drew Ming toward me.

No one tried to stop me. We had our freedom. A nagging voice whispered, *Yes, and Feng has his film.* It would have taken him less than an hour to remove the canister from the tank at the Shanghai Mansions Hotel once he had received my message; the rest of the time had been to check the contents — and, perhaps, make me sweat.

I stifled the murmur. I told myself the canister was the price I had had to pay. And I had earned the right to do so.

I slipped my arm around Ming and pulled her head into my shoulder. "Come on," I whispered. "A nice girl like you shouldn't be out so late."

Besides, my inner voice consoled me, Feng had not won everything. By no means. He had a container, certainly.

And I had another.

Containing more than half the film.

Hidden between the bricks of the new bridge over the stream a mile from where I'd abandoned my train. It would not be beyond the capabilities of U.S. Intelligence to retrieve it. When I told them.

I began to lead Ming away. She looked up and smiled gently for the first time. She didn't say anything. I guess she knew there was no rush.

We had time, now.